A Passion...

"This is madness," she murm...

"Then step with me into ma... hands aside and wrapped his ar... against him and devouring her n...

The heat rushed through then... ...ous. Billie could no more deny him than she could deny herself. She wanted him. She had wanted him since the first time he had kissed her and awakened her dormant passion.

Unforgettable.

His kiss had been that and more.

And the consequences of surrendering to her fantasies?

His kiss turned forceful, demanding she respond, demanding surrender.

She would face tomorrow when it came. Tonight she would open her heart to the ghostly lord and love.

Billie tore her mouth from his hungry one. With panting breath she whispered, "Take me into your madness and love me."

He scooped her wet body up into his arms and walked to the bed . . .

Turn to the back of this book
for a preview of

A Spirited Seduction

the next Haunting Hearts romance!

WHISPERS ON THE WIND

DONNA FLETCHER

JOVE BOOKS, NEW YORK

WHISPERS ON THE WIND

A Jove Book / published by arrangement with
the author

PRINTING HISTORY
Jove edition / March 1997

The Putnam Berkley World Wide Web site address is
http://www.berkley.com/berkley

ISBN: 0-515-12029-4

A JOVE BOOK®
Jove Books are published by The Berkley Publishing Group,
200 Madison Avenue, New York, New York 10016.
JOVE and the "J" design are trademarks
belonging to Jove Publications, Inc.

PRINTED IN THE UNITED STATES OF AMERICA

10 9 8 7 6 5 4 3 2 1

To my sister
Diane Pizzuta
with much love

WHISPERS ON THE WIND

Chapter One

CORNWALL, ENGLAND, 1808

Only the most dangerous ghosts haunt on a stormy night.

Belinda Latham's head struck the top of the coach only seconds before her backside landed with a solid thump on the floor. Her thoughts of her mother's favorite way of beginning a ghost story and scaring her usually brave daughter were dispatched in an instant. Her bonnet toppled forward, covering her eyes and pitching her into complete darkness.

"Damn, but I hate storms and ghosts," Belinda muttered, shivering away a tingle of fear. She shook an angry fist at the driver sitting outside atop the coach.

With her silent protest leaving her little satisfaction, she adjusted her claret bonnet, tying the moss-green silk ribbon loosely beneath her chin.

"Sometimes, Belinda, I wonder if you have any brains," she scolded herself. "Hiring a coach on a stormy night like . . ."

A night perfect for dangerous ghosts. Her thoughts intruded once again, sending shivers racing through her.

"Stop it, Belinda Latham," she warned herself, shaking her finger in front of her nose. "Stop being childish."

The coach suddenly tilted at a precarious angle and Belinda hastily braced her hand against the door for support. Why the devil had she hired such an incompetent driver, and why the devil had she insisted on continuing her journey in such hazardous weather?

The coach righted itself with an abrupt jerk just in time to connect with another rut. Belinda winced when her backside received another sharp slap from the floor.

Lightning splintered the night sky, the glaring light penetrating the shade-covered windows for a brief second. Belinda squeezed her eyes shut, covered her ears and braced for the thunder that would follow. The thunderclap exploded, sounding as if it had rent the earth in two. Belinda felt gooseflesh crawl frantically up her arms.

"Damn, damn, damn, I hate storms," she complained to the inside of the coach.

The horses' shrill cries mingled with the howling wind and, from the precarious sway of the coach, Belinda realized that the driver had his hands full keeping control of the frightened animals.

Belinda shook her head and remained sitting on the floor, counting herself lucky for the safety of the coach.

The driver shouted to her above the ferocity of the storm. "Hol—on—arri—soon."

She caught a few of his words, piecing together the rest. Their arrival appeared imminent. She smiled in relief or anticipation—she had yet to decide.

Another rut sent the coach and Belinda pitching dangerously to the side. The driver yelled his commands in excited anger at the horses.

Relief, Belinda decided hastily. No matter what she faced when she exited the coach, it had to be a far sight better than the beating she was taking.

Another crack of thunder shattered the night. She shut her eyes tightly for a moment before opening them, reminding herself she had been through far worse times.

Belinda, or Billie as her family had fondly referred to her since her birth twenty years ago, was made of stronger stock than that. If she hadn't been she wouldn't be here now traveling alone along the Cornwall coast to St. Clair.

No. She would be back in Nantucket, Massachusetts, probably forced, due to her awkward situation, to wed Jeremy Ulster. She shivered at the repulsive thought and recalled that Jeremy always smelled of day-old fish and ale which he consumed in equal amounts and was the reason for his big belly.

Billie's round face tightened with a frown. She hadn't wanted to leave Nantucket. It was an island that produced women who were capable of surviving on their own out of necessity, little choice being left to them. With their men at sea, some for years, they learned to rely on their inner strengths.

She was a strong, independent woman. If she hadn't possessed such hardy traits, she never would have consented to this trip.

Her bottom once again felt the sting of the hard floor as the coach wheel caught another rut. She laughed her soreness away with humor. *It's my stomach I'll be sleeping on tonight,* she thought.

Her mother had often teased her about her penchant for sleeping on her stomach, her arms wrapped snugly around her pillow and her head buried in its feathery softness.

"It's a husband you need to be tucked around," her mother had remarked with a cheerful laugh. "A big, strong husband."

Billie sadly shook her head. Her father, William Latham, had died at sea when she was five. Friends and neighbors said she bore his smile, kind and gentle in a strong way, they had insisted. Others said she had his eyes, deep brown and

filled with the luster and excitement for challenges and adventures. Her petite form came from her mother—she stood
only five feet four in her stocking feet. Her hair was also
reminiscent of her mother's, a mixture of blond and light
brown and shiny in its long length.

Billie was grateful for having inherited a special part of
each of her parents. She had loved them both equally and
her Uncle Thomas as well. It had been he who had taught
her so much about the sea. Much had changed though, when
Henry Radborne entered their lives. A short, jovial man, he
had been thought highly of by everyone in Nantucket. Her
mother had fallen in love for the second time in her life, and
she had married Henry Radborne only three months after
meeting him. Billie had been relieved when she learned that
they would remain living with her Uncle Thomas; though
she had been happy her mother had found love again, she
felt they would all fare better under Uncle Thomas's roof.

A tear stung her eye and she wiped it away. They were all
gone now, taken from her by a freak carriage accident. Her
mother and Henry had been killed instantly. Her Uncle
Thomas had lingered for a week. Billie had cared for him,
listening to him repeatedly express his sorrow to her. She finally understood what he had been trying to tell her upon his
death. She had been left in severe debt, partly due to a bad
fishing season and partly due to Henry Radborne's enor-
mous gambling debts.

The letter of inquiry from Cornwall, England had been a
godsend and she had given it careful consideration. It was
from the estate of one Maximillian Radborne. The solicitor,
Mr. Hillard, explained that Maximillian Radborne, Earl of
Strathorn, was now deceased. A search was being conducted
for a Henry Radborne, his uncle and sole inheritor of the Radborne estate. Mr. Hillard requested that either Henry Radborne or his heir produce himself—with proof, of course—at
Radborne Manor to collect the substantial inheritance. And
since Henry Radborne had taken the measure to leave a will,
dated and attested to, Billie was now his sole heir.

She had just enough money left after the sale of the fishing boat and the house and the payments of the debts to purchase a ticket for England. There was nothing left to keep her in Nantucket. And with her father's adventurous soul and the call of the sea, her decision had come easily.

The driver's sharp yell snapped Billie back to the present. The loud crack of his whip sounded like distant thunder, forcing the horses to quicken their already swift pace.

Arrival was only minutes away. Radborne Manor awaited her. She collected her wits and sensibility, picking herself up off the floor. She straightened her moss-green cape, wrapping it more closely around her to protect her claret wool dress from the inclement weather she would face upon leaving the safety of the coach. Her bonnet was back in place, her gloves secure and her traveling cases in hand.

The coach slowed to a steady, more even sway. Their arrival was obviously at hand. Excitement gripped Billie. She had been looking forward to this moment since first reading the letter. She had no idea of the condition of the Manor, or the staff which Mr. Hillard proclaimed had dwindled considerably since the lord's death. But none of that mattered to her. Her interest was in the manor, her new home. She had thoughts of the garden where she would grow her herbs, vegetables and flowers. A home where she could invite the village women for tea and local gossip and become part of their lives. She was filled with anticipation for this new beginning, this new chapter in her life.

The coach halted with much more dignity and reserve than Billie thought possible. She pushed herself to the end of the plush brown velvet seat and waited for the carriage door to open. Her eyes widened with excitement and her body shivered with anticipation.

The driver yanked open the door, admitting a flourish of wind and rain. "We're here, mum."

Billie strained to see through the sheet of rain that looked more like a downpour from a large pitcher than from the heavens above. She squinted and caught sight of a wooden sign swinging in gusty momentum. COX CROW INN.

"Pardon me, sir," Billie said as he offered her his hand. "But this doesn't appear to be Radborne Manor."

"Nay, it ain't."

Billie's voice took on an air of authority as the rain attacked her garments. "I hired you on to take me to Radborne Manor."

"Nay," he corrected with a stubborn shake of his head. "St. Clair, Cornwall is what you said."

"Yes, Radborne Manor in St. Clair, Cornwall."

"And I've delivered you here, I have," he insisted.

"It's Radborne Manor I wish to be delivered to," Billie argued, refusing to move another inch until this matter was resolved to her satisfaction.

The driver shook his cap-covered head and waved his hand in front of her. "I don't go there. Nobody does, especially on a night like this when the banshees are having a fine time for themselves."

Lord, not ghosts, Billie thought. The last thing she needed at this very moment was to hear about ghosts. Her legs began to tremble.

"Does Radborne Manor put a scare into you?" she inquired and was answered by a loud thunderclap that caused both of them to jump.

The driver cast an anxious glance over his right shoulder, to where Billie could only assume lay the direction of Radborne Manor. And where she had no intention of looking.

"That it does. Now I'll be leaving you here in the care of the good people of this inn. If you can find someone crazy enough to take you to the manor, then God go with you, mum."

Billie could clearly see his apprehension: His hands trembled and his eyes darted about cautiously. His disquietude added to her own. "I don't understand? Why do you fear going to Radborne Manor?"

The driver shook his head, crossed himself and spoke in a fearful tone. "It's haunted."

Chapter Two

The inhabitants of the Cox Crow Inn sat in rapt silence, staring at the young woman the raging storm had blown in with a gusty flourish through the front door.

Ghosts! Billie shuddered, shook the rain from her soaked garments and dropped her two stout traveling cases at her side. She untied her bonnet, slipped it off and grasped it firmly in one hand.

She stared back at the sea of inquisitive faces, her sharp brown eyes wide with curiosity. With her posture dignified and her tone tremulous, she announced, "I am Belinda Latham, the new owner of Radborne Manor."

Startled gasps and mutters raced throughout the large room. The roaring blaze in the huge hearth seemed to add its disfavor with a hiss and a sputter caused by the fat drippings of the roasting lamb that hung on a spit over the fire. Its highly seasoned scent teased Billie's nostrils and tempted her as did the tankards filled with hot cider spiced with cinnamon sticks and dollops of fresh whipped cream.

Not having eaten since the morning meal, Billie unconsciously licked her lips.

"The poor, dear girl is starving and her traveling on a night not fit for man or beast. 'Tis a shame."

The high-pitched nasal tone caught Billie's attention. A short, round woman, her gray hair piled in a group of tight curls on top of her head, waddled like a mother duck over to her and clucked her disapproval with her tongue and a shake of her head.

"You'll catch your death in those wet clothes. Now get that cape off and those gloves, and I'll fix you something to warm your innards and chase the shivers and chills from your bones."

"Best listen to Bessie, mum," a man called out. "She runs this inn and she always gets her way."

"You're right about that, George Beecham, and you won't be having supper if it's my way I get tonight," she sassed.

"Ouch," George yelled out with a laugh. "My wife is starving me again."

"By the looks of that big belly, George Beecham, I'd say that mouth of yours does more shoveling of food and guzzling of ale than is good for a man. This is no conversation to be welcoming the new owner of Radborne Manor," Bessie scolded, reaching to take Billie's cape and gloves from her.

Mutters once again stirred around the room, drifting overhead like the hazy hearth smoke that hung in the warm air.

Billie expected a certain amount of resistance, she could even understand it. She, a foreigner, had inherited land that had belonged to the Radborne family for centuries. What claim did she have to it? In their eyes, none.

Not one to back down from a challenge or adversity, Billie presented them with a dazzling smile, turning her simple attractiveness to sheer beauty. Many a man's mouth dropped open and many an eye widened at the sight of one so lovely.

Her soft voice laced with a melodius tone enthralled them even more. "I have traveled a great distance to claim my inheritance—"

"We were expecting a man," a gentleman near the hearth called out, forcing all eyes to glare accusingly at Billie.

"A simple explanation," she offered. They waited. "My given name is Belinda, but my family has called me Billie since my birth. All the documents my stepfather, Henry Radborne, had drawn up specifying me as his sole heir were written under the only name he had ever heard me called, Billie Latham."

"Mr. Hillard's going to be in a snit over this one," George said and scratched at the gray whisker stubble on his chin. "He's been boasting about the new owner being a big, strong man from America who will finally take care of the *problem* at the manor."

"Problem?" Billie asked nervously, not certain she liked the turn this conversation was taking. She hoped—no, prayed—it had nothing to do with ghosts and hauntings.

"Never you mind him," Bessie ordered, urging Billie with a gentle nudge toward a long table near the fiery hearth.

Billie relished the heat that caressed her back as she settled on the bench. She spread her skirt out so the damp wool could dry, especially the hem that dripped heavily with rainwater.

"You set yourself to rest. I'll fix you a plate of food to fill you up," Bessie said and hurried off.

Billie glanced around the room at the various faces still concentrated on her. She held their attention and their curiosity. Taking advantage of the moment she asked, "Is there anyone here who could take me on to Radborne Manor tonight?"

Silence filled the room, so cold that it sent chills through Billie, giving her the shivers. Even the hissing fire refused comment, its licking flames roasting the lamb soundlessly.

"She has a right to know," one voice whispered, though not low enough to keep from reaching Billie's ears.

"She should be told," another agreed softly.

Bessie hurried over to Billie like a protective mother duck. She placed the plate filled with slices of hot lamb, a fat potato and two thick slices of black, crusty bread in front of her, then added to it a tankard of hot cider with fresh whipped cream floating invitingly on the top.

The delicious aroma of the tempting food evaporated Billie's misgivings and she heartily dug into the mouthwatering fare.

Bessie swerved around, her hands hugging firmly to her wide hips and her full cheeks flushed red from working too near the hearth. "Will any of you fine gentlemen be willing to take the lady to the manor as she's asked?"

"She should be warned," argued one man.

"He's right," a woman agreed.

George banged his near-empty tankard of ale on the table. "She's the new owner. She should be told. What if she runs into the likes of *him* tonight?"

Shocked gasps circled the room and Billie caught sight of a few people hastily blessing themselves. Lord, she hoped this had nothing to do with ghosts. Humans she could deal with, but ghosts? She could still remember shivering beneath the covers when her mother dramatically recounted her favorite ghost tales.

"Who?" she asked hesitantly.

"*The ghost of Radborne Manor*," George bellowed and, as if adding credence to the tale, a sharp crack of thunder sounded over the inn.

Billie flinched while sipping the cider and a spot of whipped cream caught on the tip of her nose. She hastily wiped it off with her finger. She decided to test the validity of the tale, hoping it was only village entertainment for a stormy night. "Are you certain it's haunted?"

Bessie answered without hesitation. "For sure a ghost haunts the manor."

"Really?" Billie tested again and bit into the warm, tasty

bread though her stomach was aflutter from nerves, not hunger.

"Oh, it's not nonsense, mum," said a tall and thin woman whose numerous facial wrinkles attested to her advanced age. Her gait was slow as she walked over to the table to join Billie. "Marlee Dunlop," she said by way of introduction.

"Pleased to meet you, Marlee," Billie greeted the woman as she slid onto the bench opposite her.

" 'Tis the truth, mum. By all that's holy the manor is haunted," Marlee said and received a chorus of agreement from those in the room.

Billie, realizing some of these people might be new neighbors and others potential friends, didn't wish to antagonize them. She would be no worse for listening to what probably amounted to no more than a favorite tale about Radborne Manor, she hoped. After all, the stormy night did lend itself as a perfect setting for a haunting tale. The wind's howl sounded like a crying banshee while the rain pounded the windows, demanding entrance, and thunder rumbled angrily overhead.

With a speck of doubt she suggested, "As Mr. Hillard failed to apprise me in his letters of a resident ghost, perhaps someone would be so kind as to tell me of this restless spirit."

"It's only fair she knows," George said, grabbing his refilled tankard of ale. He shuffled lazily over to the table and joined Billie and Marlee.

Bessie shoved her ample rump on the bench next to Billie, placing a pitcher of ale and one of hot cider on the table. She intended to have no interruptions while the story was recounted.

The remaining occupants gravitated over to the table as well, all prepared to hear the ghost tale they undoubtedly had heard on more than one occasion.

Billie wondered who would begin the story and waited nervously.

Marlee began. "It was a shame it was."

All surrounding the table agreed with resounding "Ayes!"

Billie cupped her hands around the warm tankard of cider,

her meal left half finished, and concentrated on Marlee's soft, articulate voice, so perfect for storytelling.

"His lordship was a good man," Marlee continued. "Fair and decent in his dealings."

"Not a better man to be found," George praised, raising his drink in a salute.

"Quiet now," Bessie ordered and swiped his tankard from him. "Let Marlee tell the story."

George grumbled his dissatisfaction, but settled down.

Marlee sent Bessie a grateful nod and cleared her throat before she proceeded. "As I was saying, Lord Maximillian Radborne was a right decent man, respected by all, feared by many and fancied by every lady in the district and beyond. He was strapping in his height and width. He had the strength of twenty men, feared no man or beast and had the devil's own temper, that he did."

Billie remained mesmerized by Marlee's overly dramatic speech and her overly emphasized description of Lord Maximillian Radborne. The woman could really spin a tale.

Marlee's voice began on a whisper and intensified with each word. "It began on All Hallows' Eve." Her dark eyes wildly darted from one to the next around the table, causing most to shiver. "When the evil spirits rise and play their sinful games, tormenting the God-fearing folk and tempting the poor souls too weak to resist their immoral ways.

"Lord Radborne had hosted a lavish ball two nights before. The ladies had flocked in droves, enchanted by the lord's swarthy good looks and irresistible charm. The servants say there was much mischief-making and immoral activities afoot. An omen for sure of the tragedy to come."

Heads around the table bobbed slowly in agreement, and Billie found herself completely enthralled.

"The guests departed early on All Hallows' Eve, some fearing to be out after dark and others off to play wicked games. Quiet seemed to descend over St. Clair until late afternoon when the storm began. By nightfall the wind and rain raged out of control. Much like tonight."

Marlee paused and took a quick sip of ale. "The wrecking bell tolled at ten that night. The unfriendly Cornwall coast had claimed another ship." She blessed herself, then continued. "The villagers hurried to the rocky shore below to help survivors, if there were any. The waves crashed mercilessly against the shore, slapping viciously on the rocks and dragging from the beach whatever lay in its path.

"Naturally, Lord Radborne appeared, the sight of him taking one's breath away. He was soaked to the bone, his white silk shirt plastered to the strength of him. His polished boots rode high on his calves and his trousers were soaked to him like a second skin. His drenched dark hair was tied away from his face and his eyes . . ."

Marlee shivered and shook her head. "Some say he had the look of a madman that night and others say he acted like one. He ordered the boats drawn as the first desperate cry of a struggling survivor sounded. More cries followed. Anguished cries. Fearful cries that mingled with the roar of the brutal sea.

"The lord himself took to one of the boats and he rowed out with a crew of five. His boat made three trips out and back, more than any other. On the last return, the men spilled out of the boat exhausted, their hands cramped, their backs aching. The lord walked along the shore surveying the damage, his manservant hurrying behind him, attempting to drape his greatcoat over his shoulders.

"It was then it was heard. A lone, pitiful cry sounding like that of a lost, helpless child. It drifted in on a wave and crashed upon a jagged rock. The lord threw his coat off him and marched to the boat. Taking the oars in his powerful hands and with a shove from some still able men, he rowed out alone, into the darkness, into the mouth of the rampaging sea."

Marlee took a shuddering breath and those around her shivered.

Gooseflesh ran in fright up Billie's arms. Her breath locked in her throat and her heart hammered wildly.

"The cry soon died away and the villagers waited and waited. Morning brought with it a calming of the storm. The rain continued, though not as heavily. The sea spewed forth remnants of its rampage—barrels, pieces of the wrecked ship, trunks and, near the outcropping of rocks at the far end of the beach, the rough waves deposited the remains of the broken and battered rowboat of Lord Maximillian Radborne. The sea had swallowed him, burying him in a watery grave."

A breath of despair caught in Billie's throat. If this was no tale, but truth, her sympathy went out to Lord Radborne. He deserved a more appropriate burial for his heroism than the deep darkness of the sea. She shuddered, thinking of how alone he must have felt in his last moments of life, perhaps clinging to some hope that he would somehow be saved.

A quivering voice diverted Billie's attention.

"Listen, mum, please listen to Marlee," a young, pretty girl pleaded. "Don't go to the manor tonight. Tell her, Marlee. Tell her."

Marlee fortified herself with a stout swallow of ale and then proceeded. "His body was never found, so a service was held in the chapel and a stone marker was erected in his honor in the small cemetery." Marlee paused, obviously distressed about continuing.

"Go on. Tell her," George urged and a chorus of mumbled agreements followed.

Marlee nodded, her duty in the matter clear, though her voice was not quite as articulate as she announced, "A week later his *spirit* returned."

Those around the table hastily blessed themselves, including Marlee.

Billie swallowed the lump that had lodged deep in her throat. *He couldn't be the ghost? He just couldn't be.*

"Maximillian Radborne walks the halls of Radborne Manor, shouting and ranting his anger—his temper being what it was—his soul refusing to rest, to go peaceably to its reward."

"Or punishment," George mumbled.

"Hush up," Bessie scolded her husband.

Marlee cast George a reproachful glance and then went on. "He haunts the manor now searching for what answers, God only knows and only God can help him. On quiet, peaceful nights his distant cries can be heard in the village. They sometimes sound like whispers on the wind."

Billie trembled. Why couldn't the ghost be a weeping woman? Why was it a temperamental man? "Has anyone seen this ghost?" she asked.

Marlee wasted no time in responding. "Of course he's been seen. Hester, one of the house staff, was cleaning the lord's chamber early one evening a couple of weeks after the tragedy. It hadn't been touched since the night of his death and Matilda, the manor housekeeper, ordered Hester to clean it. Not that the young girl wanted to, but duties are duties.

"A sudden chill breeze flickered the candles' flames and sent shivers up Hester's spine. She turned from her chores wanting to rid herself of the strange room, and there Lord Maximillian Radborne stood by the blazing hearth, his elbow braced on the mantel as if he had not a care in the world. He was drenched from head to toe and wore the same clothes he had drowned in. He stared at her, his sea-blue eyes blank. He smiled, that wicked half smile the ladies all loved, and held out his hand to her. Hester ran screaming from the room, right out the manor's front door, never to return."

"It sends the shivers through you, it does," a woman at the table said and swallowed a generous gulp of ale.

Once again Billie asked a question, certain she would regret the answer. "You've all heard his cries?"

"Shouts be more like it," George amended and swiped his tankard back from Bessie. "All in the village have heard the strange sounds when passing by the manor late at night. That's why we be minding our own business and keeping our distance from the place."

"Vicar Bosworth doesn't believe the manor haunted," Bessie corrected.

A kindred spirit, Billie thought jokingly, though not laughing. "Vicar Bosworth?" she questioned.

"The vicar is new to St. Clair, being here only six months. A kind, dear man he is," Bessie said.

"The vicar would give you refuge tonight," Marlee strongly advised.

Billie shook her head though her common sense disagreed. "There is no need. I have the manor to go to."

"Didn't you listen? Didn't you hear all I said?" Marlee insisted and grabbed at the small metal cross hanging on a chain around her neck as if in protection. "It's a stormy night much like the one the lord died on. He'll surely haunt the manor tonight."

"I do thank you for your concern," Billie said and though it was a blatant lie courageously added, "I don't believe in ghosts. My journey has been long and I have looked forward to my arrival in my new home." Billie cast a quick glance around the room. "Won't someone please take me to the manor tonight? I'll gladly pay for the service."

Bessie nudged George in his beefy arm. "Take her," she mumbled softly. "We could use the money."

"Are you crazy, old woman?" George complained.

"Crazy enough to realize we need the money. In a few days you'll be out of your weekly allowance of ale money and my stitching hasn't brought in enough this month to give you extra. No ride to the manor. No ale money for the month."

George feared ghosts, but he feared going without ale for a month even more. He cleared his throat and spoke. "I'll take you," he said and added quickly. "But only to the gate."

Bessie shot him a scathing look, but George held his ground.

Billie inched off the bench slowly while strongly debating the wisdom of her decision. "I've been caught in worse downpours. A bit of a walk won't hurt me. I accept your offer, George."

"You can't be serious," Marlee protested. " 'Tis foolish to attempt such a feat."

"My arrival at Radborne Manor may not be as I fancied it, but I'll arrive nonetheless," Billie assured her while attempting to reassure herself. "A little drenching wont' hurt me. I had sent word to the manor that I would arrive tonight, and I suspect the warmth of a fire's hearth is waiting for me."

"And the ghost?" Marlee asked. All around the table grew silent as they awaited her answer.

Billie reached for her cape, which was draped over a chair near the fire, the wool almost dry. She slipped it on and fastened the clasp near her throat. "Why, I shall tell Lord Maximillian Radborne that he no longer owns Radborne Manor and he should take his leave, *permanently*."

"Ouch!" George yelped. "I wouldn't be doing that if I were you. He has the devil's own temper."

"And I," Billie said, tying her bonnet firmly beneath her chin with shaking hands, "am as stubborn as a mule. Now let's be off. The rain sounds as though it has subsided."

"A breather, that's all," George said and grabbed her two traveling cases sitting by the door. "It will be a steady downpour again in a minute or two. We'd best hurry. Wait outside the door while I bring the inn's coach around from the stables."

As heads were shaking and tongues clucking their disapproval, Billie took her leave of the Cox Crow Inn.

Chapter
Three

Billie hurried into the coach, the rain now a mere trickle.
Once situated on the well-worn brown velvet seat, she said
a silent prayer for the storm to hold its temper until her arrival at the manor door.

The ride was surprisingly short and a nervous George
rushed her out of the coach. "Leave your heavy luggage
until morning, my lady, and I'll deliver it to the manor then."
His tongue continued its rapid-fire directions. "You'd best
hurry before the rain picks up again."

After being deposited outside the coach, with a helpful
and hasty hand from George, Billie handed him several
coins. She was about to extend her appreciation for his services when he bobbed his head, ran to the front of the coach,
scurried atop the driver's seat and, with a sharp snap of the
reins, took off.

She shook her head and shivered. Marlee's storytelling

talent had certainly put the fright into him and herself as
well. She was feeling none too confident at the moment. She
turned reluctantly, her traveling cases in hand, ready to proceed.

Lightning struck, illuminating the dark sky and silhouet-
ting the manor in all its ghostly splendor.

A gargoyle. Billie gasped and stumbled back. She swore
she had seen the tiny demon creature, its grin wide, perched
near a turret.

Your overactive imagination, she scolded herself and
walked with unsure steps through the tall, open, iron-spiked
gates. The drive to the manor appeared longer than she had
imagined.

Get your feet moving, she cautioned herself and felt several fat raindrops pelt her bonnet and cape.

Her steps were quick despite the mud-soaked driveway.
Though it was difficult to see, her eyes stayed glued on the
ominous manor in the distance. Its formidable size—three
stories, turrets, adjacent wings and such—loomed like a sin-
ister foe waiting to swallow her up. The unfriendly stone ed-
ifice extended no welcome to visitors; on the contrary, it
warned them away. Did the manor somehow inherit its previous owner's disposition, intimidating those who came to
call? If so that would change and quickly. She would—

Billie's thoughts were scattered in a flash when her eyes
noticed a flicker of light in a lone upstairs window. The light
steadied for a moment as though whoever was holding it had
stopped moving and then suddenly the light vanished as if
snuffed out in haste.

Not realizing she had stopped walking, Billie picked up
her step considerably, the surrounding darkness and steady
rain most uninviting to a lone female traveler. Not to mention the shivers that raced through her as she recalled Marlee's suggestive and haunting words. *He'll surely haunt the
manor tonight.*

The thick wooden door with its roaring lion knocker was

a most welcome sight, though the animal's snarl was far from a friendly greeting.

Billie raised her hand to the metal ring, rainwater dripped from her drenched gloves and plump drops fell from the brim of her scoop bonnet. She was thoroughly soaked and had just realized it, so engrossed had she been with her first sight of Radborne Manor.

She sounded the knocker, anxious to be in out of the storm that seemed to have intensified even more with her arrival.

Fearing the thunderclap that had sounded simultaneously with her knock had caused the occupants not to hear her summons, she raised her hand to the metal ring once again.

The door flew open.

"What is it you want?" the gruff little man asked. He was shorter than Billie's five foot four inches, and his clothes gave the appearance of having been hastily slipped into. Even the few hairs on the top of his partially bald head stood up as though perturbed by her intrusion.

Billie stiffened her posture and resolve. This night had been trying enough. She was wet and tired and wanted nothing more than a welcoming bed to soothe her aches. The servant's ill manners she would deal with tomorrow. Her voice took on a decidedly authoritative tone. "I am Billie Latham, new owner of Radborne Manor."

The gruff man's stoic expression switched from one of shock to delight in an instant. He stepped aside and waved her in. "Begging your pardon, my lady. Please hurry in out of such a foul night."

Billie entered her new home soaked to the bone and dripping with rainwater. But despite her miserable state she managed a pleasant smile.

"Forgive my rudeness," the man continued, reaching out and snatching Billie's traveling cases from her along with her drenched cape. "I thought your knock was a bothersome prankster from the village. Matilda, my wife and the manor housekeeper, and myself—I am Pembrooke—my lady . . ."

Billie acknowledged his introduction with a nod.

". . . Weren't expecting you tonight, though your message indicated such. We assumed the storm would delay you."

Billie struggled to remove her sodden gloves, giving up after several useless attempts and focused instead on the disposal of her bonnet. "Being from Nantucket, Massachusetts—where a storm is no stranger—I decided the foul weather would not delay my journey here."

Pembrooke coughed, clearing his throat as though he hesitated to speak. He accepted her bonnet that she held out to him. "Excuse my directness, my lady, but Matilda, myself—and Mr. Hillard to be sure—were expecting a gentleman."

Billie sighed wearily. She wasn't up to another explanation. Tomorrow was soon enough to clarify her ownership. "I will gladly set yours, Matilda's and Mr. Hillard's mind to rest concerning my identity tomorrow. But tonight I am wet and tired and would like very much to retire to my room."

"I am sorry, my lady, you must think me not only rude, but incompetent," Pembrooke said, accepting the wet gloves she had finally managed to disengage from her fingers.

"Not at all," Billie offered. "Anyone could announce themselves the new owner. It was wise of you to question me. And if I wasn't so exhausted I would produce the necessary papers to prove my identity."

Pembrooke spoke sternly. "Nonsense. I shall see you to your room at once. Tomorrow is time enough to conclude the legal matters. Please follow me and I will have you settled in no time."

Billie, her legs aching and her body bone-tired, followed the servant, though his steps were too spry for her to keep up. Her interest in her surroundings also did much to slow her pace.

The foyer, she had observed from a quick glance, was impressive: a white marble tile floor, brass candle wall sconces, pictures in gilt frames, pieces of dark furniture heavily polished to a high shine and a cherry wood staircase that ascended up to the center of the second floor and branched off to the left and right.

Billie paused at the top of the steps and took a quick peek at the huge oval window that was centered on the landing. Its thick glass panes were being heavily hammered by the raging storm outside. She hurried off to the right, having noticed Pembrooke turn that way. It wouldn't do her any good to get lost, especially in a supposedly haunted manor.

Lightning, angrily persistent, struck again, flooding through the window and into the hallway with a brief but startling shot of brilliant light.

Billie turned to shield her eyes from the bright flash only to be greeted by an unexpected and formidable face that made her catch her breath and tore a strangled scream from her throat.

Pembrooke rushed to her side. She stood pinned against the wall opposite the portrait that glared down at her. She purposely avoided contact with it, keeping her eyes fixed on Pembrooke.

"Wh-who—" Billie bit her lip for a second to gain control of her nervous tremors. "Who is he?"

Pembrooke held the brass candlestick high, the flame's light illuminating the portrait once more, but not as sinisterly as the sharp lighting had done. "That is Lord Maximillian Radborne, God rest his soul."

Billie dared not step forward, though her eyes dared another peek. The life-size portrait of the man intimidated in every sense of the word. The artist surely had exaggerated his size and his features. No man alive possessed such blatant good looks. His nose was painted too finely, his lips stroked too temptingly, his cheeks too high and prominent, his chin too strong in character and his eyes . . .

His eyes were like the sea, a blue-green in color, and turbulent, yet haunting in their hypnotic beauty.

She shivered, an icy chill racing straight through her. Had Marlee's description of Lord Radborne been correct, or had the artist unleashed his talent and imagination to embellish the portrait in order to please the man who had posed for it?

"Come, my lady, it is bed you need and perhaps some hot tea or milk to soothe your fatigue," Pembrooke offered, stepping in front of her and breaking the mesmerizing contact of the portrait.

"Thank you, Pembrooke," she said, clearing her fuzzy head with a shake. "But bed is all I need right now."

"Very good, madam," he answered and continued on until he stopped at the double doors at the end of the hall. He pushed them open and walked in, quickly lighting candles throughout the room.

Billie entered and for an instant felt a brisk breeze rush over her. She hugged her arms around her.

"A fire will warm up this room in no time," Pembrooke assured her and busied himself at the hearth, lighting the waiting logs.

Billie hurried in the rest of the way and cast a quick glance about. She wrinkled her nose in distaste. The furnishings were too dark and heavy for her taste, and the drab plum drapes and bed coverings matched the somberness of the large, uninviting room.

"Is there anything else I can get you, my lady?" Pembrooke inquired, standing near the door.

Billie looked at the hearth. A joyful dance of flames cast warmth and light into the room and added the only bit of welcome. "Nothing, Pembrooke. You have seen to everything. I shall speak with you and your wife, Matilda, in the morning."

"As you wish. And welcome to Radborne Manor," he said and with a curt nod and a brief grin, he closed the door.

Tired and anxious to climb into the large bed, Billie hurried over to the hearth and peeled her wet clothes from her body until only her white cotton shift remained. She arranged her dress and underclothes on two chairs near the fire to dry. She took her night rail from her traveling case and shook the wrinkles out before draping it over her arm.

Then she returned to the bureau where she had spied a stack of towels. After depositing her night rail on the edge of the bed, she snatched up one of the towels to dry herself.

The journey had been long and tiresome, her arrival not at all what she had anticipated. She had had doubts that her decision to come to St. Clair had been a wise one and within the last few hours those doubts had threatened to destroy her confidence completely. But she was finally here in *her* new home. Here she would begin her new life, make friends, perhaps even meet someone, fall in love and marry. She anxiously looked forward to her future.

Billie's courage returned. Blaming fatigue for her previous worries she set about to ready herself for bed. She slipped her shift's straps from her shoulders, pushing the material down to her waist and exposing her full breasts. Her rosy nipples responded sharply to the wet cotton being brushed off them and they instantly puckered.

She toweled her upper body dry, sighing as she rotated her shoulders back to ease the weariness from them. A sudden gust of cool air swept through the room and blew out several of the candles, leaving only the two on the bureau near where she stood lighted. Marlee's tale of Hester, the manor maid, came back to haunt her and for a moment she stood frozen in place, the towel hugged tightly to her breasts.

Turn you fool, she silently admonished herself. There are no such things as ghosts. No one is standing behind you. Lord Radborne is dead, drowned and buried in a watery grave.

Her head thrown up in confidence and her legs trembling, Billie swerved around. She sighed with relief. No apparition haunted the mantel. The crackling flames were her only company.

Nonetheless, she hurried into her night rail, shaking out of the rest of her shift as she pulled the night rail over her head to cover her suddenly chilled body from neck to toes.

She blew out one candle and grasped the other candlestick so tightly in her hand that her knuckles turned a pale white.

Once again a cool breeze blew into the room, only this time the air that drifted around her stung her nostrils with the pungent scent of salty seawater.

Her legs trembled badly, her skin crawled with goose-flesh, her heart beat at a marching rhythm and she pressed her eyes shut tightly.

"I won't look. I won't look," she mumbled under her breath. "I don't believe in ghosts. I don't believe in ghosts."

The scent of sea air engulfed her and she shook her head and wrinkled her nose against the obvious. She had to turn around. She had no choice. If she didn't think about it and just—

As Billie swung around, the flame of the candle she held flickered wildly.

Her eyes instantly focused on the mantel. She gasped and the candlestick she held fell from her hand, extinguishing the flame with a whoosh.

Lord Maximillian Radborne stood in all his splendor and glory, his arm resting negligently on the mantel, his sea-colored eyes intent on her, his starkly handsome features even more striking than in his portrait if that were possible. He wore black breeches and boots and nothing else. His chest, hard and heavy with muscles, glistened with dampness from the fire's light and his dark, wet hair reached his shoulders. He was without a doubt a magnificent ghost.

"What the bloody hell are you doing in my room?"

Billie, stunned that he spoke and with such a temper, took a step back.

He took a step toward her.

"Go away," she shouted and waved at him. "Go back where you belong."

He grinned, though barely, and advanced another step toward her. *"I belong here. This is my room and that is my bed."*

Fear prickled Billie's cool flesh and she spoke with a

courage she didn't feel. "I demand you go away. This is now my room and that is now my bed."

His barely noticeable smile faded. *"This,"* he enunciated strongly while stretching his hand out around the room, *"belongs to me and* that"—he pointed to the bed—*"is where I sleep."*

He smiled then, wide and wickedly and with each word he advanced on Billie with sure and steady strides. *"And you, madam, are most welcome to join me."*

Billie's eyes widened with each step he took toward her. The air grew heavier with the scent of the sea, the blaze in the hearth hissed and Lord Radborne reached down at the fastening to his breeches when he was but two steps away from Billie.

Billie felt her breath catch, her legs give way and darkness engulf her as she dropped to the carpet in a dead faint.

Chapter
Four

Maximillian scooped her slender body up into his arms before she could hit the floor. She felt more etheral than real, so light was she in his powerful embrace. Her complexion remained pale as Maximillian walked over to the bed and rested her down upon the mattress.

Her nightdress had tangled up around her thighs exposing her slim legs and Maximillian hastened to slip the linen gown down. His hand quickly ceased the action when his fingers accidentally slipped along her naked thigh.

Soft. His mind cried and his fingers felt. He caressed her thigh, so silky and warm to his touch. Her naked skin invited more intimate exploration. After all, she had invaded *his* bedchamber. And any woman who found her way into his bedchamber always found herself in his bed. His reputation with women was notorious. He was an expert lover and a first-rate rake. And if this woman insisted on occupying his bed, then she would learn soon enough that she wouldn't occupy it alone.

Maximillian slowly stroked down along her calf, taking note of her small feet. She was a tempting morsel and he was feeling hungry.

He shook his head, hastily making a decision and with swift agility tucked Billie's night rail down over her legs and pulled the counterpane up beneath her chin. He had more pressing matters on his mind.

He stepped back from the bed and dropped into the nearby chair. He stretched his long legs out in front of him, steepled his fingers against his mouth and studied her by the candle's flickering glow. She possessed a rare type of beauty that made people stop and take notice. Her long, shiny hair was a strange combination of dark and light blond as if one color warred with the other for dominance and her deep brown eyes, so intoxicating in their darkness, had glared at him with strength and courage.

Maximillian grinned, recalling how she had stood in defiance and had challenged him. *Him.* The lord of Radborne Manor. She even had the audacity to order him to leave and go back to wherever it was he belonged.

Maximillian laughed softly, remembering the telltale shiver of uncertainty that ran through her when she spoke. But still she had faced him with more courage than most; of course, that was until he approached her and had purposely reached for his breeches.

That was rather naughty of him, but then he did want to see her reaction and she had reacted. She had fainted.

He had expected to be sitting here speaking with his Uncle Henry. He had never considered the possibility of his uncle's death and his heir arriving at Radborne Manor, especially an attractive female heir who would occupy his bed and tempt his wayward soul.

Billie moaned softly and turned on her side.

Maximillian stood in a flash and backed up slowly, al-

lowing the shadows in the room to devour him. He watched
Billie stir restlessly and knew he must take his leave.

Fate had delivered him an unexpected twist, but he was
accustomed to handling the unexpected. And a woman really presented little challenge. He smiled confidently. He
would easily handle this minor inconvenience. He anxiously
anticipated further encounters with her.

"*Until next time, my sweet,*" he whispered and bowed
with gentle grace before disappearing into the darkest shadows of the night.

The early morning sun flooded Billie's bedroom, tickling
her eyes to wakefulness. She yawned and lazily stretched
her arms above her head.

She shot up in bed and surveyed every inch of the room
with watchful eyes. Everything looked to be in place and no
candlestick and half-burned candle lay spilled on the floor.
Had the ghost been real or an illusion caused by her exhausted state?

"No reason to waste the beautiful day on nonsense," she
admonished herself and cast the covers aside to hurry out of
bed.

She paused a moment and cast a suspicious glance down
at the carpet. No boot print blemished the dark-gray wool
carpet. Had her imagination actually gotten the better of
her? She shook off her last ounce of doubt. With so much to
do and see, she was wasting time on nonsensical thoughts of
restless spirits.

Since it was early March and the weather still had a bite
to it, Billie was glad she had chosen wisely and packed her
wool dresses. She snatched a soft lilac garment from her
traveling case, shaking out the few wrinkles before draping
it over a chair.

It didn't take long for her to wash the sleep from her face,
and pile her long hair into a riot of curls atop her head. Why
she bothered to fuss was a puzzle to her. In a short time the
blond strands would fall loose and tease her neck, forehead

and cheeks just as they had always stubbornly managed to do. She in turn chose to ignore her hair's mulish nature and overlook its usual unkempt state.

She pulled her gown over her head and wiggled it down her slim body. The popular Grecian style was girdled just below her bosom, with a low square neckline and puffed sleeves that slimmed to hug her slender wrists. She quickly slipped her white stockinged feet into her pumps and was out the door, rushing down the hall to find Pembrooke.

Until she halted abruptly at the portrait of Lord Maximillian Radborne. Tilting her head, she concentrated on the life-size painting and decided the man was just as intimidating in the bright sunlight as he had been last night in the wake of the storm.

"Imagination," Billie mumbled, convincing herself that besides talent the artist had possessed a vivid—if not wild—imagination.

Pembrooke was at the bottom of the staircase, a silver tray in hand. He was about to ascend the steps when Billie rushed down to meet him.

"Good morning, Pembrooke," she said and hurried on, allowing the man no time for response. "Is that for me? How thoughtful, but unnecessary. I'll take my breakfast down here."

"As you wish, my lady." He delivered an affirmative nod with his response and turned, walking stiffly toward two wide open doors.

With quick steps Billie caught up with him. And with just as quick a glance about the room, she gave her head a decisive shake. "How depressing."

"I beg your pardon, my lady?" Pembrooke said, having placed the tray at the head of the highly polished rosewood dining table.

Billie pointed to the walls. "The color, what is it?" The somber walls appeared lifeless, the drab color robbing energy and spirit from the room. A room that could certainly, with the right touch, be breathtaking.

"Pewter gray," Pembrooke answered with an indignant flare to his wide nostrils.

"Pewter gray," Billie repeated. "Was Lord Radborne partial to drab and muted colors?"

"His taste was impeccable. People often commented about the house."

A faint smile tempted Billie's lips. "I imagine they did."

"When Lord Radborne was alive, visitors came from far and wide," Pembrooke informed her, taking the silverware from the tray.

Billie realized his intention was to set a place for her at the long table, which could clearly hold twenty people, and she gently tapped him on his arm.

Pembrooke stared down at her poking finger and then looked directly up at her.

Billie ignored his acute glare. "I'll take my breakfast in the kitchen."

Affronted by her suggestion, Pembrooke took a step back and repeated her strange request. "You wish to breakfast in the kitchen?"

"Of course," Billie answered, not at all perturbed that he found her instructions offensive. "I wish to meet your wife, Matilda. After which I intend to go to the village and speak with Mr. Hillard. So let us not waste any more time. Where is the kitchen?"

Pembrooke was about to protest when Billie reached for the serving tray. Aghast by her improper behavior, Pembrooke snatched it from her grasp and marched out of the dining room with a gruff "Follow me."

Bright white walls greeted Billie when she reached the kitchen and she smiled. Copper pots hung on overhead hooks above the worktable while herbs hung in bunches on the drying rack near the hearth. Clay pots of flowering herbs lined the wide shelf beneath the lone window under which sat a trestle-table and two accompanying benches.

Billie sniffed the warm, spicy air appreciatively. She detected the scent of cinnamon and nutmeg, a favorite blend that brought back memories of her home. The nostalgic thought left her with a mixed sense of loss and welcome.

"Have you gone daft?" Matilda scolded her husband. "Bringing the lady here?"

Billie offered a smile with an explanation. "The kitchen is my favorite room in the house. It always smells so inviting. And *your* kitchen smells deliciously inviting."

Matilda beamed, her round face blushing with the sincere compliment. She was equal in height to her husband, her figure being pleasantly round but not plump. Her gray hair was neatly fashioned in a knot at her nape. The color almost matched her starched gray dress that was brightened by a white collar and wide cuffs and a white bib apron. "It is an honor to have you here, my lady."

"I'm happy to be here." Billie returned the sincere reception with honesty. She had worried about the difficulties she would face in setting down new roots in a foreign country. But to her relief it appeared kitchens were conducive to establishing friendships no matter the location. "Won't you join me in some tea? I have tons of questions to ask you about the manor."

Matilda shot her husband a questioning glance. Pembrooke shrugged and shook his head.

"You wish me to join you for your meal, my lady?"

"Yes. With so much to learn about the manor and the area, I am anxious to start." Billie scooted in along the bench, her back to the window so the sun's warm rays could toast her.

Matilda took the tray from Pembrooke and carried it to the table after having added another cup.

Pembrooke left the room wanting no part of women's gossiping tongues.

Billie enjoyed the hot cinnamon bread spread generously with honey butter while Matilda, still reserved in her manner, explained the difficulties and joys of running such a large home.

"Help is hard to keep," Matilda said.

"Because of the ghost?" Billie asked, deciding it was time

to learn more about the apparition that supposedly haunted her chamber last night.

Matilda paled and her mouth trembled slightly when she asked, "Ghost?"

"The ghost of Radborne Manor." Billie seemed surprised by her response. She had to have been familiar with the ghost stories concerning the manor, so why the nervous tremors? "The villagers told me of him last night."

"Rumors and rubbish," Matilda snapped, though her voice still quivered.

"My sentiments exactly," Billie agreed, though a slight tremor of uncertainty raced through her.

"This old manor has drafts and chills enough to send the shivers through a person. But no ghost haunts its halls."

"Then why the stories?"

"Legends," Matilda said, and added another scoop of sugar to her tea, stirring it gently along with her thoughts. "People love to spin tales and create legends, and if there ever was a man a legend could be made of, it was Lord Radborne."

Was there no one in St. Clair who thought unkindly of Maximillian Radborne? It appeared the number of his virtues knew no bounds. He had been extraordinary, or so people recounted often enough. Billie kept her thoughts to herself and continued to listen.

Matilda surprised Billie when she stood and said, "Let me acquaint you with the main portion of the manor. You don't want to be getting yourself lost."

At that moment Billie learned two important facts about Matilda. She didn't gossip and she could be trusted.

Matilda guided her through the various rooms on the first floor. Billie was whisked through the receiving parlor, the family parlor, the library and the study. Billie left each with a dismal shake of her head. Dark colors. Portraits of pinched-faced people. Heavily tasseled drapes.

The conservatory was next and it took Billie's breath away. The glass room abounded with plants, some flowering and some rich in green foliage. Comfortable chairs and sofas with exotic jungle print cushions—*certainly not Lord Radborne's drab taste* she thought—and several tables, which held a variety of books and plants, welcomed visitors. Billie knew her visits here would be frequent.

On the second floor Matilda introduced her to the master wing where Billie resided. Off the long corridor sat an embroidery parlor, a small family parlor, the wife's quarters and of course the master's chambers which she currently occupied.

"Now for the left wing," Matilda said, and turned in the opposite direction.

"Wait," Billie called out, her voice bouncing off the walls in a soft echo. She hurried up to Matilda. "We'll tour the remainder of the house another time. I wish to speak with Mr. Hillard."

"Very well, my lady. Then I shall see to your unpacking while you are gone. George Beecham left your luggage here early this morning. I'll make certain your things are attended to properly."

Servants attending to chores she had normally handled herself would take some getting used to. And though she enjoyed some of the fuss her new lifestyle bestowed on her, she didn't wish to relinquish all her familiar ways. Especially since her mother had ingrained the fact that *idleness fostered laziness*.

She thanked Matilda for her help, receiving a surprised look from the woman as she hurried off to her room.

Billie spent a few minutes gathering the necessary papers to present to Mr. Hillard. She slipped into her matching lilac spencer jacket and tucked on her scoop bonnet, securing the ties beneath her chin. Her pale gray gloves were added just before she left the room.

Pembrooke waited at the front door for her. "The coach is being brought around front for you, my lady."

"The day is too glorious to ride. I thought I would walk."

Pembrooke shook his head like a patient parent advising a child. "That is not a good idea. The roads are thick with mud from yesterday's downpour."

Billie frowned in disappointment. She loved to walk and had done so often in Nantucket. There was always a neighbor or friend about with a smile or a bit of conversation to share. She had hoped to find the same friendly atmosphere in St. Clair. But Pembrooke was right. In her haste to make friends she had failed to consider the condition of the roads after last night's storm.

"The coach it will be," she announced and was rewarded with a satisfied smile from Pembrooke.

In minutes she was in the village, her ride having been far more pleasant and less bumpy than the previous night. Benny, a dear old man who was hired on occasion from the village, promised to return at three sharp for her.

Billie knocked at the door of the Percy Hillard's stone cottage, prepared for what she was certain would be a confrontation.

After a long fifteen minutes of reading the documents Billie had presented to him, Percy Hillard proclaimed, "I don't believe it. You're Billie Latham?"

"You have the proof in your hands," Billie snapped, irritated by his skepticism. She had communicated often through the post with this man. He had been professional and concise in his dealings, but then he had assumed her a man. Did he feel her inadequate of managing the manor and her affairs simply because she was a female? His sharply punctuated response irked her all the more.

"I still don't believe it."

"I am Billie Latham and I own Radborne Manor," she persisted. "The documents are legal and binding. You processed them yourself. Need I say more?"

Percy Hillard mopped his perspiring brow with his white handkerchief. "Good Lord, Radborne would turn over in his grave if he knew."

Billie didn't care for the man's poor conduct, or his attitude toward her gender in accepting her ownership of the manor, so her response was less than delicate. "From what I understand he's not in it."

Percy's eyes almost popped out of his head and he found speech difficult. "You-you saw his-his ghost?"

Billie stood, a silent announcement that their meeting was nearly over. "A little detail you forgot to mention?"

"Local stories with no foundation to them," Percy defended, his handkerchief mopping his brow once again.

Billie tugged her gloves back on. "I don't believe in ghosts, Mr. Hillard." She issued a short, silent prayer for her fib before proceeding. "But I do believe the documents I signed are in order. I now own Radborne Manor . . . ghost and all. I expect a full accounting of the estate in two days' time. Since there is nothing else to discuss, I shall be on my way."

She closed the door on the shaking man as he poured himself a liberal glass of brandy.

At the end of the crushed shell walkway Billie paused and released the exasperated sigh that had been bottled inside her.

The last few months had been difficult. She had lost her family, her home and her security. And just when she thought the situation hopeless, the letter from Percy Hillard had arrived and resurrected her courage with the promise of a stable future.

Radborne Manor was now her home, regardless of a less than joyful welcome and a so-called ghost with a spirited attitude.

With a spring in her step and determination in her heart, she set off to acquaint herself with the village.

Chapter
Five

The village of St. Clair was alive with activity. Carts burdened with hay, produce and chopped wood meandered down the street, the horses as lazy in their pace as the drivers themselves. Cheerful greetings sounded often in the crisp air. Carts stopped alongside each other for drivers to exchange recent news. Children chased one another in jest, while dogs joined in the game, nipping at their heels and mothers chattered in groups, spreading the latest gossip.

St. Clair was many miles removed from Nantucket, but the village scene was a common one. Billie had hoped to find similarities and she hadn't been disappointed. Mothers were mothers and children were children no matter where they lived.

She surveyed the remainder of the street, noting the Cox Crow Inn sat near the opposite end and taking care to remember an apothecary shop stood next to a copper shop. A

seamstress shop and a tin shop resided across the street
while private stone cottages mingled amongst them all.

Taking a deep breath, Billie smiled as the pungent scent
of fresh-caught fish filled her nostrils. It was a familiar odor,
and not surprising to detect, since fishing was the mainstay
of this small coastal village, much like Nantucket. More and
more a sense of coming home surrounded Billie's new, yet
strikingly similar, environment.

Billie's wandering glance caught sight of Bessie near the
end of the street. She was involved in a conversation with an
older, distinguished woman and a man. Her interest piqued
and anxious to establish friendships, Billie took herself off
to join the trio.

Bessie smiled broadly at her approach. She bobbed her
head. "Good day, my lady. How was your first night at Radborne Manor?"

"Uneventful," Billie said, aware that gossip spread
rapidly in small villages and she, more than likely, was the
main topic at the moment.

"How delightful," the older woman remarked. "I purposely took a morning stroll hoping to meet St. Clair's
newest resident and here you are."

Bessie politely made the introductions. "Billie Latham,
may I present Mrs. Claudia Nickleton."

"The town busybody, but then I have no other forms of
entertainment to occupy my time, or interesting hobbies to
keep me active. Anyway," Claudia said with a wave of her
hand, "busybodying suits me."

Billie admired her forthrightness. There was nothing pre-
tentious about her. Tall and slim, elegantly attired in a soft
powder-blue day dress with matching cape and bonnet atop
her white hair that curled softly around her narrow face,
Claudia epitomized the perfect lady. Billie took an instant
liking to her, taking special note of her eyes, the blue color
being as sharp as her wit.

"I am pleased to meet you, Mrs. Nickleton."

"Good heavens, dear, call me Claudia, or you will make

me feel ancient. Not that I'm not, but I would much prefer to think of myself as ageless."

Billie didn't hide her smile. It spread generously across her face highlighting her gentle features to stunning.

"Good Lord, you are a beauty," Claudia complimented and directed her next comment to the man who stood silently beside her. "Don't you think she is a beauty, Vicar Bosworth?"

Billie had attempted to sneak a glimpse of the vicar while conversing with Claudia, but to no avail. He had remained quiet, his head bent and his shoulders hunched. His posture appeared to be permanently positioned as though in perpetual prayer.

Vicar Bosworth raised his head slowly, his spectacles sliding to the tip of his nose while he studied Billie intently for a brief moment. His response was a simple "Yes."

Billie rarely blushed, yet she couldn't prevent the heat that rushed to tinge her cheeks. The vicar was far from a handsome man; scholarly was a more accurate description. His dark hair was severely drawn back, accentuating a complexion so pale he appeared almost a ghostly white. His height was hard to determine due to his stooped posture. He had a slight bulge to his midriff and on his chin off to the right sat a dark mole. His deep, soothing voice and simple, yet sincere response had struck a tender chord within her. He actually intrigued her. Why? She couldn't quite understand.

"John, really," Claudia scolded with a sly grin. "You are so articulate when you deliver Sunday service. A simple yes will not do—elaborate."

The vicar, made nervous by Claudia's demand, shifted his weight from one leg to another and pushed his glasses up on the bridge of his nose only to have them slide down again. When he finally spoke, his voice was once again soothing, reaching out to comfort and support. "Welcome to St. Clair, Miss Latham."

"Oh fuss and bother, John," Claudia snapped with motherly scolding. "How do you ever expect to find yourself a wife if you don't take advantage of opportunities?"

The vicar shook his head at Claudia and attempted a distraction by righting his glasses. The wire rims refused to comply.

Billie tactfully interfered, noting the vicar's discomfort and wishing to spare him embarrassment. "I am pleased to meet you, Vicar Bosworth, and I am happy to be here in St. Clair."

"Well, Bessie and I have errands to run," Claudia said in a rush while giving Bessie a gentle shove. "You two just carry on with your lively conversation. I'll be in touch soon for a visit to the manor. Ta-ta." And with a flippant wave of her hand she was off.

"Claudia Nickleton is one of St. Clair's more colorful residents," the vicar said with a faint smile.

She noticed his smile was hesitant as if he were unsure, more of himself than of her. She favored his kindly manner and felt comfortably at ease around him. "I have met only a few of the villagers and found them most friendly and helpful."

"Then you plan to remain in St. Clair?"

Billie thought his question odd, but given the gossip concerning the manor she supposed his query was reasonable. "Radborne Manor is my home now. I find it quite to my liking and have no intention of deserting it." She thought she caught the slight tensing of his jaw and his tone took on a deeper quality when he spoke.

"You are a brave woman to travel so many miles alone and to such an uncertain future."

"Uncertain?" she asked confused. Why would he feel her future uncertain? Did he, too, think so little of a woman's ability to survive on her own?

He dropped his gaze to his scuffed boots, apparently embarrassed by his remark and the need to clarify it. "I only meant that—that without family and friends and in unfamiliar surroundings your future could—could prove lonely at times."

Billie found his response thoughtful and considerate, like

that of a trustworthy friend. She would enjoy getting to know him better. "Vicar Bosworth, you obviously need to learn more about me. I love adventure and challenge, and travel to distant lands excites me. I look forward to making friends and hopefully establishing a family here for myself."

Again the vicar's smile appeared hesitant as did his response. "Please call me John and—"

"Then you must call me Billie," she interjected then waited for him to proceed.

"Billie," he said with a nod and added softly. "I would like to learn more about you."

Pleased by his willingness toward the same notion, she extended an appropriate invitation. "I would like that, John. Perhaps you could join me for supper one evening?"

His hands were instantly at his nose, pushing his spectacles up only to have them slide down again. Billie realized it as a nervous gesture and she wondered if she had somehow offended him.

She sought to correct any error she had inadvertently made. "If evening is an inconvenient time for you perhaps we could take tea together one afternoon?"

"Supper or tea would be fine," he said, his squinting eyes peering over the rims of his glasses.

Enjoying her chat, she decided to query the vicar concerning the alleged ghost of the manor. "Tell me, John, do you believe in this nonsense of a ghost at Radborne Manor?"

John folded his hands piously in front of him and rocked a bit on his heels. "I have been the vicar here but six months. I have learned that telling the story is a favorite pastime of many. The villagers seem to delight in their resident ghost. And from what I have been told of Maximillian Radborne, he was a formidable man."

"I wonder though," Billie said, her head turned away for a moment to glance at the manor in the near distance. "Was Lord Radborne the all-powerful and divinely handsome man everyone contends him to have been?"

"You have doubts about his *legendary* qualities?"

"I find that legends tend to be embellished upon, for sake of entertainment or just plain storytelling prose."

"Then you doubt the ghost's existence?"

"Do you believe it exists?" Billie challenged in return.

The vicar's expression was firm and positive. "No. I don't believe in ghosts."

"I have my own doubts as to the existence of ghosts." And doubts they were. She doubted if mere mortals could handle such daunting creatures.

"You are a sensible young lady. A most admirable trait."

"Actually," Billie said softly with a quick glance about her to make certain no one heard her confession, "I am a bit stubborn-headed, to a fault, or so my uncle had often warned me."

The vicar's pause was purposeful and his response delivered slowly. "We all have faults, Billie. But rarely do we admit them."

Bessie's return interrupted their congenial conversation. She extended an invitation to Billie to share the midday meal with a few local women anxious to make the acquaintance of the new lady of the manor. Billie gladly accepted the kind offer and bid the vicar a good day with a promise that they would speak soon.

By the time Benny arrived at three to return her to the manor, Billie had decided that St. Clair was much to her liking. The people were pleasant and treated her not at all like a stranger, though she credited their acceptance of her to Bessie. She was certain the woman had regaled them with stories of her arrival last night and the courage she had possessed in traveling on to the manor.

The day had proved fruitful after all. She had dealt fairly and firmly with Percy Hillard. She had met more of the townsfolk. And she had acquainted herself with a kindred spirit, Vicar John Bosworth.

Her doubts and fears faded and with a lighter heart she returned to the manor.

Pembrooke opened the front door for her and she entered with a flourish, discarding her scoop bonnet, jacket, gloves and reticule to a nearby chair.

"We have work to do, Pembrooke," she announced, her finger tapping her cheek as if a decision was close at hand.

"I thought my lady would care to rest some before supper."

"Rest?" Billie asked oddly.

Pembrooke seemed as confused as she. "A nap, my lady. A chance to recoup your strength for the evening."

Billie laughed and shook her head. "I never nap and I have no need to recoup. I am accustomed to rising early, working through the day and enjoying more leisurely activities in the evening."

Pembrooke rolled his eyes to the heavens. "I will adapt to your strange customs . . . in time. What is it you wish of me now?"

"I am in need of pen and paper. We are going to make a list."

"A list?" he repeated dubiously.

"Yes. I need to make a list of the changes I can institute immediately and those that will take time."

"Changes?" Pembrooke's voice rose an octave or two.

Billie walked over to the dining salon and glanced over the spacious room before turning her attention back to Pembrooke. "Yes, changes. New drapes. New wallpaper. Fresh paint. I want to add some brightness and life to the manor. The colors are too grave and lifeless. The rooms need spirit added to them."

Pembrooke cleared his throat sharply. "Lord Radborne— "

With a direct tone that brooked no opposition, Billie prevented him from finishing. "Is deceased. I am the owner of Radborne Manor now, as Mr. Hillard can certainly attest to. Would you be so kind as to bring me the paper and pen I requested?"

Pembrooke stiffened, his nostrils flaring as he spoke. "As you wish, my lady."

Billie spent the next few hours making detailed lists for the various rooms she felt needed immediate attention while jotting down notes for future reference.

She hoped she hadn't insulted Pembrooke by her remark, but she didn't wish to live in the shadow of the previous owner. One way to make certain she wouldn't was to change the manor to reflect her own tastes. It would take time for many to accept her ownership of the estate. She imagined it would be referred to as Radborne Manor for many years to come, and she had no objection to that as long as her status as owner was assured.

It was, after all, the only home she possessed. She had no desire to return to Nantucket. Her future was here. She could feel it. The very spirit of the manor settled around her like a comforting quilt, warm and sheltering. This was now *her* home. She sensed its overpowering welcome. And she would allow no one to rob her of that deep feeling of security.

Billie once again startled Pembrooke and Matilda when she insisted on joining them in the kitchen for supper. Refreshed and spirits high, Billie settled herself on the bench at the table.

"It smells delicious," she said, rubbing her hands together.

"Fresh fish stew with potatoes, carrots and wild onions for added flavor. Baked herb bread, hot from the hearth and bread pudding soaked rich with brandy," Matilda said, her smile spread wide.

Billie licked her lips. "My mouth is watering."

Matilda hurried to arrange the table, setting it more elegantly since Billie was present. It just wouldn't do to have the lady of the manor eating off anything but the best china, even if it was in the kitchen.

Surprisingly Matilda and Pembrooke quite enjoyed the meal. Billie kept a steady patter of conversation going until, feeling she had disrupted the couple's routine enough for one day, she forced a yawn, allowing for the perfect reason to excuse herself. She bid both a fond good night and retired to her room.

A fire in the hearth welcomed her and candles cast a soft glow of light around the room. The yawn that surfaced as she undressed was unexpected and she realized her busy day had caught up with her. She looked forward to the comfort of the waiting bed, its pillows plumped and the counterpane drawn back.

She changed for bed and brushed her hair vigorously. Her scalp tingled from the stiff bristles when she finished.

A sudden gust of damp wind blew the window open and howled through the room, snuffing the candles out in an instant.

Buried in the dark corner of the room, away from the friendly glow of the fire, she hastily fumbled toward the open window and reached up to secure the latch and shut out the chilling wind.

She bumped her knee on the stool when she then turned to grope her way toward the chest. Candles lay there within easy reach and with a few more tentative steps and a bit of a stretch, she undoubtedly would find them. Her fingertips grazed the wax sticks and she righted them in their brass holders as she fumbled along, attempting to light them.

A spark caught the wick and set it aflame. The simple light brought a sigh of relief and a smile to Billie's lips. She stretched her hands out near the flame, seeking the pleasure of its warmth. And then she felt it.

Unsure at first of the direction of the faint chill that crossed her back, she glanced at the window in confusion or confirmation, she wasn't certain.

The languid coolness drifted over her once more . . . from behind. Her wide-eyed expression remained fixed on the *closed* window in front of her. The window she herself had secured only moments before.

The candles flickered wildly, threatening to extinguish and racing Billie's heart to near exploding.

She froze, listening to the heavy silence of the room. The fire's hiss and crackles sounded like frantic whispered warnings, urging her to run . . . to escape!

She was too frightened to shiver. She stood immobilized. Uncertain. Unprotected.

A deep, caustic voice erupted in the silence. *"Did you enjoy my bed, madam?"*

Chapter
Six

A mixture of fear and anger raced through Billie as she turned sharply, almost losing her balance and toppling over. She righted herself in an instant and glowered at Maximillian Radborne, ghost of Radborne Manor.

He occupied his usual place by the mantel, impeccably groomed in the deepest midnight blue waistcoat and black breeches. A white silk shirt was inappropriately opened to the middle of his chest. A chest sculpted perfectly with thick muscles. And his face? Too handsome. Too arrogant. Too human . . . to even consider this man a ghost.

With a will born of pure stubbornness she threw her question at him. "What in heaven's name—" she paused, shook her head and corrected herself. "What the devil are you doing back here?"

His smile teased and tempted, and Billie was instantly reminded of the blistering sermons Preacher Neelsom delivered back in Nantucket. *Beware the man who tempts the flesh with sinful smiles and promises.*

He moved away from the mantel, discarding his waistcoat to the nearby chair with the nonchalance of one who planned to stay. *"Need I remind you that this is my room?"*

Billie stood firm though her knees knocked once or twice. "Need I remind you that you are dead?"

"My untimely demise does not prohibit me from continuing my residence here."

His towering height and autocratic manner intimidated. He was without a doubt accustomed to giving orders and having them obeyed without exception as his stern tone that expected immediate compliance implied.

Billie wondered if Heaven and Hell had both refused him admittance. "If you are a ghost—"

His deep voice boomed throughout the room, causing Billie to retreat two hasty steps back. *"What the bloody hell do you mean if I am a ghost?"*

Billie planted her hands on her hips to hide their trembling. "You look to be of sound flesh and bone to me."

He advanced another few steps, his voice much lower and softer in volume yet so much more intimidating. *"Does my flesh impress you?"*

Billie felt the flush of heat race to her cheeks. But she refused to let this ghost—or man—frighten her away. "That would depend on if your flesh is real or merely spirit."

He gripped his shirt and spread it apart, taunting her with, *"Touch me and discover for yourself."*

She would have preferred that he was a misty shroud floating in the air than this apparent man of flesh and arrogant strength. Somehow the latter appeared more frightening. Or was she being foolish to think him real? Perhaps he was a stubborn ghost and when touched, her hand would meet no hard, resistant flesh, but instead slip right through the unearthly apparition.

Shedding her fear, or at least tucking it away for the moment, her practical side surfaced and rushed her forward.

She halted abruptly when her hand slapped against rock-hard flesh. A stunning warmth radiated up her arm and drifted down to her stomach, tumbling it until it protested with a faint whimper.

He was no ghost. He was solid man and from the feel of him she harbored no doubt that his solid form extended to every part of his body.

Maximillian arched a defiant brow. *"You are bold."*

Not a question—just a sure statement that was obviously meant to intimidate. Which it did, though Billie showed no signs of just how much it affected her. Her knees were doing a fine job of that, quivering beneath her night rail.

"And you—" she said sharply and with a solid poke to his chest as if confirming for a second time that his firm flesh was real—"are no ghost."

Maximillian glanced down at her jabbing finger and then raised his head ever so slowly, as if warning her of imminent danger.

Billie knew the wisdom of retreat when necessary. She took two steps back, but refused to take her stubborn gaze off his face.

He compelled, commanded and conquered all in one look. This was no ordinary man. He was a man accustomed to power and obedience. He was a man no woman refused and a man that no man dared to challenge. But was he a ghost?

"I take solid form when necessary," he said with a touch of annoyance at having to explain his ghostly abilities.

Billie gave thought to her mother's ghost stories and with a brief tap of her finger to her lips and a squint of her eyes, she flung out her left arm, pointing her finger at the wall. "Walk through that wall."

Maximillian smiled, pushed Billie's arm out of his way and collapsed on the bed, bracing himself against the fluff of pillows. *"I don't do parlor tricks."*

Billie swung around to face him. "I want proof of your ghostly status. What about your clothing?" she asked, but allowed no time for an answer. "Ghosts remain wearing the articles of clothing they died in."

"A mere myth and I grow tired of your demands, madam. It is I who should demand an explanation as to your presence in my home."

"My home," Billie corrected, wishing he would vacate her bed. He was sure to leave a sea-scented fragrance on her linens which would cause her a fretful sleep.

"Explain yourself," he ordered boldly.

Billie acquiesced, wanting this matter clarified as quickly as possible. "My stepfather, your uncle Henry Radborne, passed on and left all his possessions to me. Therefore, Radborne Manor is legally mine."

A faint frown marred his powerful features. *"That does present a predicament."*

"In what way?"

The frown easily turned to a teasing smile. *"That by inheriting the manor you have inherited me."*

Billie stared dumbfounded at him. "You can't be serious?"

"Immensely serious. This was my home before my death and will remain my home until I decide to move on."

Billie heard her mother's warnings about ghosts that were unable to pass on due to deeds left undone or circumstances involving the death. "Why do you remain on this earthly plane, if you are a ghost?" she wondered.

He shook his head and released a dramatic sigh. *"A tragic and untimely death I have yet to accept."*

"And what will it take for you to accept your fate?"

Maximillian showered her body with a sinful gaze. *"That, madam, has yet to be determined."*

The fire's crackle followed by a sharp pop alerted Billie to the reason his focus remained on her lower anatomy. The glow from the hearth silhouetted her body beneath her cotton night dress, giving the lord of the manor an improper view.

Billie stepped to the right side of the bed where the shadows protectively engulfed her.

Maximillian released a petulant sigh.

"You must find another room to reside in."

"I think not." His voice rang with authority.

She attempted reason. "We cannot share the same bedroom."

"Why not? I am a ghost."

"Ghost or not, it isn't proper."

"I was never one to conform to convention."

"So I've heard."

He laughed. *"Tales still spin about me, do they?"*

"Embellished tales I'm sure." Although Billie wondered. "Now would you kindly be something in death that you were not in life?"

"Which is?"

Billie squared her shoulders and announced firmly, "A gentleman who vacates a lady's bedroom upon request."

His smile was barely tangible and his eyes glazed with a sensuous heat. *"Ah, madam, but I was never requested to vacate a lady's bedroom, but rather to stay and entertain."*

"You're incorrigible."

"Of course. Aren't all ghosts?"

Billie threw her hands up. "This will never work, unless—"

Maximillian raised a curious brow as he watched Billie pace in front of the bottom of the bed.

She stopped abruptly, locked her arm around one of the bed's tall posts and looked at him directly. "Unless we discover the reason you still remain earthbound, rectify it and thereby free you to finally rest in peace."

Maximillian was off the bed and stood beside her in an instant.

Her head spun, his quick movement making her dizzy and uncertain if he had floated in midair across the bed to her or he had moved so rapidly that he appeared a blur. She shivered in doubt.

His arm slipped around her waist, drawing her against his solid warmth. Their clothing established the barest of boundaries between them. She felt all of him from his muscled chest to his firm thighs and the hardness in between.

How could this wall of sculpted flesh be a spirit? He was all too male to be less than human.

His heated flesh chased the chills from her body and caused her skin to tingle in response. The strange tremors increased as his other arm found its way around her.

Cocooned in his arms she raised her face to him.

"You would help me seek peace?" His voice was whisper soft and his lips rested threateningly close to hers.

She nodded, afraid to speak, afraid her lips would brush his and afraid she would find them all too inviting.

He gave her a curious glance, his eyes questioning for one brief moment and then almost as if attuned to her thoughts he leaned down and caught her lips with his.

It was a gentle capture, but a conquering one. And as quickly as he tasted her, he stopped.

Her eyes flashed open and to her surprise she stood alone in the room, her arms wrapped securely around the bedpost. Her worried glance searched the room.

When she was certain her trembling legs could support her, she hurried to the door and opened it just enough to search the hallway.

The long, dark corridor was much too uninviting, and she shut and bolted the door. She leaned back against the polished wood and cast another glance around the room. The fire roared, her bed lay prepared for her and she was alone.

She shook her head. Had she been dreaming? Had she gone to bed, fallen asleep and walked in her sleep?

Again she shook her head. *Absolutely not.* He had been real. She had felt his flesh. His very hard and heated flesh. And his lips. Her fingers tentatively touched her lips. They were warm, full and aching with the want of him.

She walked to the bed in a daze, extinguishing the few candles that remained lighted. The hearths' flame kept the room bathed in a soft glow as Billie hurried beneath the counterpane.

Her eyes gave the room one last, quick survey and with a heavy sigh she dropped back upon the pillows. Her nostrils instantly filled with the sharp scent of the sea.

She groaned and rolled over, burying her head in the sea-scented pillow to make certain she wasn't dreaming. Confirming her meeting with Maximillian had been real and so had the kiss, she angrily flung the pillow off the bed and flopped back around to lay on her back and ponder her encounter.

"Sleep tight, Belinda." The soft whisper was followed by a gentle laugh that drifted off into the darkness.

Billie called out. "You'll not share my bedroom, Maximillian Radborne."

Another laugh followed and dissipated overhead.

Billie angrily pounded the mattress before drawing the covers over her head and shivering herself to sleep.

Chapter Seven

The bright light of morning brought with it common sense, courage and sheer determination to Billie. She planned on making Radborne Manor her home. She wanted no arrogant ghost—or man—haunting her bedroom. And therein lay the problem.

Was Maximillian Radborne an unsettled spirit or of human flesh and form?

The thought plagued Billie as she settled herself at the trestle table in the kitchen for breakfast. Her sleep had been as fretful as she had predicted and an expected yawn attacked her.

"Restless sleep, my lady?" Matilda asked with sincere concern after placing a steaming cup of English tea in front of her.

Billie nodded before inhaling the tempting scents of hot porridge liberally sprinkled with cinnamon and nutmeg and sweet rolls drizzled with honey. "I suppose my new home takes getting accustomed to."

Matilda poured herself a cup of tea and joined Billie. "You have traveled a good distance only two days past. Perhaps you would be wise to rest some."

Billie ignored her suggestion, though not intentionally. She felt the urge to explore and discover; to take the first step in solving the haunting or unhaunting of Radborne Manor.

"Have you ever seen the ghost of Max Radborne?"

Billie's blunt question and the referral of Lord Maximillian Radborne as Max caused Matilda to choke on the tea she had just swallowed.

Billie stood ready to assist her but an anxious wave of Matilda's hand sent Billie back to her seat.

"I upset you," Billie said after Matilda had regained her composure.

"It is just that—" Matilda paused and cast a nervous glance around the room. She whispered when she finally spoke. "I have never heard my lord referred to as"—again she hesitated before finishing—"Max."

Unconcerned by her improper reference to the lord of the manor, Billie continued. "Then you have never seen his ghost?"

Matilda turned her question back on her. "Have you?"

Billie brushed her fingers over her lips and thought about last night and the fleeting kiss. She shrugged.

Matilda offered a suggestion. "If you feel the need to speak to someone about apparitions why don't you visit with Vicar Bosworth?"

Billie's face brightened and she suddenly attacked her porridge with vigor. "An excellent suggestion, Matilda. Thank you."

"I'm glad I could help, my lady. And if I might add . . . ?" She waited for permission to continue.

"Please," Billie urged. "I often sought advice from family and friends back home. I miss not having it freely given."

Matilda smiled in appreciation. "This village tends to overly enjoy recounting and creating tales and legends. And this house certainly lends itself to ghostly tales with its drafty rooms and intense shadows."

"Max did have a propensity for shadowy colors."

Matilda attempted to correct her. "Lord Radborne preferred the subdued."

Billie laughed and threw her arms out wide. "That's about to change."

A brilliant grin spread across Matilda's full face and lighted her wide, bright green eyes. "A challenge I have no doubt you are up to."

Billie stood after draining her last drop of tea from the blue flowered china cup. "I shall inquire in the village as to willing workers."

"A large enough purse and promised ale and you shouldn't find yourself without volunteers," Matilda offered.

"I have heard that Bessie is the best seamstress in St. Clair."

"None better, my lady."

"Excellent," Billie said. "My day is suddenly filled with errands. By this evening I will have workers hired. The house will bloom along with the first signs of spring."

Matilda's generous grin followed Billie out of the room.

"The carriage, please, Pembrooke," Billie requested as the servant followed rapidly behind her into the large foyer.

Pembrooke almost collided with her when she halted abruptly.

"This foyer needs—" She spun around surveying it slowly.

She stopped abruptly when she came face to face with the large gilt-framed mirror and the startling image of Maximillian Radborne reflected in it.

Billie stood frozen. She stared wide-eyed and silent, looking up at him. He stood impeccably attired in tight buff-colored, wool breeches and waistcoat and a frock coat of a green so dark in color that it reminded Billie of the trees back home dressed in their evergreen winter finery.

His arms were akimbo, his back rigid, his legs stiff and his face angry. *"Leave my manor as it is, madam."*

She closed her eyes for a moment against his powerful presence and warning. "You are not really here."

"I am right here, my lady."

Her eyes flew open and rounded like soup saucers to stare at Pembrooke standing in front of the clear mirror.

"Any other instructions before you leave for the village?" He held up her heather-colored spencer jacket that matched her dress.

She slipped into it and the scoop bonnet that Pembrooke also held out to her. "Nothing further. Thank you, Pembrooke."

Billie was in the carriage and on her way, wondering quite simply if she was going insane.

Billie was in the carriage and on her way, wondering quite simply if she was going insane.

The vicarage was a modest stone house with a low stone wall surrounding it. An iron gate creaked a rusty welcome to those who entered and a crushed shell walkway directed visitors to the front door. Ivy climbed the old stone around the door and up to the second-floor windows. A plain, iron ring knocker waited to announce callers and Billie reached out eagerly to make her presence known.

Billie smiled with surprise and pleasure when Bessie answered the door.

"Come in. Come in, my lady," she urged, ushering Billie into the narrow hallway and straight to the small receiving parlor off to the right.

"Vicar Bosworth is with a parishioner. He'll be but a moment. Please have a seat, my lady, and I'll get you a nice cup of tea."

Billie removed her bonnet, fluffing the unkempt curls around her face. "You work for the vicar?"

"Laurel Smithers is the vicar's housekeeper, but she's on

a holiday visiting her daughter and family over in St. Simon. I'm looking after the vicar until her return."

"And I don't know what I'd do without her."

Both women turned and smiled at Vicar Bosworth standing in the doorway.

"I'm pleased that you have come to visit with me, Billie."

Bessie hurried out of the room with the promise of tea.

"I must be honest with you, John. I came for a specific reason."

John's smile was thoughtful and he entered the room with slow, measured strides that bespoke of confidence and consideration. He didn't appear a physically strong man, yet his soft, calm demeanor gave one the sense of comfort and of an inner strength.

He extended his hand to a grouping of chairs and tables beneath the lace-covered window. "Please have a seat and tell me what is troubling you."

She didn't show her surprise at his astute observation of her disquietude. She did as he invited, sitting stiffly on the edge of the pale blue settee.

He joined her and for an awkward moment silence reigned in the room until he reached out and gently took her hand in his. A soft reassuring squeeze reminded her of her concern.

"Trust me, Billie, I will always be here for you."

Oddly enough Billie felt a rush of heat race through her and an overwhelming sense of protection settle over her. The vicar was no Lord Radborne in looks or strength, yet he possessed a quality the lord of the manor sorely lacked. Compassion.

"Your friendship is a comfort to me, John." She gently gripped his hand and found his warmth satisfying. She held on, not wanting to relinquish such closeness. It had been too long since she had shared a caring touch. She and her mother had hugged often and her uncle had been prone to giving her bear hugs on a daily basis. She missed sharing such loving moments.

"I am sure in time you will make many friends here among the villagers, though you must understand that you are the lady of the manor and will soon be engaged in visits with other gentry of the area."

Billie's stubbornness surfaced. "My friends are mine to choose."

John peered at her over the wire rim of his spectacles. Tender concern shined in his eyes and he offered solace with a gentle squeeze to her hand. "The villagers themselves will expect certain behavior from you. It has been their way for centuries and they take pride in the lord and lady of the manor. I don't think you would intentionally disappoint or hurt them by disregarding their customs."

"I would never do that, though I could use some tutoring in regards to being a lady of the manor."

John withdrew his hand from hers and raised both hands in playful defense. "That, I am afraid, is out of my realm of expertise."

"A suggestion, perhaps?"

He thought seriously for a moment, pushing his glasses up along the bridge of his nose only to have them slide back down and rest nearer the tip. "Matilda, your housekeeper, would surely be able to tutor you in the proper etiquette."

Billie's light laughter filled the quiet room and subsided with a shake of her head when she noticed the strange look on the vicar's face.

"Your suggestion is perfect," she assured him. "As was Matilda's when she suggested I seek your counsel concerning apparitions."

John's brow furrowed in surprise. "You've seen Lord Radborne's ghost?"

"Lord help us," Bessie cried from the doorway and the tray, heavy with china dishes, teapot and biscuits, began to rattle.

The vicar stood and took the tray from Bessie, offering her a hasty reassurance and gently prodding her out the door.

He brought the tray to the table in front of the settee and then returned to the door, closing it.

Billie, accustomed to tending to her own needs, poured them each a cup of tea, handing one to the vicar as he took a seat beside her once again.

"If gossip is anything here like it is in Nantucket, all of St. Clair will be debating by this evening as to whether I have seen the ghost or not." Billie sipped her tea with a smile.

"The villagers have speculated on the ghost of the manor since Lord Radborne's death. Many have claimed to have seen him. Are you one of them?"

Billie took no offense at his question. It was not asked with malice or suspicion, only with concern. "I think I have, yet I wonder if it is but an illusion brought on by stories and suggestions."

John sipped his tea and nodded thoughtfully. "You are wise to question."

Billie laughed. "But do I question my sanity or the apparition I may have seen?"

"Think of what you have been through of late. You have traveled a great distance on your own, leaving the only home you have ever known. You arrive in a foreign land and immediately your head is filled with tales of a ghost. You take residence in a gloomy manor and—"

He paused and stared at her. "Do you dream, Billie?"

Billie sighed and rested her china cup and saucer on the silver tray. "I thought perhaps I was dreaming, but the kiss . . ."

John looked at her oddly. "The kiss?"

"Oh, dear," she said and shook her head. "I had not planned on discussing the kiss with you."

He took her hand once again. "Perhaps you should. It obviously has disturbed you."

Feeling suddenly like a caged rabbit, Billie stood and walked to the window, keeping her back to the vicar. "Lord Radborne has appeared in my bedroom on two occasions. On one occasion he stole a fleeting kiss from me or at least

I think he did. Perhaps it was all my imagination. My mother often told me that a man's kiss could be unforgettable."

"Was his kiss unforgettable?" came the vicar's soft reply.

Billie stood looking out the window at Radborne Manor in the distance. "I'm not sure," she answered honestly. "I don't know if it was the kiss I remember or his supposedly ghostly presence."

The shivers ran over her as a cloud covered the sun, pitching the morning sky into a grayish gloom. She turned to speak with the vicar and stumbled against him, for he stood so close to her.

John reached out and gently grabbed her arms, steadying her. "Do you wish him to visit?"

"What an odd question," she said, staring through his thick lenses that blurred the blue of his eyes.

John directed her back to the settee. "Actually it is a pertinent question when you stop to think of how much your head was filled with tales of this ghost upon your arrival."

Billie gave thought to his suggestion. "Are you implying that my own curiosity conjured up this ghost?"

"Coupled with your exhausted state, I would say that your apparition is a mere illusion caused by your own fears, curiosity, desires—"

"Desires?" she queried, offended, and spoke without thinking. "I don't desire a ghost. I prefer a man of flesh and blood, even-tempered, caring—a man such as yourself."

John averted his eyes, casting his glance to his boots, which were scuffed and in need of polish. "I-I did not mean th-that type of desire. I but meant your de-desire to build a future here."

"Oh," was all Billie could say. She really had made a blunder this time. Or had she offered the truth to the vicar and herself? Had she found Lord Radborne desirable? His features were unquestionably handsome. His presence commanding. His kiss . . . Billie shivered. So briefly delivered and yet so *unforgettable*.

"I should go," Billie said, standing.

The vicar stood with her. "If you need me, Billie, any time of the day or night, please send for me. I will come at once."

"And if you see the ghost of Radborne Manor, then what, John?"

He took her hand once again and raised it to his lips. "Then I shall rescue you, my lady." He brushed his lips across the back of her hand and briefly glanced at her with eyes filled with courage.

Billie smiled like a young girl intent on impressing her first beau. "You would make a perfect lord of the manor."

John shook his head, pushed his glasses up on his nose and shook his head again. "Nonsense, I am but a simple vicar. A lord requires strength and wisdom beyond my capabilities."

"Do not underestimate yourself, John. You truly are a courageous man."

"You flatter me, my lady."

"Billie," she corrected with a grin. "I will not have you addressing me so formally." She scooped her bonnet off the nearby chair and asked, "It is proper for you to call me Billie, isn't it?"

"No one will disapprove."

"Good," she said, putting her bonnet on and tying the ribbons beneath her chin. "Now I am off to hire workers."

John scolded her softly. "I thought you intended to rest?"

"I will retire early this evening. I promise," she said with a smile so sweet and sincere that it brought a blushing grin to the vicar's full cheeks.

"You are making changes to the manor?" he asked, following her to the front door.

"Necessary changes."

He opened the door and a rush of wind swept in so strong that they both turned their backs against the blustery, cold air.

"Winter has yet to leave us," he offered. "Perhaps the warmth of spring is a better time to begin work on the manor."

Billie adamantly disagreed. "Absolutely not. The manor is so drab and dull. It needs life and color added to it now. It will blossom with spring and burst into full richness with summer."

Thunder rumbled overhead as if in disagreement and Billie couldn't help but look toward the manor in the distance. It stood foreboding, framed by the dark clouds that hovered in the gray sky. If offered no welcome, but instead warned all to stay away.

"Remember, if you need me, Billie," Vicar Bosworth said and with a faint bow he turned and disappeared into the house, closing the door behind him.

Billie gathered her courage around her and hurried toward the village.

Late afternoon produced the thunderstorm that had been brewing since morning. Billie sat in a high-backed chair in the receiving parlor of the manor, her feet comfortably resting on a dark red ottoman with a lap blanket of midnight blue trimmed with a dark red fringe covering her legs.

She had given in to Pembrooke's insistence that she rest, attempting to act the proper lady of the manor. But she could still hear Pembrooke's annoyed muttering when she requested that he bring her paper and pen so she could determine the necessary changes to the receiving parlor. She had hired workers and they were to begin as soon as she detailed what work she wanted done.

"A visitor, my lady," Pembrooke announced, minus the pen and paper.

"A friend," Claudia Nickleton corrected, waltzing into the parlor in a flourish of periwinkle blue.

Billie attempted to stand but Claudia waved her efforts off. "Stay where you are. You look positively comfortable."

Claudia joined her after handing over her cape, bonnet and gloves to Pembrooke. She made herself comfortable in the twin chair that sat opposite Billie.

"You visited with John today."

Billie was uncertain how to respond. Claudia hadn't asked a question. She had simply stated a fact.

Claudia leaned closer and in a conspiratorial whisper said, "I am curious. John grows tongue-tied around women. I wondered how he fared with you. He is such a wonderful man, kind and considerate. He will make some lucky woman a good husband."

"Are you matchmaking, Claudia?"

Claudia beamed proudly. "What else does a woman of my age have to look forward to?"

"Finding a man for yourself. Age has no bearing on romance. One is never too old to fall in love."

"You are a romantic. How positively wonderful." Claudia clapped her hands in delight. "John needs someone romantic. I truly believe that beneath that shy, pious exterior of his lurks a spirited, romantic man. Far different from the man who inhabited this manor."

"You were acquainted with Max Radborne?"

Claudia laughed until she almost cried. "Good Lord, young lady, Maximillian would have positively thrown a tantrum if he heard you refer to him in such an unacceptable manner."

"Well, Max isn't here." Billie thought a moment and amended that. "At least I don't think he is."

Pembrooke entered and both women grew silent.

"Tea, my lady?"

"I think with this chilled weather a brandy would be more satisfying," Claudia suggested.

Pembrooke glared at her.

Billie agreed with a smile. "A brandy would be perfect right now."

"Pembrooke," Claudia commanded in a true lady of the manor's tone. "Brandy."

Pembrooke looked at Billie for confirmation.

She nodded her approval and with a huff and a grumble Pembrooke vanished out the door.

"What do you mean you don't *think* Maximillian is here? Have you seen his ghost?"

"What do you know of ghosts?"

Claudia shrugged and both women once again grew silent when Pembrooke returned with the brandy.

Pembrooke stoked up the fire to keep a warm heat in the room then left, closing the door behind him.

Claudia reached for both glasses, handing one to Billie. "Why do you ask?"

"I had thought ghosts were more of spirit than flesh." The brandy sent a warmth spreading through her and she relaxed, drawing the lap blanket more comfortably around her. "But Max's spirit was of solid muscle and radiated warmth."

Claudia neglected to take a sip of brandy before moving the glass away from her mouth. "You touched him? He felt of flesh? Not spirit?"

Billie took another ship of brandy as if fortifying herself against what she was about to admit. "Yes, I touched him and yes, he felt of human flesh." She leaned forward to stare curiously at Claudia. "Is that possible?"

Claudia swallowed back a generous portion of brandy before she answered. "I've never had the pleasure of meeting a real ghost so I cannot say what should or should not be."

"The vicar believes I have exhausted myself, and I but dream the encounters."

"Sounds sensible to me."

"And what if I dream of him again tonight? What if he waits upstairs in the master bedchamber for me?"

"The master bedchamber is where he haunts?" Claudia asked anxiously.

"*His* bedroom, as he reminds me."

"That's solved simply enough. Move to another room and see what happens."

Billie smiled with the delight of one who had just received a much-wanted present. "A simple yet practical solution. Thank you."

Claudia finished her brandy. "I must be off. The storm

sounds as if it has worsened. I had best return home before the roads become muddy."

Billie insisted on seeing Claudia to the door herself, much to Pembrooke's displeasure.

Billie waved to a departing Claudia and watched the coach vanish down the road toward the village.

Shutting the front door against the storm, she turned to direct Pembrooke to prepare another bedroom for her.

With fright and alarm she stumbled back against the solid wood door at the sight of Maximillian Radborne standing at the foot of the stairs. He was dressed as he was in the mirror that morning and he wore the same warning expression.

"As you can see, I appear wherever I wish in my house; therefore, it will do you little good to change bedrooms." His tone was adamant and authoritative.

Infused with the strength of the brandy, Billie stood straight and approached him. "You intruded on my conversation with Claudia."

"This is my house, madam. I will intrude where I see fit."

Billie poked her finger at his chest. "The manor is mine now, Max, and you will do well to accept that."

"Max?" he roared. His hands clenched at his side and he stormed off to the receiving parlor.

"Petulant ghost," Billie murmured and proceeded to follow him when Pembrooke stopped her.

"Matilda thought perhaps you would care to have your meal in the quiet of your room this evening after the long day you have had. Would that be acceptable, my lady?"

"Yes, I would cherish solitude this evening." She moved to climb the stairs when she stopped and turned to Pembrooke. "Please bring the brandy to my room with two glasses. I have the distinct feeling I am going to have company this evening."

"I shall make certain no one disturbs you, my lady," Pembrooke said quite seriously before disappearing down the hall to the kitchen.

Billie was almost at the top of the stairs when she stopped, turned and softly asked, "Are you coming, Max?"

"I'm already here, Belinda," came the soft reply from the top of the landing.

Chapter
Eight

"You are not to make any changes to my manor," Maximillian demanded, easing himself into the chair beside the burning hearth in the bedchamber.

Billie stood in the center of the room, her arms crossed and her toe tapping in annoyance. She ignored the tremor in her stomach and her legs and proceeded to defend her home. "This manor now belongs to me and I shall make whatever changes I feel are necessary."

"I think not." He stood and moved with swift litheness in front of the hearth. The blaze of flames behind him sent his shadow wide and long over Billie.

She shuddered but then she had a thought that brought a smile to her face and forced her forward on shaky legs to announce, "You can't be a ghost. Ghosts don't cast shadows."

He produced a witty smile and shook his head. *"Who filled your head with such rubbish about ghosts?"*

"Shadowless ghosts are a fact," she defended.

"An old wives' tale."

Billie prepared to argue when Maximillian continued. *"We can debate this issue at another time. At the moment I am more concerned with my manor's appearance and reputation."*

"Reputation?"

"I had hoped that the haunting tales would subside in time. But now with your penchant for spreading gossip—"

Billie took umbrage at his remark. "I do not spread gossip!"

"You gossiped about my appearance not only with Claudia, but with that pious fool of a vicar."

Billie bit back a scolding retort. "I sought advice from the vicar. Who is a gentle and understanding man, unlike you who are arrogant and stubborn."

He bowed ever so elegantly. *"Thank you for the compliment. A lord of a manor could be nothing less."*

"You are a *deceased* lord," she reminded firmly.

"Who intends to make certain his manor remains intact along with its reputation. You will do as I direct."

Billie's hands curled into fists at her sides and with a stubborn tilt of her head she challenged him. "I will do as I please."

He approached her while his stern voice clearly warned that she immediately comply. *"You will do as I say."*

"Or what?"

This woman who barely reached his chest in height and who he could scoop up in his arms without sparing a breath dared to contest his authority. He wondered with an insolent smile if her demonstration of courage masked the truth. Did her pretty, slender legs shake beneath her dress? Did her hands tremble beside her curvaceous hips? Was she actually afraid of ghosts? Of him?

He moved closer to her, his coat brushing her dress. *"I'll haunt you."*

The whispered brush of wool against wool unnerved her. He stood much too close. "You already haunt me."

"Not intimately."

She remained speechless for a moment before blurting out, "You wouldn't dare."

He leaned his face next to hers. *"I dare what I please."*

With a slight tremor to her voice she answered, "You are no gentleman, sir."

He stepped away from her and roared with laughter. *"Look to the vicar if it is a gentleman you want. He will pray for your soul—"* His eyes narrowed, his smile vanished and in a rough whisper that sparked the sensually charged air around them, he added—*"Whereas I will tempt it."*

Heat, warm and tingling, like fine brandy just swallowed, weaved its way through Billie, leaving her with a yearning for another taste. She forced herself to respond, not surprised to hear the tremor in her voice mount. "I prefer you seek your just reward."

He slipped out of his coat, tossing it on the chair before casually stretching out across the bed. *"I enjoy my earthly reign."*

"My mother once told me that spirits sometimes remain earthbound due to the circumstances surrounding their death."

"She's quite possibly right."

Curiosity brought Billie closer to the bed. "I was told you drowned."

Maximillian patted the spot beside him, inviting her to join him as he delivered his stunning answer. *"That I did, but there had been several attempts on my life before that fateful night."*

So shocked by his confession, she rushed to the bed without thought to her improper actions and joined him. She sat beside him, her pumps hastily discarded and her stockinged feet tucked completely beneath her dress.

"Who wanted you dead?"

"That, my dear, is the question."

Her smile was brilliant. "No, that's the answer."

He was rendered speechless by her beauty. He studied her with appreciation as he would a fine work of art. Lines, angles and shadows all blended perfectly to create a vision so lovely that a man could get lost in her radiance forever.

She continued, undisturbed by his silence. "We need to discover who intended you harm and then you will be able to rest in peace."

With his senses soaring, but his pragmatic side in control, he addressed her sternly. *"That could prove dangerous."*

"I shall seek help."

"From whom?"

She scrambled off the bed excited by the prospect of solving her ghostly dilemma. "Claudia and the vicar."

He swiftly left the bed, his movement startling Billie and sending her stumbling back. He reached out, grabbed her arm, swung her around and planted her with a firm plop on the edge of the bed.

His towering height intimidated and his sharp voice cracked like a whip, causing her to jump in surprise. *"You expect an old busybody and a pious weakling to help you solve murder attempts?"*

Perturbed by his overbearing manner, Billie stood and poked him hard in the chest. Not that it bothered him in the least; his chest was much too thick with muscle for her slender finger to do any damage. "What better person than Claudia, who openly admits she enjoys gossip. She could learn much." She poked him again, much harder. "And as for Vicar Bosworth, he is also in a position to hear much as well as being a caring soul who would willingly offer his assistance if I requested."

He grabbed her attacking finger. *"He is a weakling who can offer you no protection."*

"I can protect myself."

He turned her own finger on her, delivering a small poke to her nose. *"You can't even defend yourself against a ghost."*

"But I can," she said with a sweet smile. "I shall solve this mystery and off you will go to your just reward."

"You're so sure of that?"

"Yes, *if* you are a ghost. If you are not?" She stared at his intensely handsome features, gooseflesh rushing over her. She feared the idea of him being of sound flesh and blood, for if he was then she would find herself penniless, homeless and at his mercy. "Then I shall discover the reason for your deception and seek reparation."

His response surprised her. *"You possess much courage."*

He released her finger and took several steps away from her. He paced in front of the hearth, deep in thought. Perhaps she could help. She could go places he couldn't. She could question people he couldn't. She could also find herself in danger.

He stopped and turned a serious expression on her. *"If I allow you to assist me in this matter, you will obey me without question."*

"You aren't my husband," she challenged.

His voice grew stern. *"I am lord of this manor."*

She reminded him yet again, and with a smile, "Deceased lord."

He commanded firmly. *"Lord nonetheless, and you will obey me."*

A sudden thought struck her and her answer came swiftly. "Of course."

He walked over to her with the grace of a majestic beast skillfully bearing down on its prey. *"You acquiesce too easily. What is on that stubborn-headed mind of yours?"*

She stood her ground and offered him a teasing grin. "I realize that your spirit is bound to the manor. Therefore, once I leave here I can do as I wish with no threat of you following."

His grin was far from teasing, it was feral. *"Remember, Belinda, the manor is your home. You must return here . . . to me."*

With that he cupped her chin, leaned down and kissed her lightly. *"And I do so look forward to our time together. Don't you?"*

She opened her mouth to respond.

He whispered, *"Perfect."* And closed his mouth over hers.

Startled by the invasion of his tongue, she jumped. He stilled her with his arm around her waist and gently guided her up against him. His tongue teased hers into response.

Lost in a world of new senses and emotions, Billie slipped her arms around his neck and savored every moment. He tasted good, so very good, like nothing she had ever tasted before. And the length of him was so hard against her that he heated her to the core and brought tingles to her most intimate of places.

He gently ended their kiss and eased her away from him. He raised her hand up to his lips and placed a soft kiss across her fingers. *"Our time together will be memorable."*

She disengaged her hand from his and walked away from him, a warm shiver racing through her. She hadn't expected this. Kissing a ghost wasn't suppose to feel so . . .

She braced her hand on the fireplace mantel and stared into the flames. Kissing a ghost was impossible. Ghosts were spirits, not flesh and blood. They couldn't feel or touch and certainly not kiss. He owed her answers, plain and simple.

Billie turned.

He was gone.

She hurried to the door. It remained locked from the inside. She spun around, searching the room for any possible means of exit. She found none.

Confused by the recent turn of events, she drifted through the rest of the evening, eating little of her supper and retiring early to her bed.

With lights extinguished except for the glow of the hearth flames she lay in the large bed, sleep eluding her. Busy thoughts cluttered her mind. Why had there been attempts on Max's life?

Why would someone want him dead?

The answer that intruded upon her thoughts was not at all

to her liking. She wondered if an irate lover had wished revenge or a husband who had discovered that his wife was dallying with Max wanted justice. Marlee had mentioned how the ladies all found Max attractive and she had to agree with them.

The artist had not embellished the painting. Maximillian Radborne, Earl of Strathorn, was a stunning specimen of a man. A man or ghost, whichever the case, far out of Billie's reach.

She must keep things in perspective; dwelling on his remarkable features would do no good. She must consider the consequences and plan accordingly. She had to investigate the attempts on his life and learn the truth: Was he a ghost or man? Only then could this vexing problem be solved.

Tomorrow she would speak with Claudia and the vicar and ask for their assistance. Tonight she would get a good night's sleep.

She punched her feather pillow several times and attempted to comfortably rest her head. It took much effort and an hour of tossing and turning before she finally fell into a fitful sleep.

The rowboat bobbed and tossed in the rough sea. Billie fought hard with the oars to control it. The rain and wind attacked her scantily clad body and the cold chilled her to the bone. Her eyes searched the dark sea. She couldn't find him. Dear lord, she couldn't find him. But she had heard him call to her. Heard him call out for help. And she was here, ready to help him.

The darkness grew more heavy around her, the sea more rough, and she felt as if something were closing in around her.

"Max," she screamed. "Max, where are you?"

No answer came. Only the sound of the raging storm that grew more intense by the minute.

"Max! Max, please! Maximillian, where are you?"

"Shh, Billie, I'm here. Everything is all right. I'm here

with you." His warm arms encircled her and cuddled her against the strength and heat of his body.

She settled comfortably against him, her fretful dream fading as she finally slipped into a peaceful sleep.

"Stay," came a hushed whisper that tickled Maximillian's bare chest just before she rested her head on him.

His arms closed more strongly around her. *"Sleep. I'm here."*

But for how long? His thoughts warred. He admired and respected her spirit and courage. And his attraction to her startled him. He had desired many women over the years and had had his fair share, never involving himself in long, emotional relationships. He had always kept his distance and emotions under control.

And yet with Billie, control was nonexistent. He hungered to possess her body and to challenge her mind.

Why had she come into his life now? When it was so impossible. When soon his ghostly reign would end.

He breathed deep of her sweet scent, burying his face in her hair, the silky texture caressing his skin. She would be his for a short time and he would make their time together unforgettable. And then . . . he shook his head and hugged her tightly to him.

Chapter Nine

"Attempted murder?" Claudia Nickleton repeated in aston-
ishment.

"You did say murder?" the vicar offered as well, pushing
nervously at his glasses.

Billie continued pouring each of them a cup of tea from
the flower-sprigged bone china teapot. Her calm demeanor
and steady hand made her reference to murder sound as if it
was a normal teatime subject.

She passed Claudia's teacup to her and offered the vicar
his before taking her own and sitting back in the drab gray
high-backed chair. "I merely suggested that perhaps there
was more to Max—" She paused and corrected herself.
"Lord Radborne's death than first thought."

John stood, carrying his teacup with him, and walked to
the open door of the receiving parlor and closed it. "How do
you stand all that banging?"

"It's a delight to hear," Billie admitted as John returned to his seat opposite her. "The work has finally begun on the manor and I'm thrilled. Soon colors bright with life will welcome friends and visitors to Radborne Manor, instead of the atrocious drab grays and plums that fill a good portion of this place."

"I heard Bessie is busy sewing new drapes and chair coverings for you," Claudia said, helping herself to a sugar-covered tea cake.

Billie helped herself to one as well. "She's wonderful. She's been by several times taking measurements and going over swatches of material."

A discreet but distinct cough from the vicar caught the two women's attention. "The conversation seems to have strayed and I am curious as to why you mentioned attempted murder in connection with Lord Radborne."

"Goodness, yes," Claudia declared, snatching another tea cake off the china plate. "He bravely surrendered his life that night in the storm to save others. He was much loved. He was a true hero."

The vicar agreed with a nod. "From what I have heard of the man, he demonstrated remarkable courage."

Billie returned her empty teacup to the server. "Yes, I suppose the dear man should have a monument erected in his honor."

Claudia smiled. "The villagers have discussed it."

Billie sent a silent prayer to the heavens to help her control her tongue. "I'm sure Lord Radborne would prefer to be remembered in the villagers' hearts and, of course, their tales."

"I agree with you dear," Claudia said. "Legends are made that way and dear Maximillian was quite a legend, in more ways than one."

The vicar added his own concern. "Yes, I heard the lord was a generous man. The villagers speak highly of him."

"Especially the women."

The vicar and Claudia cast wide eyes on Billie.

Evidently her prayer went unheard. She blushed and properly offered an apology. "Forgive my hasty tongue, but I heard gossip."

"Gossip is the devil's tongue," the vicar warned.

"Then my tongue must belong to the devil himself," Claudia said with a satisfied grin. "And the gossip was true. Maximillian did have a reputation with the ladies."

The vicar nervously fiddled with his glasses. "I never meant to offend—"

Claudia dismissed his apology before he could finish it. "Oh pish, John, everyone gossips. It's the mainstay of the community. The village couldn't survive without it. It makes us a family."

Billie enthusiastically agreed. "Just like back home in Nantucket. We all looked out for one another."

Claudia nodded. "She's right. The villagers loved the stories that circulated about the lord of the manor. They gossiped with pride. Why the men beamed like peacocks that the lord was fancied by the ladies far and wide. And the women enjoyed warning them that there would come a day when Lord Radborne would lose his heart to a beautiful lady and . . ."

Claudia's voice faded and she raised her lace-trimmed napkin to wipe the tear from her eye. "I'm sorry. I did so love Maximillian and wanted more than anything to see him fall in love, marry and have a passel of children."

The vicar placed a comforting hand over Claudia's. "I'm sure he was well aware of how deeply you cared for him and returned it in kind."

"You are a dear man, John, thank you." Regaining her composure, Claudia held her empty tea cup out to Billie. "Now, what of attempted murder?"

Billie poured the steaming hot tea into her cup. "I've been thinking." And that she had. She needed to enlist their aid without informing them of Max's ghostly interference; otherwise they would probably think her quite insane. Of course, too, there was the very real chance that Max was not a ghost at all, which would make her look more the fool.

Billie decided to embellish on the gossip she had heard. "I learned Lord Radborne met with a few mishaps before his death."

The vicar looked at Claudia. "I was not in residence at the vicarage until after his death and have heard of no such mishaps."

Claudia sipped at her tea, her brow furrowed. "I know there was an accident or two, hunting or some such thing." She placed her cup on the server and looked directly at Billie. "Did you know that Oran Radborne, Maximillian's father, was murdered only a few months before his son's death?"

"What happened?" Billie inquired, empathizing with Max, having experienced the same loss herself and knowing the difficulties and heartbreak one suffered.

"Oran came upon smugglers in the caves that run beneath part of the manor. They shot him." Claudia once again dabbed at her eyes with her napkin. "He was a gem of a man. I loved him so very much."

Billie watched the vicar reach out to Claudia and comfort her not only with his touch, but with softly spoken words of kindness. She settled and relaxed under his consideration.

Her curiosity piqued, Billie asked, "What caves beneath the manor?"

Claudia obliged her with the information. "Since smuggling and wrecking are common in the surrounding area, many of the manor lords had avenues of escape and shelter built beneath their homes, mostly for protection. Sometimes the gentry participated in a bit of smuggling themselves. Fine brandy. Tobacco. Spices from the Far East. Many times the local magistrates turn their heads at the unlawful practice for a part of the smuggled bounty."

"Are the caves still accessible from the manor?"

The vicar stumbled over his words. "Y-you don't in-intend to investigate them, do you?"

"They are part of the manor and, therefore, I should be aware of them."

"I have made you aware of them, Billie. Stay away. The caves are dangerous," Claudia cautioned.

"I agree," John said, his fingers fidgeting with his glasses.

Claudia stood. "I must be going. I have an appointment with my solicitor. John, you stay and make certain you convince her to keep her distance from the caves."

Billie assisted Claudia with her black cloak. "I would like to learn more about Oran Radborne's death and his son's. Will you help me?"

Claudia smiled. "It would give me pleasure to help you as long as you don't place yourself in any danger."

"Agreed," Billie said and gave Claudia's hand a squeeze.

Claudia gave her a motherly hug before hurrying out the door.

"Does Lord Radborne's ghost have anything to do with this sudden interest in the father and son?" John asked, remaining in his seat.

Instead of returning to her seat Billie walked over to the window draped with heavy plum velvet curtains. She sighed and wrapped her arms around her waist, watching the gray clouds gather in the sky. It would rain again. She wondered if it ever stopped raining here in St. Clair.

"It is the ghost that disturbs you. Tell me about it," John offered gently.

Billie turned around, her own arms still comforting her. "You won't think me a fool?"

"Never," he said and held his hand out to her.

She went to him eagerly, needing the sincere support he offered. She took the chair beside his and his hand encompassed hers.

"Tell me," he urged in a whisper.

"What can I say?" Billie held onto him as she spoke. "The ghost visits me at his whim. Day or night. He dictates to me what I shall or shall not do to his manor. And he—"

Billie pulled her hand from his. She turned away from him to gaze at the flames in the small hearth, embarrassed by what she was about to discuss with him.

"You can talk to me about anything, Billie," he said softly.

Feeling safe and secure with John, she admitted, "He kisses me."

"And you enjoy my kisses immensely," came the bold retort.

Billie whipped around, her wide-eyed stare frantically searching the room for Maximillian.

"Billie, what's wrong?"

John's gentle voice turned her attention to him. "Did you hear anything?"

"I heard you," he answered.

Billie remained silent, expecting Max to add his opinion. When silence reigned, she stood and slowly walked the perimeter of the room while she spoke with John.

"I sometimes wonder if I'm going slowly insane."

"I doubt insanity has anything to do with your visions. I daresay they are more dreams than not. You push yourself much too hard. You should rest more and not worry so about the manor or its history."

"I feel that if I could but settle these inquiries that disturb me then perhaps the ghostly visits would cease."

"And the restless spirit would be at peace."

She smiled graciously at him and continued her patrol of the room. "You understand."

"I offer my help freely and unconditionally. Whatever you need from me, you only need to ask."

"He's a useless fool who can offer you nothing but prayer."

"Shut up this instant," Billie shouted without thinking at Max's comment.

"I beg your pardon," John said nervously.

Billie rushed to him, dropping down beside his chair on her knees. "I'm so sorry, John. I didn't intend—" She shook her head, not able to offer a rational explanation. "Forgive me. I need your help and I deeply appreciate your willingness to give it to me. Thank you."

With a slight tremor in his touch, John caressed Billie's face. "I will always be here for you, Billie."

"That comforts me more than you know."

He hesitated briefly and then, as though finding the courage and afraid of losing it, he bent his head down and kissed her.

Surprised by his gentle play of lips against hers, she stilled. His kiss continued, undemanding and softly sensual, sending a shiver racing through her.

He eased his lips from hers slowly as if unwilling to relinquish the taste of her. He rested his forehead to hers and murmured, "Forgive me for being presumptuous, but I have so wanted to kiss you."

Billie planted a light kiss on his cheek. "Your kiss was delightful and I wouldn't find it at all presumptuous of you if you should feel the inclination to kiss me again."

John smiled, cupped her hands in his and moved a respectable distance away from her. "I would like that. Would you join me at the vicarage tomorrow for tea?"

Billie didn't hesitate. "I would be delighted."

"Good," he said, releasing her hands and standing. "I must leave now. I have business to attend to."

Billie hurried to the nearby chair to retrieve his gray scarf and gloves. "I'll walk you to the door."

"Why can't the fool find his own way out?"

Billie turned around, forcing a smile. "On the other hand, would you mind if Pembrooke showed you out? I have a pressing matter to see to."

"Of course," John said with concern. "All this work going on in the manor must keep you busy."

"My hands are full, all right." She walked him to the door, casting a quick glance around the room as she went.

Pembrooke was in the hall and dutifully took charge of the vicar, leaving Billie to shut the receiving parlor door with a solid thud.

"Show yourself this instant, Maximillian." When he didn't answer, she stomped her foot. "At once. Do you hear me, Maximillian? Show yourself this minute."

"I think not." His deep voice held much more authority than her angry one.

Billie marched to the center of the room, spinning around slowly in an attempt to determine his whereabouts. At the moment he sounded as if he surrounded her, his voice resounding from every corner of the room.

Frustrated, Billie shook her finger. "I demand that you show yourself now!"

His laughter rolled like thunder in the quiet room. *"Demand?"*

Billie spun around, thinking him behind her. "You intruded on my privacy," she said to the empty room. "And now you hide from me like a petulant child."

"Petulant child?" his full voice echoed.

"You have no right—"

"You forget who you speak to, madam. I am the lord of this manor and you shall respect my authority."

Her anger mounting, Billie argued back. "I am now the lady of this manor and you shall respect my position. Don't you dare intrude upon my private conversation with friends again."

"I dare what pleases me and that fool of a vicar irritates me."

Billie turned again, catching a sound to the left of her. "John is a gentle, caring man who you would do well to heed."

"He is an idiot. What man apologizes to a woman for kissing her and what the bloody hell were you doing kissing him?"

Billie shouted loudly as if addressing someone outside the room. "I enjoyed his kiss."

A discreet knock sounded before Pembrooke opened the door slightly, peeked his head in and asked if she was all right.

"I'm fine," she snapped. "Now leave me be."

Pembrooke hastily retreated, shutting the door firmly.

"Now see what you've done," she cried. "You've made me irritable with my staff."

"The staff matters not. Explain yourself."

She turned once again, directing her voice to the hearth, and threw her hands to the heavens in frustration. "What am I to explain?"

His voice rumbled with a mixture of anger and annoyance. *"Why you kissed the vicar."*

"The vicar kissed me, which is none of your concern."

"Everything in this house is my concern."

"Fine," she sighed, feeling close to surrender but deciding a change of subject might help. "Then tell me about the caves beneath the manor."

His deep voice filled every corner of the room. *"You will stay away from those caves, Belinda."*

"But perhaps I could uncover something of importance down there."

"Danger is the only thing you'll find. The caves are not safe to explore. You are not allowed down there."

Tired of his commands, she retaliated, "I will go where I wish."

"I think not."

Billie shivered from his warm breath that whispered across the back of her neck. He stood behind her, directly behind. If she turned, she would brush against him. If she stepped forward she would be too close to the hearth, her cheeks already flushed red from the flame's heat. Chairs stood to the right and left of her. He had expertly trapped her.

No choice but to confront him. She turned slowly.

He stood almost on top of her and the size and appearance of him made her gasp. He looked positively magnificent. He wore a smoky gray waistcoat and jacket with pale gray breeches, a white linen shirt and a gray-and-black-striped cravat knotted at his neck. His black hair was pulled straight back and fastened securely. His sea-blue eyes resembled the rich colors of a turbulent sea. And he wore no smile. His features were sharp and unflinching and heartbreakingly handsome.

Billie grabbed the folds of her fawn-colored cashmere dress and held her head up, annoyed at the strands of unruly hair that fell loosely around her face.

"I will say this one time, Belinda," he said calmly but sternly. *"You will not go to the caves."*

Billie found speech difficult given the fact that she couldn't take her eyes off his lips, thin and powerful and oh-so-delicious. She ached for him to kiss her.

The soft flutter of her eyelids and a gentle sigh of longing brought an ungentlemanlike smile to his face.

He slipped his arm around her narrow waist and brought her up against him. *"A vicar's kiss could never satisfy you. You're too full of passion."*

His lips took hers and demanded she respond.

She did, her arms slipping around his neck, her body pressing firmly against his and her tongue mating with his in a wild frenzy she couldn't deny.

His hand roamed down her body, cupping her bottom, moving her against him intimately. She felt the swell of him, bold and powerful, and her head swam with wicked thoughts.

The loud knock sounded at the door just before it sprung open to admit Matilda.

Billie stumbled and stared wide-eyed at the woman in front of her, her mouth still aching and her body trembling. She cast an anxious glance about the room but saw no one save her and Matilda.

"Stay away from the caves," came the stern whisper.

Billie looked at Matilda. The woman smiled at her.

"I beg your pardon, my lady, I thought you were finished in here and I could clean up."

"Of course," Billie said, walking over to the window and touching her still swollen lips. Whatever was the matter with her? She had melted at the sight of him and become soft clay in his hands to mold as he wished. Was she crazy? Before she knew it he would have her obeying his every command and whim.

The first raindrop fell against the window as Billie turned around swiftly. "Matilda, tell me about the caves beneath the manor."

Chapter Ten

Billie secured the leather belt around her slim waist, buttoned her black wool jacket and slipped the red knitted stocking cap on her head, shoving all of her hair beneath it.

She looked in the full-length mirror in her bedchamber and took stock of her appearance. With her brown wool skirt and black boots, a fisherman's thick knit sweater beneath her jacket and her hair tucked away she looked like a young girl, ready and willing to attempt . . . an adventure.

The workers were busy in the dining salon and the main parlor. Their hammers droned away with monotonous bangs. Pembrooke and Matilda had gone to the village for food staples, though Billie imagined it was an excuse for them to escape the constant clatter.

The vicar had cancelled their afternoon tea, which they had shared each afternoon for the past few days. He had been called to the house of an ailing villager and was expected to be gone until early evening.

That left Billie to her own devices, and she intended to explore the caves. She grabbed the gray wool gloves on the bed and hurried out of the room.

Her steps were quiet yet hasty as she took the stairs down to the first floor. She hoped Maximillian was otherwise occupied and would not notice her presence in the caves.

He had been a tyrant of late, demanding she cease all refurbishing of the manor, that she curtail her visits to the vicar and that she place more effort on his problems. Yet he refused her admittance to the caves and warned her to be cautious of who she spoke with concerning him.

Afternoon clouds gathered outside as Billie readied a lantern in the kitchen. A distant roll of thunder warned of another impending storm. John had informed her that all the current rain only aided in bringing to life the spring beauty of the Cornish coast. He told her of the wildflowers that would grace the land and how the beaches would be strewn with smooth stones and driftwood in the oddest shapes.

She looked forward to the transformation, for she honestly had begun to detest the rain. And when raindrops began to hit the window she childishly stuck her tongue out at them.

Content with her petulant action, she grabbed the glowing lantern and walked over to the cupboard. Slipping her hand behind the almost undetectable crack, she activated a lever and the cupboard slowly squeaked open.

Thunder rumbled closer and a spine-tingling shiver raced through Billie. She reminded herself that she possessed her father's adventurous soul and most importantly his courage. He had told her many times that fear was an emotion easily controlled. The unknown and uncertainty was what caused fear in many. Knowing life was abundant with both and having the courage to face either was what conquered the fear.

She was about to conquer.

Billie held the lantern high, recalling Matilda's warning

that the descent to the caves could be dangerous and she should mind her steps. Actually Matilda, like everyone else, had warned Billie to keep her distance from the caves. But she, unlike the others, had informed Billie of the secret entrance.

The steps were narrow and made of stone. They wound their way down as if descending into a pit, narrowing at intervals and making Billie wonder if all of the Radbornes had possessed a thin physique.

The air grew damp and dark. Billie brushed cobwebs that hung like fine threads out of her way and was grateful for the gloves she wore, especially when the stone wall she braced her hand against for balance grew moist.

Just when she thought her descent was drawing her down into Hell, she came to a wooden door bolted with a thick metal latch. She placed the lantern on the bottom step and attempted to lift the latch. It didn't budge. She needed more strength behind her to move the heavy, rusted metal.

Leaning down and bracing her shoulder beneath the latch, she shoved all her weight against it. It rattled and creaked, but didn't open. Another effort fueled by her grunts and groans found the latch opening in protest and Billie's shoulder aching. She would surely be bruised tonight.

She braced her heels against the bottom stone step and laid her hands flat against the heavy door and pushed. The door opened slowly with a tortured creak.

Cold, damp air rushed around her, stealing her breath for a moment. She stepped back and reached for the lantern. Holding the flickering light high above her head, she proceeded cautiously into the cave.

The stone floor became a dirt floor and the deeper she traveled, the wider the passageway became until its width was the size of a small room. Here she found broken crates and barrels. Giving them a quick inspection and finding nothing of relevance, she moved on.

The passageway again grew narrow and veered to the left, then suddenly opened up on to another room-sized cave.

Here crates and barrels were stacked high. None were broken. All were nailed tightly shut.

She could hear the roar of the sea sounding as angry as the thunder that boomed like arguing voices overhead. She assumed she was close to the entrance of the cave from the beach. If she investigated and found where on the beach it opened to, perhaps it would prove beneficial for future reference.

A squeal and scurry of feet along the crates gave her a start and she turned, catching sight of several rats racing across the crates. She grabbed for the lantern, knocking it off the barrel. She stumbled, grasping for it and catching the handle before the lantern hit the ground.

A sudden rush of salty sea air swirled around her. The tangy scent was all too familiar. She righted herself and with confidence she swung the lantern high, turned around and faced . . .

"You're not Maximillian." Billie stared wide-eyed at the older gentleman standing a few feet in front of her. Impeccably dressed in black-and-gray attire, he stood a good six feet tall with pure white hair and a mustache.

"I'm Oran Radborne," he said with a pleasant smile. *"And you are?"*

"Dead."

"Oh dear, you are, too?"

Billie shook her head and closed her eyes. "This isn't happening. He isn't here. There are no such things as ghosts."

"Oh, but there are, my dear," he assured her, justifying his belief with a serious nod of his head. *"When alive, I thought as you. Ghosts were a figment of a storyteller's mind. One had to be insane to believe in ghosts. Unfortunately, I died and I found I became a very real ghost."*

Billie collapsed onto the barrel behind her, dropping the lantern on the top crate, stacked three high beside her.

"Are you all right?" he asked, sitting himself on a barrel a short distance to her right.

Billie sighed, pulling the cap from her head. Her thick

hair fell in a mass of waves past her shoulders. "How many ghosts haunt Radborne Manor?"

He cleared his throat with a brief cough. *"I can't be sure."*

"I can't believe I'm sitting here talking to another ghost. I must be insane to believe all this nonsense." Her eyes shot open wide. "How do I know you're Oran Radborne and not just some smuggler or lunatic?"

Oran smiled broadly. *"A beautiful and intelligent woman. How delightful."*

Billie's hands went up in surrender. "You must be Max's father."

"Max? Oh Maximillian. Yes, dear I am Max's *father."* He hid a chuckle behind his raised hand. *"Of course if you would like to make certain of my identity, there is a portrait of me in the hallway not far from Max's portrait."*

"I think I recall seeing it, though briefly. I'll take a look when I return."

"What are you doing down here in the caves? They are dangerous for a woman."

Billie noticed that he spoke with fatherly concern, unlike his demanding son. Was she actually speaking with the ghost of Oran Radborne? Or was someone out to play tricks on her, perhaps make her appear crazy. But why? What would the person gain? She decided to proceed with caution and tell no one of this meeting.

"Do you only haunt the caves?" she asked. "You've never shown yourself above in the house."

A sadness washed over him, his shoulders sagging with the weight. *"Rarely do I go above to the manor. Too many memories."*

Sorrow tugged at Billie. He was alone. His spirit doomed to walk these caves for how long? "Why can't your spirit rest?"

"A need to protect."

This was one explanation she hadn't hard. " Protect who?"

"Protect those involved."

"With your death?"

"The innocent ones, yes. The wrongdoers I wish to see punished."

For some reason Billie felt this information was important. Why? She couldn't say, but like a puzzle she needed to sort all the pieces before fitting them together and seeing it clearly.

She pursued. "Who are the innocent ones?"

"The people who loved me. I fear they may be in trouble." He frowned and his voice grew firm. *"I want no harm to befall them."*

"Who are—"

He stopped her. *"I cannot tell you everything. I can only assist you in finding the answers."*

Confused, she shook her head. "Why?"

"You will come to understand everything in time. Trust me."

"A ghost?" she asked, furrowing her brow. "You expect me to trust yet another ghost?"

He smiled like a kindly old gentleman offering advice. *"Trust your intelligence."*

She nodded with a grin. This ghost she could get to like. "Good advice. Now what else *can* you tell me?"

"Listen closely to what people say. They offer much more information than they realize. And find out what you can about one Derry Jones. But be careful—he is an unsavory character."

"Could this Derry Jones have anything to do with the attempts on Maximillian's life, before his death?"

"Much is involved. All of it must be solved to be settled. And you, a stranger to St. Clair, will see more clearly than those who have spent a lifetime here."

"You should tell that to your son," Billie said. "He has a problem with his lordship status and issuing commands."

Oran chuckled, not bothering to hide his mirth. *"Maximillian has much to learn."*

"I couldn't agree with you more."

"Then teach him," he challenged.

She held up her hand in defense. "No, thank you."

"Too much for you?"

She bristled for a moment and then she laughed and shook her finger at him. "You're a sly one. But you're not going to trick me into teaching Max anything."

"Not even how to let go?"

She saw the sorrow in his eyes.

"He needs to say his good-byes and move on. Help him."

She had her doubts, too many doubts. "I don't know if I can."

"You will try?"

He didn't request, he pleaded. How could she say no to this old man who wanted nothing more than for his son to accept his own death and go on to rest in peace? And if she didn't rid the manor of these ghosts, she would be living with them for a lifetime.

She made the decision quickly. "I'll try."

"You must go back," he said, standing. *"The cave is growing more damp from the storm and I don't wish to see you become ill. We'll talk again."*

Billie stood and picked up the lantern. "Shall I visit with you down here or will you—"

She stopped talking when she realized she was alone. "I hate when they do that. Poof, off they go into thin air."

She shook her head and made her way toward the narrow passageway.

"Billie," the soft voice called.

She turned, but saw no one.

"We shall visit again—be careful. And put your trust in the vicar. He will help you."

His voice drifted off, sounding like whispers on the wind. She shivered and hugged her middle with one arm for warmth before heading back in the same direction from which she had come.

John stopped by the manor after his visit with the ill parishioner. Billie offered him food though the hour was past the evening meal. He declined and they both settled with tea in the receiving parlor.

"Was your day eventful?" he asked, relaxing in the gray high-backed chair with his teacup.

She thought about her day, exploring the cave and talking with a ghost. She couldn't stop her smile from spreading. "Yes, very."

He appeared pleased by her response. "What kept you occupied and obviously pleased?"

She was about to blurt out everything about her adventurous day and then thought better of it. She sent a silent prayer to Heaven, asking for forgiveness for lying to a vicar. "I was busy deciding on various patterns, materials and colors for the other rooms."

"An eventful day is always pleasing," he said and gave his wire-rimmed glasses a familiar push. "You look weary, Billie. Are you sure you didn't swing a hammer with the workers?"

Noting his teasing smile, Billie produced one of her own. "I made myself familiar with the manor. The tour was exhausting." At least that wasn't a lie. The caves were, in essence, part of the manor and upon her return upstairs she quickly had changed her clothes and took herself off for further investigation of her home.

"And what did you come across?"

She stood and held her hand out to him. "I'll show you."

He placed his teacup on the silver server and stood, taking her hand.

Billie opened the door with John in tow and almost collided with Pembrooke.

Pembrooke took a step back. "My apologies, my lady."

"No harm done, Pembrooke. The vicar and I are off to the conservatory."

"The conservatory has been closed off until spring." He sounded as if he were ordering her to stay away from it.

"I opened it this afternoon. It's much too lovely a room to

be shut off," she said and tugged at John's arm. "Come, I'll show you."

Pembrooke appeared flustered. "My lady, the conservatory should remain—"

"Open," she finished and walked off, dragging an unresisting John behind her.

Billie hurried across the foyer and down the hall, releasing the vicar's hand as they came upon wood-framed glass doors that Billie reached out and flung open.

She waltzed into the room, spinning around gaily, her moss-green wool dress wrapping around her slender legs. "Isn't it wonderful? Can you imagine it in the summer, bursting with colorful flowers?"

John stood and watched her face grow bright with excitement.

She continued explaining to John as if he couldn't see for himself. "The glass ceiling and walls make me feel as though the outside is inside, and look here," she said, hurrying over to the white orante metal table and two chairs. She ran her hand lovingly across it. "A perfect spot for afternoon tea."

She wished it were daylight so John could enjoy the beauty of the room. She was glad at least that the storm clouds had drifted off and a bright full moon sprinkled its rays over the glass, infusing it with enough light to see by.

"It must be a beautiful view during the day," John commented.

"Fantastic," she cried, spreading her hands out to the windows. "You can see the gardens. I can't wait to begin changing the flower beds and planting a larger herb garden."

"Change the gardens?"

"Yes," she nodded. "And look at this beautiful white wicker furniture." She plopped down in the rocking chair with the exotic print cushion. "How lovely it would be to rock a child to sleep here or spend a summer evening with a husband."

"You take too much work on yourself."

Having been lost in the image of a family sharing an evening together in the conservatory bright with lights and laughter, she had to ask, "What was that you said, John?"

"You talked about changing the gardens," he explained softly. "And you haven't even finished the inside."

"Oh pish, John," she said, walking over to him and hooking her arm through his. "This is my home now and I so enjoy creating a warm and welcoming manor."

He looked down at her strangely.

She held firmly to his arm, smiling and surprised by the strength she felt beneath the dark material.

His eyes transfixed on her face, he whispered, "I missed you."

A tremor rushed through her stomach and she realized she was glad he was here with her. His presence comforted her and surprisingly stirred her. She wished he would kiss her.

He obviously felt the same way since he leaned over and gently captured her lips. He lingered in his pursuit, tasting her with a tenderness that sent shivers racing through her.

He kept her at a proper distance, not allowing their bodies to touch but not allowing their lips to part. He lingered in his sweet assault until both their bodies trembled and he eased himself away.

He took her hands in his. "You're very special to me, Billie."

Her lips tingled and she could still taste him on her. It felt exquisite. "The feeling is mutual."

"You will have tea with me tomorrow at the vicarage?" he asked hopefully.

"I wouldn't miss it for the world," she agreed readily.

He walked with her out of the conservatory. "You're right about that room. It would be a wonderful place for a husband, wife and baby." It sounded to her as if he longed for a family to love. "Now I must take my leave. The hour grows late."

She accompanied him to the door and he brushed a brief kiss on her cheek. "I'll see you tomorrow."

"I look forward to it," she said and watched him walk out into the night, the darkness swallowing him up. She closed the door and leaned against it.

Her thoughts rushed through her. He would make a good husband and a good father. He would be thoughtful to his wife and treat her with respect, not order her about.

"Pardon me, my lady," Pembrooke said, interrupting her mental survey of the vicar. "Is there anything else you require this evening?"

"No, thank you, Pembrooke. I'm off to bed." She headed for the stairs and stopped, turning back around to address Pembrooke once again. "Why didn't you want me to go into the conservatory?"

Surprised by her directness, he stumbled over his words. "It's . . . that is . . . it's draft . . . terribly drafty. I wouldn't want you becoming ill."

She nodded, accepting his explanation. "Perhaps I shall look into having a hearth installed in there and then it will be available to use year round."

"Yes, my lady," he said and walked away, mumbling.

By the time Billie climbed the stairs and closed the door to her bedchamber, complete fatigue had claimed her. Every limb ached and every muscle protested, and her shoulder had begun to pain her. She would now suffer the consequences of her exploration of the caves.

With slow movements she began to undress. She carefully hung her dress in the wardrobe and attempted to make hasty work of her remaining garments. Her protesting limbs prevented her from rushing.

After several painful minutes she finally managed to slip on her white linen, lace-trimmed night rail. She collapsed with fatigue onto her vanity bench and proceeded to take her hair down.

She wondered at Maximillian's whereabouts. She had expected him to pop up when she was down in the caves, and she had thought for sure when the vicar had visited he would make his presence known to her. She was surprised to find herself upset by his absence.

"Are you crazy?" she asked her image in the mirror, picking up her hairbrush and running it through her long hair. "You finally have a solitary, peaceful moment. Enjoy it."

She smiled at her own admonishing and applied more pressure to her brush. She winced and dropped the brush onto the silver vanity tray. Carefully, she eased her night rail off her shoulder.

She winced again and looked in surprise at the large purple-and-black bruise on her shoulder. She recalled the metal latch and her determination to open the door, then glanced again at the results.

The candles' flames suddenly flickered, a rush of sea air swept in the room and a deep voice demanded, *"How the bloody hell did you get that bruise?"*

Chapter Eleven

"I earned it," she said proudly, watching his reflection in the mirror as he approached. Dressed in black breeches, a white linen shirt, his dark hair free and wild around his shoulders and wearing a taut expression, he descended upon her.

He dropped to one knee beside her, his hand going instantly to her bruised flesh.

She cringed and he growled like an angry bear.

He stood, walked over to the dresser that held her evening pitcher of water and poured some into the ceramic bowl. *"Explain,"* he demanded, dropping a cloth into the cold water.

She sighed, too tired to fight him, but intelligent enough to skirt the truth. "I moved a heavy object."

He returned to her side, again dropping to one knee. Without a word he applied the cold cloth to her swollen shoulder.

Her breath caught at first and then the cold seeped into the bruise and began to dull her pain. She stared at him, his look so intense and his face so finely sculpted that she thought for a moment he couldn't be real. He had to be a dream.

Her hand went to his face, needing to feel his flesh beneath her fingers. Her fingers tingled from his warmth and he made no move to distance himself from her. Realizing her action was improper, she dropped her hand and said, "Thank you, that helps."

"Come," he ordered, holding his hand out to her and offering no reason for his demand.

She placed her hand in his, her fatigue reminding her she was in no condition to argue.

He guided her to the bed and once she was seated on the edge he removed the cloth and walked over to the bowl of water. He dropped the cloth in and carried the bowl to the small stand beside the bed. He then proceeded once again to bathe her shoulder with the cold cloth.

"Where were you all day?" she asked. The contrast of his warm shirt brushing her bare arm combined with the chill of the cloth sent gooseflesh rising along her skin.

He sent her a look that quelled her curiosity and he asked, *"What object did you attempt to move?"*

She chose to ignore him and ask another question. "Do you like the changes to the manor?"

"No," he snapped at her, soaking the cloth once again and reapplying it.

"I suppose a person with your taste for drab colors wouldn't care for the richness of the colors I chose."

"Answer my question," he warned her in a soft tone.

That this large, demanding man could be so tender in caring for her and that he saw to her needs as a husband should, unnerved her. "What que—"

"You know very well the question."

And she knew very well she could not supply him with the answer. She considered that a partial answer might appease him.

"A stuck latch," she said indifferently. "Why don't you like the colors?"

He dropped the cloth to the bowl once again and studied her bruise with a gentle touch of his fingers. *"The colors are not to my liking. My manor suited me just fine the way it was."*

"Drab with not a speck of life to it." She attempted to keep the tremor from her voice. His gentle exploration of her bruise made her insides quiver.

"Defiant and full of strength," he corrected, rinsing the cloth and returning it to her shoulder. He grabbed her face firmly in his hand. *"Now you will tell me exactly what latch caused you so much difficulty."*

"An old, stubborn one," she said, pulling free of his grasp.

He locked his eyes with hers. He would not be denied his answer. His intense gaze penetrated, searched and found the truth. His satisfaction produced a brief smile before he simply and calmly said, *"You went to the caves."*

She shrugged. Why deny it? "Yes, I did."

He stood and paced beside the bed, his hands fisted and his jaw tense. *"I recall ordering you otherwise."*

"I'm not one to take orders and I have a terribly curious nature."

"So I see," he said, sitting back down opposite her. He removed the cloth and gently probed the darkened flesh. *"Curiosity can hurt."*

"You feel too alive to be a ghost," she whispered, her skin heightened in awareness from his soothing touch. She was tired in mind as well as body and wanted answers of her own. "Why do you play this game with me?"

"I have no choice."

"Are you a ghost?" she asked softly.

"An unsettled spirit searching for peace." His hand moved to stroke her silky neck.

"You play with words, Max."

"You try my patience, Belinda."

"Will I have an answer?"

"Only if you find it yourself."

She smiled, dropping her head forward as he massaged the back of her neck, relaxing her tense muscles. "A challenge. I love a challenge."

He worked his fingers around her throat and gently eased her head up. *"The caves are dangerous. I want you to promise me you'll stay away from them."*

"You challenge me to uncover the truth and then tie my hands." She shook her head. "I can't promise you I won't go to the caves again."

She possessed a strong will, one that matched his own and he admired her for it. *"What am I to do with you, Billie?"*

Without thought and not knowing why, she answered, "Kiss me."

He smiled and with his hands firmly around her neck he drew her to him. *"With pleasure, my lady."*

His lips claimed hers and she was swept up in his assault, losing all coherent thought. His tongue had speared her lips on contact and taken her with an erotic force that made her limbs quiver and sent a rush of sweetness between her legs.

She felt the soft feather pillow behind her and realized he had eased her back on the bed and lay partially stretched across her.

Perhaps she dreamed. Perhaps none of this was real. Perhaps she only willed this arrogant lord to appear in order to appease her own desires. *Fantasies.*

If so, she intended at this moment to enjoy him. Her hands rode over his back, reveling in the taut muscles beneath his shirt. She arched her head back to accommodate the kisses he rained along the sensitive column of her throat, and when his hand cupped her breast and squeezed with a gentle forcefulness, she groaned.

His touch softened with the gentling of his kiss. Soon she found his rhythmic caresses soothing her into a sleepy state. Her last thought of him before drifting off into a peaceful slumber was of him cradling her protectively and whispering, *"Free me."*

*   *   *

Maximillian's words echoed in her head most of the next day. The sun was bright and no rain clouds threatened and for this she was grateful. And she was most relieved that the ground was dry enough to walk to the village and the vicar's house for tea.

She needed thinking time. A chance for thoughts to take hold and work through. Back home in Nantucket she had used washing time, baking time and walking time for her thinking time. Here in St. Clair she was deprived of all that. Matilda baked, a woman from the village attended to the wash and walking had been impossible due to the rain.

Today, when her prayers that the sun would remain shining were answered, she almost ran from the manor.

Pembrooke had rushed after her with her forgotten bonnet and reminded her to keep to the road and watch her step.

The man worried like a father and it was quite nice to know he cared. Now she was on her way with her thoughts on last night and Max.

She had always thought this ghost business was simple, thanks to her mother's expert storytelling abilities. A ghost was a misty shroud that floated in the air, never spoke a word and frightened the devil out of people.

Now having become acquainted with two suspected ghosts, one appeared harmless and the other . . .

Frightened the devil out of her.

How could she have asked him to kiss her last night?

Because she wanted him to.

Her own answer caused her to pause in her tracks. She had to be the most sinful woman. Only a short time before she had kissed Maximillian, she had kissed the vicar and enjoyed it.

And her kiss with Max?

Unforgettable.

She had thought briefly this morning that she had dreamed the whole incident. But when she had groaned in embarrassment and buried her face in the pillow beside her, the scent of the sea invaded her nostrils, reminding her of his lingering presence.

She even recalled to her dismay cuddling against him during the night. How long had he stayed?

Billie shook the troubling thoughts from her head and marched on. She must settle this ghostly dilemma. It was her only hope of retaining her sanity.

She remembered him whispering, *Free me*. Free him from what? His earthly reign? His charade? She needed to intensify her investigation. She hoped Bessie would still be at the vicar's when she arrived. She would ask her for help in locating this character called Derry Jones.

Her meeting with Oran would remain her secret. If she began hinting that there was another ghost at the manor people were certain to think her crazy.

She refused to hurry her pace though she was anxious to talk with Bessie. It had been too long since she had taken a solitary walk and she found her own company delightful.

Once at the manor gate she stopped and turned, staring at the manor in all its splendid gloom. Even with the bright sun beating down on it, the manor still retained a sense of unwelcome about it.

Whatever could she do to change it? She paced in front of the open iron gate, considering possibilities.

Color was a definite necessity. She would make certain the window treatments were bold in color. Flower beds rich in assorted colors would do well sprinkled across the lawn and bordering the entrance drive. Ornate stone containers bursting with a mixture of flowers and herbs crowding the manor steps would be a welcome greeting for visitors, as would scented wreaths of lavender decorating the front doors.

Her decision made and noted, she walked through the gates, halted and cast a quick glance over her shoulder. "Ivy for the gates," she told herself, certain the green clinging vine would definitely soften the harshness of the black iron that warned away rather than welcomed visitors.

In no time and with a feeling of vigor, Billie was knocking at the vicar's door.

"Bessie, how wonderful," she said when the plump woman opened the door. "Just the person I wanted to see."

"What can I do for you, my lady?" She took Billie's bonnet, cloak and gloves and directed her to the small parlor where the vicar usually took his afternoon tea.

Billie seated herself on the ivory settee, adjusting her garnet dress at the wrists before patting the seat beside her. "Come join me for a moment, Bessie. I have a favor to ask."

Ready to please the new lady of the manor, Bessie obliged.

"First I must tell you how pleased I am with the work you have done for me at the manor. The dining room chair covers are lovely. I can't wait to use them."

" 'Tis the colors, my lady," Bessie said with a bob of her head. "You have a special eye that blends colors perfectly."

"Thank you." Billie accepted the compliment gracefully. She had always loved vibrant, rich colors that favored the best of nature. "But there is much work yet to be completed."

"And I'm pleased that you've chosen me to do the work. The money will surely help George and me."

"I'm glad," Billie said sincerely, realizing that she had provided much-needed work for several villagers and would continue to do so with the various improvements she had planned for the manor. "I was hoping you could help me in another way."

Bessie nodded. "What can I do, my lady?"

"I don't know many people here or in the surrounding area. And I am curious to discover the whereabouts and information on one Derry Jones."

"The name has a familiar ring to it."

"I have been told he possesses a dubious nature."

"Then he could prove dangerous," Bessie warned, sounding like a protective mother.

"I only require the information," Billie assured her.

"What information?" John asked, entering the room.

Bessie immediately vacated her seat. "I'll see to the tea." She sent Billie a conspiratorial wink before departing.

Billie smiled at Bessie's clear message and at John as he joined her on the settee. "My search to solve the mystery of Radborne Manor continues."

He took her hand and kissed her cheek. "Do be careful."

She patted his hand. "I'm always careful."

The familiar nudge of his glasses reminded Billie he was nervous, but surprisingly he addressed his concerns.

"You sometimes take on more than you should."

"Never more than I can handle," she assured him.

A further adjustment of his glasses and a tug of his gray waistcoat over his slightly rounded belly had him once again speaking his concerns. "You should have a man's assistance. A woman should not have to face difficulties alone."

"Where I come from women were more often than not on their own. Their men took to the sea and they had no choice but to be independent."

"It is different here, Billie," he said. "Especially being the lady of a manor."

Billie held up her hand in defense. "I am on my own, John. There is no changing that."

"Change is always possible," he said softly and stood. "Come walk with me in the garden. It is such a beautiful day."

Bessie appeared at the door with the tea tray.

"Please keep it hot, Bessie. Billie and I are going to take a spot of fresh air." He held out his hand to Billie.

"It will still be piping hot on your return," Bessie assured him and took her leave.

Billie took his hand and shortly she was draped in her cloak, he in his jacket, and off they walked along the paths of the carefully tended garden that lay dormant in winter sleep.

The sun was bright and radiated a long-forgotten warmth.

Spring was almost upon them and Billie looked forward to it.

"Look," she cried and left his side to drop down along the shell path. "A crocus breaks through."

John joined her, kneeling beside her and brushing winter's debris away from the tiny bud that graced the path's border. "Billie," he said softly as he finished, dusting dirt from his hands. "I-I find th-that I ha-have feelings for y-you."

Billie looked at him. His glasses sat perched correctly on the bridge of his nose, his eyes a blur from the thick lenses. Her heart flip-flopped. His sincerity was tangible. He actually cared for her. Had feelings. *Love?* Was it possible?

The image of Maximillian raced before her eyes, the power of his lips, the strength of his embrace, his demanding nature.

"Give me a chance," John said, interrupting her thoughts. He stood, pulling her up along with him. "I care for you, Billie."

She shivered, though not from the chill breeze, but from the thought that she could have a normal life with John. He would treat her well, be a good father and a loving companion.

"You're cold. We'll return," he said, folding her arm over his and leading her back to the house before she could protest.

He summoned Bessie, directing her to bring the tea and a blanket. He soon had her lap and legs tucked snugly with a wool blanket and he handed her a hot cup of mint tea with a shortbread biscuit balanced on the saucer's edge.

"You're too kind, John," she said and relaxed in the settee, enjoying his attention.

"I care," he reiterated and sat back himself with his teacup. "Tell me of the ghost. Any more visits?"

She didn't want to be reminded of Maximillian now. He interfered far too often in her life and at the moment she found pleasure in being with John.

But she realized she couldn't lie to him, so she spoke the truth. "He visits me often."

John listened.

She found him easy to confide in so her words flowed freely. "He becomes familiar with me at times."

"How so?"

"He kisses me." She couldn't admit that he touched her intimately. It wasn't proper.

John spoke candidly. "Have you given thought to what I once suggested, that he is but a dream?"

Billie sipped her tea and slowly returned the delicate china cup to the saucer on her lap. "I have considered it."

"Is he perhaps what you desire in a man?"

His question troubled her. What type of man was she attracted to? John was tender, understanding and of common features. Max was stubborn, overbearing and terribly handsome. Where John's touch was tame, Maximillian's touch denoted courage, protection and virility. Characteristics Billie had found seductive.

Yet she found comfort and safety when in John' presence. Combined they would make the perfect man.

John waited patiently for a response or perhaps he required none. Did he just wish to set her mind to thinking?

She decided to answer him. "I'm not certain what I desire. I know not if Maximillian is a dream or a true ghost or perhaps he is of flesh and blood and but plays a game. I only know I must solve the mystery or the manor will never truly be mine."

"I will assist you in any way possible."

"Your help means much to me as do your feelings." She reached for his hand. He grasped hers. "I care for you in a special way, John. But I need time—"

He stopped her with a gentle finger to her lips. "We need not rush anything. We only need to learn more about each other and see what grows from there."

She smiled. "Like the tiny bud in your garden."

He nodded and returned her smile. "Nature shall nurture

it until it bursts into full bloom. We shall nurture our relationship and wait for the results."

Two hours later Billie returned to the manor, the sound of banging hammers greeting her.

Pembrooke welcomed her with a frown and a protest. "They are completely destroying the dining salon."

She deposited her cloak over his arm and hooked her bonnet's ties on his fingers. She assumed he referred to the workers. "They follow my instructions."

"My lord would not be pleased," Pembrooke said with a firm shake of his head.

Billie calmly addressed the issue. "Pembrooke, I understand your loyalty to Lord Radborne. I have heard many speak of his courage and kindness, but he is gone and I am now lady of Radborne Manor."

Wide-eyed wonder seized him as if he only realized her words bore truth.

"I know you don't approve of the changes, but they are necessary, for me and for the manor. Please try to understand my sorrow for your loss and my hope for your acceptance of my ownership. I do so want you and Matilda to be happy and stay on with me. But I can no longer tolerate you reminding me that Lord Radborne wouldn't be happy with the changes. He is *gone*. I am *here*. The manor will see changes."

Pembrooke seemed to accept her directive. "As you wish, my lady, though I request that you instruct the workers that they are to follow my rules. One being that they are to finish an hour before sunset so they do not disturb your evening meal."

Billie smiled, realizing this was Pembrooke's way of accepting her as lady of the manor. "I shall inform the workers that they are to receive their instructions with regards to starting and finishing times from you."

"Cleaning up as well," he added. "They leave their tools

scattered like children leave their toys and neither I nor Matilda shall abide such untidiness."

"I shall so instruct them."

"Thank you," he said with a quick nod. "Is there anything you require now, my lady?"

"No, thank you, Pembrooke. I have some correspondence to see to. I will be in the study."

Pembrooke was about to take his leave when he paused. "Do you plan changes to the study, my lady?"

Billie knew all too well that the study had been Lord Radborne's ultimate domain. No one had entered the hallowed room without his strict permission. She had to insist after being there two weeks that she be allowed to enter and even then Pembrooke had protested vehemently.

"I haven't decided yet," she answered, not wanting to admit that she favored the dark colors in the room. The dark green walls and highly polished dark wood trim blended beautifully together and the beige, green and garnet oriental rug that covered nearly the whole wood floor added that perfect touch of color.

Pembrooke took his leave without comment, though she was certain a protest rested near his lips.

She hurried off to the study, planning to answer the few letters she had received from friends in Nantucket and the letter she had received from Jeremy requesting her hand in marriage yet again. He even suggested that he wouldn't be adverse to joining her in England and becoming lord of the manor.

She laughed at the thought and entered the study, surprised that a lamp was already lighted. She approached the large desk, oversized for her small frame, though she was certain it had accommodated Maximillian perfectly.

She noticed as she neared the desk that her letters lay spread open on top. She didn't recall leaving them as such and glanced about the room.

She was alone and yet someone had been reading her letters.

Maximillian?

A sudden gust of wind swept the room, extinguishing the lamp and sending a chilling shiver through Billie.

"Maximillian," she called, annoyed that he toyed with her.

No answer came and the chill grew stronger, racing gooseflesh over her cool skin along with a sudden pinch of fear. The dark grew darker and she could see nothing. The blackness swallowed her whole along with whoever else occupied the room.

"Maximillian?" Her call turned frantic.

She heard a scurry like someone rushing about, but she was unable to detect the sound's direction. A table toppled over and glass shattered just as a shaft of light speared the room. A crouched, dark figure jumped up and raced full speed toward her, knocking her down as he bolted past her.

Before her head hit the floor she could have sworn she saw the powerful figure of Maximillian silhouetted in the doorway, speared by light, but the doorway wasn't where it was supposed to be and darkness was fast engulfing her, confusing her senses.

She only had time to reach her hand out and whisper, "Max," before being swept away into unconsciousness.

Chapter
Twelve

Billie heard voices as if off in the distance. Whispers and mumbles. She strained to hear more clearly but her head hurt terribly. She groaned pitifully, the sound an aching vibration at the base of her skull.

"Open your eyes, Billie," she heard Max demand harshly.

She wanted to shake her head. Refuse him. But the murderous throbbing in her head robbed her of speech.

"Now, Billie, do you hear me?" He continued his bullying tirade. *"Open your eyes now!"*

Her mind shouted all sorts of nasty retorts at him and with her head still protesting she lay in forced silence. She tried to recall the reason for her faint, but the pain hammered incessantly in her head, giving her little room to think of anything else.

"You'll do as I tell you, Billie." His voice rang loud and

clear and Billie was certain it echoed in the room, reverberating in her own head.

"This minute, madam, this very minute. Open your eyes. I am still lord of this manor and you will obey me. Open—"

She couldn't stand to hear another command from his annoying, blaring mouth. With great effort and her eyes remaining closed she said, "Be quiet, please be quiet."

"I beg your pardon, my lady."

Matilda's soft voice caused her eyelids to flutter and fight their way open. "Matilda?" Her voice sounded weak and barely audible.

"Yes, my lady, 'tis me," Matilda answered with a hand on Billie's shoulder to prevent her from attempting to rise. "You've had a nasty fall, my lady. Please don't try to move. Pembrooke and I have sent for the vicar."

Billie cringed, more from the pain that lanced her head than from the couple's decisive action. "You shouldn't have disturbed John." Her voice blared in her head though Matilda strained to hear her.

"Rest, the vicar will be here shortly and—"

"Billie," came the concerned shout that caused Billie's hand to seek her head and hold it, afraid it was about to explode.

John dropped down to his knees beside her where she lay on the floor.

"It's the back of her head where she took the bump," Matilda explained, standing out of the vicar's way so that he could tend her.

"Does it hurt?" John asked, easing his hand beneath her head.

"Like bloody hell," she replied without thought, her eyes clamped shut.

She heard Matilda chuckle. Pembrooke suppressed his laughter with a forced cough.

And the vicar cleared his throat before saying, "Then I suggest we get you upstairs to your bedchamber so you may rest."

She groaned in protest.

"Open your eyes, Billie."

The familiar arrogant voice had her eyes shooting open. "No," she cried as the pain speared her head.

John's hand cupped the back of her head and he spoke softly. "Let me help you to the chair first and then we'll see about getting you upstairs."

Before she could voice her objection, John slipped his arm around her waist and as he stood her up he leaned her body against his own.

Soft like pillows, she thought, cushioned against him.

Gently he moved her to sit in the chair near the desk.

Her head still throbbed but she was regaining her wits.

While John issued instructions to Matilda and Pembrooke, Billie scanned the room for Maximillian. She had heard his voice. She wasn't imagining things. He had been there, she was certain of it. Why, she could still detect the slight scent of the sea.

Her hand sought the back of her head. Unable to find the source of the pain due to her swept-up hair, she removed the combs, allowing her hair to fall freely over her shoulders.

She was then able to run her fingers through her hair and locate the source of her distress. She winced when she connected with a large bump.

"A cold compress will help," John offered, coming to rest on one knee beside her.

"I'm sorry to have troubled you," she said, reaching out to him.

He took her hand in his. "Nonsense. I would have been upset if Pembrooke hadn't summoned me. I told you, Billie, I'll always be here for you."

She squeezed his hand, happy he reiterated his promise. It felt so good to have someone care for her as much as he did and she was beginning to feel a strong stirring of emotion for him as well. She wondered over it often. It was as though she were long familiar with him, and yet they had only recently met.

"Can you tell me what happened?"

Billie began to nod and then stopped, thinking better of it. "I came into the study to tend to my correspondence. The lighted lamp blew out. I heard a noise and knew I wasn't alone. Then a flash of almost blinding light pierced the room. That's when I saw a figure run toward me. He sent me toppling to the floor."

She omitted the vision of Max silhouetted in the stream of light, certain John would surely think that the bump on her head was the cause of her delusion.

John looked at Pembrooke. "Did you hear anything?"

"A crash, which brought me rushing in here. I found my lady lying unconscious on the floor."

"No one was in the room?" John queried.

"No one, sir, and the door was closed."

"Is there any other way out of this room?" Billie asked, surprising both men.

Pembrooke looked at her oddly. "There's only one door, as you can see, my lady."

Billie recalled the hidden entrance to the caves behind the cupboard in the pantry. If one hidden exit existed, then why not others?

Not prepared to share her opinion on hidden passageways just yet, she sighed dramatically and raised her hand to her head. "I'd like to rest now. This whole ordeal has greatly upset me."

She didn't catch the three wide-eyed looks sent her way.

John assisted her in standing, "I will help you to your bed-chamber with Matilda's assistance, of course."

Matilda stepped forward.

Billie objected immediately. She didn't require nurse-maids. She was more than capable of taking care of herself. "Nonsense, John. You have done more than enough for me. I'll take myself directly to bed and rest."

John, as if not trusting her, turned to Matilda and instructed, "Please see that she is settled comfortably for the night."

"Yes, sir."

"I'll look in on you tomorrow," John said and with a gentle squeeze of her hand, he followed Pembrooke out the door.

"Now, my lady," Matilda started. "I'll help you upstairs and then I'll fetch a nice bowl of beef broth with—"

"I appreciate your concern," Billie interrupted. "But I don't require any help." She walked toward the door, her steps slow and shaky. "Though I would enjoy the beef broth."

Matilda grinned at the young woman's tenacity. "With fresh-baked cheddar bread?"

Billie kept walking and held up two fingers. "Big slices."

Matilda didn't bother to follow her and insist on tending her. She would do fine. Strong and resilient. Billie was a match for anybody and any ghost.

Billie took the stairs slowly. She wasn't fool enough to think she could maneuver the steps at her usual pace. She had suffered a serious bump and if she recalled her mother correctly she shouldn't seek sleep for a while. Rest, yes, but sleep wasn't a wise choice at the moment.

The throbbing increased as she climbed the stairs and she paused once or twice, steadying herself with her hand on the bannister to regain her strength. By the time she reached the landing she felt dizzy and weak.

She paused for a few minutes and then headed down the hall to her bedchamber. The passageway to her door appeared much farther away than she remembered. Much too far a journey for her to make in her weakened condition.

She leaned against the wall and rested her head back. Her eyes caught sight of Maximillian's portrait hanging above her.

Jokingly, she admonished, "Where are you when I need you, Max?"

"Right beside you, Billie," he whispered in her ear and effortlessly scooped her up into his strong arms.

Relief rushed through Billie. He was there. He had come to help her.

His shoulder cushioned her head as he walked at a considerate pace so as not to cause her more pain.

"I heard you," she murmured, feeling content in his protective embrace.

"I should hope so. I shouted loud enough at you."

She smiled at his arrogance and the hint of concern he failed to keep from his tone.

He carried her to the bed and gently placed her down, resting her back against a fluff of white pillows. *"Stay put."*

He crossed the room, returning to the door to close it. He then searched her chest of drawers.

"Whatever are you looking for?" she asked.

"Your night rail." He pulled a soft white cotton gown from the bottom drawer and marched toward her.

She attempted to move. The pain prevented her from doing so, forcing her to speak firmly from her reclining position. "I can't undress in front of you."

"I'll turn my back, but I want you in this night rail and in bed resting."

"An order?" she asked with a touch of defiance.

He leaned over her, his nose touching hers. *"A strong suggestion."*

"And a good one," she said, her voice breaking with a quiver. It wasn't that she was afraid of him. She was more afraid of her response to his presence. She had allowed him to kiss and touch her intimately. What else would she allow him to do? What else would he seek from her?

Maximillian eased her to the edge of the bed and helped her to stand, giving her time to steady herself. He unfastened the ties of her dress, warned her to inform him if she required help and then moved away from her to stand at the hearth.

Billie hastened to make fast work of her clothes, discarding her garments at the end of the bed. Feeling vulnerable naked, she hoisted her night rail over her head and shoved her arms through the armholes. Unfortunately her aching head couldn't find the neck of her gown and she soon became tangled in the garment.

Fighting it only made her more dizzy and her bare legs shivered with a chill, the gown resting just below her bottom.

Mortified at her predicament and feeling close to fainting, she called out to Maximillian.

He spun around at her weak cry and hurried to her side. *"Relax,"* he ordered gently. *"I'll free you."*

His strong voice and tender hands worked their magic. She was safe. He was there with her. He would help her.

He eased the gown over her head and untangled her arms in the sleeves. His hands inched the gown down along her body until at her thighs he released the material to drop to her ankles.

Her body sagged against his. "I'm so dizzy, Max."

She closed her eyes as he tucked her into bed and a light knock sounded at the door.

Billie opened her eyes to look up at him, but he had already vanished. She hadn't wanted him to leave her. She wanted him right there beside her, holding her, caring for her.

Matilda entered the room, carrying a bed tray filled with food. "You look exhausted, my lady," she said on closer inspection.

Billie only nodded though the effort hurt. Her mind remained on Max and this sudden need for him.

Within minutes Matilda had her sitting up, a mound of pillows supporting her back and head and a cold compress applied to the bump. The tray sat across her lap and the rich aroma of beef broth, thick cheddar bread, chunks of white cheese and chamomile tea made her mouth water.

Matilda busied herself with seeing to Billie's discarded garments, though Billie suspected that the woman wanted to stay close by should she need assistance.

Coincidentally, Billie finished her meal at the same time Matilda finished tending the room.

Making certain Billie required nothing further, Matilda took her leave.

Billie closed her eyes but only for a moment.

She sensed his presence before he sat beside her on the bed.

"Why did you leave me?" She sounded as if she scolded him.

He pushed away the strands of hair from her eyes. *"I didn't leave you. I was here the whole time you ate so heartily. Now open your eyes, you should not sleep yet. I've known too many who have suffered a bump to the head and fell into sleep never to awaken."*

"My mother told me similar stories, yet I grow tired." A yawn affirmed it.

"Then we shall talk."

"About what?"

"About the bump on your head."

Billie poked his chest. "You were there."

"Afterwards I was, demanding you open your eyes," he admitted.

"But I saw you," she said, though she wondered if the bump had actually caused an illusion.

"I was not in the room, Billie. Perhaps it was another ghost come to your rescue," he teased.

She wore a worried frown. Could Oran have ventured upstairs?

He sought to ease her concern. *"The bump on your head could have caused you confusion and misinterpretation of what you actually saw."*

She chose not to disagree, planning to work out this strange turn of events on her own.

"Did you see the person who ran into you?"

"No, I can't even be sure of his size. He appeared bent over as he ran toward me and battered me like a ram. It all happened so fast I didn't have time to think or react. What troubles me most is that I don't understand what he was searching for."

"Coins probably."

"I don't think so, Max. My letters to family and friends lay opened and scattered across the desk as if read and discarded in haste."

Maximillian didn't care for what he heard and his deep voice reflected his concern. *"The thief seeks knowledge about you."*

A yawn attacked her and she shrugged. "I've made no secret of my background, and most in the village know my origins."

Max's expression grew dark, his eyes narrowing. *"Does anyone know of your family?"*

Sadly, she answered him. "I have no family. They're all gone. I'm alone."

"An aunt? Uncle?"

"No one. I either had to journey here to St. Clair and claim my inheritance or marry a man I could not abide. My choices were limited, though not difficult. I realized I could not commit myself to a man I did not love. And I often dreamed of traveling to distant lands, so my decision was an easy one. I chose to come to St. Clair."

"You have me."

Billie wasn't certain she had heard him correctly. "I have you?"

"Me," he reiterated softly.

She smiled without it hurting her head. "I never imagined a friendly ghost."

"Friendly isn't exactly how I would describe our relationship." He slipped his hand over hers linking their fingers.

"Describe our relationship," she urged with a teasing smile.

He didn't hesitate. *"Unusual."*

She laughed. "We finally agree."

His fingers tightened around hers. *"I want you to be careful."*

"I'm alw—"

He brought their clenched fingers up to her mouth to silence her words. *"I'm serious about this. If that person did not find what he was looking for this evening, he may return. If he did find what he was looking for . . ."* He paused and skimmed her lips with their entwined fingers. *"Then you may be in danger."*

"You're confusing me," she said and shook her head, forgetting the bump. She winced when the pain struck.

She didn't notice that his jaw clenched and his free hand fisted at his side. *"Enough about this evening. Tell me about Nantucket."*

"You'd like it," she said, relaxing against the mound of pillows and still clinging to his hand that he rested in her lap.

They spent an hour talking of Nantucket and St. Clair, comparing the towns' similarities and differences. They smiled, laughed and conversed easily until Billie could no longer keep her eyes open and drifted off to sleep.

Maximillian left her side only for a moment, stoking the fire to make certain the room remained comfortably warm. He returned to the bed, easing himself down alongside her, not wanting to disturb her, yet not wanting to leave her alone.

The thought that she had no one, that she had traversed an ocean alone to come to a foreign country and begin a new life made him admire and respect her all the more. She could have planted herself in a loveless marriage like many women did when finding themselves on their own. But instead she saw an opportunity for herself with her stepfather's inheritance and although it meant giving up all she had known and was familiar with, she took the chance.

She was strong, resilient and beautiful.

He reached out and ran the back of his hand across her cheek. Her skin was silky soft, the color of rich cream and tasted just as sweet. Her eyes, hidden in contented slumber, were of the deepest brown like the fresh earth when dark and ripe and ready for planting. And her hair was a contrast in color ranging from a light, faint brown to the richest blond.

Her body was an area he had best not dwell on; such intimate thoughts would do him no good.

Why? Why had she entered his life now?

He shook his head at his disgruntled thought and tapped her cheek with his finger, waiting for her protesting groan. He stopped as soon as she responded. He didn't want her slipping into an eternal slumber. She was too full of life to allow it to carelessly slip away.

He had been careless and now had to face the results. He had lost so much and thought to reclaim it so easily. He had not judged his situation wisely and had paid dearly.

He thought to chase her away, assure her safety, but now . . .

He selfishly wanted her with him.

She stirred, sighing his name.

He comforted her with a soothing caress to her neck and soft words of reassurance that he would not leave her side. She settled once again.

How had she become so important to him? So fast? When had he realized he ached to touch her every moment he was with her? When did he realize it was only a matter of time before they became intimate? And when did he begin to worry about the consequences of bringing his restless spirit to rest?

She turned and slumped down into the pillows. Her awkward position would only cause her neck discomfort in the morning. He reached over her and cupped her head in his hand, avoiding the area around the bump. He tossed several pillows aside so she could rest her head more comfortably on one pillow rather than a mound.

He told himself she no longer needed him but, unconvinced by his own words, he remained, stretching out beside her on the bed. He would watch over her, nudging her occasionally to make certain that slumber only had claimed her.

Billie cuddled up against him in the middle of the night burying her face against his linen shirt.

When morning finally peeked through the windowpanes, the only proof that Maximillian had ever been there was the scent of the sea on the pillow that Billie hugged closely to her.

Chapter
Thirteen

Two days later rain returned to St. Clair. Billie watched it run against the windowpane in the kitchen. She was busy cutting vegetables for the fish chowder she was cooking, happy to have finally found some time to prepare a favorite dish of hers.

Matilda and Pembrooke had gone to the village; actually Matilda had all but dragged her husband out of the house. He, not his wife, had strongly voiced his opinion about the lady of the manor working in the kitchen like a common cook.

His wife didn't share his rigid views, having spent time chatting with Billie and learning about her life in Nantucket. The poor girl was accustomed to doing for herself, not born to the pampered life of the gentry. She befriended who she pleased and had earned the respect of more villagers than any lady Matilda had ever known.

Pembrooke even attempted to use the excuse that Billie still required attention, the bump on her head not being completely healed. But with two days past since the incident and the bump on her head nearly gone, his objection was dismissed as nonsense by a stern Matilda and out the door and into the carriage the couple went.

Billie had eagerly slipped into the gray wool dress she had worn for chore time in Nantucket and had borrowed one of Matilda's large white bib aprons. She tied it twice around her waist and set to work cooking.

The broth, heavily seasoned with herbs and spices, was stewing in the iron kettle over the open flame while her hands busily sliced potatoes. She felt like her old self, having rested the past two days. Now it was time to return to her daily routine and to her ghostly investigation.

The front door's lion knocker echoed through the manor and had Billie hastily wiping her hands on her apron and rushing to see who visited.

"Claudia," Billie said with a smile, and hugged the woman when she entered.

"You are the most unconventional lady," Claudia said, but returned her hug with enthusiasm.

Billie took her cloak, gloves and bonnet, depositing them in the receiving parlor on a chair.

"Join me in the kitchen," Billie said and led a startled Claudia to the room that was filled with such rich scents that it made one's mouth water.

"It smells delicious," Claudia said with an unladylike sniff of the air. "Whatever are you cooking?"

Billie put the kettle on and arranged teacups on the trestle table. "Please sit," she offered and answered, "Fresh fish chowder."

Claudia watched in amazement as Billie hurried around the room, collecting all the paraphernalia that normally sat in readiness on a serving tray. She arranged the items in their proper serving places on the table and then added a plate she had artfully grouped with slices of fruit bread.

She attended to the boiling tea, brewing the leaves like a woman long familiar with the process and sat the teapot on the table to steep.

"I need to finish cutting the potatoes so they finish cooking with the other vegetables. Do you mind if I work while we visit?"

Claudia, completely enthralled by Billie's charming and unpretentious manner, simply nodded.

"I'm so glad you stopped by. In Nantucket friends would often drop in for a chat."

"When John told me of your accident I wanted to come right over, but he insisted you needed rest. He just informed me today that you were well enough to have visitors."

"I feel much better." She dropped the chunks of potatoes into the pot, stirring the chowder. With a quick wash of her hands in the ceramic basin, she hung her apron on the peg on the wall by the door and eagerly joined Claudia.

They enjoyed the tea and fruit bread and chatted like neighbors sharing an afternoon visit.

"I talked with Bessie about finding out the whereabouts of a man named Derry Jones who may have information concerning Oran's death."

Claudia's eyes rounded as wide as large coins. "Oran's death? I thought you were curious in regards to Maximillian?"

"Don't you find it strange that the son died only a short time after the father was murdered?"

"It was an accident caused by a wrecking, something not unusual around here."

"But no body was found?"

Claudia offered a reasonable explanation. "It washed out to sea."

"Have most drowning victims washed out to sea?" Billie inquired.

Claudia's mouth opened and closed so fast it was as if she bit back her retort. She cast a pondering glance at Billie and then spoke. "Come to think of it, most of the bodies wash up along shore here or along one of the other villages' shores."

Billie mentally filed that bit of important information away for future use.

"What are you suggesting?"

Billie shrugged. "I don't know. It's too early to piece together such fragmented facts. I need to learn more about Oran's murder and the events that followed. But something doesn't seem right. And I won't feel properly settled here until I can lay to rest this uneasiness that gnaws at me."

She wished she could discuss seeing more than one ghost with Claudia, but since the woman was the self-proclaimed busybody of the village she knew that wasn't a wise choice. Hearing that the new lady of the manor talked with ghosts would challenge her credibility, not to mention her sanity.

Claudia patted her hand. "I'll do what I can, Billie, but you must promise me that you will be careful in your search. You never know what unsavory characters you may come up against."

Ghosts. If she could face ghosts, she could face anything.

"I promise I'll be careful," she assured her and then asked, "Were the caves below used by smugglers?"

Claudia frowned. "I'm afraid so."

"With Oran Radborne's knowledge?"

Claudia nodded, her frown deepening. "He only dealt with insignificant smugglers, no one who the authorities were concerned with. I wouldn't be surprised if the magistrate wasn't involved as well, accepting a few bottles of foreign brandy and cigars as payment to ignore the illegal activity in the caves."

"What happened?" she asked, recalling Oran was limited in the information he could supply.

"I don't know." She shook her head, her eyes misting with tears. "He was found shot to death in the caves. He was such a dear man, thoughtful and kind." She laughed sadly. "Arrogant and demanding as well. He expected obedience as all lords do."

Billie at first thought, like father like son, but after becoming more familiar with her new home, she realized just how important heritage and titles were. A lord of a manor demanded a certain amount of respect, and though it appeared tyrannical to her since she came from a country where nobility was nonexistent, here it held great importance.

She also realized that Claudia had loved Oran Radborne. It was written in the sadness that claimed her eyes and the tremble in her lips.

"Oran loved his son dearly. He wanted so much to see him marry and have a family. He was in the process of securing a good marriage contract for him when he died."

"Marriage contract?"

Claudia took a sip of her tea before she answered. "Titled families arrange marriages for their sons and daughters. One cannot marry below their station and then, of course, there's the dowry a wife brings to the marriage. Many a family has tripled their wealth and holdings by arranging a lucrative marriage."

"What about love?" Billie asked, stunned.

Claudia cast a wistful glance at Billie. "Love is something a woman dreams about in her youth, discovers that it is far beyond her grasp as she matures and when she grows old finally realizes that she shouldn't have settled for anything less."

"I won't settle for less," Billie said with a firm resolve that turned Claudia's frown to a smile.

"I'll remind you often that you said that." She finished her tea and promised to contact a few people who could provide information concerning recent smuggling activities in the area before she took her leave, thanking Billie for a most delightful visit.

Billie returned to the kitchen after seeing Claudia to the door. Her entrance was brought to an abrupt halt when she spied Oran standing over her bubbling fish chowder, sniffing at it.

"Smells simply delicious, my dear. I only wish I had retained my earthly appetite in spirit form."

Startled that he stood there, it took Billie a few moments to find her voice. "You and your son have drastically altered my opinion of ghosts."

"We're not the conventional type of ghosts. The misty shroud, rattling chains, moaning and groaning don't appeal to me. After all, I am a lord and must maintain my dignity."

Billie had to laugh—she couldn't help it. A ghostly lord that felt himself a class above the regular ghost. She curtsied politely. "Do sit down, my lord, and visit."

Oran held his head high and gave his deep blue waistcoat a tug. He sent her a rakish smile that reminded her of Maximillian's smile. *"I would be delighted to."*

He sat in the same spot Claudia had vacated and glanced ruefully at her empty cup. *"I miss her."* And before Billie could tell him that Claudia missed him as well, he shifted the topic. *"You promised to be careful."*

Her hand instantly went to the back of her head, understanding he referred to her accident. "A thief—"

He interrupted. *"Was anything stolen?"*

She recalled her conversation with Max. Had the thief discovered what he came for or had his search been interrupted? "I'm not certain."

"You must consider all the possibilities," Oran warned. *"Don't overlook anything, even if it appears insignificant."*

Billie intended to get some answers of her own from Oran. She joined him at the table. "Why were you involved with the smugglers?"

"A harmless group, hardly worthy of the title smugglers. They dealt in trivial trade."

Billie shook her head in disbelief. "One of those smugglers shot y—"

She halted when he furrowed his brow, studied him a moment and calmly spoke. "It wasn't one of your smugglers that shot you, was it?"

He didn't confirm her suspicions. *"Look where you least expect to find the answers."*

"From Maximillian," she said with a teasing smile.

"Maximillian has much to offer you, if you but listen."

"Listen to him demand and dictate."

"He's a lord," Oran reminded.

Billie corrected him as she so often corrected Max. "A deceased lord."

"Things aren't always what they seem."

Billie attacked. "Aha, he isn't a ghost is he? He just plays at one. But for what purpose?"

Oran stood, shaking his head. *"You must solve this puzzle on your own. I have said too much already."*

"I will find out, you know," she challenged.

"You will solve the puzzle, I have no doubt. But when you finish, then what? Perhaps you will find yourself with a piece that fits in more than one way."

"One piece that fits two?" she asked, attempting to understand.

His expression was overly cheerful. *"Or two that fit one."*

A knock at the front door prevented any further discussion. Oran stood. *"I will visit with you again."*

"Perhaps you could knock next time," Billie teased.

"A ghost never announces his arrival, my dear, at least not a lordly ghost."

Billie laughed and headed for the door. "Next time we visit I will have solved some of the puzzle." She turned back around at the kitchen door. Oran was gone. She wasn't surprised.

As she hurried to the front door, his voice, filled with fatherly concern, trailed after her. *"Be careful."*

"I will. I will," she repeated, opening the door.

John stood there, potted crocuses clutched in his hand. "You will what?"

"Flowers for me?" she asked, purposely avoiding his question while urging him in with a wave of her hand and anxiously closing the door behind him.

He offered them to her. "I wanted to bring you a bit of spring."

Billie felt the thrill of his thoughtful words race through her. She took the flowers, inhaled their fragrance and then hugged the plain white pot to her chest. "Thank you so much," she said and, without conscious thought, kissed his cheek.

She saw that her unconventional actions made him nervous and she grabbed his hand. "Come with me." She towed him behind her until they entered the kitchen.

"Sit. You must try a bowl of my fish chowder. It is one of my best recipes." She talked while she placed the bright buds on the table and rushed to collect dishes and such.

John remained standing in the doorway, watching her hurry about. "I have never met a lady of a manor that cooked."

No one but Matilda could understand her need to tend to daily chores. She was raised with the necessary skills to make a man a good wife. She enjoyed polishing wood to a brilliant shine, washing linens clean, stitching a fine garment and cooking a meal that would please a husband. She was proud of her talents and found it difficult to allow other people to do for her when she could do for herself. She was a strong, proud American.

"Please sit," she repeated, removing the cups and plates left from Claudia's visit.

John obliged her. "I realize the cultural change must be difficult for you."

Billie took soup bowls from the corner cupboard. "Very difficult." She ladled steaming chowder into each bowl. "But I promised myself that once every so often I would do the things I so enjoyed doing in Nantucket. Cooking was one of them."

John watched her slice thick black bread, place it on a plate that she added to the serving tray set with soup bowls and carry it to the table.

He stood to assist her.

"Please," she said, placing a gentle hand on his arm. "Let me do this for you." She wanted him to understand that it was her way of showing her appreciation for his thoughtfulness, and because she cared for him. She wanted to share the intimacy of a couple sharing a meal. It was strange,. but she recalled when she was little how pleasant it was to watch her mother and father talk and laugh at the table. They had shared something special. She wanted to share that closeness with John.

John studied her a moment, patted her hand, took his seat and with a sheepish grin said, "I really can't wait to taste it. It smells heavenly."

Billie beamed with pride. "My chowder is known as the best throughout all of Nantucket."

He waited for her to join him at the table, then he folded his hands in prayer. She did the same. He said a simple yet generous grace and they ate.

They talked eagerly, John complimenting her profusely on her chowder. He soon had her talking about her life in Nantucket and when she mentioned a marriage proposal, he casually interrupted.

"Why didn't you accept this Jeremy Ulster's proposal?"

Her answer came fast. "I didn't love him."

"Love sometimes grows with time," he suggested in a soft tone that confirmed his preaching skills.

"I agree that love can grow, but only if two people care for and respect each other. If there is no emotion involved, there is nothing to build on."

"You could not marry without love?"

Billie put her spoon down and cupped her chin in her hands, her elbows braced on the edge of the table. She gave his question thought. "I always dreamed that I would meet a man and instantly fall madly in love with him. My mother called it a childhood fantasy."

"And is it still a dream?"

She laughed and threw her hands up in the air. "I'm all grown up now."

"Grown-ups dream, too."

Lately her dreams had been of ghosts, haunting her with unforgettable kisses. And emotions she didn't quite understand. What did she feel for the ghostly lord? Love? Or pure passion?

"Love is important to me," she responded as if reminding herself. "I was raised in a family that gave of it freely and generously. I wish the same sense of emotional security when I marry and have children. What about you?"

He shrugged. "I don't have much to offer a future wife."

"Of course you do," she disagreed.

"My yearly vicar's stipend is small—"

"Nonsense," Billie interrupted. "You yourself have much to offer a wife."

He shook his head firmly and voiced his opinion just as firmly. "I am not what a woman looks for in a husband."

"You are," she insisted and proceeded to detail why. "You are kind and considerate. You care deeply." She smiled and placed her hand over his. "And you listen to me speak of ghosts, yet you don't judge me. I trust you, John. I know if the need arose I could turn to you and you would be there for me. You are a special man."

John reached out and gently ran his finger down the side of her face. "You are very special, too."

His voice was whisper-soft, his touch gentle as a breeze and her reaction instantaneous. Her insides quivered.

Hesitantly, he brought his face nearer to hers, giving her a chance to deny his advances. To his surprise and pleasure she inched her face closer to his and when their lips met their reaction was mutual.

He kissed her with the sweetness of a man introducing a woman to the first steps of pleasure. Tenderly his lips passed over hers inviting her to enjoy and partake.

She did, tasting him and wanting more. She parted her lips in invitation and he slowly slipped in. His tongue teased hers playfully and she found herself responding, her desire budding in the most intimate places.

Raised, squabbling voices broke them abruptly apart and had the vicar moving an appropriate distance away from Billie.

Matilda and Pembrooke burst through the kitchen door.

"You are a stubborn fool too set in his ways to see that—" Matilda ended her scolding immediately upon seeing the vicar and Billie seated at the table.

Pembrooke's mouth dropped open and he glared at Billie, obviously appalled that she entertained the vicar in the kitchen.

John addressed the situation to the relief of everyone. "Billie cooks the most wonderful fish chowder. I simply couldn't eat enough of it."

Matilda joined in his praise of Billie. "My lady is a wonderful cook. Her biscuits are light and tasty, melting in your mouth."

Pembrooke stared at his wife as though she had just sprouted three heads.

Matilda ignored him and proceeded to salvage the situation. "My lady, you must be tired from your busy day. Allow me to serve you and the vicar tea in the receiving parlor."

John stood. "I must be going, but I am certain a bit of rest wouldn't hurt Billie."

Outnumbered, Billie wasn't about to protest. "I'll see you to the door, John."

A disgruntled cough from Pembrooke alerted her to her error.

"Pembrooke will see you to the door, John," she corrected with a sweet smile.

John bid her a pleasant evening and followed a stiff Pembrooke to the front door.

"Tea, my lady?" Matilda asked, cleaning off the table.

"I've had my fill," Billie said and stifled a yawn. "I think I'll rest some. Will you wake me before nightfall?"

"Of course, my lady."

Once in her room Billie stripped down to her white linen chemise, freed her hair to spill over her shoulders and slipped between the bedcovers. Her busy day and the rain rhythmically tapping at the windowpane combined to lull her into a gentle slumber.

She dreamed of John, his gentle kisses, his tender touches, his caring ways and his mild temperament. He would love his wife with compassion and warmth, never raising his voice to her.

She snuggled deeper beneath the covers, fantasies of love, happiness and forever after filling her head. Forgotten was the thought of love at first sight, racing heartbeats, quickened breath and *unforgettable* kisses, until . . .

A warm whisper teased her ear. *"You forgot passion."*

Chapter Fourteen

His fingers breezed across her nipples; the faint touch puckered them to life. His lips paid homage to her neck with faint kisses while he whispered a litany of erotic promises.

Billie drifted on the verge of wakefulness, too tempted by passionate pleasure to leave her dream. He haunted her with intimate touches, excited her with spirited kisses and tempted her with the devil's own tongue.

"Touch me, Billie," he urged, taking her hand and slipping her trembling fingers inside his shirt. *"I need you to touch me."*

She moaned as her hand connected with his warm, hard chest and then she explored, her fingers inching ever so slowly over him. His own nipple puckered as the palm of her hand brushed over it and she rested there a moment, rubbing the orb to a hardening madness.

"Enough," he groaned in her ear and nipped at her lobe before proceeding down along her chin to her lips.

Empty and aching, her mouth greeted him, devouring him with a hungry passion. Reason and sanity escaped her. She wanted nothing more than for this maddening moment to never end.

His hand raced along her body over her linen chemise, touching, teasing, torturing. She arched against his hand when he cupped her between her legs and they groaned together.

He moved over her, his hands rushing to capture her face, deepening their kiss while his body moved in an erotic rhythm that brought her unspeakable pleasure. She could feel him nestling against her, hot and heavy, even through the clothes that barely separated them.

"I want you, Billie. I want you," he repeated over and over between kisses that left her writhing.

A gentle knock and a soft, distant voice calling *my lady, my lady,* intruded on Billie's dream, but before she fully woke, she distinctly remembered her hand brushing him intimately.

He was no ghost, she thought, shaking herself awake. He was built too powerfully, too large, too hard to be anything but a man of flesh and blood.

Those thoughts haunted her over the next few days as did he. He stole kisses, tender caresses and stared at her with eyes filled with such heated passion that Billie thought he would melt her.

She turned quiet, her thoughts troubling her. If he was no ghost then he would eventually reclaim the manor—but when? What did he hope to gain by this charade?

She wished there was someone she could talk to about her problem, but she couldn't turn to John with such intimate details and Claudia was out of the question. She had become friendly with Matilda, but the woman continued to remind her of the differences between common people and gentry and how she must tread lightly along that line.

Maximillian, however, saw no problem in crossing the

line. He wanted her and, from her response, she wanted him. But no words of love were spoken between them, and she was a fisherman's daughter, he a nobleman playing at being a ghost. What future was there for her in such a bizarre relationship?

She sighed, rubbing her head. Even the completion of the dining salon hadn't helped ease her worry.

"What the bloody hell have you done to this room?"

Billie's eyes popped opened and she took a step back, bumping into a dining table chair. She grabbed the back so it wouldn't topple over and so that she would have support while her racing heart calmed down. He had scared the wits out of her. She had thought by now she would be accustomed to him popping in and out of rooms.

That, she thought, was her next project: discovering how he managed to enter rooms as if from out of thin air.

"Answer me," he bellowed again.

She continued holding on to the chair; the sight of his tall, powerful form outfitted in shades of gray that reminded one of a brewing storm was much too intimidating.

She finally spoke up though her voice didn't project the volume she had intended. "I gave it life." And with her courage returned, she added, "Something you know nothing about."

That definitely stung him. He marched further into the room and pointed an accusatory finger at her. *"You've made this room—"*

She finished for him, her smile generous. "Stunning."

He was about to shout at her again when she lifted her butternut wool dress just above her black pumps and marched over to him with the determination of a soldier heading into battle.

She stopped a few inches in front of him and poked him in the chest. "Stop your meaningless blustering and take a good look. This room is filled with rich, soft colors that invite guests to relax and enjoy their visit."

He grumbled and cast a quick, unobservant glance around the room. He was prepared to deliver another reprimand when he caught sight of his mother's favorite crystal pieces artfully displayed in the built-in corner cupboards that were painted a soft apricot color.

His eyes studied the room further. Wallpaper with gentle white birds, apricot-colored flowers and deep green vines against an ecru-colored background covered the walls while the apricot color continued along the wood trim. The deep green and ecru colors were carried over onto the dining chairs' velvet cushions, and the pattern of wide green stripes followed by a paper-thin ecru stripe repeated itself on the velvet curtains at the windows.

The beautifully embroidered table scarf that his mother had labored over for so many months when he was a young boy was draped over the middle of the dark wood table and a large, shining crystal bowl filled with a mixture of fragrant dried herbs sat in the center. The sideboard glistened with two crystal candle holders and a three-tiered crystal fruit server.

Maximillian remained speechless, his thoughts on how Billie had lovingly and considerately displayed and put into use so many items his mother had loved so dearly.

Billie, as if reading his thoughts, broke the silence. "I discovered so many beautiful and useful treasures stored away that I just had to find places for them. Wait until you see what I do to the receiving parlor, the main parlor, the conservatory, the bedchamber—" She stopped. "Did I forget any rooms?" And with a wide grin directed at Max she added, "The study."

He glared at her. *"I think not."*

She had no intention of disturbing his study; she loved it just the way it was, but he needn't know that. She shot back. "We'll see."

"Belinda, if you wish to alter a few rooms to keep yourself occupied I have no objections—"

"You like the room," she interrupted.

"It is—" His glance fell on his mother's table scarf. *"It is*

lovely. But," he added more firmly, *"you will not touch my study."*

She tapped her finger against her cheek and sighed dramatically. "Lord Radborne, you do remember that you are a ghost?"

"What difference does that make? I am still lord of this manor." And before she could open her mouth he said, *"And don't remind me that I am a deceased lord again."*

"Then if you are d—" She paused, not repeating the word. "What difference does it make if I change the manor?"

"The manor belongs to me."

She shook her head. "No, it belongs to me now."

Maximillian attempted to hold his temper. *"I still occupy the manor."*

"Only until I can settle your restless spirit and send you on your way," she corrected.

"And if my spirit never rests?"

She knew he challenged her and enjoyed it, but then so did she. "I am alive, therefore, as lady of the manor I give the orders and people obey. You are a *ghost*; no one will listen to you, you would just frighten them away." She brushed her hands together as if the matter was settled. "So, I'll do as I please."

Maximillian stared at her with eyes the color of a raging sea after a mighty storm. He issued his words slowly and with a firmness that made her pay close attention. *"If you were my wife, you would obey me without question."*

Her voice was just as firm and so was the poking finger she jabbed at his chest. "If I was your wife, I would do as I please and you, my lord—" She paused and ran her poking finger slowly down his chest, "—would like it."

She deposited a quick kiss to his cheek and hurried out of the room, her light laughter trailing her.

He cursed soundly and rushed after her. He was brought to an abrupt halt by voices in the foyer and he turned in the opposite direction and slipped away.

Pembrooke handed Billie the note that had just been delivered. She read it and asked, "Who brought this?"

"A boy from the village."

"Please get my cloak and bonnet, Pembrooke, I need to
go out."

Pembrooke nodded. "Will you be needing the carriage,
my lady?"

"No, I'll walk," she answered and within minutes was
tugging on her gloves and rushing out the door.

The Cox Crow Inn was empty. The fire held a bubbling
cauldron of seasoned lamb stew and several loaves of fresh
hearth bread sat cooling on a nearby table.

Billie surveyed the empty room just as she had done upon
her first night in St. Clair only this time there was no sea of
faces judging her; only Bessie, red-cheeked and smiling as
she hurried over to greet her.

"Come, my lady, and sit," she urged. "We only have a
short time before this place will start filling up and I have
news for you."

Billie took a seat and Bessie joined her after insisting on
getting Billie a cup of hot tea.

"Your note said you found the person I'm looking for?"

Bessie nodded her head. "That I did, though he hasn't
been heard from in quite some time. Many thought him
dead, but news is he was away—hiding from the law some
say. Heard he's a bad one, fast to use his fists and his knife.
Found out that he's over in St. Simon at the Cove Inn most
nights, bragging into the wee hours to whoever will listen.
But talk has it that he'll be leaving by week's end, possibly
for good."

Billie had no time to hire a man to handle this matter. She
couldn't let Derry Jones just slip away. She needed to ob-
serve him in his own environment and if she listened, she
was bound to learn something if the man bragged.

"Are you familiar with the Cove Inn?"

"It's no place for a lady," Bessie warned.

Billie's disappointment was evident.

"I could have my friend ask around and see what he can find," Bessie offered, wanting to please the lady of the manor.

Which meant it would be necessary to confide more in Bessie, and she couldn't very well tell her that a ghost had advised her to investigate the man. No, she had to handle this herself.

Her mind churned with different ideas while she sipped her tea until finally she grinned wide. "You sent a boy to deliver the note?"

"That I did," Bessie confirmed.

"Do you think the lad would like to make a few coins?"

"The Cove Inn is no place for a boy, though Samuel is a wild one."

Billie shook her head. "I only want his clothes."

Bessie raised a startled brow. "You can't be thinking to—"

"With the help of your friend, of course," Billie said, knowing Bessie would never allow her to go off alone disguised as a boy.

Bessie attempted to talk her out of such an outrageous act. "You can't be serious, my lady. This is too dangerous and you could get hurt."

"I will be careful and I will have your friend nearby to help me in case there is trouble."

"Bart is a big man, thick-muscled and thick-brained." Bessie shook her head, still uneasy with the insane idea.

Billie sought to reassure her. "I have donned men's clothes before when I helped my uncle on his ship. I will keep to myself and out of harm's way, and if Bart is as big as you suggest, then I shall be well protected."

Bessie softened. "If Bart went along—"

"I would be fine," Billie finished and leaned closer to the woman, ready to discuss plans for her adventure as a boy.

Maximillian sat in the chair before the burning hearth in his study, his legs stretched out and his steepled fingers resting against his lips. He hadn't expected this revolt of his emotions. He had always controlled himself where women were concerned. He had never allowed any one female to become too important to him.

He had understood in his youth that a beneficial marriage would be arranged for him and he would be expected to do his duty to his family. He was the only heir to his father's title, his parents never having been blessed with other children.

Therefore, he steeled his emotions, not wishing to hurt himself or an innocent young woman prone to romantic notions of love. Even the mistresses he had kept over the years were relegated to a safe distance.

He had been proud of the painstaking preparation he had taken in building an uncomplicated future for himself. He had never counted on this turn of events so far beyond his control, or for the willful and beautiful young woman who was thrust upon him.

She had, in fact, turned his life upside down. He was still attempting to make sense of his feelings toward her—strong, passionate feelings. Uncontrollable feelings. Protective feelings. Insane feelings. He could go on forever describing how his emotions fluctuated.

It perplexed and delighted him all at once. He found himself looking forward to hearing her voice, to arguing with her, to challenging her to . . .

He stood and walked over to the window, casting a worried glance out at the rumbling clouds. He had seldom considered falling in love. Love wasn't meant for nobility; sacrifice was.

And yet . . .

He chased his inconceivable thoughts away with a shake of his head. He had long ago believed that certain things were impossible and then . . .

"You resemble a tortured man."

Maximillian turned around and greeted his father with a smile. *"Tortured by the new lady of the manor."*

Oran settled in the high-backed chair by the hearth, motioning his son to join him in the chair opposite him. *"A sweet torture if you ask me."*

Maximillian stoked the dying flames before taking his seat. *"Sweet? I think not."*

"She is beautiful and so . . ." Oran paused as if searching for the right word. *"Courageous."*

"That she is," Maximillian agreed, but hurried to add, *"To a fault. I worry what trouble she'll get herself into. She talks to anyone and thinks nothing of visiting whoever she wishes. She has no sense of propriety."*

"That may be a blessing, but why allow her to help you with your dilemma?"

"I have no choice. I have no one else to turn to, nor do I trust anyone. Billie is our only hope."

"She's an innocent dragged into this mess. I worry about her."

"As do I, but her stubborn nature may help in solving this puzzle."

Oran sighed. *"I grow weary and wish to rest."*

"I have discovered most of the pieces to this puzzle, but one is missing. One person masterminded the wreckings and the smuggling. His plan was brilliant and his identity undetectable."

"And you think Billie will uncover this mystery person?"

"She has enlisted the aid of Claudia, Bessie and the vicar. Any or all of them could prove useful."

"Keep her out of harm's way," Oran ordered. *"She's already suffered once when she shouldn't have."*

Maximillian sought confirmation of his suspicions. *"You were in the study."*

"I heard her anxiously call your name," he explained and cast an angry shake of his fist at the far wall. *"But the blasted wall separated us. Took all of my power to pass through and my bloody spirit energy exploded once I made it, shedding a brilliant light on the situation and scaring the devil out of the fellow."*

"You didn't catch his identity?"

"The damn light blinded me."

Maximillian laughed.

Oran shook his finger at his son. *"It's not a laughing matter. Spirits should be misty shrouds that float about as the stories all these years dictated. Instead I discover I can walk about in death as I did in life only with a few added amenities, propelled by my spirit energy, of course, which I have yet been unable to control."*

"I've explained to you that it is a matter of concentration."

"I'm too busy concentrating on more important matters." Oran moved to the edge of his chair, reaching out to grasp his son's arm. Tears misted in his eyes. *"We are almost out of time, Maximillian, and I wish to leave knowing all is settled and the manor and its holdings will endure."*

Maximillian placed his hand over his father's and squeezed. *"I will see that all is how you wish it."*

"And Billie?" Oran asked, almost reluctantly.

Maximillian dropped his hand away. *"What of Billie?"*

"You aren't being fair to her."

"I am handling this as I feel necessary."

Oran leaned back in his chair and asked, *"Then when do you plan on telling her the truth?"*

Chapter
Fifteen

"She's no fool. She knows the truth," Maximillian said, turning his attention to the flames in the hearth.

"You've told her?" his father asked, followed by an audible sigh of relief.

Maximillian looked at his father and smiled. *"You like Billie don't you?"*

"I admire the young woman. She faces adversity with the strength of a man and meets challenges head on even when fearful. A man would be lucky to have her as a wife, but then it would take a special man to be able to deal with a woman of such formidable strength." And with a smug grin stated, *"The vicar appears to be gaining her attention."*

"The vicar is a thorn in my side," Maximillian complained. *"He has posed more of a problem than I could have ever imagined. Billie trusts him and confides in him and . . . I wonder if she is beginning to care for him."*

Oran grew short-tempered. *"Then tell her the truth and be done with it."*

"I can't," he responded with bitter sadness. *"If I reveal the truth it may place her in danger and that I would never do."*

Oran stood and patted his son's shoulder. *"Time, my son, time."*

The vicar arrived at the manor an hour after Billie returned from the village. Pembrooke showed him to the larger receiving parlor where Billie sat on the floor among bolts of various colored material.

"John, how wonderful," she said when he entered. "You must help me decide on colors for the different rooms." She patted the space beside her on the floor.

Pembrooke shook his head, more baffled than distressed. "Does my lady wish tea served?"

"Hot cider," she said matter-of-factly.

Pembrooke repeated her as if he hadn't heard her correctly. "Hot cider?"

"Yes," Billie said, offering John an assisting hand. "With plenty of that fresh whipped cream that Matilda made and slices of the gingerbread cake she baked."

John eased himself down awkwardly, folding his legs beneath him and adjusting his black waistcoat that rode up above the slight bulge of his belly.

Pembrooke grumbled incoherently before he asked sharply, "Is that all?"

Billie was about to answer, unoffended by his crisp tone when John spoke up.

"My lady wishes hot cider instead of tea. Does that present a problem for you, Pembrooke?"

Pembrooke stiffened and responded in a much more respectful tone. "No, sir, I shall bring the items my lady requested immediately."

"He needs time to adjust to me," Billie said in defense of her servant. "He grumbles, but he's thoughtful."

"Regardless," John said firmly, "he must respect your authority and his station."

"Do you like these colors?" Billie asked, changing the subject and anxious to get his opinion. She tossed the silk material over him and it floated down gracefully on his lap.

He fingered the delicate silk. Tiny, soft blue flowers fringed with gentle green leaves were cast against a pale yellow background.

"I thought the bedchamber," she informed him and leaned over to show him a crimson silk. Unable to reach it, she got to her knees and stretched her hand out. "I thought this color perfect for—"

Pembrooke interrupted with a choking cough and a raised brow. "The hot cider, my lady."

Billie realized her bottom was practically swaying in the vicar's face and didn't look at all proper. She hastily plopped herself back on the floor.

Pembrooke placed the tray on the table in front of the gray silk settee and stood beside it as if waiting for her to correct her impropriety.

John stood after untangling himself from the material and extended his hand to her. She gratefully accepted it.

"That will be all, Pembrooke," she directed pompously, once seated on the settee with John.

"Very good, my lady." And with a formal bow he took his leave.

"You handled that like a true lady," John complimented.

Billie smiled appreciatively. "Thank you. I did rather enjoy it."

She handed John a plate with a slice of warm gingerbread.

"I have learned of some problems at the manor just before Maximillian's death."

Wide-eyed, Billie hastily chewed her bite of gingerbread and asked, "What have you found out?"

"It appears that there were several accidents at the manor a few months before Lord Radborne's death. The magistrate had been called here on at least three occasions."

"What kind of accidents were reported?"

"That's where it becomes unclear. Hunting mishaps were listed, attempted theft was another and, of course, there was All Hallows' Eve when the magistrate was summoned to the manor. The reason is unknown and the magistrate remains oddly silent on the subject, though there is rumor and speculation."

"Which is?"

"Most villagers believe a lovers' argument ensued and that someone was killed, presumably the husband of the woman believed to have been Maximillian's lover."

Billie recalled talk of Lord Radborne's reputation with the ladies and for an inexplicable reason it irritated her. "Max was a scandalous devil with the ladies, wasn't he?"

"If you believe the rumors."

Naturally, the vicar would give the person the benefit of the doubt, offer guidance and help and condemn only if warranted. Billie, on the other hand, was familiar with Max's arrogance and autocratic manner. He was a man accustomed to having his way in all things, and she had no doubt that he always had his way where women were concerned. Why women probably swooned at his feet.

Irritated by her own thoughts she snapped at John. "I believe the rumors. Maximillian is overbearing, stubborn, impossible, demanding, temperamental—"

"Billie," John interrupted, bringing Billie's accusatory tirade of Max to an abrupt end. "You speak of the man as if he were alive."

She almost shouted, *He is*, but thought better of it and held her tongue.

"He still haunts your dreams?" John questioned softly.

Billie dropped her glance to her clenched hands in her lap. If she blushed, she would die of embarrassment, and yet how could she keep her cheeks from reddening when her body immediately responded to the memories of Max's intimate touches.

"Billie?" John probed gently yet firmly.

"He haunts me night and day," she admitted reluctantly, but with a sense of relief.

"It isn't only at night you think you see him?"

"I *think* I see him?" she said, affronted by his insinuation that she but imagined him.

"Now, Billie." John spoke calmly and reached out to reassure her with a pat of his hand to her arm.

She yanked her arm away and stood, taking several steps away from him before pacing in front of the table. "So you *think* I but dream these visions?"

"I never meant to imply—"

"That I'm insane?"

"I never meant to upset—"

Again she didn't allow him to finish. "Upset me, by telling me that you never actually believed me from the beginning." She turned her back on him and marched over to the window.

"You tell the idiot, Belinda."

Maximillian's laughing voice caused her to swing around in alarm. She saw no one but John, who was fumbling to hoist his glasses up on the bridge of his nose with trembling fingers.

"Please, Billie, I'm sorry if I offended you," he said sincerely.

Billie glanced past the vicar surveying every inch of the room as she turned in a slow circle.

"Send the fool off."

"Shut up," she shouted and turned to face a shocked John. She rubbed her head, her temples suddenly throbbing.

"Do as I say, Belinda."

The laughter was gone from his voice and he had issued his demand sharply. She thrust her chin up. "I will do as I please."

"Then would it please you to know that I am deeply sorry for upsetting you and that my choice of words was poor but my intentions sincere," Johns aid, holding out his hand to her. "Please, come sit by me and we'll talk."

Billie shut her eyes against the pounding that increased in her head.

"Your head aches, get rid of him and join me upstairs."

Again his voice rang with authority and with an emotion Billie was beginning to easily recognize—passion. He wanted her and she found herself wanting him. She shook her head, warning herself that he was no ghost, that he but played games with her, and yet when he spoke no one heard him but her. And as usual he demanded and as usual she didn't take well to demands, though her body responded quickly enough. She felt all the more confused.

She opened her eyes and forced a smile. "I'd like to talk with you, John." And with that she joined him on the settee.

"Tell me what troubles you," he urged, giving her hand a supportive squeeze.

"I once feared ghosts, due mostly to my mother's excellent storytelling skills, but now . . ." She shook her head. "Now I fear that ghosts will rob me of my sanity."

John remained quiet and listened.

She squared her shoulders and stared him straight in his eyes, distorted by his lenses. "I don't believe Maximillian is a ghost."

John appeared confused. "Then what is he?"

"He is alive."

John seemed to find her statement almost as incredulous as her belief in ghosts. "If he were alive why would he pretend himself dead?"

Billie didn't have enough facts to prove her theory correct and she suddenly realized she could not confide in anyone until she had garnered more proof.

"I'm being foolish," she said. "I suppose the idea of seeing a ghost is something difficult for me to accept and I'm searching for a more reasonable explanation."

"You find it difficult believing in ghosts?"

"I was raised on ghost stories." She smiled, recalling fond memories. "My mother was a wonderful storyteller. She often enthralled neighbors and friends with her skill. On rainy nights she would never fail to weave the most haunting and frightening ghost stories. Afterwards, in my bed, I would shiver beneath my blankets, fearful that I would see a ghost."

John returned her smile and shared his own memories. "I had an aunt that possessed the same skill, although I would bravely tell her that I didn't believe in ghosts and that she couldn't frighten me. She warned me to beware, for surely a nonbeliever such as me would one day be visited by a ghost."

"But you still don't believe, do you?"

John took her hand in his. "I believe in you, Billie, and I will help you in any way possible. If it means facing a ghost and sending him on to his reward, then so be it." His smile broadened. "I would slay dragons for you, my lady."

Her heart rushed with emotion upon hearing such endearing words. He was so thoughtful, so considerate and so very much alive.

"Have you ever slain a dragon, dear sir?" she asked playfully.

He attempted to square his hunched shoulders and hold himself erect. "In my youth I slayed many a fire-breathing dragon and always saved the damsel from distress."

"With a wooden sword?"

He held his hand out as if grasping an imaginary sword hilt. "One made with my own hand."

Billie beamed with pride. "I made one of my own, too."

"You slayed dragons?" he asked incredulously.

She squared her shoulders, her firm breasts sitting high and full. "Just because I was a girl didn't mean I couldn't slay dragons. My father told me I could do anything if I but conquered my fear. So I made a sword of the finest wood, wrapped a pink rag made from a worn-out petticoat around the handle and went in search of dragons."

"I would like to have known you as a child," he said seriously. "We could have had some grand adventures together."

"We could have some adventures now," she suggested.

He chuckled. "I think we already are."

Billie locked her fingers with his. "And I'd like them to continue. I cherish our friendship."

John shifted uncomfortably and stalled a moment as if uncertain that he should speak. Gathering courage he proceeded. "I had hoped our friendship would grow in . . ." He took a deep breath before continuing. "I had hoped we could establish a relationship that might lead to a more permanent arrangement."

Billie spoke more bluntly. "You wish to court me with marriage in mind."

He nodded, his cheeks flushing bright red.

Billie thought about the prospect of marriage to the vicar. He would be good to her. He would not suppress her independent nature and he would make an excellent father. And, of course, she had to consider that if Maximillian wasn't a real ghost she would eventually be left to his mercy. What would he expect from her then? She very much liked John and he was very much alive. He made her feel warm, comfortable and content. A courting relationship would allow those attributes to possibly evolve into love.

"I accept your courting proposal, John," she said softly.

"As you have no parents for me to speak with, I have no choice but to formally seek approval directly from you." With a clear and distinct voice he asked, "May I call on you with intentions of marriage?"

Her response was quick and sure. "I would be honored." And possessing such a spirited nature, Billie leaned over and kissed his cheek.

John smiled and shook his head. "You are the most unconventional lady."

"Then I will never bore you," she assured him happily.

His expression grew serious and he raised his hand to cup her chin. "No, Billie, you shall never bore me. You shall fill me with life." He brought his lips to hers and kissed her with a richness that had her knees trembling and her insides quivering.

He reluctantly ended their kiss, depositing short, sweet kisses along her lips as he pulled away.

"I must be going," John said with obvious regret. "I have appointments at the church."

She stood with him. "You will come for tea tomorrow?"

"Yes, with delight," he beamed.

They walked to the door and while Pembrooke hovered nearby, Billie saw the vicar out, waving as he walked down the drive and out of sight.

She turned and addressed Pembrooke firmly, though her wide smile negated her authoritative tone. "Please bring another hot cider to the study."

"Whipped cream, my lady?" he asked.

She was much too happy to allow his haughty manner to bother her. She most improperly hooked her arm with his and spoke. "Of course, and you should try some. The sweet fluff is sure to bring a smile to your downturned lips."

With a grumble and mumble, Pembrooke disengaged himself from her and marched off.

Laughing lightly, Billie took herself to the study. She slipped into the large chair behind the desk with thoughts of purchasing a smaller one since this one completely devoured her when she sat in it.

She moved her correspondence aside, removed a ledger from the side drawer, opened it and began going over the columns of numbers.

Pembrooke came and went without a word, leaving her hot cider with a fat dollop of whipped cream floating on top beside her to the right.

The sharp voice cut the silent air, ripping a shiver through Billie. *"Whatever do you see in that meek man?"*

She glanced up from the ledger and fought for the breath that lodged in her throat at the sight of Maximillian, standing in front of the desk. Tall, arrogant, self-assured and dangerously handsome, he could capture any woman's heart with a mere smile. He dressed in a perfect blend of grays and black and his dark hair was tightly bound at the nape of his neck with a silver clip.

"Does the vicar have any *attributes?"*

She grew annoyed that he should fault such a good man as John, so she spoke tersely. "He's alive."

He stiffened at her cutting remark. *"You would do well to remember who you speak to."*

"A ghost?" She waited for confirmation.

He denied her an answer and instead said, *"He can offer you nothing but a tedious and burdensome life."*

Billie corrected him. "He can offer me companionship, support and love, not to mention kindness."

Max smashed his hands flat on the desk. *"You need more."*

Billie's hand trembled nervously and she gripped the handle of the cider mug for support. "Really? And what more is it that you think I need?"

"Passion!" he exploded.

The word jolted Billie and raced through her, igniting her flesh like dry kindling caught by a flame.

"How would he know how to bring your body to life? He is a pious man without knowledge of the intimacies of a woman. You require a skilled touch that will fulfill your deepest, darkest dreams."

She tightened her grip on the mug and stared directly into his eyes. "What do you know of my dreams?"

"You come alive in your dreams, Billie. You free yourself of all restraints and enjoy pleasures and emotions women were made to enjoy."

She feared he spoke the truth, but accused him otherwise. "You lie."

"I'll prove it." He walked around the side of the desk and pushed her chair out from beneath, her hand slipping off the mug handle. He reached over to swipe up a finger full of sweet whipped cream.

She stared with rounded, unblinking eyes at him.

He leaned down in front of her and slowly spread the

whipped cream over her lips, running a thin line down her throat. He then proceeded to lick his finger clean, drawing his long tongue up his finger in leisurely strokes that kept her glance glued to his suggestive action. And when she thought him finished and that her heart could race no faster, he stuck his finger in his mouth and slowly sucked it clean.

"Now for you," he whispered with an anticipated lick of his lips.

She moved back against the chair, for once appreciative of its generous size and prepared to lick her own lips clean, but he would have none of her attempts to foil their fun.

"No, no," he warned harshly and licked at the corner of her mouth before urging in a sensual whisper. *"Let me taste you and bring us both pleasure."*

She stilled all movement as he braced his hands on the chair arms, effectively capturing her with his body as his tongue thoroughly and methodically licked the whipped cream from her mouth.

Short licks, long licks, teasing licks, rhythmic licks, his tongue tasted and she was soon reduced to a quivering mass of highly aroused passion.

When he finished at her mouth, he moved to her neck. At the same time his hand found its way to her breast and cupped it forcefully, bringing a flare of pleasure so strong it tightened her nipples to hard tiny buds.

"Bloody hell," he mumbled against her mouth. *"I want to taste your nipples."*

Passion shot through her, quivering her womanhood to a frighteningly sensual height that was at once unfamiliar and yet so devastatingly familiar.

"Tell me to taste them, Billie. Tell me," he urged, trailing demanding kisses down along her neck to the modest neckline of her dress and sending a mass of shivers over her entire body.

She so badly wanted him to taste her, needed him to, ached for him to, but reason reared its practical head and reminded her of the commitment she had just made with John.

And also reminded her that although John had made his intentions clear, this ghostly lord had not.

"No," she whispered with regret.

"Yes," he repeated with a playful squeeze to her nipple.

She took a fortifying breath and urged her body not to betray her. "I don't want this."

His hand slipped off her. *"You deny the obvious. Why?"*

She was grateful that he distanced himself from her, leaning back against the desk. How did she explain that she feared the outcome of this matter? Whether spirit or flesh she would never become part of his life. And he spoke only of passion. Did he not at least care for her as John did?

She answered with more honesty than she realized. "Passion is fleeting. I want more."

He stared at her incredulously. *"You prefer the boring bed of a kind vicar?"*

She held her chin high. "He would slay dragons for me."

Maximillian stood tall and proud. *"I would make love to you until you screamed with pleasure. The choice is yours."*

Chapter
Sixteen

The choice is yours.

Those words had echoed in her head for the last few days. When she and John shared tea, when they walked hand in hand along the shore and when he kissed her with tenderness, Maximillian's words returned to haunt her.

They haunted her still as she approached the back entrance of the Cox Crow Inn. She needed her wits about her tonight. Now was not the time to be thinking such disturbing thoughts. Tonight she needed a clear head. Tonight she would go to the Cove Inn with Bart.

A worried Bessie hurried her through the back door and down the hall to a small room filled with barrels, smoked meats and drying herbs. There amongst the inn's provisions Billie transformed herself from the lady of the manor into a young boy.

Bessie had secured Samuel's clothing for her, washing the

few articles to remove the grime and stench. Billie slipped the brown coarse wool breeches on, added the dark stockings and boots and allowed Bessie to help her into the white linen shirt after binding her breasts with a thick, long strip of cotton cloth. She then finished her attire with a black worn wool jacket and a black knitted cap that snugly captured all her hair beneath it.

Bessie fussed over her like a concerned mother. "I shouldn't be aiding you in such a dangerous scheme. The vicar will have me in penance forever if he discovers my participation."

"John will not find out," Billie assured her. "I will be there and back before anyone discovers me gone."

"A storm is brewing," Bessie said as if the weather were a deterrent to her plans.

"When doesn't it storm in these parts?" Billie asked jokingly.

"The roads could get bad and the storm could worsen and make your travel difficult."

"I'll take my chances," Billie said. She needed to learn more about Derry Jones. So far her search had led nowhere. The pieces to her puzzle had been few and insubstantial. Nothing to grasp onto or direct her to the right path. She had to learn more.

"You need to dull that fresh, pretty face of yours," Bessie suggested and scooped up dirt from the floor with her fingers and smeared streaks on Billie's face.

Billie wrinkled her nose and sneezed.

"You'll be sneezing all the more if you're caught in the storm tonight," Bessie advised. "You'd best tend to business and be on your way."

A sharp rap at the door silenced them both.

"Bessie? You in there?" came a deep, raspy voice.

"Bart," Bessie informed Billie before she swung open the door.

Billie followed Bessie out the door into the hall. She

stared in wonder at the man twisting his cap in his hands and respectfully bobbing his head at her.

Thick and solid as a stone wall was the best way to describe Bart. Barely three inches over five feet, the man was a barrel of muscles. He was completely bald, but sported a thick, dark moustache.

"You'll make certain my lady is well protected, Bart," Bessie ordered with a warning shake of her finger in his face.

"Aye, mum, that I will," he said with a firm nod. "I'll see no harm comes her way."

Billie sent him a wide smile.

Bart shook his head madly. "Don't be doing that, my lady. You look too pretty and even for a young lad that could mean trouble."

Billie blushed, understanding all too clearly his warning. "I'll be a good, quiet lad tonight."

"That would be wise," Bart said. "We'd best be going if we're to be back before the hour grows too late."

Bessie gave her one last brief inspection, nodded her approval and then sent her with a "Godspeed" on her way.

Almost an hour later Bart was giving her last-minute instructions as they sought cover from the rain beneath a large drooping tree only a few feet outside of the Cove Inn.

"Keep your head down, your mouth shut and do as I say, my lady," he ordered with concern. "You'll stay safe if you follow my instructions."

She nodded, tucked her head down, pulled her shoulders up and shrugged her hands into her pockets.

"You're a smart one," Bart said with a smile. "Follow me."

The inn was fairly crowded, the wooden bar full across and the few tables occupied except for one or two. Smoke hung heavy in the air as did the smell of ale and unwashed bodies.

Billie followed Bart to an unoccupied table in the back corner of the room. No one paid them mind; they looked like a father and son out for a pint of ale.

Billie itched to discover Derry Jones's identity, but minded Bart's warning and remained silent.

The barmaid deposited two tankards of ale on the table and when Bart raised his to his lips he whispered, "Listen and learn."

She did as told and it wasn't long before she heard someone yell, "Jones, got anything for me?"

Billie followed the man's anxious glance as it landed on a tall, skinny man with a pox-scarred face.

Jones jerked his head toward the table in front of Billie and Bart. He chased away the three men sitting there with a flash of his knife and filled two of the glasses with the remaining liquor from the bottle on the table.

The pint-sized man who had called out to him joined him. "You got anything?"

"I got a big one planned, though the timing ain't set." Jones swallowed back the liquor.

"Your boss in St. Clair tying your hands again?" the man asked with a nasty laugh.

Jones flashed his blade again, dancing it in front of the man's startled eyes. "I'll be rid of that one soon enough."

The man lowered his voice, but Billie could still hear him. "Like you rid yourself of your last problem?"

"I do what needs being done. I won't let no one stand in my way and I'm tired of taking orders."

"You know anything about the wreck over in Gulley's Cove last month? Talk is that the spoils were rich."

"Should have been mine," Jones grumbled. "But it don't matter. The one I have planned will make that one look like a mere pittance."

"Tell me," the man urged and their voices grew too low to hear.

"Come on, son," Bart said and stood. But Billie didn't want to leave, she wanted to hear more. She wanted to learn the identity of the person who ordered the wrecking activities. But the hour grew late and the rain more heavy, pelting the inn's windows like angry fists.

Billie hurried along behind Bart, her mind busy digesting the revelation that someone in St. Clair was the mastermind behind the wrecking operation. And from the sounds of Jones's boasting, he had disposed of another problem. Could he have murdered Oran? Her thoughts too occupied to mind her feet, she tripped over outstretched legs and was quickly grabbed by the back of her collar and given a rough shake.

"Watch where you're going, boy," the drunken man warned and shoved her sprawling flat on her face.

Thick hands hoisted her up. "Mind your feet, boy," Bart yelled and slapped her in the back of the head as he followed her out the door.

Bart hauled her around the side of the inn. "I'm sorry, my lady, but I feared a brawl with the drunk if I took to defending a clumsy lad."

Billie rubbed the back of her head and laughed. "I deserved it for not paying attention."

Bart searched the night sky, rain drenching him. "Don't look like it's going to ease up. We'd best be on our way."

Billie already felt the heavy rain begin to soak through her jacket. It would be a long ride home on the back of Bart's old mare.

Three hours later Billie all but dragged herself up the steps of the manor to the front door. It was well past the time that Billie had informed Pembrooke and Matilda that she would be home from visiting Claudia.

She was soaked to the skin and her body ached so badly she didn't expect to make the last two steps. Bart's old mare had thrown a shoe shortly after they had left the Cove Inn and they had to walk the remaining distance home.

Her legs, though accustomed to walking, protested profusely the long stretch of miles she had been forced to cover. The heavy rain had only managed to hinder an already difficult journey. Now she finally leaned against the manor door, the metal lion knocker pressed to her cheek, wondering what explanation she would offer her staff.

Her hand barely banged the knocker when the door was thrown open and an upset Pembrooke stood there, shocked speechless by her appearance in boy's clothing.

Finding his voice, he demanded like an indignant parent, "Where have you been?"

Billie managed to lift her head high, though her neck ached, and strode past Pembrooke, delivering her answer tersely. "*That* is none of your concern. See that a hot bath is prepared in my bedchamber and bring me a pot of tea."

Startled by her sharp orders and recalling his position, Pembrooke changed his tone. "Does my lady require anything else?"

Her manner softened along with his. "I am so bone tired besides being soaking wet that all I want is a hot bath and my bed." A loud and most unladylike sneeze followed.

"Good heavens, you're drenched," Matilda cried entering the foyer and hurrying over to Billie. She didn't question Billie's odd state of dress. She simply ordered her husband to prepare a bath and rushed Billie upstairs.

"You'll catch your death in those wet garments," Matilda scolded after entering the bedchamber and she quickly helped strip Billie out of them.

She sat on the bed, shivering beneath the warm blanket wrapped around her and watched as Pembrooke dragged a large brass tub into the room and deposited it in front of the burning hearth. Water, Pembrooke carried up in buckets full, was heated over the flames in a deep iron pot hanging over the open hearth flames.

Matilda shoved a hot cup of tea into Billie's trembling hands and ordered her to drink it all. She didn't object to Matilda's motherly fussing; she actually enjoyed it.

Pembrooke left the room after being forced out by a bossy Matilda and within minutes Billie eased herself down with a grateful sigh into lavender-scented, steaming hot water.

"I'll leave you to relax," Matilda said. "Your drying towels are hung over this chair beside the tub and close to the flames to keep them toasty warm for you. I'll be back shortly to see if you need anything more."

Billie shook her head, her eyes closed as her head rested back against the rim of the tub. "That won't be necessary, Matilda. You've done more than enough already and the hour grows late. I can tend to the rest myself."

Matilda hesitated. "Are you certain, my lady? You look so weary."

"My own fault," Billie said with a laugh. "Which this bath shall remedy. And then it will be off to bed for a much-needed night's sleep."

"I'll bring your breakfast up in the morning," Matilda said, walking to the door.

Billie was about to protest, but thought better of it. "Thank you, Matilda, for everything."

With a nod, Matilda bid her good night.

Billie eased down further beneath the hot water, allowing the heat to penetrate her aching bones. She didn't want to think about tonight's adventures, or the consequences of returning to the manor in boy's clothing. She wanted to forget about everything and concentrate on the pleasure of her steaming bath.

Before the water cooled, she soaped her hair and washed it thoroughly and then she soaked, too tired to do much more. In a few short minutes her eyes drifted closed and she hovered on the brink of sleep, thinking only of the hearth's crackling flames.

"Where the bloody hell *have you been?"*

Billie almost jumped from the tub before realizing the water was the only thing between Maximillian and her nakedness.

Her eyes widened like round, full moons and she stared at him not blinking. He was mad—no—he was furious. He stood anchored to a spot a few feet in front of the tub, his stance rigid, his hands fisted at his sides, his jaw tense and his eyes . . .

Raging.

"Answer me." He said that too softly.

Short and to the point, she said, "Out."

Billie gave brief thought to the idea that smoke actually billowed from his nostrils, but it was only an angry flare.

He walked over to where her clothes lay in a wet heap on the floor near the bed. He reached down and hooked the breeches on his finger, holding them up for her inspection. *"What were you doing garbed as a boy? And* where *did your charade take you?"*

He had her cornered and the truth was her only option. The bathwater would soon cool considerably and become uncomfortable. She felt vulnerable enough naked beneath the warm water, but once it turned cold and chilled her skin she would feel even more trapped. She spoke with more re-solve than she felt. "I discovered that a man who might have information concerning the wrecks here in St. Clair would be at the Cove Inn and . . ."

She continued with her story, detailing the whole evening from her arrival at the inn, the conversation she overheard, the slap in the back of the head and her unexpected walk home.

"So you can understand my fatigue," she finished with an exaggerated yawn, hoping he would take the hint that she wished him to leave so she could rest.

"You little fool," he shouted, incensed. *"Have you any idea the risks you took?"*

So much for hints. She said bluntly, "I am tired and sore. I want only to crawl into bed and sleep. We can discuss this another time."

"You will not dismiss me as if I were a mere servant," he warned, taking several steps toward the tub.

She halted him with a quick outstretched hand. "Stop. This is not the proper time for me to be discussing this mat-ter with you."

"Oh, we shall not discuss the matter, Belinda," he said firmly. *"I will tell you exactly what you are allowed and not allowed to do from this point on."*

She flung his own familiar words back at him. "I think not."

Maximillian lost all control. *"You stupid little fool. Do you have any idea of the danger you placed yourself in tonight?"*

He didn't expect an answer and paced where he stood, a few short steps from the tub. Too close to Billie's way of thinking. She was as far beneath the water as she could go and if he stepped any closer . . .

"Dressing like a common boy, drinking like a man, walking in a thunderstorm and leaving yourself prey to thieves, cutthroats and highwaymen! Have you no sense?"

His shouts echoed in the room and he continued to berate her for her irresponsible actions.

Billie grew more annoyed at his raging tirade. She had placed herself in jeopardy to help him and here he stood, reprimanding her like a child. And besides, the water was growing uncomfortably cool while she grew more irritated.

"Do you realize any manner of danger could have befallen you? You could have been robbed."

"I carried no money."

"You could have been molested."

"I was dressed as a boy."

"You could have been murdered," he shouted.

She smiled sweetly. "Then we could have haunted the manor together."

Her sarcastic remark spurred him into action. He advanced on her like an enraged beast, his low growl all the more intimidating. Instinct jolted her into action and she jumped up, water splashing over the rim onto the carpet. Her hand shot out in front of her. "Stop!"

He halted in his tracks, staring at her in rapt silence.

In her nervous confusion she ignored her naked state and attempted an explanation. "I went to the inn to help you. If I can discover who in St. Clair is involved, then you may have your answers and then . . ."

Her words drifted off as she realized the flames' heat licked her wet backside and that Maximillian was staring at her nakedness.

Their eyes met and Billie shuddered from his slow, intimate perusal.

"You're beautiful," he said softly and took a step toward her.

Her heart beat like a wild drum. "Don't," she cried regretfully.

He took another measured step, his own heart racing wildly. *"Why?"*

Coherent thought slowly slipped away from Billie. She forgot the towel sat only inches from her hand and she shook her head and answered, "Because."

His step was short but it brought him closer. *"Because why?"*

Her hand quivered, continuing to ward him off. "It isn't right."

He remained still. *"How could it not be right, Belinda, when you come alive to my touch? I ignite the flames of fantasies deep inside you. They sputter and spark until you shiver with the sheer heat of unbridled passion. Your body was made to be loved."*

His words worked their magic, lighting the tiny flame inside her and allowing it to flicker and tease.

Her protest sounded weak. "No."

"Yes," he argued, taking another step. *"Your breasts are high and full, a perfect fit to my hand, your nipples rosy and quick to respond."*

"Maximillian, please," she pleaded, his blatantly intimate words stimulating her already aroused state.

"I want to please you and pleasure you. I want to bring your body alive. I want to make love to you."

He had stepped closer with each word spoken. The last step he took brought his chest flat against her outstretched hand.

"Feel me," he urged and slipped her wet hand inside his shirt to press against his chest. *"My flesh is heated with the want of you."*

"This is madness," she murmured.

"Then step with me into madness and free me." He pushed her hand aside and wrapped his arm around her wet waist, yanking her against him and devouring her mouth.

The heat rushed through them both, fast and furious. Billie could no more deny him than she could deny herself. She wanted him. She had wanted him since the first time he had kissed her and awakened her dormant passion.

Unforgettable.

His kiss had been that and more.

And the consequences of surrendering to her fantasies?

His kiss turned forceful, demanding she respond, demanding surrender.

She would face tomorrow when it came. Tonight she would open her heart to the ghostly lord and love.

Billie tore her mouth from his hungry one. With panting breath she whispered, "Take me into your madness and love me."

He scooped her wet body up into his arms and walked to the bed.

Chapter
Seventeen

If she was dreaming, she never wanted to wake up. This was her fantasy to tuck away inside her mind and heart and cherish forever and ever. This was her choice.

Billie moaned with the onslaught of his lips rushing over her mouth and racing over her nipples, budding them into sharp ripeness.

Maximillian stood back from the bed and shed his clothes. Billie thought his nakedness magnificent. She assessed him with the eyes of an appreciative lover, admiring his firm muscles, his fine curves and his full manhood.

"Come to me," she said, stretching her hand out to him.

"With pleasure, my lady."

To her surprise he approached her from the bottom of the bed, his hands sliding along her legs, spreading them slowly apart and descending down on her with a wicked grin.

She tensed when she realized his intentions.

"Easy, love," he said, stroking her inner thigh. *"Let me teach you the ways of love."*

He didn't wait for an answer, as his mouth covered her intimately.

Billie's tense muscles relaxed within seconds and she soon found herself lost in a world of exploding passion. His tongue and fingers worked an erotic magic that left Billie panting and breathless. In her wildest dreams she would never have imagined such exquisite and torturous pleasure.

Her hands grasped at the pillows beneath her head and her body rose and fell with each taste and touch he delivered. He had invited her to step into his madness and she most certainly had, for only madness could produce such potent feelings.

She felt within herself a flame burning too brightly, ready to burst into a shatter of sparks. The feeling grew stronger, her moans became louder and she begged him . . . for what? She wasn't certain. She could only repeat his name, crying for him to . . .

She exploded and shattered in mindless pieces and before she could gather her senses he was covering her with his hot, hard body.

His demanding kisses left her even more senseless. He nipped, licked and bit and she responded in kind, losing herself again to the all-consuming emotion that rushed over her.

"You belong to me," he said with such fervor that Billie shuddered beneath him.

He continued his sensual assault, robbing every ounce of free will from her until she once again heard herself plead with him for release.

He eased himself between her legs, ordered her to hold on to him and entered her so swiftly that she gasped from his sharp entrance. Her breath was further robbed from her as he moved with such a steady and intense rhythm she could think of nothing else but matching his thrusts.

Their movement was as one, fluid and precise.

"You'll always belong to me," he said, his voice harsh and panting from his sensual exertion.

She didn't doubt his words. After tonight she would belong to him body and soul. She was surrendering a part of herself she had only dreamed of . . . she was surrendering her love.

They erupted together, their cries released in unison, their shuddering pleasure simultaneous. And their sighs of satisfaction drifted away like whispers on the wind.

Maximillian eased himself up to lay beside her and gather her close against him. He pulled the counterpane over them and wrapped his arms around her, placing a gentle kiss on her forehead.

"Are you all right?" he asked, his breath still heavy.

Her response was rapid and short. "Yes."

He rubbed her arm and draped his leg over hers locking her more securely to him. She faded against him, stealing his heat and strength.

Talk seemed unnecessary. They lay fulfilled and content like sated lovers long involved.

Billie's eyes drifted closed, her mind unable to focus or comprehend the consequences of her actions with the ghostly lord.

His lips once again touched her forehead before brushing over her closed eyes. *"We aren't finished, my love."*

"So tired," she mumbled before he kissed her lips.

His wicked laugh rumbled in her ear. *"Not yet you're not."*

And then his hands began to introduce her to a slow, tormenting pleasure.

"My lady. My lady," the anxious voice called with gentle firmness.

Billie pushed the counterpane down far enough from her face to peek through squinted eyes at Matilda standing at the foot of the bed holding a breakfast tray.

She blushed profusely, recalling who had stood at the foot of her bed last night, and she groaned, yanking the covers back up over her face.

"Are you all right, my lady?" Matilda asked. "It's almost noon. I've come up several times to check on you this morning, but you slumbered so deeply I couldn't wake you."

"I'm fine, Matilda. I was very tired." Of course, she thought, who wouldn't be after a night of constant lovemaking? A move of her legs and an unfamiliar soreness brought a moan to her lips and a reminder of her intimate activities.

"Your muscles ache?" Matilda asked, placing the tray on the nearby chair so she could assist Billie.

Billie nodded as Matilda folded back the counterpane. "I'll help you to sit up," she continued. "Hot porridge, sweet bread and good strong tea will help to strengthen you."

Billie didn't argue. In minutes Matilda had the pillows fluffed, Billie sitting up and braced against the mound, the coverlet folded back across Billie's lap and Billie's hair brushed and tied back with a ribbon.

The woman was an absolute wonder, especially when she placed the full tray across Billie's lap.

"I'm starved." Billie realized how hungry she was when the succulent scent of food wafted beneath her nostrils.

Matilda poured the strong brew into her cup. "Eat to your heart's content and if you wish, rest some more. I will return to check on you shortly."

Billie was thankful for Matilda's generous nature and she eagerly dug into the much-appreciated food before the woman closed the door behind her.

Filling her stomach gave her more balanced thoughts and she looked down at her night rail as she munched appreciatively on a generous piece of sweet bread.

She wore her night rail. But she hadn't been wearing it when Maximillian had carried her—still wet—to the bed, and she hadn't put it on after they had made love the first time, or the second or the third, leaving only one explanation.

Maximillian had dressed her in her night rail before he left her last night. Was it so that no one would know that all evening she had been naked and making mad, passionate love with the ghostly lord of Radborne Manor?

Ghost?

"I think not," Billie said between munches.

Funny thing was that she felt no regret in her surrender to him, only that he would not confide the truth to her.

She could not honestly believe him a ghost, not after last night. He had felt so alive, so solid and real, so much a part of her.

He was a noble lord with much influence and power. The talk in the village was that he had many prominent friends. If this truly was a charade, what was he hiding?

The other thought that haunted and disturbed Billie was the emotional tug to her heart. She had felt it upon meeting Maximillian. And anytime thereafter she had experienced the same strange feeling around him. Though he was arrogant to a fault, she found him intriguing, interesting and irresistible all rolled into one.

But therein lay another problem. Maximillian was a lord, and she a commoner from Nantucket. Her provincial background did not suit his noble upbringing. They were not at all compatible except, of course, in bed.

She shivered and sipped at the strong, hot tea as she recalled last night and what she and Max had shared. She had been shameless in her actions, and he as wicked as the devil himself.

Not one time did she find herself shy and withdrawn. She had thought her first time with a man might prove difficult, but with Max it had proved *unforgettable*.

"Dreams," she whispered. "Only dreams." Her pragmatic side surfaced and reminded her that she had awakened in bed alone. Max was nowhere to be seen. He hadn't remained to rain sweet morning kisses on her or to soothe her concern or to tell her he cared very much for her. She was alone.

Billie moved the breakfast tray to the opposite side of the bed and slipped out from beneath the warm covers. Her bare feet barely felt the chill of the floor as she rushed across the room to her closet.

She had survived much, so now was not the time for self-pity. Now was the time for decisive action. If she could handle all the affairs after her family's death; she could manage one haunting lord.

What other choice did she have? No matter what the results, she would still remain the strong, resilient woman she had become. No one could take that away from her; she wouldn't allow it.

She chose to sleep with the ghost of Radborne Manor and the consequences were hers and hers alone. But then she was never one to accept the logical; she always looked beyond. Her hopes and dreams proved her unrest with the ordinary.

Now she was involved in a most unusual circumstance and she would use her wits to find a plausible solution.

She chose her dark blue Empire-waist dress trimmed with a faint touch of ecru and hurried into it. She managed to twirl her hair into a messy knot at the top of her head while frantic strands slipped free and graced her neck and ears.

She put on her pumps, grabbed the tray from the bed and rushed out the door.

Matilda met her halfway down the stairs. "My lady—"

Billie, in her usual haste, didn't let her finish. "I have much to do." She pushed the tray into a startled Matilda's hands and hurried the rest of the way down the stairs.

She rushed to the small closet beneath the stairwell to retrieve her black cloak and bonnet. Holding them securely in her hands, she swerved around and collided with Maximillian.

He grabbed her by the shoulders to steady her and when certain she was surefooted, he took her firmly by the arm and hauled her into the study, releasing her and closing the door solidly behind him.

"Good morning, it's a pleasure to see you, too," Billie said, dropping her cloak and bonnet on the chair.

He walked over to her with such fierce determination that he caused Billie to take several steps back. When she could go no further, her back up against the desk, her hands braced on the edge, he stopped, reached out and brushed the frantic strands of hair away from her face.

"You need a lady's maid," he said. *"Though I do favor the careless way you do your hair. It definitely suits you."*

"I assume that was a compliment, so I'll say thank you."

"And I thank you," he said softly.

She detected the hint of passion that he subdued and her own voice trembled when she spoke. "Thank me for what?"

"Last night." His whisper brushed her cheek as he bent down and kissed her like a lover introducing her to his lips for the first time. Sweet, gentle, considerate. Far different from the demanding, passionate, crazed man of last night.

She discovered she liked both sides of this dual lover.

"Did you enjoy me?" he asked candidly, bracing his hands on either side of her and pressing his body to hers.

His blunt question did not disturb him in the least. He actually looked pleased with himself, wickedly pleased. He wore that arrogant smile that made him appear all the more handsome and his body, pressed so intimately against hers, warned her that his passion was far from under control.

She kept her wits, though her body ached to arch against him and feel his hardness sink into her. "You were quite pleasurable."

He pressed his forehead and nose to hers. *"Detail pleasurable."*

She looked at him strangely. "Detail?"

He rubbed their noses slowly together. *"Precise detail."*

She grew nervous thinking of the intimate words needed to comply with his command. How could she tell him how much she had enjoyed the way he tasted her so intimately or that his touch sent tingles and shivers through her or that his kisses were unforgettable?

"Tell me," his whisper urged when she hesitated.

His nose no longer touched hers but his face remained only a fraction away. He watched her with intent eyes that promised he would not be denied his answer.

Where to begin? What to say? She shifted uncomfortably and searched for appropriate words.

"Let me help you," he offered, as if sensing her discomfort and wanting to ease it. *"Did my kisses please you?"*

Her eyes widened with her smile. "*Very* much."

"And when I touched you," he said, brushing his knuckles across her nipple, *"did you find that enjoyable?"*

Her breath caught and held momentarily as she nodded vigorously.

"And when I tasted you," he said, pressing his hard manhood to nestle between her legs, *"how did you feel?"*

The same way it was making her feel at this moment, hot and bothered. She kept that observation to herself and answered in a whispered reluctance, "As though I was in a dream that brought me endless pleasure and I never wanted to wake up."

He bent his head. She pressed her finger to his lips, preventing him from stealing a kiss.

"I woke up."

He took a step away from her. *"And?"*

"And I would appreciate an answer."

"To what question?"

She braced herself for his response. "Are you a ghost?"

"What do you think?" he asked, his arms folded across his chest and with an arrogant rise of his brow.

She stood straight. "I think you play games with me."

"Then you have but one choice."

"Which is?"

"Uncover the secrets of my death and set me free."

She sighed and threw up her hands. "You always talk in riddles."

"Solve them," he challenged. *"You're intelligent."*

"Another compliment," she gushed. "You'll be turning my head before I know it."

"You don't need a man to fill your head with empty compliments. You need a man to match your sharp wit, your stubbornness and to satisfy your unbridled passion."

Passion. He always spoke of passion. Did the man never think of love? She walked around him and snatched her cloak and bonnet off the chair. "Since you mention my wit and stubbornness I might as well put them to good use."

She slipped on her cloak and placed her scoop bonnet on her head, tying the ribbons firmly beneath her chin. "I'm off to uncover secrets and reveal the true ghost of Radborne Manor."

His strong voice halted her at the door. *"Billie, will you be able to deal with the truth?"*

Her smile did not hide the sadness in her eyes. "I have no choice."

Maximillian collapsed in the chair before the hearth, which burned with a low flame. He had never expected this turn of events. He had never dreamed he would find a woman of such strong will and attractive spirit. But then he hadn't counted on Belinda Latham entering his life.

She had completely turned his world upside down. He had been focused and direct in his mission and now his thoughts were . . .

He shook his head, confused. He hadn't had a sane thought since she entered his life. If he wasn't concerned over her improper behavior, then he was concerned with his uncontrollable urge to possess her. His feelings for her ran deep, so deep he wasn't even certain he understood them.

He had lost complete control with her last night and he had never lost control with a woman in his life. But when he had seen her standing there naked, her softly curved body glistening with droplets of bathwater, he had succumbed to his raging desire to possess her body and soul.

He wanted her more than he wanted any woman he had ever been with and her intimate surrender to him only made matters worse. Their lovemaking had been so completely satisfying that he found himself thinking in terms of love.

Love. A word he had strongly and purposely avoided over the years. He had not even believed in its existence. To him it was as real as ghosts. And now that . . .

His father materialized through the hearth, startling Maximillian.

"Must you do that?" he snapped, his relaxed posture turning rigid.

Oran gracefully took the seat opposite his son. *"I am a ghost; that is what I do."*

"It's quite unnerving."

"I daresay that Billie would agree with you," he said with a laughing grin. *"Having a ghost pop in and out of your life at his will can be a tad disturbing."*

Maximillian stood, walked around to the back of the chair and braced his hands on the top. *"I have no choice."*

"You have more of a choice than I do," Oran said sadly. *"You should use it wisely."*

"I am attempting to."

His father grew annoyed. *"Confide in Billie, let her help."*

"She could also be hurt," Maximillian argued. *"I do not want to see her become so embroiled with this problem that she places herself in danger."*

"The day she arrived at this manor she placed herself in danger," he warned. *"When will you listen to me?"*

"When will I listen to you?" Maximillian repeated incredulously. *"When will you listen to me and not give Billie useless information?"*

"Derry Jones is not useless information."

Maximillian rounded the chair and paced in front of the hearth. *"I told you he is unimportant and as for the mastermind of the group residing in St. Clair"*—he shook his head—*"I've come up with nothing on that, not even a suspect."*

You're not looking in the right places, not talking to the right people."

"I spoke with almost everyone in the village and no one knows anything."

"You haven't spoken with the right people," Oran insisted, sternly.

Maximillian stopped his pacing and stared at his father. He sounded like he used to when Maximillian was but ten and had not handled a task to his satisfaction. He had never raised his voice or hand to Maximillian. Calmly and forcefully he would reprimand him and explain he expected more from him, the heir to Radborne Manor. *"I am doing all I can."*

Oran shifted in his chair. *"I realize that, my son. And I realize you are limited in your approach. That is why it is so important for you to trust Billie."*

"And endanger her as well."

Oran looked at his son with weary eyes. *"She could be in more danger not knowing the truth. What if she unknowingly becomes involved with the very person you seek?"*

"I don't know who that person is so—"

Oran interrupted anxiously. *"Precisely, and neither does Billie, leaving her vulnerable."*

"My protection of her now is more than adequate, actually more adequate than if I confided in her," Maximillian offered.

"And what if she discovers the truth before you can offer an explanation?"

Maximillian cringed. *"I don't plan on having that happen. When the time is right she will be told."*

"And what then?"

Maximillian smiled broadly. *"By then she will belong to me completely and will have no choice but to accept the inevitable."*

Oran laughed. *"Billie doesn't strike me as the type of woman to accept a man's dictate. She possesses too strong of an independent nature and is too sharp of wit to bow to any man."*

His father's words angered Maximillian. *"She'll have no choice. She traversed an ocean to a new destiny and she will* accept it. She has no family to return to. Her future is here and here she will stay."

Oran raised his brow. *"You have decided all of this for her?"*

"I know what is best."

"For her or you?"

"I am lord of this manor," he reminded his father.

Oran smiled. *"But she is presently lady of the manor and no ghost."*

Maximillian groaned and dropped down in the chair. *"I tire of being a ghost."*

"I know the feeling."

Maximillian glanced with worry at his father. *"I wish—"*

Oran held up his hand. *"What's done is done. Let us finish this and find peace. Now tell me what Billie has discovered and what she is up to."*

Maximillian shook his head. *"She's off to—"* He jumped out of the chair, startling his father.

Oran laughed. *"She's up to something, isn't she?"*

"Bloody hell, yes," he said and stormed out of the room.

Chapter
Eighteen

Several heads turned when Billie entered the Cox Crow Inn. She smiled at all the startled faces and made her way around the tables to where Bessie and Marlee sat in the far corner near one of the two windows.

"My lady, what are you doing here?" Bessie asked with concern.

Billie slipped off her cloak and bonnet and joined the two women at the table. "I've come to talk with you."

"At the inn?" Marlee stared wide-eyed at her.

Billie glanced curiously from one woman to the other. She then cast a quick peek over her shoulder. A sea of surprised faces stared back at her.

She turned back to the two women. "I suppose it isn't proper for the lady of the manor to frequent the local inn?"

Both women nodded.

Billie shrugged. "Well, I'm not your customary lady of the manor. I'm an American and my customs differ. So, St. Clair will have to abide by my strange ways."

"Then it will be an ale you're having," Marlee said with a smile, raising her tankard high.

"An ale it is," Billie agreed, wondering if it was as strong a brew as the American ale.

Bessie served her a full tankard and Marlee raised her own in a salute. "To the new lady of Radborne Manor."

All the tankards were raised along with a cheer for Lady Radborne. Talk returned to normal after that and no one seemed to find it peculiar that Lady Radborne sat among them; she had been accepted like no other lady before her. The thought pleased her.

"Now what is it you wanted?" Bessie asked.

Billie lowered her voice. "Have either of you heard of anyone in St. Clair being involved with the wreckers?"

Marlee shrugged. "There may be one or two who would help for an extra coin or two."

Billie took a sip of her ale before she shook her head. "No, more involved than that, like someone who would actually command a group?"

Both women shook their heads vigorously. "No one here is that involved."

Billie finished another swallow, the generous brew tasty. "Are you sure? Couldn't someone have kept their unlawful activity silent?"

Bessie answered. "St. Clair is a small village. Everyone here knows everyone. If someone was heavily involved with wreckers the village would have heard about it."

"And neither of you have heard anything?"

Marlee added her thoughts. "Nothing. Gossip flies around here. We surely would have gotten wind about such activities."

"There's something going on here in St. Clair," Billie insisted and took another swallow of ale. "Derry Jones wouldn't have mentioned the place otherwise."

Bessie gulped back a hefty swallow and then spoke with a tremor in her voice. "He was probably bragging like men do."

"Sure enough," Marlee agreed. "A man's not a man unless he brags about something."

Billie wondered if it was the light-headedness from the ale she drank that made the women appear nervous. "I suppose if something was going on you both would know about it?"

Marlee boasted. "There's nothing that goes on in St. Clair that we don't know about. Right, Bessie?"

Bessie seemed reluctant to agree, but she finally nodded in agreement.

Billie continued. "Then you both were aware of the smuggling activities in the caves beneath Radborne Manor?"

"How did you find out about that?" Marlee asked.

"I took myself on a tour of the caves," she admitted proudly.

Bessie almost choked on the ale she had just swallowed. "You went to the caves?"

"Yes, and saw the stacks of barrels and crates, which leaves me to believe that the smuggling activities are still going on."

"What else did you discover?" Marlee asked with what she assumed was an innocent voice, but sounded heavily riddled with guilt.

Billie was about to admit that she met Oran Radborne's ghost but thought better of it. "Only that it is a perfect place for smugglers to hide their spoils. How long has this been going on?"

Bessie reluctantly answered. "Lord Oran Radborne had an agreement with some men who smuggled goods from time to time."

"What kind of agreement?" Billie asked, wondering if Claudia had neglected to tell her everything about Oran and the caves.

Marlee explained. "The cave was a drop-off point for their shipments. Oran would be given a percentage of whatever goods he favored; in turn the men had the use of the cave. No one was hurt. It was strictly a business arrangement."

"What went wrong?" Billie asked, sensing the two women knew a lot more than they admitted.

Bessie took over. "We heard something about a larger smuggling and wrecking crew attempting to take over the smaller one."

"I assume the small crew didn't favor this?"

Bessie and Marlee cast anxious glances toward each other.

Bessie continued speaking. "They didn't have a choice and neither did Oran Radborne."

"So one of the new crew murdered Oran."

Both women nodded, Bessie confirmed. "It's assumed that's what happened."

"What about Maximillian? Did he know anything about his father's illegal dealings?"

Marlee answered. "He was probably aware of it. This type of dealing is not unusual. Some manors fall on hard times and have no choice but to resort to this type of unlawful trade."

Billie recalled the financial papers Mr. Hillard had supplied her with. Radborne Manor was in no jeopardy of financial loss now or in the near future. So why had Oran agreed to such nefarious dealings?

"Maximillian must have halted all dealings after his father's death," Billie said.

Marlee supplied her with detail. "He was in a fury. He had the old magistrate removed and a new one assigned. He spoke with other lords in the area and got them to agree to bring a halt to the illegal dealings. They were about to organize an association to help bring about the demise of all wrecking and smuggling activities in the area when Maximillian Radborne met with his death."

Billie tipped her tankard up for another swallow and was surprised to see it empty. Bessie hastily refilled it from the earthenware pitcher on the table.

"The crates and barrels now in the caves would mean that the smuggling is still going on," Billie said, speaking aloud her thoughts.

Bessie offered her own conclusion. "More than likely since the manor has sat empty for about eight months except for Pembrooke and Matilda being there."

Marlee frowned at Bessie.

Bessie ignored her. "That's why you should be cautious and stay out of the caves."

Marlee piped in as well. "That's right, my lady, stay out of the caves."

Everyone wanted her away from the caves. Why? What secrets lay locked beneath the house? Billie was now more determined than ever to discover what was going on, no matter the cost to her. She had been drawn into a game, a dangerous game, and she intended to be one of the players who emerged a winner.

"The manor belongs to me now," Billie said firmly, "Therefore, the caves also belong to me. I'll have no smuggling going on beneath my own home."

The women's eyes rounded like milk saucers. Bessie found her voice first. "You're only a woman, there's nothing you can do. It's best if you leave it to a man to handle."

"What man?" Billie asked after taking a drink of ale.

Marlee smiled sweetly. "Vicar Bosworth."

"I cannot disturb him with my problems," Billie said.

"You can disturb me with any of your problems, Billie. I will always be here to help you."

Billie turned fast in her seat, setting her head to spinning and her body to swaying.

John reached out and grabbed hold of her arm, steadying her before she toppled off the bench. "Careful," he said and righted her in her seat.

He sent Bessie and Marlee a reproachful glance and both women blushed and hung their heads.

"You've been enjoying St. Clair's infamous ale?" he asked, noticing her flushed cheeks and glazed eyes.

"Bessie and Marlee have been nice enough to share a tankard or two with me."

The vicar spoke firmly to the two women. "I will see you at church services tomorrow."

This time all color drained from the two women's faces and they stumbled over each other as they jumped up, making excuses for their hasty departure.

John took Billie's hand firmly in his, concerned that her small drinking binge with the two women had left her anything but steady on her feet or backside. "Join me at the vicarage for tea."

Billie glanced up at him. His eyes blurred behind his glasses, his smile was soft and his shoulders hunched over. He didn't appear to be a man of strength and yet his grip on her hand denoted otherwise. His fingers wrapped around hers with a firmness that surprised her. His taut grip offered support, protection and made her feel safe.

She smiled and squeezed his hand. "Tea sounds good."

She attempted to stand and found herself swaying on her feet. John slipped his arm around her waist. "Let me help you."

She leaned against him for support and whispered near his ear, "I think I drank too much ale."

He smiled and whispered back, "I think so, too."

He held her while he reached for her cloak and bonnet and then helped her on with both. His arm remained around her waist as he escorted her to the door, cries of good day sounding from each person they passed.

The cool air and sunlight startled Billie for a moment and she almost lost her balance as they exited the inn.

John tightened his arm around her waist. "Are you all right?"

She rested her head on his shoulder. "Just give me a minute and I'll be fine."

"Are you sure?" His voice was filled with concern.

She laughed. "As long as you don't let go of me, I'll be fine."

John squeezed her waist. "I'll never let you go."

Billie felt a tremor run through her. Why did this simple man make her feel so protected? So loved?

She walked along with him in silence, her mind too consumed by her thoughts to speak. She wondered with concern if she was a wanton woman. How could she make love with a ghostly lord one night and the next day feel so compatible with, of all people, a vicar? Did she have no morals? Was she one of those women who possessed unnatural desires for men? Whatever was the matter with her? And who in heaven could she speak to about such intimate thoughts?

Her glance went to John's face.

He instantly stopped walking and looked down at her over the rim of his glasses. "What's wrong?"

She couldn't very well blurt out her wicked thoughts. She paused in her response, searching in haste for an acceptable explanation. Her words spilled out before she could pull them back. "Are you upset with me?"

John looked at her strangely. "Whatever for?"

She thought of admitting her betrayal, confessing that she had been intimate with another man, but how did one admit she had slept with a ghost or a man posing as a ghost and who everyone believed to be a ghost?

She shrugged, locking away her worries, and admitted, "My behavior was improper for a lady."

"Nonsense, Billie, you were being yourself and you have yet to learn all the ways of the English gentry." He urged her along with a nudge of his hand.

"I sometimes wonder if I ever will," she confided.

"Don't be so harsh on yourself," he scolded softly, reaching the gate of the vicarage. He pushed it open, the familiar squeak of the rusty hinge welcoming them. "This is all new to you and you have plenty of time to learn."

They entered the house and John saw to her cloak and bonnet before depositing her on the settee in the small parlor. Then he went off to fetch tea.

Billie looked about the small room and recalled the lovely backyard garden. The house was small, but warm and comfortable. A loving couple could raise a happy family here. The wife of a vicar would have more freedom to mingle with the villagers than the wife of a lord. And John was gentle and caring, not arrogant and demanding.

Passionate.

The word caught her unaware. Max was fiercely passionate. How would John be? She blushed at thoughts of John making love to her as Max had. Somehow she couldn't see the shy vicar tasting or touching her in the intimate places that Max had tasted and touched.

A rattle of dishes sounded John's approach and she attempted to push her scandalous thoughts aside. They refused to stay suppressed and as John walked in the room, shaking tray in hand, glasses perched on the tip of his nose and a gentle smile, Billie instantly realized his lovemaking would be completely the opposite of Maximillian's.

"This strong English brew will set you right," he said, placing the tray on the table in front of Billie and sitting down beside her.

She watched him pour the tea and add sugar, one teaspoonful, the way she favored it. He handed it to her and she accepted it with a grateful smile. "Thank you for rescuing me. You are a true hero."

He fiddled nervously with his glasses and then with jittery hands poured himself a cup. "Nonsense, I but offered you assistance."

"At a most opportune time. I daresay I don't think I would have been able to walk out of the inn on my own accord. That brew was much stronger than I am accustomed to."

He sipped the well-steeped tea. "St. Clair has a reputation for potent ale."

She laughed lightly. "I must remember that and I shall remember your rescue."

John placed his cup on the silver tray. "I would rescue you from the devil himself if necessary."

Billie felt her cheeks heat with color. Could his prophetic words come to pass? Max was a devilish soul, and John a pious man of the Lord. So opposite in nature and yet she was attracted to both men. It puzzled her.

"What took you to the inn?" John asked.

Relieved he changed the subject, Billie eagerly offered an answer. "I was seeking information about smuggling in the area." She returned her empty cup to the tray.

"And did you find any answers?"

Billie sighed and shook her head slowly. "No, but I had the strangest feeling that Bessie and Marlee knew more than they cared to share."

John eased his glasses up on his nose. "What makes you say that?"

She shrugged. "I don't know. It's just that they appeared nervous and uncertain when they spoke."

He slipped her hand in his. "And you appeared into your cups."

She watched his lips open and close ever so slightly as he spoke. They fascinated her. Warm and gentle came to mind. Thoughtful and tasty, she thought, too. Kissable was another and she realized a kiss was what she wanted from him.

Her intimate musings startled her and her breath caught in surprise.

"I didn't mean to offend," he offered, having assumed his remark caused her distress.

"No, John, you didn't offend. My mind was elsewhere."

"Where?" he asked softly, his hand turning hers over and gently tracing circles in her palm.

Shivers raced up her arm, across her chest and down to her stomach. His touch was far from demanding but it sparked her passion nonetheless. Small, tingling tremors raced through her and she wanted more than ever for him to kiss her.

"What were you thinking?" he repeated.

"How I would like you to kiss me," she said without thought to her audacious remark.

He didn't appear at all upset by her confession. "You are a most unconventional lady."

Encouraged by his response she continued. "Then will you kiss me?"

He bent his head down to hers. "I would be delighted."

Their lips met briefly, brushed and then consumed each other. Billie was astonished by his commanding actions. He tasted her like a man long deprived. His hand went around her waist and drew her closer to him as his tongue thrust in her mouth and mingled eagerly with hers.

The sensitive tingle continued to heighten and she suddenly felt the need to have him touch her more intimately. She slid closer beside him and pressed herself against him, her breasts buried in his gray frock coat.

Too many layers of clothes separated them and she wanted to reach out and rip his clothes off and make love with him. She wanted to feel his hands on her, his mouth, his words of love.

"Billie."

She heard the anxious voice, but paid it no heed. She hungered for more from him, so much more than a simple kiss.

"Billie." John's stern voice jolted her foggy mind and she sat back to stare at him wide-eyed.

"I'm sorry," she murmured, ashamed of her improper actions.

"Don't be," he said, cupping the side of her face. "You make me feel so wanted, so desirable, so loved. If I could I would carry you to my bed and make tender love to you, but without the sanctity of marriage, intimacy is prohibited."

Billie felt a fool and again John soothed her obvious distress.

"You feel so good against me, Billie, so right. I have never felt this strongly about a woman. I have never been more tempted."

"I didn't mean to tempt you," she said hastily.

"Which makes me all the more pleased. You reacted naturally and I am most honored that you should feel so strongly about me. I had hoped—" He paused and squeezed her hand, but kept a proper distance from her. "That you would find me appealing since I am not the most handsome of men."

Billie felt a stab to her heart. "Oh, but I think you are most attractive or else I could not have behaved so wantonly."

John smiled. "You are not wanton."

She turned playful. "With you I am."

"I am pleased it is with me you lost control and no one else."

Billie forced her smile to remain solid on her face, but her heart once again felt a stab. A stab of betrayal.

"Perhaps it would be wise of us to consider how fast we would like our relationship to proceed."

How fast did she want their relationship to grow and to what end results? There was so much to consider. And what if Max proved to be no ghost? What then? How could she confess her sins to John?

"I think that is a wise decision," she said and stood. "And I think it wise for me to leave now."

John kept her hand in his as he stood. "You don't have to rush off."

"A walk home in the fresh air will do me good," she said, easing her hand from his and reaching for her cloak. She needed time alone to think and a walk provided her with just such solitude.

"Are you sure your head is clear?" he said, concerned.

Her head was far from clear, but it wasn't the remnant of ale that fogged her senses. "As clear as necessary," she said with a laugh.

John walked Billie to the front door and kissed her lightly on the cheek. "Please join me for tea tomorrow so that we may talk further."

Always the gentleman, she thought. He wouldn't dare suggest that her brain was too muddled by ale to seriously discuss their relationship.

"I would love to," she said and kissed him on his cheek. Then she hurried down the walkway, sending him a hasty wave as she closed the gate behind her.

Her walk had been slow and contemplative and when she reached the manor much later than a walk from the village would normally have taken her, she found herself filled with energy.

The rest of the afternoon she filled with strenuous activity. She had Pembrooke move furniture from various rooms to the conservatory where she arranged the many pieces he carried in and out.

By nightfall she was exhausted, as was Pembrooke, and after an enjoyable meal with Matilda and a yawning Pembrooke she took herself up to bed.

It took only minutes for her to change from her clothes into her night rail and slip into bed. She was about to douse the candle's flame when she heard: *"I prefer you naked in my bed."*

Chapter
Nineteen

"This is my bed and I prefer me clothed," she argued and snuggled deeper beneath the covers. "Now go away, you pesky ghost."

He laughed, a full-bodied laugh that rumbled off the dark plum walls. *"You think to dismiss me like a servant?"*

Billie refused to glance down at the bottom of the bed where his voice drifted up from. "No, like a supposed ghost who doesn't at all behave according to ghostly standards."

"I behave by my standards," he reminded sharply. *"Now get out of bed so we may talk."*

Billie groaned and threw the covers completely over her head. She was tired and wanted no part of his demanding attitude. Her muffled voice drifted out from beneath. "I will speak with you tomorrow at a decent hour."

"I think not." His voice retained its sharpness.

"I will—"

He interrupted her. *"Do as I say or I will drag you from that bed."*

She shot up, the quilt dropping to her waist where she sat. "You're insufferable."

"You finally understand me."

He stood in dark gray breeches, a white linen shirt unfastened to the middle of his chest and his dark hair spilling down to his shoulders. His stance was arrogant, rigid legs, arms crossed and head high. *The lord of the manor.*

She shook her head. "I will never understand you. Must you always demand?"

"I am accustomed to obedience."

She threw her hands up in frustration. "I'm not a dog."

His arms relaxed and he smiled. *"No, you aren't, but you are a most unusual young woman."*

She raked her fingers through her tousled hair and it fell in further disarray around her shoulders giving her a look of unquenched passion. "A compliment?"

"You're beautiful."

His soft yet sincere words stole her breath and raced her heart. "A compliment?" she repeated, sounding breathless.

He walked over to her, slipped his hand around her neck and brought his lips down to meet hers. His kiss was tentative, searching, longing.

"So beautiful," he whispered against her mouth.

She robbed the words from him with her own kiss, her arms going up around his neck. She fed on him, enjoying their play of tongues and the heated pleasure it rushed through her body.

With his knee braced on the bed, he brought his hand around her waist. As he dropped back on the bed he pulled her with him, drawing her on top of him.

His hand ran down her back, cupping her buttocks, pressing her against him, feeling her heat, her desire. She felt good, so very good. He could touch her forever and never grow tired of the feel of her. He hungered to possess her, to make her his, to unite in passion and pleasure.

Stolen moments were all they had until . . .

Their kiss became more frantic, more uncontrolled.

He reached down, lifting her night rail, running his hands beneath, racing over her bare backside, urging her against him.

She responded by pressing herself into him, feeling his readiness, aching for him to satisfy her lusty need.

Tenderness had no place in their urgency to possess each other. They both nipped and bit and tugged until Billie found herself beneath him, her night rail tossed up and his fingers freeing himself.

Her legs were lifted high over his broad shoulders and he plunged fast and furious into her sweetness, a mingled cry of delight bursting from them both.

Their frenzied coupling tore strangled cries from them as they matched thrust for thrust and soon exploded into a raging climax that shattered their souls.

Max collapsed on top of her, his breathing rapid, his heart pounding and his need of her temporarily quenched.

When the aftermath subsided he raised himself and looked down at her, pushing the damp strands of hair away from her face. *"Are you all right?"*

Billie still found it difficult to breathe, let alone speak, so she nodded.

He pushed more of her hair aside. *"Don't fight for your breath. Relax, let it come naturally."*

She followed his wise advice and soon found her breathing returning to normal.

He eased off her to the edge of the bed and pulled her night rail down over her legs. He stood and adjusted his own clothes before walking to the water pitcher and pouring a glass.

He returned to her, holding out his free hand to help her up. She locked her hand around his wrist and he easily pulled her up, offering her the water.

She drank greedily as if parched and handed the glass back to him. "Thank you," she said softly.

He walked over to the pitcher once more and downed a full glass himself before returning to the bed where Billie had safely ensconced herself beneath the quilt. He sat on the edge of the bed beside her.

She waited for him to say something, anything. To tell her that he cared, that he was alive, real, that he loved her.

The silence was unnerving and she ran her fingers through her hair drawing it back and twisting it tightly to rest down her back. Unable to endure another moment of the quiet tension she spoke. "Our relationship is strange."

"I'm not at liberty to offer you more."

His honest remark only disturbed her further. He made no promises, he declared no love, he talked of no future. Where did that leave her?

Her pride surfaced. "I didn't ask for more."

"I have never met a woman that didn't demand something in return."

She smiled and shrugged. "If you insist . . . I demand the truth."

He didn't smile. *"I have also never met a woman as intelligent or quick-witted as you."*

She leaned back with a gentle sigh, relaxing against the mound of pillows. "There you go with those compliments again and you do recall where that led us."

Maximillian chose safer ground and changed the subject. *"What were you doing at the inn today?"*

"Drinking the most delicious ale."

He tsk-tsked before remarking, *"Shouldn't you amend that to drinking* too much *ale?"*

"How did you know?"

"Village gossip travels," he said, abruptly and again maneuvered the conversation. *"Did you discover anything significant?"*

She countered his question with one of her own. "Did you know of your father's smuggling involvement?"

"I learned of it in its later stages."

"Did you approve?"

"One did not agree or disagree with my father. He was the lord of the manor and his decision was law."

"But you ceased all involvement after your father's death."

"Of course I did," he said indignantly. *"I wouldn't very well assist the men who murdered my father."*

"I've been told that the smugglers he dealt with weren't involved in the murder."

Max appeared perturbed. *"There were no witnesses. No one knows for sure."*

Billie's mind churned with possibilities, spewing them out as fast as they came. "What if there was someone here in St. Clair who aided the smugglers or commanded them? What if that person gave your father an ultimatum and your father, being as pompous as you are—" She paused to smile at his scowling face and then continued, "Refused to agree to his demands, so he was murdered."

"Have you any evidence that this mysterious person exists?"

Her disappointment voiced itself in her sighing response. "No," she said, pointing her finger at him, "but I'm still investigating."

"Which is what took you to the inn. Where, I should remind you, is the perfect place to hear the town news."

"What you're saying is that if I can't find out anything there, then it probably doesn't exist."

"Precisely."

"Unless," she piped up. "The villagers fear this person."

"The only person they feared was me."

She giggled. "I can certainly understand that."

He sent her a sharp-eyed glare. *"I was a good lord who provided well for the village. Circumstances didn't always warrant their like for me, but they did respect me."*

"That I know for a fact. They all speak highly of you."

"See, so—"

She cut him off, speaking with excitement. "What if the villagers protect instead of fear the person?"

"This is complete nonsense. There is no one in St. Clair who masterminds the wreckers."

"You're so sure?" she asked, annoyed that he should dismiss her claim.

He explained. *"After my father's death, I thoroughly investigated that premise. I found nothing to substantiate that claim."*

"But Derry Jones spoke of someone he answered to in St. Clair."

Maximillian shook his head. *"He's a thief and liar, not to be trusted. I wouldn't be surprised if he was more involved than evidence indicates."*

"I agree he's not to be trusted, but he's also angry with someone and I think that someone is here in St. Clair."

Maximillian disagreed. *"I don't think you should concern yourself with that, there's no proof—"*

"Then I will find proof," she stated confidently.

"You are wasting your time."

"Where would you suggest my investigation take me now?"

He snapped at her. *"Not in the caves, not dressed as a boy and not drinking ale with the locals."*

"Who then could I possibly go to for help?"

"Claudia might prove useful and then there's that pious vicar of yours."

She wondered if his sarcastic tone when referring to the vicar was due to jealousy. The thought pleased her. "The vicar is mine?"

"He calls on you regularly, though I can't understand why you would enjoy his company. He's boring and weak."

Billie immediately jumped to John's defense. "He is not boring. We have interesting and meaningful discussions, and he's a gentle soul, but far from weak. He possesses a sturdy grip and speaks with a strong command when needed."

"You favor this passionless man?" he asked in surprise.

"He is not passionless," she defended again.

"Do his kisses stir you?"

"Yes, he is gentle and kind—"

"And he lacks the spark to set that unbridled passion of yours to a roaring flame."

"I will not discuss this with you, it is none of your concern."

He reached out and caressed her hand. *"It is my concern. We're intimate."*

"You're a ghost, it doesn't count," was her hasty reply, not voicing her worry that if he wasn't, what then?

He laughed, sure and strong. *"Wit, beauty and passion, what more could a man want?"*

"Life?"

He shook his head slowly and crawled up and over her. *"Taste,"* he whispered and nibbled on her pouty lips.

She pressed her hands to his chest. A mistake. He felt so warm, so inviting that her hands slipped inside his shirt and over his hard muscles.

It took only seconds for them both to become lost in a world all their own and they were soon naked beneath the sheets, nibbling each other in the most intimate of places.

The next afternoon Billie sat with John, having tea and riddled with guilt. Last night with Max had been wonderful, breathtaking, *unforgettable*.

She feared she was becoming a promiscuous woman. She desired Max much too much. She could make love with him every day and never grow tired of sharing such intimacy. Was this love? Or was she a woman who just enjoyed intimate pleasures?

"Your thoughts trouble you?" John asked, peering at her through his glasses.

Billie debated confiding in him. He had frequently offered his help. And he was accustomed to villagers confessing their troubles to him. That was his job, listening and counseling.

She tested the waters with carefully chosen words. "Yes, my sleep has been restless." She didn't add that it was because the ghostly lord kept her occupied most nights.

John nodded, sitting back beside her on the settee and folding his hands in his lap. He waited, not pressing her to continue, not urging her to confess. He just waited like a patient, pious man of the cloth.

She continued. "Would you think me strange if I told you that I still have visions of the ghost?"

"Not at all," he said calmly. "I had suspected as much."

"Why?"

"Your intense interest in Lord Radborne."

"He's impossible," she said, resting back beside John. His willingness to listen and his nonjudgmental manner eased her concern in talking with him and she relaxed considerably. "He's demanding and arrogant to a fault. He feels that he is this mighty lord who must be obeyed in all things. His judgment must never be questioned and his word is law."

"You speak with him often?"

"We talk at least every day, sometimes more than once, and he usually visits with me in the late evening." Realizing her last remark revealed more than she had intended, she blushed.

John made no reference to her pink cheeks or her remark. "You speak of him as if he is real."

"I sometimes feel he is," she admitted.

"Billie," he said softly, taking her hand. "His grave is marked for all to see."

"And empty of his remains," she reminded.

"You can't honestly think him alive. What reason would he have to fake his death and resurface as a ghost?"

Billie yanked her hand from his. "That's it," she cried with excitement and shook a pointed finger at him. "The missing piece, I need to find out why he would go to such extremes and then all the other pieces will connect."

"Perhaps you should ask yourself if you find him desirable, a phantom who fills your fantasies."

She looked with wide eyes at him. "You still think I dream all this?"

He chose his words with care. "I think you are an intelligent and imaginative woman who has survived much loss and unexpected change. Hardships such as those can affect a person in various ways."

"What ways?" She found his deductions curious.

He offered his explanation with the familiar sound of a preacher delivering a sermon. "Sometimes a person will create a situation in their mind that they seek in reality. It provides a measure of safety until—"

She stopped him, asking, "Are you suggesting that I desire a man like Max?"

"According to village stories he was the type of man who women found irresistible."

"He certainly is that, but irritating and a few other choice descriptive words also come to mind. He pales in comparison to a man with your qualities: sincere, trustworthy, caring."

He stumbled over his words. "You co-compare m-me to Lord Radborne?"

She had and realized she meant every word. "Yes, and your qualities far outshine his." She frowned in thought. "Actually, I wonder if he possesses any good qualities?"

"Villagers talk highly of him. He must have had some good qualities."

She was about to shake her head when vivid memories of last night assaulted her and with a wicked grin she said, "Perhaps one."

"Is it one you would look for in a man?"

Her eyebrows arched and her lips pursed. "Ahhh." She hastily turned the question on him. "What would you look for in a woman?"

He clarified her question. "It is what I would look for in a wife and the answer is simple."

She waited with stilled breath as if his answer was her salvation.

"I would want someone who would love me as much as I love her."

Her eyes drifted closed briefly, the truth of his words disturbing her. Love was important. Love connected two peo-

ple more deeply than passion. Passion was fleeting, love
was forever.

"You're right," she said with a nod and fought the urge to
shed a tear. "It is simple."

"Do you love this ghostly lord, Billie?"

She stared at him, this virtuous man who cared with a
gentle passion for his fellow man. This man with hunched
shoulders and glasses that forever slid down his nose and
who possessed a tender strength and loving soul. This was a
man she could love.

She shook her head. "No, it is nothing but a fleeting fantasy that shall pass, but not endure."

He took her hand. "Perhaps it has already begun to fade."

His touch was warm and reassuring. He linked his fingers
with hers and inched his way toward her as if giving her the
option of rejecting him.

She had no such thought. At that moment she wanted very
much for him to kiss her and when their lips finally met, she
felt the softest of tingles run along her skin.

He eased a response from her, not rushing, not frantic,
only seeking. She answered in an unhurried play of her lips
to his and they savored each other as their kiss deepened.

His undemanding manner and her anxious response to
him alarmed her. Max and John were such opposites and yet
she responded to both with the same degree of intensity. The
idea that she could be attracted to two such opposing men
frightened her.

She attempted to ease away from him, but his fingers
stroked her neck and his lips stubbornly pursued. She shivered when his hand slipped around her waist and drew her
against him, her breasts connecting with his chest.

His small display of intimacy surprised her and it must
have surprised him as well since he abruptly ended their kiss
and moved a proper distance away.

He took a deep breath and she sensed he was about to
apologize.

She spoke first. "I enjoy your kisses and the closeness we share, John."

He sighed heavily and smiled, pushing his glasses up on his nose. "I am glad, for it makes what I am about to ask easier."

She looked at him strangely.

He reached for her hand. "Billie." He stopped to clear the squeak in his voice so that he could speak more articulately. "Billie, I love you."

Her eyes rounded, full and wide.

"I love your sincerity, your kindness, your thoughtfulness. I admire and respect your courage and I could think of no other woman I would want to spend the rest of my life with."

He took a deep breath and plunged on. "Billie, will you do me the honor of becoming my wife?"

Chapter
Twenty

Billie sat on a stone bench in the garden, her soft wool blue shawl draped around her shoulders, her glance focused on the purple irises that had burst into full, glorious bloom and her thoughts on John's marriage proposal.

She had requested time to consider it and he had agreed it was best she not rush into a decision. That was two days ago and she could think of nothing else.

With her mind so preoccupied she had decided a walk outside would be beneficial. The sun had stayed bright in the sky since early morning, chasing the spring chill from the air. A time of new blooms, new growth and abundance.

It was time to begin anew. She looked out on the freshly dug earth primed for planting and on the rows and circles of flowers and shrubs that had been carefully cleaned of winter debris and surrounded with mulch. All was in readiness for the new growth.

Was she?

Max had visited her last night and she had managed to keep her distance from him. They had spoken about hiring a man to further investigate Derry Jones and she had argued that more investigation was needed in St. Clair itself. He had left, annoyed with her.

She wondered what he would do when he learned of John's proposal. Would it matter to him? Would he confess all to her? Or would he disappear in a puff of mist?

She shook her head at her ridiculous thoughts when a white mist drifted through the bushes a few feet in front of her. It thickened almost to a fog then developed slowly into . . .

"Oran?"

Oran Radborne tugged on his waistcoat and flecked a speck of dust from his mustard-colored frock coat before he walked toward Billie.

"Magnificent entrance wasn't it?" he said and leaned down to kiss her cheek before joining her on the bench.

Billie eyed him suspiciously. "Why doesn't Max make such grand entrances?"

"He's not familiar with the technique. He requires more practice."

"He's a novice?" she inquired skeptically.

"Most definitely. He lacks the experience to perform the smallest of ghostly abilities."

She grinned and quirked a brow. "Hmmm, I wonder why that is?"

Oran hastily changed subjects. *"I heard about the marriage proposal you received."*

"Ghosts gossip, too?"

Oran puffed out his chest. *"We see much and know much."*

Billie's expression turned serious. "Then be honest with me and tell me what is really going on. I know that you know much more than you are admitting."

"I cannot confide all I know," he said regretfully. *"I cannot."*

A chill ran over Billie, sending gooseflesh crawling along her skin. She got the distinct feeling that Oran could not bring himself to tell her what he must, that somehow the knowledge pained him.

"I can tell you not to ignore the obvious," he warned. *"Follow your instincts; they will guide you wisely."*

"According to your son my instincts are all wrong." She sighed heavily releasing some of the frustration she had been carrying around. "I can't help but think that Bessie and Marlee were nervous when I spoke with them as if they knew something but were afraid to tell me."

"Then by all means follow your feelings," he urged. *"And"*—he paused covering her hand with his—*"marry the vicar, but remember looks can deceive."*

"What is that supposed to mean?" she asked, another chill coating her skin with gooseflesh.

He patted her hand reassuringly. *"Only that there is more to him than you suspect."*

"The vicar has secrets?" she asked jokingly.

"We all have secrets, Billie," Oran said seriously.

She spoke just as somberly. "I think the whole village has a secret."

"Then discover it and set them free," he said with a sadness that upset her.

He kissed her cheek once again and stood. *"Be careful,"* he warned and walked toward the shrubs, waving before he faded into a misty shroud and evaporated before her eyes.

Billie returned to the house, brewing a pot of mint tea and filling a plate with honey cookies against Matilda's objections.

"I can do that for you, my lady."

"Nonsense, Matilda. You're busy preparing supper and I enjoy doing for myself at times."

Matilda smiled, her pudgy fingers expertly kneading the bread dough on the flour-covered surface of the table. "I wonder if I will ever grow accustomed to your unusual ways."

"We have plenty of time for you to get used to me."

"Yes, plenty of time," Matilda agreed with her smile widening and a vigorous shake of her head.

Billie took her tea and cookies to the study, happy that at least Matilda was pleased she would be around for a while. Pembrooke, on the other hand, at times made her feel that he would not be at all distraught if she announced she was leaving the manor permanently. And then there was Max.

She set the silver serving tray on a small table, which was flanked by two high-backed chairs in front of the burning hearth. The rooms still required fires to warm them even with the weather change. The old house retained a constant chill and until summer came fires were essential for comfort.

A book and her tea were good distractions from her weighty thoughts. She had brought a favorite gothic tale from America along with her that normally gave her a fright. Now she imagined it would amuse her.

She settled comfortably in the chair, the book waiting in her lap as she munched on a cookie and sipped her tea.

The click of the metal door lock echoed in the room and Billie froze, fearful that her attacker had returned.

"When did you plan on telling me?" Maximillian said, his voice raised considerably.

Billie calmed her trembling hands by wrapping them around the cup and sipping the tea, her jittery stomach needing the soothing brew.

"Tell you what?" she said, returning the cup to the tray.

He stood before the hearth, his dark attire making him appear a silhouette in front of the flames' bright light. He looked powerful and majestic in his arrogant stance.

"Marriage proposal stir your memory?"

"I wasn't aware I was required to discuss such a personal matter with you," she informed him, calmly wondering if the prospect of her marrying someone else upset him.

"You promised to help me," he accused as if she had betrayed him.

"My marriage to the vicar would in no way infringe upon my promise to you." She spoke sharply, annoyed that he cared not a whit that she might marry, only that it might interfere in resolving his dilemma.

"You will not marry him," he demanded.

She relaxed back in the chair. "I wasn't aware that I required your permission."

He leaned over her, bracing his hands on the arms of the chair and effectively locking her in. *"You are required to use common sense."*

"Common sense?" She almost laughed in his face. "Marrying John would be the most sensible thing I've done since arriving in St. Clair."

"I think not."

Her bravery ebbed with his closeness, her voice becoming small. "John is a good man."

"But not the man for you."

She attempted to challenge him, but her voice faltered. "I think he would make the perfect husband."

He stepped away from her, throwing his head back in a roar of laughter. *"Perfectly boring."*

Billie jumped to her feet. "John is not boring. I enjoy his company."

Maximillian turned on her swiftly, standing nearly on top of her. *"And his kisses? Do you enjoy them?"*

John's kisses certainly didn't possess the scalding fire of Max's kisses but she enjoyed them nonetheless. "Yes, his kisses are pleasurable."

"Liar."

"How dare you—"

Maximillian swept her up against him and planted his lips to hers so swiftly that he stole her gasped breath. He kissed her with an erotic fury that she couldn't deny or fight. He didn't relent until she melted voluntarily against him and her arms snaked up around his neck.

He eased his taste of her, savoring her sweetness until he reluctantly separated their lips, gently kissed the tip of her nose and set her away from him, holding her arm with a steady hand while she regained her balance.

"He will never kiss you like that." Maximillian released her and with two steps put a safe distance between them.

Billie breathed deeply, her concentration returning and her wit as sharp as ever. "But he will love me."

"Will he?" Maximillian challenged. *"Perhaps his love is born more from your fortune than his feelings."*

"You pompous idiot!"

Max's brow shot up.

She stormed over to where he stood and shook her finger in his face. "How dare you suggest that John is after my money—"

"My money," he interrupted.

She continued. "He is too kind and generous a person to care about *my* money. He cares about me, not the Radborne fortune."

"My fortune shall not pass to a weak-willed vicar."

Billie crossed her arms solidly over her chest. "My fortune shall be shared with whomever I choose to marry."

"Whomever you choose to marry will control Radborne Manor, not you."

"That is one reason why John would make the perfect husband. He would not interfere in my control of Radborne Manor. He would be too occupied with his duties as the vicar of this village."

He raged at her, his fist thumping his chest. *"And how will you explain me?"*

She grinned and rocked on her heels. "John doesn't believe in ghosts."

His look turned lethal. *"I wasn't referring to my spirit."*

She stopped rocking and hugged her arms around her waist, warding off the chill that suddenly descended over her. "What do you mean?"

"I mean," he said, taking two steps toward her and running his finger down her cheek. *"How will you explain the intimacy we've shared?"*

She shoved his hand away and walked over near the hearth. "If he doesn't believe you exist, then how could our intimacy?"

"What you're saying is that you have no intentions of telling him."

"He would believe me crazy if I confessed a torrid intimacy with a ghost."

"You are being foolish to even give his proposal consideration," Max chided.

"I must think of my future."

"Then think on it," he snapped, *"and don't throw your life away on a penniless and passionless vicar."*

Billie responded defensively. "I will do as I wish."

He groaned and threw up his hands. *"You're stubbornheaded to a fault. Do as you must, but make certain you don't neglect your promise to me."*

He marched past her.

She shook her head as she turned around, thinking him worse than a child who had just thrown a temper tantrum. "I will—"

He was gone.

She cast a quick glance at the door. It remained locked. She eyed the room suspiciously and with determination she walked over to the wall and began to knock, her ear pressed to the wall as she listened for hollow spots.

Two weeks passed without much fanfare. She took tea every afternoon with John and spent most nights in Maximillian's arms. This odd situation could not continue.

Her investigation of various rooms in the house turned up no secret passageways. She could neither prove nor disprove whether Max was a ghost or a man. And her inquiries into Derry Jones and St. Clair were at a standstill.

Her life, though, needed to move forward. She had found herself eagerly anticipating the time she spent with John as she did now, walking hand in hand along the shore with him.

The sun shined brilliantly, the water lapped softly and the sea birds entertained overhead with a squawking tune.

Billie glanced at the silent man who kept step beside her. His head hung down, matching his stooped shoulders and his glasses perched precariously on the edge of his nose. His dark hair was drawn severely back and tied with a black leather strip. His steps were sure and steady and his hand firm around hers.

He glanced at her and smiled, squeezing her hand. "I cherish our time together."

She tugged him to a halt. "Wait, I have something to say."

"Are you all right?" he asked anxiously.

"I'm fine," she smiled. "Actually better than fine. I'm in love."

John looked at her with hopeful eyes.

She stepped closer to him and slowly brought her lips to his, kissing him gently. "I would be honored to be your wife."

His arms moved around her, drawing her against him while his lips met hers and sealed their future with a tender kiss.

"Billie, would you mind if we married right away?" He offered a reason for a hasty marriage. "I have no family and neither do you and I miss you when you're not with me and—"

"Is next week soon enough?" She wanted a hasty wedding just as much as he did. She hoped his presence in the manor would settle her ghost problem.

"That would be fine," he said, his grin generous. "I shall contact the vicar over in the next village and make all the preparations for us to wed in the church."

"I will speak with Matilda about a small reception at the manor and invite . . ." She paused and shook her head. "I'd like to invite the villagers to the manor. Would that be proper?"

"I think it would be most fitting."

Billie, most unladylike, threw her arms around John's neck and kissed him soundly.

He stumbled back, holding on to her, and after briefly returning her enthusiasm, he eased her a proper distance away. "With so much to do and so short a time to do it in we should return and set to work our plans."

Billie nodded, her smile not nearly as enthusiastic as before. She silently cursed Maximillian as she and John headed back to the manor. His words echoed in her head, warning her of a passionless man. Or was she a woman who desired more than she should?

Upon their return to the manor, Billie summoned Matilda and Pembrooke to the small receiving room and with John standing beside her she announced their intention to marry.

Matilda squealed with excitement and hugged Billie to her buxom chest like a mother thrilled for her daughter. Pembrooke shook the vicar's hand and—to Billie's surprise—he even smiled.

John left shortly afterwards, promising to return early tomorrow so they could finalize plans. On parting he gave her a peck on the cheek.

Billie had grown suddenly tired and explained to Matilda that she needed a nap. "Decide on an appropriate menu for the wedding and we shall discuss it later."

"You look pale, my lady. Are you all right?"

"It's the excitement," Billie lied and turned to climb the steps. When she reached the landing that divided the stairway, she stopped and glanced out the window. The sun had disappeared behind a large storm cloud and an overcast sky promised rain.

"So much for sunshine," she said and headed down the hall to her bedchamber.

Max was waiting for her.

"You're a fool," he said calmly.

"No," she said with equal calmness and a shake of her head. "I am a woman who understands what is best for her."

He remained where he stood by the hearth. *"And this marriage is best for you?"*

"The absolute best," she said with a sudden smile, as if just remembering why she had agreed to marry him. "John is wonderful. He cares to a fault, and I love him."

"You hardly know him," he argued.

"You're wrong. I know him very well." Her smile widened. "He's a man strong in his convictions and one who would never turn his back on a friend. He will always be there for me. He loves me."

Maximillian pushed away from the hearth and walked straight toward Billie. *"What of passion?"*

Billie didn't retreat from him. She remained where she stood and he stopped mere inches from her. "Passion is elusive. It doesn't last forever. Love and commitment do. John offers me both. What do you offer me? Nights of pleasure and days of emptiness?"

Maximillian gently cupped her chin. *"What do you want me to offer you?"*

She stepped back, his hand falling away. "It isn't what I want, it's what you're willing to give. John gives without request. He knows what I need and what I feel and offers his emotions and support freely. *You* won't even tell me the truth."

"Would it make a difference?"

"You tell me." She waited.

He looked at her strangely, his eyes concentrated on her, his lips almost aching to speak but hesitant, as though inside he waged a private battle.

She felt the urge to comfort him, to let him know it was all right no matter what he confessed. She took a step forward and as she did, so did he.

The knock at the door shocked them both and Billie turned around, wanting desperately to chase away whoever was there.

"My lady," Matilda called. "You have a visitor."

She turned back to Max, but he was gone. She shook her

head as she walked to the door. A few minutes, just a few, and she was certain he would have confessed all. And then what?

She shivered, since the answer possibly held even more unanswerable questions.

Billie was greeted with an enthusiastic and congratulatory hug from Claudia when she entered the receiving parlor.

"I am so happy for you and John," she gushed. "He's perfect for you, absolutely perfect. Of course, I never expected him to gather the courage to propose—and this soon. And to marry so quickly? Why he surprised the daylights out of me."

Billie finally managed to direct the chattering Claudia to the chairs so they could sit.

"We decided that since neither of us had family there was no reason to wait."

Claudia smiled. "The faster you marry, the faster you can start a family. And besides the manor needs children to fill these empty rooms."

Billie decided to probe. "Had Maximillian planned on filling the manor with children?"

Claudia nodded. "It was his duty."

"What about love?"

Claudia reached over and patted her hand. "Love rarely enters an arranged marriage. Oran had often commented to me how difficult it was to arrange a marriage for him. Maximillian found fault with every candidate his father chose. And of course Oran, loving his son the way he did, never forced the issue."

"Why was it so difficult?"

"You would have to be familiar with Maximillian to understand."

Billie knew Max all too well, but she wanted to hear Claudia's opinion. "Tell me about him."

Claudia grinned. "He was a devil with the women. They loved him. He was charming, arrogant and demanding and every woman that met him was enthralled with him. Oran once commented that it would take a woman with courage and strength to love and marry his son. And I think that is exactly what Maximillian was searching for in a woman: courage and strength. A woman much like yourself."

"Like me?" Billie asked, surprised.

"Most definitely. Maximillian would have found you intriguing, but you are much better off with a man like John."

"Why?"

"John is quiet and tender and will treat a woman with care. Maximillian was the complete opposite of John. He possessed a fiery passion and his wife would have known no peace. You could feel it when he walked into a room. His presence overpowered. No man argued with him and few women denied him." Claudia shook her head. "Perhaps if he had been here when Oran . . ."

It was Billie's turn to reach out her hand to Claudia in support. "I'm sure he felt the same way."

"Oh, he was furious," Claudia said. "Furious with himself because he had returned to London to resume a dalliance with a well-known stage actress."

"He blamed himself for not being here when his father needed him the most?" Billie asked, knowing full well the answer.

"He was beside himself when he returned, locking himself away in the manor for several weeks before he emerged and began a full-scale investigation into his father's death."

"Then he had to have uncovered Derry Jones's involvement."

Claudia stared bewildered at her. "How do you know about Derry Jones?"

Billie wasn't about to detail her escapade as a boy. "I heard about him from someone."

"He's a good one to stay away from and besides, Maximillian found nothing connecting him to the wreckers."

"But I heard Derry answered to someone in St. Clair."

"Being the town busybody I would certainly know if someone was masterminding a wrecking ring in St. Clair."

"But—"

Claudia interrupted. "No buts. You need to concentrate on your wedding, not the likes of wreckers and smugglers. Now let me explain what type of wedding reception would be appropriate for the lady of the manor."

Chapter
Twenty-One

It was her wedding day. The sun was shining, the birds were singing and the manor was abuzz with activity. So why did she feel so melancholy?

Billy stared at herself in the full-length mirror Matilda had moved into her room from the lady's bedchamber down the hall. Bessie had surpassed her own seamstress skills in creating the most stunning of wedding dresses within one week's time. The soft white silk girdled just beneath her breasts and fell softly to rest at her ankles. The bodice was trimmed in an intricate design of beadwork as were the cuffs of the long sleeves. The design was repeated around the four-inch hem. A cloak of white wool trimmed with white rabbit fur around the collar and cuffs was laid across the chair, waiting.

She had insisted on fashioning her hair herself, only this time the unruly strands blended in perfect harmony with the bits of baby's breath she had added throughout.

She made, as Claudia had tearfully announced only moments ago, a beautiful bride.

She imagined it was the fact that her mother, father and uncle were not here to share this special day with her that she suffered from this melancholy. She was truly alone and within the hour she would begin her future as the wife of Vicar John Bosworth.

Tears stung her eyes. She had never felt so isolated since losing her family. There was no one, not even Max. He had deserted her the day he learned she had accepted John's marriage proposal. She had not seen him at all since then and she was beginning to wonder if he had ever existed.

She wiped away her tears with her fingertips and took a deep breath. This should be a happy day. She and John had spent many pleasurable hours together this past week in preparation of this very moment. He had been kind, caring and so very thoughtful of her emotions. He wanted, as he expressed so many times, for this day to be memorable for her.

She realized, too, that she wanted to make him a good and loving wife and hopefully a good mother to their many children. She attempted to not dwell on her concern that their relationship lacked the lusty passion she had shared with Max. But then . . . perhaps she had but dreamed it all.

The coach waited outside for her, Matilda waited downstairs to accompany her and John was at the church. Everything was in readiness for her. She reached for her cloak.

"I came to wish you well."

Billie swerved around, almost toppling herself. "Max . . ."

Her smile faded briefly when she watched Oran fully materialize before her. Recovering her composure, she showered a brilliant smile on him. "Oran, I'm so pleased you came." And she was; he was almost like a father to her, offering advice and caring like only a parent could.

He walked over to her and gave her a fatherly hug and kiss on the forehead. *"I could not allow you to marry without my best wishes."*

"I'm so happy you are pleased with my decision."

"More pleased than you realize." His smile was genuine.

"I am a bit nervous," she confessed, hugging his cold hand.

"Only natural, my dear. Why, the day I married I had the chills and shivers. I was afraid my teeth would rattle when I spoke my vows."

She laughed. "Did they rattle?"

He shook his head. *"No, I took one look at my lovely bride and realized how very lucky I was to have her as my wife and how very much I cared for her. The shivers ceased and I spoke my vows loudly and clearly."*

"I am lucky to have found John," she said, though a hint of doubt trailed her words.

Oran cupped her hands in his. *"You are very lucky, Billie. He will be a good husband to you and he will love you deeply like no other man could. He is a special man, always remember that, no matter what happens. Always."*

Billie felt a chill race through her. "I'll remember," she promised. "I was wondering if you've seen Maximillian."

"Pay him no mind, he sulks."

"Why?" she asked.

"Because he cannot have that which he wants," Oran said and reached for her cloak. *"Now hurry before you are late for your own wedding."* He rushed her into her cloak, gave her one last quick kiss and hurried her out the door with a whispered, *"Good luck, my daughter."*

The small stone church overflowed with villagers and neighboring friends. Everyone was decked out in their Sunday finery waiting for the lady of Radborne Manor to arrive.

Cheers sounded when she descended from the coach and she waved to the sea of smiling faces. Once she was inside the church foyer, her stomach began to quiver. Claudia assisted her in removing her cloak and handed her a beautiful bouquet of a variety of white flowers speared with dark green ferns.

Billie clung to the beribboned stems, the music sounded and Claudia urged her forward. She walked down the aisle alone, not familiar enough with anyone to request such a personal favor.

She caught sight of John, resplendent in black, standing poised and ready, his glasses balanced perfectly on his nose, his smile wide and his hand extended out to her.

She walked forward and grasped his fingers.

"I love you so very much," he whispered and gently pulled her forward to take her place beside him.

The ceremony was splendid and over with before Billie realized it had passed so quickly. She and John were soon receiving well-wishers at the entrance of the church and she stared in disbelief at the plain gold band that circled her marriage finger.

It was over. She was now Mistress John Bosworth.

With a hail of good wishes following them, the newly-weds hurried inside the coach and headed back to the manor to receive their wedding guests.

"You are happy?" John asked, taking her hand and pressing a lingering kiss to her palm.

A tingle rushed over her and she smiled. "Very happy."

"Good," he said followed by a sigh of relief. "I feared that you might reconsider at the last minute."

She had, but didn't wish to upset him, so she kept her last-minute doubts to herself. "We are now husband and wife," she confirmed.

"Forever," he whispered and leaned over to brush her lips with his.

She ached for more as he eased away, carrying his kiss no further than a simple, delicate touch of their lips. She hoped this evening he would prove to be more passionate.

The manor soon overflowed with guests. Food and drink were served in abundance. People laughed and raised their voices in well wishes. Billie received a generous number of comments on how bright and lovely the manor looked; "so much more welcoming" was the most often heard compliment.

She had hoped to have work started on the master bed-chamber this week but with the wedding she postponed the work, instead having the workers finish all the rooms on the first floor. From the many compliments she received, she was pleased with her decision.

John and she were rarely together during the entire reception. The men kept him occupied and the women fussed over Billie, sharing wifely tales with her that made her blush on more than one occasion and brought good-hearted laughter to the women.

Matilda and Pembrooke had seen to the hiring of staff for the day so the serving and clearing away was going smoothly. And Pembrooke was in his prime, issuing orders to the small army of servants.

Billie smiled with contentment, taking in the scene before her. Her home was filled with friends who came to help her celebrate this special day and she had a husband who loved her. She was deeply blessed.

John glanced her way, catching her eye with a hasty wave. She waved back and he smiled.

Yes, all was good and could only get better. She looked forward to this evening and the intimacy she and John would share.

The hour grew late and guests began to take their leave, again bestowing meaningful best wishes on the happy, wedded couple. Claudia was the last to take her leave. With a tearful embrace she bid them good night and wished them a long and fruitful marriage.

The couple were finally alone. They stood hand in hand, smiling at each other.

"My lady, shall I assist you?" Matilda asked from the doorway of the receiving parlor.

Billie was about to tell her that she required no help, wanting only to be alone with her husband, when John answered, "By all means, Matilda, please see to my lady."

Billie moved to protest, but a tug of her hand brought her attention to her husband's face. "It is only proper she see to your needs this evening."

"It isn't necessary," she said and boldly added. "I have you."

He shut his eyes tightly and his jaw grew firm. She wondered if she had angered him.

His eyes opened and he spoke softly, "Matilda should see to you. It is only proper."

She nodded, her disappointment evident. "If you wish."

He held her close as she moved to leave. "I wish many things, Billie. Give us time."

His soft plea tugged at her heart and she kissed him softly on the cheek and whispered, "I'll be waiting."

She hurried from the room to follow Matilda, hoping her words had been the cause of his barely audible moan.

Matilda fussed over her, talking incessantly and telling her not to be nervous that the vicar was a kind and good man.

Billie sat on her vanity bench, dressed in a white linen night rail with ties of white silk ribbons crisscrossing her breasts. She brushed her hair, smiling at the older woman who was attempting, most endearingly, to ease Billie's bridal nerves.

"I'll be fine," Billie said, hoping to ease her concern.

Matilda rushed over to her and embraced her to her ample bosom. "Of course you will, my lady." She stepped back. "Now I'll be off and a good night to you." She blushed profusely and hurried out the door.

Billie laughed and ran her hands through her hair, shaking the shiny strands so that they rushed around her face wild and free. She walked over to the end of the bed, toying with the ribbons at her breasts.

Would she appear shameful if she loosened a few?

Better not to, she decided. John was probably nervous enough about this evening. She didn't wish to add to his anxiousness and she didn't want to appear improper.

A soft knock alerted her to John's entrance as he pushed the door open. He stood on the threshold of the room, uncertain, his hand tightly fixed on the metal latch.

"Do come in and join me, dear husband," Billie invited with a smile and patted the spot on the bed beside her.

John cleared his throat with a rough cough and entered, shutting the door behind him.

"Shall I help you undress?" she asked, about to stand.

He halted her with a brisk, "No, that won't be necessary."

She hid her disappointment behind her forced smile.

John took his coat off and folded it neatly on the back of the chair near the hearth. He fumbled with the buttons on his waistcoat, his fingers visibly trembling.

Billie took her courage in hand and walked over to him, gently brushing his hands aside. "Let me be a proper wife and see to my husband's needs."

"I-I-I c-ca-can—"

She hushed his nervous stutter with her finger to his lips. "Shhh, let me," she whispered.

He shut his eyes and took a deep breath.

She unbuttoned one, then two and before she could release the last button, his hand captured hers. She looked up at him and he raised her hand to his lips, tenderly kissing her wrist, her palm, her fingers . . . She closed her eyes, lingering in the sensual pleasure.

"You are so beautiful," he murmured and released her hand to capture her lips. Short, light kisses were followed by probing gentleness and culminated with his tongue slipping with haste between her lips to finally mate with hers.

It was a serene blending, both enjoying the simple sensuality of their foraging tongues. Tingles shot through Billie, radiating along her sensitive flesh and settling intimately between her legs.

He moved his hand to the ribbon ties at her breasts and tugged gently, freeing them. His hand slipped in and his fingers brushed her already hardened nipples. His hand shook as he attempted to intimately acquaint himself and accidently squeezed the puckered bud too hard, causing Billie to jump.

"I'm sorry," he whispered near her ear.

She steadied her uneven breath. "It's all right, I like it when you touch me."

Encouraged by her words, he continued, only to once again cause Billie discomfort. He tried to further loosen the ties but fumbled and accidently knotted them.

Abandoning his unskillful efforts, he returned to kissing her while easing her night rail up and running his hands over her bare bottom.

They felt so good to Billie; warm, tender and intimate. Thinking to help him, she reached down and further lifted her night rail up. John, seeking to assist her, joined her hands in ridding her of the garment only to become entangled in the ribbons and cloth.

Billie, lost in a world of white linen, finally cried, "Stop, John, please, let me do it."

He immediately ceased his help and stepped back. Instead of taking the night rail off, she eased it down over herself. Flushed from her ordeal and having lost the tingle of sensuality he had first stirred in her, she looked at her husband.

He fumbled with his glasses, his fingers attempting to catch them before they fell off his nose. Righting them, he admitted, "I am not very good at this. I lack experience."

She couldn't very well confess her own experience and at the moment she felt guilty for wishing he was more widely educated in the way of women. She had not thought that she would need to instruct her husband in the ways of making love.

She kept her disappointment to herself and offered encouragement. "We have time to learn together." She held her hand out to him, intending to guide him in his next attempt at passion.

He stared at her for several silent moments, his strange look unreadable and then he took a step back, fastening his waistcoat buttons. "I think perhaps we should give ourselves time to become better acquainted."

Billie shivered and wrapped her arms around herself. He

had no intentions of consummating their marriage and the thought chilled her. "We are acquainted."

He avoided direct eye contact with her. "Not enough, I fear."

At a loss to answer, she remained silent. How did a bride react when her husband rejected her? She had no idea what to do.

"It is for the best," he assured her.

Hiding her disappointment behind her courage, she nodded. "As you wish."

John stepped around her, sweeping his coat off the back of the chair. He slipped it on, walked back beside her, kissed her cheek and walked to the door. "I shall sleep down the hall in the lady's bedchamber. Good night."

She didn't respond, and she barely heard the click of the closing door that shut her husband away from her. Tears filled her eyes and she fiercely fought them, but their persistence prevailed and they soon broke loose to roll one after another down her flushed cheeks.

Alone with the crackling fire, the only sound in the empty room, she gave in to her tears and wept. Not loud sobbing cries, but soft whimpers that no one heard but her.

Powerful arms suddenly slipped around her, turning her, pressing her against the warmth of a solid naked chest and her own arms broke free, wrapping around the man who knew her all too intimately.

"Max," she cried and buried her head against his chest to spend her tears.

"It's all right, I'm here."

His embrace was filled with a power that protected and his voice soothed like an old, familiar lullaby. He held her, rocking her gently from side to side, whispering words she barely heard but understood completely. He was there for her when no one else was and he always would be.

He let her cry, never once insisting she stop and when she finally finished he walked her to the bed, freshly laundered and turned down in preparation of her wedding night. He tucked her beneath the counterpane, sat beside her and with his finger gently wiped the remnant of her tears off her cheeks.

"Your eyes are much too beautiful to shed so many tears."

"What did I do wrong, Max?" she asked between heaving sobs.

"Hush," he ordered sternly. *"You did nothing wrong. He is a fool to wait to bed a wife as lovely and willing as you."*

"He doesn't know how," she offered in defense of her husband's odd actions.

His devilish grin set Billie's heart to palpitating and her guilt to rise several degrees.

"It isn't that hard to learn."

Her own wicked grin surfaced. "No, it isn't."

"I've missed you," he admitted, much too directly.

Her grin faded and she caught the spark of passion in his eyes. She noticed, too, that he wore only a pair of black breeches, no shirt, no stockings and his hair was loose about his shoulders. He looked as if he had rushed into the one garment, having been disturbed in the middle of . . . what?

"Where have you been?" It was her turn to be direct.

"I thought it best I stay away for a while, but I see now that it doesn't matter."

"What do you mean?" She struggled out from beneath the covers bracing herself up against her pillows.

He bluntly informed her, *"You want me as much as I want you and your marriage doesn't change that. Why it probably only worsened matters since your husband is an inadequate lover."*

"He lacks experience."

"Courage is more like it."

"He feels we should—"

Max snapped at her. *"He should feel like a man unable to keep his hands off you. He should be hungry for your naked flesh, not fumble like a young schoolboy."*

She was about to take umbrage of his opinion when she suddenly shouted, "You were here in the room with us!"

He hastily vacated the bed.

She jumped out herself, racing up to him where he stood in front of the hearth and poked him hard in his chest. "You spied on us."

"I did not spy," he said, casting a warning glance at her jabbing finger.

"Were you here?" She shot him another jab.

"This is my bedchamber." He spoke in a calm and controlled tone.

"It is mine and my husband's and what goes on in here is no concern of yours." She stressed with several pointed jabs.

He had enough. He grabbed her finger. *"Nothing goes on in here, so I have nothing to concern myself with."*

"He'll come to my bed," she told him with a defiant lift of her chin.

He grabbed her jaw. *"And disappoint you. I, on the other hand, will always be here and always make you burn with the want of me."*

She attempted to argue, but his tight grasp wouldn't allow her to speak.

"Are you going to try to deny the truth?" His voice was soft and his grip slipped away, his fingers moving languidly down her neck.

His touch devastated as always and she couldn't deny it. He set a fire in her blood and he soon would have it raging out of control.

"Your skin is so soft, so silky, so touchable," he whispered and ran one finger down her chest, beneath the loose ribbons.

She forced herself to remain as still as a statue when his finger brushed her nipple.

"And the taste of you." He moaned like a man deprived too long, then lowered his head, his fingers expertly and quickly untying the ribbons, pushing them aside and covering the semi-hard orb with his mouth.

She tangled her fingers in his dark hair, drawing him closer, her ache unbearable.

He feasted hungrily, his need as unbearable as hers.

She groaned with unquenched passion. His tongue, teeth

and lips skillfully tormented her to breathlessness. She wanted this, needed this, expected this . . . tonight was her wedding night.

The realization struck her like an unexpected blow and she shoved him away, stumbling backward.

He reached out, grabbing her by the shoulders. *"Don't deny us."*

"I'm married."

"To a fool," he snapped and shook her. *"You won't find passion with him."*

"I will," she insisted and struggled to free herself.

He released her and she rushed around him to jump back in the bed beneath the covers. "Don't enter my bedchamber again."

He stared at her with eyes of fury, his shadow rising in exaggerated length and width and resembling a dark demon on the wall behind him.

She shivered at the raw, masculine power he exuded. It overwhelmed, captivated and intoxicated. How would she ever deny him?

She warned him once again, though with much less fervor, "Stay out of my bedchamber."

He issued his own warning. *"I am lord of this manor and will go wherever I choose. And, my lady, I shall finish what your husband so inadequately started."*

She yelped in fright or expectation—she was uncertain which—and threw the covers over her head as he advanced on her.

When he failed to pounce on her, she peeked from beneath the covers.

He was gone.

She pounded the bed with flying feet and fists. He purposely didn't carry out his threat tonight to give her cause for worry and frustration. Now she wouldn't know when he'd next show up.

That was it, she'd had it. Tomorrow she would tell John they were moving to the vicarage.

Chapter
Twenty-Two

"Move to the vicarage? Whatever for?" John asked, bewildered, as he and his new wife shared their first breakfast together in the dining salon.

Billie had slept little last night. Every creak, every pop of the burning log, every rattle brought her fully alert, fearful that Max had returned to make good on his promise. Her sleeplessness had given her time to think through her motive and she presented it most confidently.

"The vicar of the village is usually a common man, living a common life. I worry that the villagers will find you inaccessible here at the manor."

"Nonsense," John said, unconcerned by her suggestion. "I will take my appointments at the vicarage and make it clear that anyone is welcome at the manor."

Billie felt her carefully formulated plan slip away.

John reached out and patted her hand. "You worry over

the unnecessary. All will be fine. And besides, this manor is yours and you deserve to reside here."

She certainly couldn't confide the truth about Max so she attempted to implement her alternate plan. "John, about last night."

His hand began to tremble and he returned the teacup he held to the saucer. "We should discuss this later in privacy."

Billie glanced about the room. "I see no one here but you and me. We have all the privacy we require."

He lowered his voice. "This is not a proper topic to discuss over breakfast."

She grew annoyed. "When is it proper to discuss? This evening in our bedchamber?"

"Early this evening in the study will do fine," he informed her, a little too sternly to her way of thinking.

"I think not," she said and almost winced recalling that the phrase was a favorite of Max's.

"Belinda," he said firmly.

"I have something to say and I intend to—"

Pembrooke walked into the room and John shot her a look that warned her to remain silent.

She spoke up. "Pembrooke, the vicar and I wish to be alone, please leave."

So startled was he by her unexpected and sharp orders, Pembrooke took his leave without even a "yes, my lady."

"That was rude," John said, tossing his white linen napkin to his plate.

"I intend to finish saying it." Billie completed her statement and carefully folded her napkin beside her plate.

John had other thoughts. "Our intimacy should not—"

"What intimacy? We have none and we will continue to have none if you sleep in the lady of the manor's bedchamber. You are my husband and I would like you to share my bed."

"A lady in England does not share her husband's bed nightly, only occasionally."

"I'm not a lady from England. I am an American and in America husbands and wives share beds nightly." She hoped getting him into her bed would solve two problems. It would keep Max away and it would help them establish, slowly if necessary, an intimate relationship, culminating in the consummation of their vows.

To her surprise his frown turned to a smile. "You are a most bold and unpretentious woman."

She grinned. "Qualities you admire in me."

He leaned over where she sat to his right and took her hand. "I do admire you, Billie, much more than you realize."

She locked her hand with his and whispered, "Then sleep with me."

His smile vanished, a blush rose to tinge his cheeks and he remained silent as if he was deep in thought and she wondered why such a simple request should trouble him so. After all, he was her husband.

"We need to take this slowly," he said, reaffirming the fact that he had no intention of consummating their vows anytime soon.

"If slow is what you want," she said, perplexed by his response.

"I think it wise," he said, offering no further explanation.

"Then slow it is, but you will share my bed?"

He didn't hesitate this time. "Yes, I will share your bed."

She smiled with the exuberance of a young girl who has just received a most wanted gift. Now Max would find it more difficult to pop up in her bedchamber. Her husband's presence would afford her protection.

Obviously relieved, John stood and held his hand out to her. "Come. I have planned a small excursion over to Granville. The village has the most wonderful bookshop and an inn that makes the best meat pies."

Billie joined him, taking his hand and speaking low. "Shhh, we mustn't let Matilda hear. She may not let us go if she hears we favor another cook."

He whispered close to her ear, his warm breath tickling her sensitive skin. "Then we must make a secret pact to never admit to our traitorous ways."

"Agreed," she said and planted a chaste kiss on his cheek, then turning her cheek to him she waited for him to seal the pact with an identical kiss.

He hesitated briefly before skimming her cheek with his lips.

She heard his sharp intake of breath and felt his arms wrap around her just as she caught a fleeting spark of passion ignite in his eyes.

He kissed her then with precision and power, surprising her, and her need for him kindled.

His softly spoken words only fueled her desire for him. "I want it to be right for us, Billie. I want you to always remember our first moment together as husband and wife."

He kissed her again before she had a chance to comment and then he tugged her alongside him as he hurried out of the room with a shout to Pembrooke to have the coach brought around.

Though the sensual tingles lingered inside her, she felt pleased. Time and patience were needed for now. Eventually they would share an intimate life together. Her marriage had been a wise choice. All would be right.

Those words haunted her three weeks later. Their marriage had taken on a common routine and the part that irritated her the most was when John climbed into bed in his nightshirt that trailed on the floor, turned on his side and fell fast asleep. And need she forget that she never woke with him beside her in the morning? He was always gone before she opened her eyes.

Tonight he had been called away to pray over an ill villager. He would probably be gone most of the evening.

Her investigation into the wreckers had yielded nothing. Bessie and Marlee changed the subject every time she attempted to question them, and she was growing more suspicious of them by the day. What, or better yet *who*, were they protecting or frightened of?

And Max had grown unbearable to tolerate, though he

had managed to keep his distance from her bedchamber. He harped incessantly on the changes that were still going on in the manor. He frequently offered derogatory comments on her husband's inadequacies in being a *proper* husband and he kissed her much too often in demonstration of what she was missing from a man who was well aware of husbandly duties.

Billie climbed the stairs with a heavy burden on her mind. She did love John dearly. He had proven to be an excellent husband in all areas except one and she had no idea how to rectify the problem. She only knew it could not continue in this fashion.

She yawned, closing her bedchamber door behind her.

Max popped out of the corner shadows, startling her. *"Alone again."*

"My husband shares my bed as you well know." She brushed right past him to plop down on her vanity bench and began to pluck the pins from her hair.

Max walked up behind her, focusing on her reflection in the mirror. *"And his husbandly duties? Has he seen to them?"*

Billie fought with a pin tangled in her hair. "That is none of your business."

He pushed her hands away from the mass of unkempt waves and untangled the pin with steady and gentle fingers. *"This manor is my business."*

She tried not to think about the way his fingers rummaged so tenderly in her hair or about the tingles that shot through her body when his fingers stroked her scalp as he disengaged the captured pin.

He tossed the pin to the vanity table and his hands returned to her hair, running up from the nape of her neck to the top of her head, around the sides and back down again. He repeated his slow and steady massage and Billie relaxed considerably.

He spoke softly and yet with a firm resolve that captured Billie's attention. *"You possess a passion for life in all things you do. You embrace every moment and challenge every day. You require a man of equal strength and character. One who can enhance your passion, not bury it."*

His fingers moved to her neck and he skillfully massaged the tense muscles.

She moaned from the exquisite feeling of her tight muscles melting away. "John is my husband," she said, unable to think of any other argument to offer.

Max dropped down behind her and kissed along the column of her silky neck before whispering in her ear, *"Not yet he's not."*

He continued to apply the most ardent of kisses to her neck and shoulders while his fingers worked to free the back of her garment. He eased it down over her shoulders, the straps of her chemise joining the plunge.

"I love the taste of you, so womanly."

She watched in the mirror as his lips traced a path over her shoulder and his hands further freed her from the confines of her garment.

"Beautiful," he whispered and cupped her naked breast in his hand.

Billie stared mesmerized by his play of fingers to her breast and nipple. His touch felt so good, so right. His gentleness turned forceful, his fingers squeezing her nipple to hardness.

"Look at the way you respond to my touch," he urged.

She shut her eyes, embarrassed to watch her own desire quickened so willingly to his command.

"Look, Billie, look," he whispered and moved alongside her to tease her nipple with his tongue.

Her eyes drifted open, catching his intimate action and she was unable to pull her gaze away. The tip of his tongue flicked across the hardened bud unmercifully and then he suckled like a man who would not be denied. She watched until she thought she would go mad with the want of him.

John, a small voice in her head reminded her. *John.*

Max raised his head and stared at her wide-eyed expression in the mirror. *"Don't deny us this."*

"Deny us what?" she asked regretfully. "We share nothing but passion. You deny me even the simple request of the truth. I made my choice."

"To marry a fool," he said, standing and walking away from her.

She hastily slipped her dress up and over her shoulders before turning to face him. "I married a good man and I will be a good wife."

"And what if you lost this manor and wealth, what then?"

She answered quickly. "I would still have my husband's love. No one can take that away from me."

He looked at her with sorrowful eyes. *"Then perhaps it is I who am the fool."* He stepped back, the deep shadows swallowing him whole.

"Max?" She called out to him and when she received no response she knew he was gone.

Her heart ached for him and for herself. This had to end, she had to discover the truth. And the truth was hidden somewhere in St. Clair. Someone had to know something and if she dug deep enough she would surely find it.

The other matter that needed immediate resolution was the consummation of her marriage. She had hoped by now the problem would have resolved itself. She had begun to fear it never would since John never took their relationship past anything but a kiss.

He had never even attempted to touch her intimately and she wondered the reason for his strange behavior. Too many things had seemed strange to her since her arrival and she had become too complacent in her attempt to discover the truth of things.

It was like a puzzle: All the pieces were there, she just had to fit them together properly and then she would have her answers and solutions.

Determined to wait up for her husband in hopes of at least an attempt at seduction, Billie changed into her night rail and climbed beneath the covers, bracing herself against the pillows. She reached for her book on the night table beside the bed and began to read.

Two hours later John found her fast asleep, the book laying open across her chest. He moved the book away and tucked the quilt around her.

He bent over her, brushed her hair away from her closed eyes and was about to deposit a kiss to her cheek when he focused on her lips, so soft and plump like young fruit ripe for the taking.

He groaned, the sound reverberating low in his chest. He tore his eyes away toward the ceiling. "Dear Lord, give me strength," he prayed.

But when his gaze descended once again to his wife he realized the Lord was on her side. He leaned down and brushed his lips across hers, gently so as not to wake her but enough for him to torture himself with the sweet taste of her.

Helpless and unable to deny himself, he tasted her more fully, nudging his tongue between her lips, teasing her to open to him and slipping in the moment she surrendered. He kissed her like a starved man, knowing his time was brief, yet needing this intimacy he had craved so badly.

She moaned and he drew away in a flash, stepping back from the bed.

Billie licked her lips, her tongue searching for its mate and with a disappointed sigh she snuggled beneath the covers and mumbled, "Go away, Max."

John shook his head and walked behind the dressing screen to change into his nightshirt as was his custom each night. He removed his glasses, leaving them on the night table by his side of the bed. He extinguished the candle, slipped beneath the covers and stayed on his side of the bed.

"John?" Billie asked sleepily.

"Shhh, Billie, go back to sleep," he said softly.

Boldly she curled up against his back, forcing her hand beneath his arm to hug his chest.

"I missed you," she whispered, her hand stroking his chest.

"And I you. Now go to sleep." He removed her hand, tucking it back beneath his arm to her side.

She yawned.

"You're tired, sleep," came the stern order.

"Go away, Max," she whispered with a slumbered breath and cuddled closer to her husband.

Chapter
Twenty-Three

Pembrooke coughed upon entering the conservatory, alerting Billie to his presence before he spoke. "My lady, a—" he paused a moment as if in search of an adequate word and then continued. "A villager wishes to speak with you. He was actually quite adamant about it."

Billie looked up from her perch on the floor where she sat, surrounded by various size planting pots as well as flower bulbs, herb plants and a wooden bucket filled with soil. She held a small shovel in her gloved hand and carefully cradled a plant barely two inches tall in her other hand.

"Did he give his name?" She ignored Pembrooke's snort of disapproval before he responded.

"Bart," he announced with distaste.

Billie's brilliant smile irritated him all the more. "Send him in."

Pembrooke was about to express his opinion when Billie firmly added, "Now."

With a curt bow, Pembrooke mumbled, "As you wish," and left.

Billie was on her feet, her gloves and apron discarded on the wooden bench when Bart was ushered in.

Bart, cap in hand, bobbed his head and addressed Billie as soon as Pembrooke took his leave. "I'm sorry to disturb you and I would never have come to the front door of the manor if I hadn't thought it important—"

Billie interrupted his rushing speech. "It's all right, Bart, you're always welcome at the manor."

He bobbed his head again. "Thank you, my lady, but it's news I brought you, important news."

"Tell me," she encouraged, walking up to him so they could speak more quietly.

Bart's glance darted around the glass-walled room and, satisfied that no one spied on them, he spoke. "I heard that Derry Jones has a meeting with someone tonight near the caves here in St. Clair."

Billie grew excited, sensing that a break in solving this mystery was imminent. "Where on the shore?"

"Near the manor, by the caves," he whispered.

"And the time?"

He shook his head. "Sometime after dusk—the person I learned it from wasn't sure."

Though the time span was wide, Billie didn't mind. This was finally a chance to possibly uncover the identity of the mystery person who Derry answered to.

Bart nervously asked, "My lady, do you plan on going there tonight?"

She nodded, already formulating a plan in her head.

With worry in his voice he told her, "I have work in St. Simon tonight, I can't go with you."

"I'll go alone." She thought nothing of the solitary excursion, but Bart did. He twisted his cap until Billie thought the wool would knot.

"It ain't safe," he warned.

"I'll be careful," she promised. "Now come with me, I have something for you."

Bart protested. "It ain't necessary, my lady. I don't mind helping you."

Billie persisted. "You went through a great deal of trouble for me and I wish to extend my appreciation." And with a smile she added, "Please?"

Bart blushed and nodded. "If you insist."

"I do," she said and hooked her arm to his to lead him to the study where she kept extra coins.

Billie planned well and fast. She informed John that she would be visiting Claudia after supper to discuss a possible dinner party at the manor.

Being preoccupied with his paperwork, John wished her an enjoyable evening and reminded her to take her cloak since there was a chance of rain, the sky having been overcast all day.

Billie informed Pembrooke that Claudia's coach would return her this evening and waved good-bye as she descended the steps.

Seconds after Pembrooke shut the front door, Billie flew around to the back of the manor and into the stables. There among the horses, who stared at her oddly while they munched their hay, she changed into boy's clothing.

With her clothes folded neatly in her cloak and hidden behind a bale of hay, Billie tugged her stocking cap down around her ears and drew up the collar of her jacket. She then set out on her spy mission.

A light mist had begun to fall by the time Billie reached the appointed area. She glanced about for a good spot to hide herself and chose an outcropping of rocks close enough to the shore that she could see—and hear she hoped—what was going on.

She settled herself on the damp ground, glad she wore the heavy jacket that would protect her from the moisture, and waited.

The mist turned to a light rain and the sea began to take on a rough roar that Billie hoped wouldn't drown out the voices of the meeting pair.

Her wait was brief, to her relief. She edged up, peering between two rocks, catching sight of Derry and clearly distinguishing his voice. She waited impatiently for the other person to speak and attempted to catch a peek, but was unable to see him from her cramped position.

She strained to hear the voice and shook her head when she thought she caught the high-pitched voice of a woman. Thinking the rough sea and her distance must have garbled the voices, she attempted to inch closer.

The voices raised as if in an argument.

"You will do as I direct," the decidedly feminine voice shouted.

"The bloody hell I will," Derry argued.

Shocked by the female voice, Billie moved closer, hoping to learn the woman's identity. Was it this mysterious woman who was the leader of the wreckers? Billie's curiosity itched at her and slowly she crept forward.

The rain had turned heavy and she stayed low, maneuvering her way around rocks and tall grass. She took careful steps, approaching with caution, wiping the rain from her face and hoping she would reach a spot where she could see the woman clearly.

The voices began to fade as if they were walking in the opposite direction and Billie hastily followed in an attempt to catch up. Her quick actions made her careless and her foot grazed a slippery rock, causing her to lose her balance.

Wisely she bit her lips to stop from crying out and alerting the pair to her presence as her legs went out completely from under her and she landed with a hard, jaw-rattling slap to the ground.

The last thing she recalled was her head snapping back before all went black.

"Billie. Billie, do you hear me?" the voice urged.

Gently, hands raced over her body.

"Billie!"

She recognized the frantic voice of her husband and fought to open her eyes though the pain that speared her head warned her not to.

"John," she mumbled, his name reverberated in her pounding head. She caught a quick glance of his rain-speckled glasses sitting on the end of his nose before her eyes closed of their own accord.

"Yes, Billie, it's me," he assured her. "I'm here, don't worry."

The next thing she was conscious of was being carried in strong, powerful arms and cuddled against a solid chest. His heartbeat was rapid against her ear, but the strength of its mighty beat made her feel safe.

She forced her eyes to flutter open and she caught a clear sight of Maximillian's sharp features. "Max," she sighed with relief.

"You little fool," he snapped. "I would throttle you if you weren't so injured."

She winced when she attempted to smile.

"Don't move," he ordered sternly. "You've taken a severe blow to your head. I must get you home."

"Where's John?" she asked with difficulty, feeling herself on the edge of unconsciousness again. "He found me."

"That fool of a husband should have been watching you."

Billie attempted a protest, but the darkness claimed her before the words reached her mouth.

She woke next in her bed, dressed in her night rail, the covers tucked around her, an icy cold cloth helping to relieve the pain that throbbed incessantly in the back of her head and her husband on his knees beside her bed in prayer.

She tried to say his name but the darkness began to descend on her once more and all she could hear was his urgent prayers for her full recovery.

"Billie, fight. Open your eyes. Do you hear me? I demand that you open your eyes."

She fought the urge to stay in the safety of the dark cocoon. She was annoyed that Max should dare disturb her throbbing head. With a great effort she squinted her eyes open.

"Fight, damn you," he said, though he sounded as if he shouted.

"Shut up," she barely whispered before her eyes forcibly drifted closed.

"You will fight and get well," Max insisted angrily. *"Do you hear me, Billie? Fight. I dare you to."*

When she woke again it was to John easing her head up and replacing the cloth that had warmed with a cold one. He tended her gently, speaking softly and reassuringly to her. Telling her in a tempered voice that all would be well.

He held her hand, his head bent, praying fervently to the Lord. "Please, dear Lord, I love her so, don't take her from me. Life would not be worth living without her. Please. Please, I beg you to spare her."

His aching plea touched her heart and she returned to her dark slumber, content with the new knowledge of how deeply her husband actually loved her.

Accosted by a sweep of cold air Billie hurried to wrap her arms around herself.

"No," Max sharply demanded. *"I need to change your gown. Don't fight me, Billie."*

She shivered and he quickly dispensed with her damp gown before easing a clean, dry one gently over her head and down her chilled body. He laid her back down on the bed and hastily tucked the covers around her.

She listened to his tirade of demands that she get well and when he tired of tormenting her he turned his demands on the Lord.

"I will not tolerate You taking her from me. She is mine

and I refuse to relinquish her. She is to get well. Do you hear me? She is to get well."

Funny, she thought, floating slowly into a slumber, Max assumed she belonged to him. Why? She belonged to John. He was her husband, and a wife and husband belonged to each other. Poor misguided Max.

Billie fully woke from her stupor late the next morning. John was seated in a chair that had been drawn up beside her bed and he dozed in sleep.

"John," she said, not in a strong voice, but audible and without a pounding madness in her head.

Startled, his head shot up. "Billie? Thank the Lord," he cried and reached for her hand that inched out from beneath the covers. "I was so worried."

"Water," she almost begged, her throat felt dry as though she hadn't had a drop in days.

He released her hand and fumbled with the pitcher of water on the night table until he finally filled a glass. He eased his hand under her head, being considerate not to apply pressure to the bruised area. He tilted the glass to her lips.

She drank slowly, finishing half the glass.

He fussed with the covers around her after bracing a few more pillows behind her head. "How are you feeling?"

"My head hurts and I'm hungry."

"Your head will probably continue to ache for a few days and being hungry is a sure sign that you are on the road to recovery."

She smiled at him.

"I will have Matilda heat some broth for you." He leaned down and kissed her forehead. "I feared I had lost you and that I could not tolerate."

His eyes were strained with pain and worry and too little sleep. Billie felt the need to comfort him, to let him know how much he meant to her, how very much she loved his gentle soul.

She said the only words that mattered. "I love you."

"And I you." He kissed her forehead again and pressed a soft kiss to her lips before moving toward the door. He stopped with his hand on the latch. "Billie, when you are better we must talk."

Her eyes questioned why.

He understand her silent query. "I want to know why you were on the shore dressed in boy's clothing, and I want to know why you lied to me."

Guilt attacked her as soon as he closed the door. Now she had no choice but to tell him the truth, but how much of the truth? Should she include Max? Oran? Where to begin and what to omit?

Later that evening John had an appointment at the vicarage. He intended to cancel it, feeling he still belonged at his wife's side. Billie insisted she was fine, especially with Matilda fussing about her, and urged him to keep it, offering to wait and share a pot of tea with him upon his return.

He agreed and after seeing she was settled comfortably he left for his appointment.

Billie was grateful he hadn't questioned her about last night's escapade. She was in no condition to speak of it just yet. She required time to heal and time to decide just what to tell her husband.

"What the bloody hell were you doing on the shore alone and dressed as a boy?" Max demanded, walking out of the shadows in the corner of the room.

Billie winced, shut her eyes and cupped her head with her hand. "Must you yell?"

He walked over to her, dropping down in the chair that remained by the side of her bed. *"I'm sorry I caused you discomfort, but you damn well had me upset. I thought I had lost you and that I could not tolerate."*

For a moment Billie thought John sat beside her, Max's words echoing her husband's early sentiments. Both voices sounded similar, but then her head had been bruised and her senses confused. She could almost see the two men blending as one.

"Are you all right?"

He sounded like John again. She peeked one eye open to make certain that Max occupied the chair. He sat there, broad-shouldered, heavy-chested and handsome as ever, this man who was not her husband.

"I'm fine," she finally said.

"Good, now answer me," he said, poised on the edge of the chair as if he were ready to pounce on her.

Billie could barely put a coherent sentence together without her head protesting, and he wanted an explanation? "I think not."

He was about to erupt again when Billie, with great effort, poked him in the chest. "Quiet."

He looked down at her finger, then up at her and then took her finger gently in his hand and pressed it to his lips.

She smiled at his complete surrender and ran her finger over his soft lips. "Thank you for helping me."

He took her hand in both of his. *"I told you I would always be here for you. Now tell me what you were doing on the shore, alone, in boy's clothing."*

"Investigating."

He placed her hand on the quilt and held up his own. *"Is this going to anger me?"*

She grinned. "Probably."

"Then perhaps we should postpone it until you are well enough for me to raise my voice."

"A wise decision," she said, knowing full well he lacked the patience to wait.

He already shifted uneasily in the chair. *"Of course, if you feel it is imperative, I could attempt to control my temper."*

"Is that possible?"

He leaned forward. *"You're teasing me."*

"And enjoying every minute of it."

"It always pleases me to bring you pleasure," he said in a

low, deep voice that hinted at a much different form of pleasure than they spoke of.

His suggestive words disturbed her and she immediately directed the conversation elsewhere. "I think I've found the leader of the wreckers."

She instantly caught his attention. *"What do you mean?"*

"I learned of a meeting yesterday between Derry Jones and someone from St. Clair."

"From who?" he almost shouted, but caught himself and spoke more civilly. *"And why ever did you go alone? Why didn't you tell me?"*

"First, who I learned it from isn't important," she said, counting off his questions on her fingers. "Second, I couldn't very well ask my husband to accompany me and third, it isn't as though I can knock on a door and ask for Maximillian Radborne. You pop in and out at your whim."

"So you take it upon yourself to go off in the night to investigate criminal activity that could possibly get you killed."

"To discover the identity of the leader," she corrected, firmly.

Max shut his eyes briefly, shook his head and obviously fought to control his temper. The question that followed was not what Billie had expected.

"How did your parents ever control you?"

She chuckled. "They indulged me."

"Spoiled you is more like it."

She held her head up as high as she could without causing herself pain. "I could do anything I set my mind to."

"You still do," Max said with what Billie thought sounded like admiration for her.

Billie offered him a more practical reason for her foolish actions the previous night. "I had a chance to possibly help you solve your problems and I just couldn't ignore the opportunity."

"I don't like the idea that you placed yourself in danger because of me."

Her expression turned as serious as his. "We need to settle this Max, one way or the other. We can't go on like this."

He nodded. *"You're right, it must be settled."*

The pain in her head was nothing compared to the pain that struck her heart. Soon their time together would end and the thought that she might never see him again brought a pain-wrenching ache to her soul. How could she care so strongly about two men? How could she love both as much as she did?

"Tell me who this mysterious person is," he said, his eyes steady on Billie and filled with regret.

She hid her ache well and fought back the tears that threatened to spill. "I was unable to see the person, but it was a woman."

His brow raised. *"A woman?"*

"Yes, a woman," she reiterated.

"You're telling me that you think a woman is the mastermind behind the wreckers?"

"Why? Don't you think a woman capable or intelligent enough to do so?" she challenged.

He stood, towering over the bed. *"I know one that is devious enough."*

That angered her and she shot up in the bed. A big mistake. Her head felt as if a thousand drums beat opposing tunes while the room around her spun out of control.

"Max," she cried, reaching out for him.

He was at her side instantly, bracing her against him and leaning her back upon the mound of pillows. *"Easy,"* he whispered. *"The feeling will pass."*

He reached to the bowl on the stand beside the bed and with his free hand squeezed the cloth that rested in the water bowl. He gently wiped her face with the cool cloth. *"You moved much too fast. Give your head a chance to settle."*

Billie relaxed against his chest, her arms draped across his flat midriff. She turned her face up to him slowly and he continued to ease the cloth over and around her still pale complexion.

"You need to rest and get well," he urged.

"You don't believe me, about the woman, do you?" she asked slowly.

"You suffered a severe bump to your head —"

She didn't allow him to finish, though she interrupted softly, "And you think I am confused about what I heard."

"It's possible." He rinsed the cloth and settled it on the back of her neck.

Billie almost sighed loudly in relief. "But it's not what happened."

"We will discuss this another time." He spoke in his authoritative tone.

She realized there was no point in arguing with him. His opinion was set and there was no changing it. She would have to discover the woman's identity and find proof as to her involvement. Once presented with the facts, he would have no choice but to accept the obvious.

As soon as she was well enough, she intended to seek out Oran and speak with him. He had to have known the woman's identity; perhaps the answer even had something to do with his death. Had he perhaps discovered something he shouldn't have?

Her head had stopped pounding and spinning and she suddenly felt exhausted. She cuddled deeper against Max and hugged her arm more tightly around him, settling herself comfortably.

"Stay with me," she whispered and a yawn followed.

"Always," he promised and circled his arms around her protectively.

"Don't make promises you can't keep," she murmured as her eyes drifted closed.

His answer penetrated her sleep. *"I never do."*

Chapter
Twenty-Four

Billie sat in the conservatory, enjoying the beauty of spring in full bloom outside the wall of glass windows. Several weeks had passed since her accident. She had thoroughly rested, due to her husband's forceful restrictions and was just beginning to return to her daily routine.

John had made her feel so guilty with his tirade of how he could have lost her and how he couldn't face life without her that she submitted, though grudgingly, to his demands.

Max had even sung the vicar's praises, insisting that he was finally beginning to behave like a husband should.

But she felt restless, bored and anxious. Her investigation had been stalled and she feared she had lost valuable time. With time at a premium during her recovery she had repeatedly recalled the voice she had heard on the shore. It seemed faintly familiar to her and yet she had difficulty connecting the high-pitched tone to anyone recognizable.

Matilda waltzed into the room with a smile. "Tea, my lady, before Pembrooke and I are off to the village?"

"No, I'm fine. I don't require anything." And with a yawn Billie settled more comfortably in the wicker chaise.

"Rest then, my lady, you have the manor to yourself. No one will disturb you."

"The vicar had gone for the day?" Billie asked, knowing John had informed her he would not return until early evening, but wanting to confirm the same with Matilda.

"He'll be back for supper."

"I'll just nap until you all return," Billie said with a tired voice.

Matilda grabbed a moss green wool throw from a nearby chair and placed it over Billie, tucking it around her. "Pleasant dreams, my lady." And out the door Matilda went.

Billie waited until she heard the couple's voices fade out of the house and then waited several minutes more before she tore the blanket off her and hurried to the receiving parlor in the front of the manor. She peeked out the window to see the couple walking out through the gate.

Satisfied she was safe, she hurried to the kitchen, prepared a lantern and pressed the lever to open the secret passage. She cursed the fact that John had taken the young lad's garments away from her and had refused to return them. She had no choice but to descend to the caves in her dress.

At least she had managed to hide boots in the pantry and she slipped the sturdy pair on before picking up the lantern and making her way down the stone steps to the caves.

Now familiar with the terrain she hurried along until she reached the room where she had spoken with Oran. The crates and barrels still occupied the space and she set the lantern on a crate.

"Oran," she called. "Oran, I need to speak with you."

"Good heavens, child, what are you doing down here?"

Billie turned to find him standing behind her. "I need to speak with you."

"*But you've been ill,*" he chided. "*You should never have come down here.*"

"That isn't important now," she urged and sat on one of the barrels, patting a crate top beside her for him to join her.

Oran obliged. "*Does your husband know you're here?*"

Billie shook her head, feeling guilty. "I didn't lie to John, I just didn't tell him that I was coming down here."

"*He's going to have a fit,*" Oran warned.

"John never has a fit, he only lectures."

"*Trust me, he'll have a fit.*"

Billie shrugged. "I can't worry about that now, I need to know if you know anything about a woman in St. Clair who was connected with the wreckers and Derry Jones."

Oran stood, obviously agitated. "*Don't ask me this, Billie, just follow the trail you're on. You will find your answers, but be careful.*"

"Why won't you help me?"

"*I can't,*" he said regretfully. "*You'll understand soon enough. Now you must go. These damp caves are no good for your health, especially dressed as you are.*"

"John took the lad's garments I had used," she complained.

"*And rightfully so.*"

Billie stood. "Then if you don't wish me to come down here will you come upstairs to visit with me?"

Oran walked over to her. "*I promise I will venture upstairs soon to speak with you.*"

She smiled and kissed his cold cheek. "Good, I'm glad."

"*Now go,*" he urged, pointing her in a different direction.

"This isn't the way back," she said.

"*Trust me, Billie, and take this path. It is a bit out of the way and you will need to return in this direction, but you will find answers at the end, and remember one thing . . .*"

She waited for him to finish before approaching the passageway.

"*Love makes us do foolish and heroic things.*"

She looked at him oddly and he waved as he vanished in a puff of mist. She shook her head, not understanding in the least what he meant, and held the lantern high as she entered the dark passageway.

She walked some distance, the passage twisting and at times narrow, thinking that perhaps Oran had sent her on a wild goose chase when she suddenly came upon a wooden door, thick and scarred with age. She opened it slowly, the metal latch and joints rusted. She bore no fear, only antici- pation, realizing Oran would never place her in danger.

Surprise showed on her face when she entered a well- lighted room filled with lanterns and outfitted with chairs, pegs of clothing, a vanity table and bench and containers filled with a variety of makeup most often worn by stage ac- tors. She had become familiar with the paraphernalia from an acting troupe that had passed through Nantucket and who she had befriended.

Curious, she searched through the creams, fake hair, fake moles, cotton that enlarged an actor's mouth or nose and padding that added bulk to a body, changing the shape. A tall bottle contained dye that altered hair color until washed out.

Who did this belong to? Who was not who they seemed?

Billie searched the clothing on the pegs. She looked them over slowly, testing the material between her fingers and spreading the clothes out to take a better look. Realization hit like a mighty blow to her abdomen. The clothes were a blend of her husband's and Max's.

She spun around, dizziness stilling her for a moment and then she raced over to the vanity table, rummaging through the container until she located the fake moles. She held one up and placed it to her chin, staring at herself in the vanity mirror.

Her eyes widened in disbelief, she tightened her jaw, she tossed the mole to the floor and muttered, "A stage actress for a mistress."

She spun around again and grabbed the padding on the chair, wrapping the band around her stomach and casting a suspicious eye in the mirror. "Stomach padding."

She grumbled like an angry animal and threw the padding back on the chair. She rummaged through the room until she pieced two entire sets of clothing together and there in front of her on each chair sat John and Maximillian. Her husband and . . .

Her husband?

She groaned a furious growl. Max and John were one. Max was masquerading as the vicar and as a ghost. She had her suspicions, but Max being her husband? She his wife? That was a hard fact to comprehend. He had tricked her. Why?

Could he love her? John often told her how much he loved her, made a point of it almost every day. Was it Max who was proclaiming his love for her? Did he use John's sentimental nature as a ruse for an emotion he had difficulty voicing?

She stamped her foot hard like a petulant child angry with her parent. "Bloody hell," she cried. "How could he do this to me?"

Where did the consequences of his deceit leave them? What did all this mean? She shook her head slowly, rubbing her forehead.

She looked once again at the two outfits, clearly visualizing her husband and Max blending as one. She grinned, not at all pleasantly. She intended to get answers and she intended for Maximillian to pay for his deceit.

Billie hastily arranged the room as it had been when she had entered. Curious as to where the door on the far wall led, she walked over and quietly opened the latch. Peeking around the heavy door she was surprised to see lanterns hanging on pegs that were jammed at spaced intervals in the stone wall. She climbed the narrow, twisting stairway slowly and cautiously. Another wooden door greeted her at the top of the stairs and she eased it open only a crack.

Familiar voices floated toward her and she instantly but softly shut the door. Her hands shook and her temper raged.

She was in the vicarage. She had heard her husband's calming voice and that of the housekeeper Laurel Smithers.

She retraced her steps and made her way back to the room below. She cast a hurried and frustrated glance around the place and then moved quickly to the door that led her back to the caves.

It was with determined strides that she returned to the manor, and it was with angry steps that she climbed the stairs to change her soiled dress, the hem damp and dirty from the earth floor in the caves.

Max had caused her a great deal of torment and frustration and now she had learned that she was his wife.

His wife!

She still could not believe his duplicity. He had actually warned her against marrying himself and yet he himself had proposed to her. And then he attempted to seduce her, his own wife.

She threw her hands up in absolute fury and futility. The more she considered the strange dilemma, the more angry she became and the more determined she was to make him suffer.

She finally smiled. She now knew of his dual identity, but he was unaware of her newfound knowledge. This could prove very interesting. *Very interesting.*

While Billie slipped out of her dress, her mind focused on a plan, a plan that surely wouldn't fail and would surely bring her satisfaction.

Billie sat to her husband's right at supper that evening. She wore a congenial smile and dark blue dress that dipped so dangerously low that every time she leaned forward to converse with him her breasts looked as if they would spill from their inadequate restraints.

John patted his perspiring brow with his handkerchief more than once during the meal and more than once ran his finger beneath the collar of his linen shirt.

"Are you warm, dear?" Billie asked with overly sweet

concern. "The weather has altered considerably and summer isn't far off. Why, soon we won't be needing a fire at night."

"Yes, yes, you're right," he said and downed his entire glass of wine.

A fake smile remained glued on Billie's face, her jaw beginning to ache. But her discomfort was a small price to pay for watching her husband squirm uncomfortably in his seat.

"Do you like my dress?" she asked, leaning over the table so her breasts practically rested on the table's edge.

She almost laughed when he pushed his glasses far up on the brim of his nose. She realized that they had purposely rested on the tip of his nose so that he could see properly since there wasn't a thing wrong with his eyesight. Now that he didn't wish to view her revealing neckline, he blurred his vision with the glasses.

"It's very nice," he said and made a point of breaking his boiled potatoes into small pieces with his fork.

She lowered her voice to a suggestive whisper. "I thought we might spend some time alone together tonight."

He almost choked on the potato he had swallowed.

Billie didn't waste a minute. She rushed out of her seat and pounded him heavily on the back while making certain she stuck her protruding breasts as close to his face as possible.

His cough worsened.

Pembrooke came rushing in and when he saw what was amiss his eyes widened in shock. Billie, seeing his highly agitated distress, understood immediately that Pembrooke was all too aware of John's true identity.

"Get him some water," Billie ordered sternly.

Pembrooke looked from his lord to his lady, uncertain what action to take.

"Water, now, Pembrooke!" She almost barked the command, causing the flustered man to rush out of the room.

"Easy now," she said much more soothingly to her husband and rubbed his back slowly. "You'll be fine."

Pembrooke looked as if he flew into the room. The water in the pitcher spilled over the edges as he rushed to the table.

"Sir, an urgent message was just delivered for you. You're needed in the village."

John was about to stand, but Billie's firm hand on his shoulder prevented him from moving.

"I didn't hear anyone at the front door," she said, looking directly at Pembrooke.

"He came around back, my lady."

"Who?" she asked, innocently.

She caught Pembrooke off guard and he stumbled over his own words until he finally said, "A boy from the village."

"Nothing serious, I hope?" she asked, her hand still planted firmly on her husband's shoulder. A shoulder she realized that was well padded, making him appear hunched over.

"I'd better go," John announced sternly.

"Yes, of course, you're needed, do go," she agreed, stepping away from him and wondering just how long it would take for Maximillian to make his appearance.

He dropped his napkin to his plate and stood.

"I'll wait up for you, dear." Her smile was blatantly sexual.

"I may be late." He rushed toward the door.

"I'm not sleepy. I'll wait," she said and sent him a wave.

He waved back and without a word hurried out the door.

Billie was ready and anxious for Max to appear. Her plan had worked perfectly so far. She had no doubt the rest would succeed.

She finished the wine in her glass, summoned Pembrooke and ordered brandy to be brought up to her bedchamber and climbed the steps with a confident smile.

Billie wore a white silk night rail with a bodice of fine lace that allowed her puckered nipples to faintly peek through. The lace ran down the arms of the billowing sleeves and around the hem with a lace insert running up between her legs. It was a daring and tantalizing piece that she had discovered amongst her mother's clothing. It was much too beautiful to discard, so she had kept it and was about to put it to good use.

She lounged against a mound of white pillows on the bed in a decidedly sensual pose, showing enough bare calf and spread of legs to allow the lace insert to hint at her treasure beneath.

Her hair was a riot of unkempt waves rushing around her head, making her all the more sexually appealing, and that was the first thought that popped into Maximillian's head when he stepped from the secret passageway beside the closet near the corner of the room, the shadows concealing him as he stared at his wife.

He wanted her.

She had aroused him to a most uncomfortable state at the supper table and now seeing her spread so invitingly, he wanted her even more, so much so that he swelled with a raging intensity that he hadn't experienced since he was a young boy in his first throes of ecstasy.

But Billie thought she belonged to the vicar. His plan had succeeded in its duplicity, though with dire results. He competed with himself for his wife's affection.

This evening, however, would belong to Maximillian. His hunger for his wife was ravenous and he had every intention of quenching his insatiable desire.

He stepped out of the shadows.

Billie appeared startled, bolting up in her bed, her hand flying to inadequately cover her breasts, but she kept her legs temptingly spread.

"Whatever are you doing here?" She hid her satisfied smile behind a concerned frown.

"I thought I'd visit since your husband was called away again." He walked closer to the bed, halting at the bottom to stare at the lace that teased beguilingly between her legs.

"I am waiting for his return," she said, leading him exactly where she wanted him to go.

268 DONNA FLETCHER

"He'll not hurry, as is his way." His hand itched to run up her leg beneath the silk and lace to her sweet heat.

Billie sighed dramatically. "I don't know what to do, Max."

He looked at her strangely, coming up alongside the bed to sit down beside her. "About what?"

"My husband," she said with another heavy sigh and squeezed her eyes shut for a brief moment as if fighting back tears.

He attempted to ignore her hard nipples almost poking through the white lace bodice. "What troubles you about him?"

He hoped he kept the husky desire out of his voice though he wondered if that was possible, his mouth was so ready for the taste of her.

She shook her head, raking her fingers through her hair while her heavy sigh jutted her breasts forward. She snatched her smile back before it broke free, tucking it behind a frown. She was satisfied that from his round-eyed expression and dropped jaw she had succeeded in arousing him.

And then, of course, there was the mighty bulge in his pants that attested to her success.

She finally continued. "He just doesn't seem interested in consummating our marriage. I don't know what to do."

"Give him time," he urged, his hand finding its way over her ankle to caress it soothingly.

She kept focused on her plan, trying with great difficulty not to admit how much she enjoyed his touch. How much she had missed it.

"Our marriage vows are not valid until we consummate the marriage. I feel unwed. I feel he doesn't want me." With a tearful cry she added, "I feel he doesn't love me."

Max instantly sprang to John's defense. "Nonsense, the man loves you so much it's ridiculous."

"He does?" she asked anxiously, realizing now that he

spoke for himself as well as John and wanting desperately to hear him speak his love for her.

"The man is absolutely besotted. He worries senselessly about your safety, crumbles to your every whim, except for the lad's clothing," Max smiled. "It did my heart good to see him take a firm stand. And the way he watches you?" Max shrugged and shook his head.

"How does he watch me, Max?" Her heart swelled with love for this arrogant, caring, sneaky man who was her husband.

His voice softened. His hand stroked up her leg. "He watches you with the eyes of a man deeply in love. There is no one but you for him. His love knows no limits. He would do anything for you. He would even die for you."

Billie felt her breath catch. "You think he loves me that much?"

"I know he does."

She leaned closer to him. "Then why deny us the intimacy of marriage?"

He moved nearer to her, his hand skirting the inner regions of her thigh. "His inexperience probably makes him nervous, unsure of his ability to perform as a proper husband."

"It matters not to me."

His hand stilled as it slipped between her thighs. "You don't mind his fumbling?"

"He'll learn," she argued.

"Some men never do. They are inept lovers all their lives."

"But you—"

"You cannot compare me to him. His life has been cloistered, whereas mine has been free."

"You defend him."

"I feel sorry for him. A passionate wife and an inexperienced husband. He must feel inadequate."

"He isn't," she insisted, her plan working perfectly.

"He must feel that way if he keeps his distance."

She moved closer, his hand brushing the junction of her thighs.

He felt the wisps of hair, felt her heat and his arousal soared.

"Max," she whispered, her lips moving over his.

He moved to claim her mouth, but she pulled away.

"Max," she repeated with an achy need.

He reached out, his hand slipping around her neck, wanting to hear that she needed him as much as he needed her. "What do you want from me, Belinda?"

She licked her lips slowly and with a hint of a smile said, "Teach me to seduce my husband."

Chapter
Twenty-Five

Maximillian bolted off the bed, repeating her unbelievable request. "Teach you to seduce your husband?"

"Yes," she said eagerly, holding her hand out to him. "You could teach me exactly what to do to him to make him want me."

He glared at her. "You mean this?"

She folded her hands in her lap and released an exasperated sigh. "Of course I do. What other option do I have? I cannot allow my marriage to continue on in this fashion. It isn't proper. And you—" She paused, sending him a smile that dripped with sensuality. "You have the knowledge that I require. Teach me," she requested again and extended her hand to him.

Maximillian stared at her. She wanted him to teach her to seduce *him*. This whole matter was becoming exceedingly awkward, but then again . . .

He gave her offer serious consideration. After all she could only succeed in seducing John if he allowed her to. He was in control here. He could handle this small dilemma easily and benefit from it. He would have the pleasure of tutoring her in the ways of seduction. But what would happen when she discovered the truth? How would she react?

By then they would be so deeply involved, he reasoned, that nothing else would matter, only their love. But who did she love more? Maximillian or John?

That was an answer he intended to discover.

He summoned her with the snap of his hand. "Come here, Billie."

Billie eyed him skeptically.

He turned a grin on her that melted her insides and resolve simultaneously. She shivered from the gooseflesh that prickled every inch of her sensitive flesh and gave serious thought to her next move.

"Do you want me to teach you?" His voice dared.

She nodded against her better judgment, praying that she would be able to control the already raging desire racing through her and focus on her plan.

"Then come to me and let me show you how to tempt a man until he can think of nothing else except making love to you."

Billie took a deep, fortifying breath and slipped off the bed slowly, standing completely still for a moment as if indecisive and then, with trembling legs, she walked toward him.

His hand circled her neck and he leaned down to steal a brief but conquering kiss. "You will do as I direct," he said, his hands cupping her neck and his lips a mere inch from hers.

He would forever be a lord, she thought, always expecting immediate obedience and compliance. She nodded her consent.

"Undress me," he ordered, taking a short step back from her.

This was going to be a little more difficult than she had thought. "I beg your pardon?"

He reached for her hand, pressing it against his shirt.

"Part of the pleasure of seduction is undressing your partner, slowly and teasingly. Inch by inch. Stripping away layer after layer of protection and leaving each one vulnerable to passion."

Billie tingled with the suggestive picture his words painted.

"Now take my shirt off."

Hesitantly, her shaking hands reached up to unfasten his shirt.

His hand moved over hers, halting her inadequate progress.

She glanced up at him.

He stared down at her. "Go slowly, there's much pleasure in anticipation and . . . what waits beneath. You do want to feel my hard flesh, don't you, Billie?"

She nodded without reluctance.

"Slowly," he repeated. "Let your fingers brush my flesh, tempt me, tease me and you, as you spread my shirt and slip it off."

His words mesmerized and fanned her desire.

She did as he directed. Her fingers ran playfully over his buttons, twisting and twirling them apart. And as each one opened she teased his warm flesh with the tips of her fingers.

"Spread my shirt apart," he said with tremendous effort, as if attempting to catch his breath.

She gave no thought to his obvious reaction to her touch; she was too intent on how much pleasure she derived from undressing him.

Her fingers slipped beneath the linen shirt, running over his hard, muscled flesh, feeling his nipples pucker as she brushed over them.

His sharp intake of breath made her realize just how much he was succumbing to her inexperienced yet determined hands. She trailed her fingers down to his breeches where his shirt ends were tucked inside and she slowly but sharply tugged the material free. Her fingers crawled inch by inch up his naked chest to slip his shirt off his shoulders while she settled her lips against his bare, hot flesh and tasted.

His shirt fell to the floor and her hands continued to explore along with her tongue, licking, nipping, kissing every inch of muscle.

Maximillian attempted to control the rage of desire that shot through him. But it soared out of control and it took every ounce of willpower he possessed not to grab her, toss her on the bed and bury himself inside her.

Whisper soft and with her fingers inching down his breeches, she asked, "Shall I remove the rest?"

His arousal swelled even stronger against her hand and his hand shot out, instantly covering hers.

"If you do that, Billie, I won't be responsible for what follows."

The dampness between her legs warned her that she was as passionately aroused as he and if she chose to continue, her lesson would surely culminate with their making love.

With a strength she didn't think she possessed, but a determination to see her plan succeed, she stepped away from him. "This one lesson shall do me well. When John returns this evening I will assist in undressing him."

Max took several deep, calming breaths and when he was finally able to speak, his voice held a tremor. "He may not react as you wish at first."

"But you—"

He interrupted sharply. "You and I strike passion in each other."

She walked away from him, fearing if she stayed near, if she inhaled the scent of the passion that drifted like a sensual spice around them she would beg him to strip her and make love to her.

"It is a beginning. I will try."

Max grabbed his shirt off the floor. "Do not be disappointed if you fail."

She shot him a challenging look. "You think me incapable of stirring passion in my husband?"

"He is a pious man with a strong will."

She almost laughed at the word pious, but instead she smiled. "And I am a passionate and patient woman. I will tempt him slowly and thoroughly until his arousal is as potent as yours."

Max wore a winning grin, knowing full well he would deny her. "Don't be so sure."

"If I have no success with lesson one, surely lesson two will benefit me," she said and added as if daring him. "Meet me in your study tomorrow afternoon. John will be at the vicarage and we can continue our lessons."

"Each lesson will eventually have a price that you may not be willing to pay."

"What price?"

"We'll make love and not the soft, slow kind, but the hot, passionate, untamed type that robs you of your very soul. Are you willing to pay that price?"

She closed her eyes feeling breathless and her voice trembled. "With my husband, yes."

He didn't answer and when she opened her eyes he was gone. But he would soon return as John and she would be ready and so would he, she had made certain of that.

Billie didn't have long to wait. Within the hour Max returned as John. She waited in bed as she had for Maximillian.

"You needn't have stayed up," John said, sitting in the chair near the hearth that burned with a low flame and kept a chill from the room.

She left the bed to wander over to him, her bare feet treading lightly and cautiously across the dark carpet. "I wasn't sleepy. A difficult evening?"

"More than you know," he mumbled.

Billie heard him and smiled. "Let me help you off with your coat."

He didn't object, sitting forward while she eased his arms out and then folded the gray garment to rest over the top of a nearby chair.

She walked around to stand in front of him, certain the fire's warm light accented her body beneath the silk gown. She reached down and slipped his glasses off, placing them carefully next to the chair.

"You look so tired," she said with genuine concern and leaned forward to rub his temples, her breasts resting only inches from his lips.

He shut his eyes against the lusty temptation and recited a silent prayer, thinking that he certainly embodied John's pious character at the moment.

Billie settled herself on his lap, bringing his eyes to full alert as she purposely wiggled her way to nest comfortably against him. She smiled at his raised brows and whispered, "Poor baby." And continued to rub his head.

She allowed herself the time to fully study him, having berated herself for not noticing the similarities sooner. She grudgingly admitted that his makeup was applied with a skillful hand, but then she assumed he had been taught by a professional.

He had lightened his skin to appear pale and his eyebrows were made to look fuller, more overgrown. The mole on his chin was placed to distract the eye and his nose appeared broader than Max's. His hair was drawn tightly away from his face and looked tinged with a dye that muted his usually shiny black hair.

His glasses had been the perfect finishing piece, another distraction, especially since he had fussed with them constantly.

And then there was his body.

"Better?" she asked and lowered her hand to rest on his shoulder. She felt no padding; he was obviously prepared for her.

"Much," he said, squinting his eyes as if he had trouble seeing her without his glasses.

She ignored his ruse and proceeded to toy with his shirt buttons. "Tell me about your night."

"There is nothing to tell," he said, his tone controlled and measured.

Much too controlled to Billie's way of thinking. She purposely, yet with wide-eyed innocence, squirmed in his lap, pressing her bottom invitingly against him.

His groan was barely audible but Billie caught it.

"Did you not help someone?" she asked, resting her head on his shoulder while her finger remained at teasing odds with his buttons.

"Yes, I did help someone," he answered and to her surprise brought his hand to rest on her backside. "I provided a young woman with necessary guidance."

Billie bit her lip to prevent herself from laughing. And decided she had tarried long enough. She opened several of his buttons and slipped her hand inside against his warm skin.

"What guidance?" she asked, running her finger around his nipple and feeling it rapidly respond.

He took a deep breath. "On how to be a proper wife." His hand moved down slowly over her backside, giving her firm cheek a gentle squeeze.

"She doesn't know how?" She followed her question with a soft lick and a kiss to his chest.

"She assumes too much and does not obey her husband as is her duty," he warned, much too forcefully.

"And you helped her to see the error of her ways?" Billie tasted her husband once again, discovering that she quite enjoyed playing the temptress.

"I hope I did," he said softly.

She tasted his hard nipple and found it much to her liking. Her mouth closed over it.

"Billie."

He called her name with such a soft power that her head shot up.

"You are a wicked woman," he said before grabbing the back of her head and claiming her mouth roughly.

Shocked by his passionate assault it took her a moment to comprehend that she had actually caused her husband to lose his self-control and the victory suddenly tasted mighty sweet.

She moved her arms around his neck and feasted on him as demandingly as he did on her. She pressed her breasts to his chest and reveled in his hand squeezing her backside.

Time stood still as they found pleasure in one another. And Billie gave no thought beyond this moment and this time of magic she shared with her husband.

When she felt him attempt to end their encounter she begged in a whisper, "Make love to me, John. I want to feel you inside me."

Her words delivered a potent blow. He groaned loudly and swelled beneath her. She knew he wanted her, he couldn't deny it. There was no way he could refuse to make love to her, no way.

She whispered again. "Please, John, I need you inside me."

He groaned again like a man who had suffered too long and was about to surrender. Raise the white flag. Give up.

Victory was hers.

The loud knock at the bedchamber door startled them both and John stood, lifting her with him.

"Come in," he said with a stern shout.

Pembrooke entered cautiously, peeking around the door before walking fully into the room. "I'm sorry, sir, but another urgent message from the village."

Billie glared at the small man so murderously that he retreated several steps to the open door.

"I'll be right there, Pembrooke," John said, all traces of passion gone from his voice.

Pembrooke nodded and hastily left the room, closing the door behind him.

John eased her out of his arms to stand while he quickly retrieved his coat.

"You can't mean to leave me now," she said, furious that he had purposely arranged for Pembrooke's interference.

"I must go," he insisted firmly, bending down to grab his glasses from beneath the chair and slipping them on.

"What about us?" she said, with an angry stamp of her foot.

"Patience, my dear," he said and rushed out of the room.

Billie ran to the bed, grabbed a pillow and flung it at the door. "Damn you, Max," she yelled, having caught his grin before he fled the room.

Maximillian locked himself in his study, poured himself a liberal glass of brandy and took a generous swallow. He shed his coat, glasses, freed his hair from its tight binding and dropped into one of the two chairs that faced the hearth.

"Bloody hell," he muttered and took another swallow.

"Difficult evening, my son?" Oran walked out of the shadows.

"I don't know whether to be angry or pleased that I have such a passionate, determined wife."

"A woman that favors her husband's attention is a rare find. I'd be pleased."

"But it's John's attention she's after. The only thing she wants from me is to teach her to seduce him—I mean me." Max shook his head. "I don't know what I mean anymore."

"Why not tell her the truth?" Oran asked, sitting in the chair next to his son.

"Not yet," he insisted. "I need to make certain of her safety before I announce to all that I'm alive."

"And how do you think she will respond to this news?" Oran steepled his fingers and relaxed back in the chair waiting for his son's answer.

Max ran his hand over his face. "I don't know. I only know that I love her more than I ever thought I could possibly love a woman and I can't see living my life without her.

Perhaps once she understands that and the reason behind my deception, she'll be able to forgive me."

"And how long do you think you can continue this deception before she discovers the truth?"

Max threw back another generous swallow of brandy before answering. "After tonight?" He shook his head. "Not long. Not long at all."

Chapter
Twenty-Six

Maximillian relaxed back in the large chair behind his desk, his two fingers steepled and pressed to his lips and his mind deep in thought. His plan had been so simple and now . . .

Nothing was simple. He had fallen in love with a spirited and intelligent woman who would shortly discover the truth about him. What then? Why had he allowed his plan to escalate to such outrageous proportions?

When the attempts on his life began, he had thought them mere accidents and then, when it became blatantly obvious that someone was out to kill him, he had assumed the reason stemmed more from his female dalliances than the manor. He had not given serious thought to the problem, having been emotionally distraught over his father's death.

He folded his arms across his chest and shook his head. He could clearly recall the day his father's ghost had first appeared to him. It was only a few days after the funeral. He had been alone in the study as he was now, drowning his sorrow in whiskey when his father had materialized right through the wall.

His father had scolded him for feeling sorry for himself and had ordered him to take care since his life was in danger. With that, his father had disappeared.

He had thought the strange occurrence the results of the liquor, but his father had made several more appearances until Max began to accept his ghostly presence and finally realized his father's warning rang true.

But who wanted the manor? And why make attempts on his life and why kill Oran? He had not been able to discover any relevant information in the last few months. The Derry Jones lead proved futile as did the suggestion that someone in St. Clair headed the wreckers. He had uncovered no proof.

Even his charade as the vicar, a villager people trusted and confided in, hadn't provided him with information into the wreckings along the coast. He felt at a dead end.

And then of course Billie had entered his life and complicated it even more, though he had to admit her type of complication and involvement proved interesting. Not to mention exciting and passionate.

He just wanted to make certain that she was kept out of danger and that whoever had made attempts on his life and caused his father's death did not threaten Billie's safety.

His dual identity had at least provided him with the ability to be around her most of the day and then, of course, his father kept a steady watch over her. Then there were those times she had managed to slip off and behave in the most unseemly manner while placing herself in danger.

Max smiled. Billie possessed a spirited soul that no amount of taming could control. He realized that was the very quality that drew him to her. She challenged him when no other woman ever did. And she didn't deny her passion; she embraced it, welcomed it, welcomed him.

He had not thought overly long about marrying her under

the disguise of John. He hadn't wanted to lose her, so marriage was the simple solution, especially since he was so deeply in love with her. He smiled to himself again. He actually had his given name placed on the marriage certificate, having filled the document out himself and having the visiting vicar sign it in haste. Billie had only questioned him once about the certificate and he had informed her he had placed it away for safekeeping.

She was legally and eternally his.

When the time was right, all he had to do was explain his charade.

"You're here," Billie said, entering the study and closing the door behind her before locking the latch.

"You did instruct me to meet you here this afternoon if I remember correctly." He kept his smile focused on her. She looked stunning in the soft blue Empire-waist dress, her blond hair riotously escaping from the pins that failed to hold the wild strands.

Billie clapped her hands like a happy child. "I'm so pleased with last night's instructions."

Max played ignorant. "You succeeded with only one lesson in getting your husband into bed?"

"Not exactly," she said with less enthusiasm. "But I did manage to arouse him sufficiently enough and I feel things would have progressed most successfully if he hadn't been called away to a needy villager."

Max got up and walked around to the front of the desk, bracing his long, lithe form against the shiny wood. He leaned his hands against the edge of the desk, making certain Billie was treated to a full view of his body.

He had purposely worn extra-tight black breeches, with black riding boots that hugged his calves and he had left this white linen shirt opened sufficiently enough to entice and invite. His dark hair was loose and free around his shoulders and he knew from the heat in her eyes that his tempting appearance sparked her passion.

"Then perhaps with another lesson you will succeed."

Billie fussed with a loose pin in her hair. "I have no doubt. John is such a dear and so caring and loving, I don't see how he'll be able to stop—"

"From fumbling," Max finished.

Billie turned a cute smile on him. "He didn't fumble last night. His hand turned quite intimate and his caresses evoked a deep yearning within me. I ashamedly begged him to make love to me. I desperately wanted him."

Max recalled her plea, the words so plain and simple yet they had flamed him to a maddening arousal that had taken him the rest of the night to bring under control. And which was presently beginning to return in full force.

"Perhaps you don't need another lesson," he said, thinking any temptation right now might push him beyond the point of control.

Billie shook her finger at him. "You promised you would help me. I do so want to surprise John this evening. He does so many wonderful and endearing things for me that I want to make our first intimate moment together easy for him."

Max grew annoyed at the way she spoke so lovingly of John. "He should be concerned over making your first time together easy for you."

Billie immediately defended her husband. "John would. That's why he is hesitant about consummating our marriage. He wants to make certain that we know each other well enough, leaving us comfortable and completely trusting of each other."

"He's not a saint, he's just a man," Max snapped.

"A shy man. A man who sometimes cares too much," Billie said and as she looked at Max, her husband, she realized that he could only demonstrate those qualities as John, never as the lord of Radborne Manor. And she suddenly swelled with love for her two decidedly different but so very much alike husbands.

She walked over to him and eased herself against him, her head resting on his chest, her legs slipping between his spread ones and her arms encircling his waist.

"Teach me more."

A shiver that felt like teasing and tempting fingers crawled up his spine. She sounded like a lustful woman begging for fulfillment. And his blood raged with a passionate fury.

He wanted her naked and stretched out beneath him.

His voice was low and harsh when he spoke. "Rub against me."

She didn't hesitate. She obeyed, moving her body in a slow, steady rhythm exactly where he had intended her to.

He swelled rapidly and pressed into her, roughly cupping her buttocks and pushing her closer against him.

Her lips found his bare chest and she proceeded to taste him as she had done last night.

"That's it, Belinda, show me how much you want me, let me feel it, taste it," he urged with a ragged breath.

Her hands slipped inside his shirt, running wildly over his flesh, licking and kissing wherever her mouth wandered.

"Feel how hard I am for you," he whispered roughly, urging her against his bulging erection. "Feel how hard you made me."

Billie was quickly losing control of her senses; if she wasn't careful she would beg Max to take her here and now on the carpet. The thought of them rolling naked on the dark brooding colors inflamed her even more and she realized she needed to regain control. She had a plan that she had to follow, no matter how difficult. No matter how aroused her husband felt against her. No matter how much she wanted to feel him penetrate and pulsate inside her.

He kissed her temples, her forehead and she lifted her face to him. He took her lips and she let him. She had to taste him just a little, just briefly.

Max feasted like a starved beast on her.

Bloody hell, but he wanted her, ached for her, needed her.

"Billie." Her name spilled with agonizing torture from his lips.

With a willpower Billie cursed, she pulled away from him and caught and steadied her heavy breath before she spoke.

"Good Lord, that's a fantastic lesson. I'm certain John will be thoroughly seduced to the point of aching madness and beg *me* to make love with him."

Max felt the fury rage inside him. He bloody hell was preparing her for himself and this charade was completely and utterly driving him out of his mind.

He didn't know who he was anymore or if Max or John should make love to her. He only knew that if he didn't bed his wife soon he was going to go stark raving mad.

He sent Billie an angry growl and stomped out of the room, fearful if he remained he'd throw her on the floor and take her like some wild primitive animal in the throes of heat.

Billie watched with startled eyes as he fought with the lock, flung the door open, smashing it against the wall and marched down the hall out of sight.

"I guess he forgot he's a ghost and should disappear in a puff." She laughed to herself, deciding her plan was proceeding nicely. Right now, though, she needed to clear her mind and stem her passion and a brisk walk to the village would do just that.

The day was warm and sunny, a prelude to summer's fast approach. Billie draped a white knitted shawl around her shoulders, having discovered even on warm days the coastal breeze could prove cool.

She inspected the ornate stone planters arranged along the manor's front steps, smiling cheerfully at the rich, perfumed scent and barrage of colors the numerous plants produced. She had artfully mixed wildflowers with the more pampered garden variety and the match had proven successful; the colorful plants thrived.

Billie took her time walking, stopping to admire plants that sprouted here and there along the roadside. She wanted to learn as much as she could about St. Clair's growing climate so she would better understand the planting season and the area plants themselves.

Once in the village she stopped at the apothecary shop

and purchased a few healing herbs for various ailments, deciding it always paid to be prepared. She moved on, exchanging pleasantries with several villagers before she reached the Cox Crow Inn.

She entered the inn, the scent of freshly baked scones filling the air. Bessie and Marlee occupied a corner table, enjoying afternoon tea and hot scones.

Bessie stood. "Would you care to join us, my lady?"

Billie hurried over to the table. "I'd love to. The scones smell positively delicious. Did you make them, Bessie?"

Bessie poured Billie tea and placed a warm scone on a plate then put it in front of Billie. "I surely did."

Billie spread a generous portion of honey butter on the scone and took a bite. She sighed appreciatively and after taking a sip of her tea she spoke. "Exquisitely delicious. You truly are a wonderful cook."

Bessie beamed with pride.

Marlee agreed. "That she is."

Billie decided it was best to probe for answers in a more indirect way. "The village appears to be prospering."

"Thanks to you," Marlee said. "You have created much-needed work for the villagers. Bessie has hired two extra women to help her fill your sewing orders and you have kept several of the men busy with the work on the manor."

It was Bessie's turn to compliment. "You've also hired a gardener, stable help and extra house staff."

"The manor is too large for Matilda to see to the numerous duties herself. She requires help during the day," Billie said, attempting to explain, though she had learned from conversation with Matilda and Pembrooke that the manor had supported a good portion of the village and with Max's supposed death St. Clair had suffered. She had decided to remedy that immediately.

"The villagers are grateful," Marlee said with a nod.

Billie sent her a smile. "I appreciate their gratitude. It's nice to be part of a village that cares so closely for each other."

"That we do," Bessie agreed. "We always look out for one another. That's how we survive."

"You all must know each other well," Billie said.

Bessie was about to answer when Marlee interrupted. "We know enough, but we don't pry."

Bessie heeded her subtle warning. "Everyone has a right to private matters."

"I agree," Billie said. "In Nantucket we respected one another enough to know when to offer help and when to know a matter didn't concern anyone but the family. Of course gossip still made its rounds, like it or not."

"Here as well," Marlee agreed with a slow smile.

Bessie filled Billie's empty teacup. "We always share a bit of gossip."

That left an opening for Billie. "I heard some myself recently."

Both women leaned forward ready to listen.

Billie continued. "I heard two men over St. Simon's way were taken in by the magistrate for aiding in a wrecking."

"Rubbish," Bessie said and failed to catch the wide-eyed warning that Marlee sent her. "Most wreckings along the coast are done by women."

It was Billie's turn to stare at Bessie. "Women?"

Marlee jumped in. "We heard tell from time to time."

Bessie realized her mistake and rushed to correct it. "That's right. We've heard women get involved as well as men."

Billie nodded. "Really, how interesting." Her casual response hid her excitement. The two women had provided her with much-needed information. She was almost certain now that a woman in St. Clair was involved with the wreckings and the villagers were protecting her and perhaps even helping her.

She finished her tea and scone, turning the conversation to everyday chatter and shortly bid the two women good day. She strolled back to the manor, her mind busy with her recent discovery.

Why would the manor be involved with the wreckings? Oran had aided smugglers, but wreckers were another matter. The caves were in perfect access to the coast and were readily available for storing smuggled goods and moving the goods from there as well.

Wreckers could just as well make use of such an advantageous position. Had the wreckers threatened Oran?

She highly doubted Oran would have taken such threats lightly. He would have immediately seen to the matter and to his favor.

Billie shook her head as she walked through the open gates of the manor. She ignored the newly planted ivy that clung to the iron fence and that eventually would wind its way around the gates' spikes. Her mind was just too busy and confused. The only common denominator in this mystery was the manor; therefore, she had to assume it was the manor's strategic position that the wreckers sought. And of course, if the manor's owner would not oblige the wreckers then the answer was obvious: dispose of him.

She stopped in her tracks, wrapping her shawl more snugly around her, feeling suddenly chilled. She presently owned Radborne Manor. Did that place her in danger? Had the supposed thief that knocked her unconscious been after information regarding her and not coins?

Her eyes searched out the manor, so different from when she had first viewed it, so dark and foreboding to visitors. Now it called out a friendly welcome.

The front door opened and John stepped out and waved to her. She returned an eager wave and realized she wasn't the sole owner of the manor, nor had she ever owned the manor. Maximillian was not dead; therefore, the manor remained his. But no one was aware of this, leaving her the existing owner—along with her new husband, John. Had Max planned this all along? She had many questions for him to answer, though at the moment they could wait. She had more pressing matters to attend to.

She hurried her steps toward her waiting husband, anxious to proceed with her own plans.

Tonight she would unmercifully seduce her husband.

Chapter
Twenty-Seven

"Enough," John said with a shout and rolled out from beneath his wife with such a force that he rolled right off the bed.

Billie inched her head off the edge of the bed to peer down at her husband, who lay sprawled on his back, his glasses crooked across his face. "Are you all right, dear?"

John sent her a scathing look. "Whatever the devil has come over you, behaving so—so wantonly?"

Her lips pouted. "I assumed it was my duty to please you."

John stood, stuck his shirt back in his breeches, straightened his skewed glasses and took several steps away from the bed, placing himself a safe distance away from Billie. She had pleased him all too well; he hurt in his desire for her.

"We need to learn more about each other before we attempt intimacy."

Billie rolled back on the bed, twirling the open ties that exposed her plump breasts. "Intimacy will teach us more."

Bloody hell, but she was too intelligent, he thought. His eyes fixed on the ends of the white silk ties that she purposely brushed across her nipples. She didn't need any lessons in seduction. She was far more knowledgeable in the art than she realized.

"Not yet," he snapped, annoyed with this god-awful predicament that didn't allow him to make love to his wife in either disguise.

Billie sat up in the middle of the bed, crossing her legs and draping her nightdress just high enough over her thighs to offer a peek. The thin strap of her night rail drooped off her shoulder and the ties across her chest fell loose, leaving her breasts exposed to his full view.

"I grow tired of waiting, John. I want you. Don't you want me?" Her voice was softly seductive and highly persuasive.

The bulge in his breeches clearly demonstrated his need, though his response denied the obvious. "Not yet."

"Why?" she asked with feigned disappointment. "Don't you love me?" She hugged herself as if his rejection of her hurt and she needed comfort.

He silently berated himself for causing her distress and he reluctantly returned to the bed. He reached down and with his one finger tipped her chin up. "I love you more than you will ever know."

She ran her hand up his arm, caressing him. "Then join with me and seal our love."

He wanted nothing more than to join with her. He ached to bring their bodies together as one and settle this charade, but the time wasn't right.

"Soon," he assured her in a whisper and leaned down to kiss her gently. He pulled away before she could arouse him any further and walked to the end of the bed.

"I don't understand," she said, playing the part of the young, injured wife all too well.

"You will," he said convincingly. "Now get some sleep

while I go prepare my sermon for Sunday services tomorrow morning."

Billie sighed her disappointment and slipped beneath the counterpane. "Will you be long?"

"Yes," was his quick reply. "Very long. Now sleep."

Billie watched as he almost ran from the room and she burst with laughter when the door closed behind him. She was having a grand time seducing him, though she grew tired of the seduction never ending in fulfillment. She would have to rectify that soon.

Yes, very soon she would allow him to discover the truth and then . . . She snuggled beneath the covers, a smile spreading across her face.

Billie ushered Marlee into the receiving parlor, having been all prepared to leave for Sunday services. John had left for the church over an hour ago and she had little time to spare if she was to arrive on time.

Marlee refused the offered seat and stood wringing her hands. "I knew you'd be alone now. I waited until I saw Pembrooke and Matilda leave."

Her nervousness worried Billie. "Is there something wrong, Marlee."

She bobbed her head and squinted her eyes, the numerous wrinkles highlighting her age. "I had to come."

"What is it?" Billie urged in a gentle tone.

"I've come to warn you to mind your business when it comes to the wreckings. You're placing yourself in far more danger than you know."

"What danger? Why?" she asked, curious that this woman should make a point of warning her. Her actions demonstrated her concern, which lead Billie to believe that she knew much about the wreckings and possibly the identity of the person in charge.

Marlee shook her head. "Don't ask questions, leave it be."

"How can I?" Billie argued. "When it affects the manor and possibly my safety."

"No harm will come to you," Marlee assured anxiously.

"How can you be sure? Oran Radborne is dead and so is Maximillian." She crossed her fingers behind her back as she lied.

Marlee grew agitated and shook her head as she headed for the door. "Just mind your business and all will be well. Please, my lady." With that last plea she hurried out of the room and out the manor's front door.

Billie watched her rush down the path and wondered what brought her to deliver such a blatant warning. Something was going on, she was certain of it and she had every intention of finding out.

Her eyes caught the time on the tall encased clock in the foyer. She would be late for services and tardiness in the vicar's wife for Sunday service would not look well for John. Unless . . .

Billie looked to where her white shawl and blue bonnet lay on the intricately carved wood chest beneath the gilt-framed mirror and reached for both. She tossed the shawl around her shoulders and threw her bonnet on her head, tying it loosely beneath her chin and rushed into the kitchen. She would take the passageway in the caves to the vicarage. If she hurried she would arrive just in time.

Her steps were spry, having exchanged her black pumps for boots. She held her pumps in one hand and a lantern in the other and made her way without incident down into the caves and to the scarred door.

Easing it open, she peeked in and found the room deserted. She smiled and hurried through the room to the other door, opening it slowly and listening for voices. Discovering none, she proceeded up the narrow steps. Once at the top she listened again for voices, easing the door open but a crack.

Silence greeted her and when she was certain the room beyond was empty she stepped in. It was John's office, where he spoke with villagers and handled the business of being a vicar.

She extinguished the lantern and after exchanging her

boots for her pumps she deposited them on the top step of the secret passageway to collect later.

With a tug of her shawl and a pat of her bonnet, Billie hurried from the vicar's office, through the small vestibule where John always emerged from into the church and where Billie quietly exited, taking her seat in the vicar's family pew.

John stood at the pulpit about to start services when he watched his wife hurry into her seat. He smiled at her, having been concerned by her tardiness and worried over her safety.

She returned his smile, folded her hands in her lap and directed her full attention on him.

He realized she was attempting her best behavior, probably feeling guilty over last night and the way she unashamedly had—

His thoughts ceased in an instant and he turned his head casually to his right before turning back to focus on the congregation that waited patiently for him to begin.

She had entered from the vicar's vestibule, not through the front doors as she normally did and she had been late. There could only be one reasonable explanation for why she entered from where she did. She had to have come from the caves, through the room below and through the vicarage. Which meant . . .

He turned another smile on his innocent wife who sat so proper and pious with folded hands. She *bloody hell* knew his secret. She knew he was Maximillian Radborne. That explained why she had asked him to teach her to seduce John and why she was wickedly tormenting him with her seductive ways. She was punishing him for tricking her.

His expression turned somber and he grasped the edges of the pulpit firmly as his strong, stern voice carried out across the sea of intent faces. "Today I will speak on the duties of marriage and the role of a proper wife to her husband."

The men bobbed their heads and the women tried to keep from shaking theirs. Billie retained her smile, never taking her eyes off her husband as he delivered his reproachful ser-

mon on wifely duties with a strong emphasis on obeying
one's husband.

Later that evening, Billie invited her husband to join her
in bed, suggesting that the day had been most tiring and they
both could use the rest.

John claimed that he had work to do and that he would
join her later. Billie didn't argue. She assumed that Max
would make his appearance instead and that was fine with
her. One way or another her husband would join her in bed
tonight.

Billie didn't have long to wait. She had just discarded her
garments and slipped on her silk, lilac, full-length robe
when Max stepped out of the shadows.

She greeted him with a smile. "Just in time for a lesson."

"I was thinking the same myself," Max said and proceeded to shed his clothes.

Startled, Billie knotted her silk belt at her waist. "Whatever are you doing?"

He gave a careless toss to his boots and stockings, landing
them near the foot of the bed. "I'm advancing our lessons
since what we've covered thus far hasn't proven successful." He tore his shirt off, sending it flying to drift down over
the chair near the cold hearth.

Billie put a safe distance between them, avoiding the bed.
"I'm satisfied with the lessons thus far."

Max shook his head and began to strip off his breeches.
"I'm not."

Billie turned her back on him. "Well, I am. Now leave
your clothes on, this is not at all proper."

"You want your husband in bed, don't you?" His warm
breath flushed her neck and she shuddered.

"I—oh!"

He yanked her back against him and through the silk she
could feel his complete nakedness. His fingers worked on
the knot at her waist while his teeth nipped along her sensitive neck.

"I'm certain this lesson will end with you and your husband making love," he said between the soft nips that he continued down along her shoulder.

Billie agreed with him. This lesson would result in their coupling, but this was Max, not John, and he had yet to learn his lesson.

"You feel so good, Belinda," he whispered against her ear as his fingers freed the silk ties at her waist and eased the garment off, the silk drifting down her body until it pooled at her feet.

They both stood naked.

His hands roamed over her slowly, exploring every inch, caressing every curve and mound.

She attempted to retain her sanity. "You're seducing me when you're supposed to be teaching me to seduce you."

He spun her around to face him, steadying her with his hands at her waist. "Reverse the roles then, and touch me."

If she touched him she would never stop. "No!" The harsh whisper rushed from her lips and she forced herself to pull away.

His hands remained at her waist and he matched each step she took back. "But you want your husband naked in your bed, don't you?"

"Yes—*my husband*," she said, continuing to step back.

He continued to follow. "Then this will surely drive him to your bed. He'd have to be a monk to deny you."

She kept her eyes on his face, fearful that if she glanced over his perfectly sculpted body and his full erection she'd be lost. She took several more anxious steps away from him and was about to speak when she felt the bed brush against the back of her legs.

She glanced over her shoulder and then back at Max.

"I told you this lesson would end with you and your husband in bed." He leaned down to claim her mouth.

She yelped in shock, ducked beneath his outstretched arm and hurried over to where her robe lay crumpled on the floor. She picked it up and slipped into it.

"Damn you, Max," she cried. "You know."

He stood with confidence and blatant disregard to his nakedness, making him all the more majestic. "Know what?"

She shook an avenging finger at him. "That you are no ghost and that you are John Bosworth, my husband."

"Which makes you my wife and means you owe me obedience." His smile was sinfully assured.

"*I* owe you?" she said incredulously and before he could respond she continued, her voice rising. "*You* owe me an explanation for this trickery of yours. Why did you lie to me?"

"I owe you only what I wish to tell you," he snapped and walked toward her.

Her finger shot out at his chest when he approached. She poked him with an emphasizing jab. "You owe me the truth and I will settle for nothing less."

"You forget I am your husband," he warned sharply.

Each word she spoke was matched with a solid jab to his hard chest. "You forget that I don't play by British rules. I'm an American."

He grabbed her finger.

She raised her chin. "I want answers and I want them now. Why did you pose as a ghost? Why as the vicar?" And with a pause to gather her courage she asked, "And why did you marry me?"

Maximillian released her finger and stood glaring down at his courageous wife. He loved her fiery nature and her strong-willed determination. And now was the time to admit all.

"My plan had been simple until you showed up."

Billie listened.

"I had assumed my uncle, being the sole heir to Radborne Manor, would return home. Several attempts had been made on my life after my father's death, the last one on All Hallows' Eve being the most blatant."

"What happened?"

"A man entered the manor and shot a friend of mine,

assuming he was me. I knew then that whoever wanted me dead would go to any extreme to succeed. So I enlisted Pembrooke's help the night of the wreck. It was a perfect time to stage my death. Afterwards my solicitor sent the letter to my uncle. I had hoped to have him help me search for the culprit, but I couldn't wait for his arrival and I wanted access to the village and its gossip, so I became the vicar, John Bosworth."

"Why didn't you just tell me all this upon my arrival?"

"I couldn't," he said with a shake of his head.

"Why not?"

"At first I didn't know what to do with you, especially after I discovered you had no family to return to. Then I found your presence suited me."

"Suited you?" she repeated.

"Yes, suited me. I discovered I liked your stubborn, quarrelsome nature."

"I am not quarrelsome."

"But I am," he said with a smile. "And you challenged that side of me, a rare quality in a woman. Normally women immediately succumb to my will. Not you. You defied me at every turn and I admired your courage.

"The changes to the manor were even beginning to grow on me. The vivid colors added life to an otherwise dull home. And, of course, I enjoyed the relationship you and the vicar shared. It allowed me to get to know the special woman you truly are."

"But why continue it, why marry me under false pretenses?"

Max's expression grew somber. "I realized you were the type of woman I wanted as a wife, the type of woman I could love more deeply than I ever thought possible. But you spoke so endearingly about John that I began to worry that he was the type of man you wished to marry."

"But you are him."

"Only part of me was him, a small part. Maximillian is who I really am and our passion was obvious, but I wasn't certain if you could love Max as much as you obviously loved John. I was jealous of myself."

"You needn't have been," she said softly. "You could have confided the truth in me."

"No, I couldn't. I feared for your safety. If anyone had uncovered my charade and realized that I was alive not only my life would be in danger but my wife's as well. So I chose to continue the charade for your protection."

He reached out, his hand cupping the side of her face, his thumb stroking her lips. "Life without you, Billie, would not be worth living. I would slay dragons for you, my lady, and gladly give my life for yours. I love you with all my heart and soul."

Tears filled Billie's eyes and her heart swelled. Max loved her, John loved her, her husband loved her.

She discarded her robe, stepped forward to press her naked body against her husband and slipped her hand behind his neck, drawing his lips to hers as she whispered, "I love you, Lord Radborne."

Chapter Twenty-Eight

Max scooped her up in his arms, carried her to the bed and lowered her down, following after her. "You've driven me to insanity, my lady."

Billie purred like a wild feline and nipped playfully at his neck. "However did I do that?"

After delivering his own teasing nips to her breasts, he answered, "You tormented me unmercifully with your lessons."

She laughed and grabbed his face in her hands. "And I loved every minute of it."

His eyes twinkled with a sensual playfulness. "Now it's my turn to torment."

She writhed beneath him and stretched her arms above her head. "I'm all yours."

"You're wicked." He laughed. "And I love your wickedness . . . and you."

He stretched his arms over hers, locking their fingers and matching her rhythmic writhing. He claimed her lips greedily and she responded with the same rapacious force.

Their overwhelming need fueled their frantic response for each other and their sensual moans blended into an erotic rhythm that matched their titillating movements.

Max used his body to arouse her while his mouth worked unforgettable magic on her senses. When she thought she would burst with the want of him, he released her hands and used his own to drive her to the brink of sensual madness, touching her with the precision of a master lover.

She shamelessly and urgently pleaded for him to take her this very instant. She insisted he take her, needed him to take her.

She paused briefly to catch her breath and cried, "You must take me. I want you deep inside me."

He smiled as he whispered, "Not yet." And lowered his head to taste the sweetness of her passion.

Billie almost jolted off the bed from the thrust of his tongue. She grabbed the bedcovers, called him names only used by seasoned seamen and begged him to end her torture.

"As you wish, my lady," he said with a soft laugh, and slipped over her, easing himself inside her until he himself could stand no more and ended his tender entrance with a forceful plunge.

They both lost complete control and mated with the primitive fervor of jungle animals in the throes of heat, wild and potent.

They lay still, drained and breathless. Tremors rippled through them and they shuddered with the aftermath of intense lovemaking.

Max rolled off her, remaining silent in an attempt to control his heavy breathing and calm his racing heart. He reached his hand out to his wife lacing his strong fingers with her limp ones.

"I gave you what you begged for. Are you satisfied?" he teased with a ragged breath.

With her breathing labored, she answered, "Extremely satisfied."

He gave her fingers a reassuring squeeze.

"Not fair," she said with a weak smile.

"What's not fair?" His question hinted at ignorance but his smile suggested otherwise.

Her breathing returned to almost normal and she answered, "You've had more lessons than me. I need more practice."

He laughed with delight and kissed her gently. "You are too precious, my love, and I am lucky to have found you, and I am lucky to have you love me without restraints."

"I'll always love you, Maximillian, and I'm glad that you are no ghost."

He threw the bedcover over them before gathering her to rest comfortably in his arms. "I must remain a ghost."

"Why?" she asked, confused, and then suddenly realized the reason. "You would still be in danger."

"As well as you. Your marriage to the vicar affords you some protection and I had hoped the culprit would approach John and make him an offer."

"What offer?"

"Payment to use the manor as a central point for wrecks and smuggling."

"He would never," she said indignantly.

"Thank you for the confidence."

She laughed. "I forget you both are one. What would you have done if approached?"

"I would have proudly fumbled my way through the exchange, making myself appear the passive, frightened fool and then, having discovered the person's identity, taken the appropriate steps to see him and his cohorts jailed for life."

"Were you approached after your father's death with such a request?"

He shook his head. "My actions and outspoken condemnation of such abhorrent activities made it clear that I would not tolerate such a ludicrous proposition."

"Put your foot in your mouth, did you?" she teased with a poke of her elbow to his ribs.

"That I did, but my father's senseless death left me livid and I sought nothing but revenge."

She offered her sincere sympathy. "I'm sorry about your father. He is a wonderful man."

"Billie," he said calmly and with regret. "You do realize my father is dead?"

She sprang up and jabbed him in the chest. "Your father is truly a magnificent ghost. I love when he materializes through the bushes and walls and . . ."

He looked at her strangely while she tapped her finger to her lips and searched the room with an intent stare.

"Where is the secret passageway which enables you to enter this chamber?"

"To the left of the wardrobe near the corner of the room and where the shadows conveniently seal my entrance."

"Where else in the house?"

"Secret passages run throughout the house, connecting room after room."

"That was how I heard you that day in the receiving parlor when you visited as John?"

"Yes," he said and explained. "Instead of leaving the manor, I slipped through the passage behind the foyer mirror—"

She interrupted. "Where I saw you the day after my arrival."

He grinned with guilt. "If you hadn't been so shocked and intimidated you would have realized there was no glass. The glass is on a panel that slides into the wall where I keep a change of clothing for John and Max."

"And where you changed that day into Max."

He nodded. "Correct. I needed time to make the transformation, so I changed in the passageway in the receiving parlor while we spoke."

"And when we were alone—"

He finished for her. "I waited until you were distracted

and not facing me and I transformed my gentle vicar's tone to—"

It was Billie's turn to finish. "Max's demanding one."

"Correct again," he said and pulled her down across him. "And Max the demanding one is now going to demand that you keep your nose out of this investigation. I will handle it from this point on. I don't want any harm to come to you."

Billie ignored his orders. "I assume that since Pembrooke aids you in your charades that Matilda is also familiar with your dual characters?"

"Of course, and I must add that she was thrilled when you and John announced your intentions to marry."

Billie gasped. "Our marriage, is it legal?"

Max caressed the small of her back with his hand. "I made certain of it."

"Then I am legally your wife?"

"Yes," he said and tugged her back into his arms. He kissed her gently, running his hand intimately over her soft flesh.

She sighed contentedly, her own hand searching his nakedness.

"Billie," he whispered near her ear as his hand slipped between her thighs.

"Mmm" was her only response.

"You will obey my orders and cease all investigations into this matter. *I insist.*"

"Mmm," she answered again, arching up to greet his fingers and purposely ignoring his warning. He would learn soon enough she would not follow his dictates.

Her moans of pleasure and urgent response to his touch drove all rational thought from his mind. He wanted her and she him; nothing else mattered, nothing. But a tiny nagging voice echoed a reminder that his wife was far from obedient and dutiful even when it came to their lovemaking.

And with a pleased smile he proceeded to make love to his wife.

* * *

Billie and Claudia sat in the conservatory; sharing afternoon tea.

"I always loved this room," Claudia said, choosing a small cherry fruit tart from the silver serving tray. "And you have managed to only add to its beauty."

Billie chose a raspberry tart and sat back in the white wicker chair to enjoy it. "I really only added a few choice pieces of furniture from the attic and naturally, with the onset of summer, a multitude of plants."

"Stunning," Claudia said before taking a bite of the cherry tart and glancing around the room, which was brimming with hanging planters of greenery and an explosion of color. Soft pinks mingled with deep pink flowers that sprawled over the pot's edges peering down on admiring viewers. White and red dovecotes complemented each other beautifully in overflowing baskets bunched together beside tables and chairs. Daisies, bright as the summer sun, peeked between spiked greens in Chinese ceramic planters that sat atop several tall marble column plant stands.

"I love flowers. They give such pleasure and beauty," Billie said, after finishing her tea. She decided to discover just how much Claudia knew about village gossip. "I had the strangest warning yesterday."

Claudia observed her with motherly concern. "Warning? Someone threatened you?"

"No, it was a warning . . . from Marlee."

Claudia appeared confused. "What in heaven's name would Marlee warn you about?"

"In all honesty I think I am getting close to discovering the identity of the person in St. Clair who commands the wreckers."

"Nonsense, my dear," Claudia said with a gentle pat to Billie's hand. "I would be aware of any nefarious activity of a local. You are searching in the wrong place."

"Then why the warning?"

Claudia shrugged. "I couldn't say. Perhaps she's searching for a good tale to spin."

"She appeared serious to me."

"Who appeared serious about what?"

Startled by her husband's unexpected and suspicious entrance, Billie jumped.

Claudia patted her own chest. "Good gracious, John, your entrance was much too light-footed; you would almost think you were a ghost."

Billie sent him a skeptical glance. "Wherever did you come from?"

"The church," he said softly, and leaned down to kiss her cheek.

She whispered in his ear. "That's not what I meant."

He smiled and kissed her again, this time lightly on the lips. "I've missed you."

Claudia beamed. "I knew you would be good for him, Billie. He was so stodgy that I feared he would never meet a woman. But marrying you has changed him."

Billie decided to tease her husband. "If the women of the village only knew the other side of him." She reached out to where he stood beside her chair and took her husband's hand.

Claudia raised a curious brow and Max squeezed her hand in warning before unlocking their fingers and taking the seat beside her.

Billie ignored him. "He's so tender, so loving and . . ." She paused briefly, running her hand slowly from his padded shoulder down his arm. Her thoughts rushed to his muscled flesh that lay hidden beneath the padding of the gray garments he wore and she finished with a whispered ". . . And so passionate."

Claudia coughed softly, her hand covering her smile.

Her remark had the desired effect: John blushed, though she was certain Max steamed.

"This is not a proper conversation, Billie," he warned and fumbled with his glasses.

Billie appeared contrite, her hand moving to his chest, slipping inside his coat and stroking him much too personally. "I'm so sorry, it's just that I love you so very much."

"How very lovely and so romantic," Claudia said with a sigh.

"I can't get enough of him," Billie said, her hidden fingers brazenly teasing his taut nipple beneath his shirt.

John closed his hand over her wrist and slowly pulled her hand away, but not before she flicked her thumb across the hardened peak and felt her husband shudder.

"I love you just as much, my dear," he said, though his voice sounded strained.

"This does my heart good," Claudia said tearfully. "I had so hoped my matchmaking was accurate and now . . ." She patted her tear-filled eyes with her white lace handkerchief. "I see that you two are truly in love."

Billie reached across to caress her husband's leg. "We're just two lovebirds." Her dramatic sigh matched the one that Claudia released.

John patted his wife's hand a little too sternly before clamping it down on his leg with his own hand.

He spoke softly but with strength and verve. "You have no idea, Claudia, the extent of the emotion that I feel for my wife."

Billie smiled with exuberance and leaned over to kiss him on the cheek and whisper in his ear. "Are you aroused? I am."

He turned his head quickly to kiss her cheek and responded, "You'll pay for this."

She grinned and licked her lips suggestively and with a flourish turned to grab the serving tray, holding it up in front of her husband. "A tart?"

"Do have one, John, they are simply delicious," Claudia suggested.

He accepted the tart politely, thinking that his wife purposely acted the perfect tart and that she was blatantly aware of how much she had aroused him. He wanted her so badly that he strained against his breeches and she knew it as well. She had graciously and with a wicked smile placed a white linen napkin across his lap, concealing his bulge.

Billie fixed John a cup of tea while Claudia chatted incessantly about the qualities of a marriage filled with love.

Claudia took her leave ten minutes later, hurrying off in a flourish, having forgotten an important appointment she was to keep.

Billie as usual walked Claudia to the door to the usual disapproval of Pembrooke.

When she turned her husband stood behind her, standing straight and tall and minus his glasses, coat, waistcoat and padding.

She smiled sweetly.

He grabbed her by the arm and propelled her along the hall to his study where he released her and slammed the door, bolting it.

"You think to tease me in front of guests?" he asked, his voice sharp and his hands shedding himself of John. He yanked the mole from his face, freed his hair to fall loose and almost ripped his shirt off his body using it to wipe the makeup away and reveal Max's darker complexion.

She backed up nearer to the desk. "Now, Max, I meant no harm."

He laughed and strode toward her. "No harm?" He grabbed her hand and placed it over his swollen manhood. "You call this no harm?"

He waited for her to apologize, to weep her regret, to . . .

She stared him straight in the eyes and daringly cupped him in her hand, squeezing ever so gently.

He dropped his forehead to rest softly against hers. "You will drive me to madness."

"Can we go together?" she murmured and reached to unfasten his breeches and slip her warm hand inside to more intimately stroke him.

He moaned and shuddered as he responded to her touch, swelling and pulsating in her hand.

"I love touching you," she said in short, anxious breaths as she sought his lips.

He met her eager mouth with his impatient one and his hands sought the back of her garment, ready to tear the dress off her.

"Am I interrupting anything?" came the familiar voice of his father from behind.

Max moaned.

Billie instantly removed her hand and hastily fastened her husband's breeches to his disappointment, whispering to him, "Don't you just hate when ghosts drop in uninvited?"

Chapter Twenty-Nine

Billie walked around her husband and greeted her father-in-law with a hug and a kiss.

"I've interrupted," Oran said contritely.

"Whatever made you think that, Father?" Max said, turning around, bracing his backside against the desk and crossing his arms over his bare chest.

Oran shrugged and took a seat in one of the twin high-backed chairs in front of the cold hearth. *"Could it be your near state of undress?"*

Billie kept her smile to herself when she dropped down into the chair beside Oran.

Max mumbled beneath his breath and marched to the door, unlocking and opening it. He summoned Pembrooke with an angry shout and in moments Max was slipping into a clean shirt.

"You should knock before you enter," Max warned his father, seating himself in a chair opposite them.

"The way you always did, dear?" Billie asked with a laugh.

Max shook his head. "As you can see, she is not an obedient wife."

"But she is *the perfect wife for you,"* Oran said proudly.

Max ran a reflective glance over his wife. She was undeniably beautiful, undeniably willful and wickedly passionate . . . and she was all his. "That she is, Father."

Billie smiled with glee. "You both are so much alike, it's delightful to watch you two together."

"I am more delighted that you two *are husband and wife. I only wish . . ."* His words trailed off and he wiped the tear from the corner of his eye. *"There isn't much time left."*

"What do you mean?" Billie asked anxiously. She didn't care for his sense of finality.

"You, my dearest daughter, are going to help lay my soul to rest."

Billie felt her husband's sorrow, it was tangible and it matched her own. She didn't want to lose Oran; she loved him dearly and yet she realized that only an unselfish love could free him. It wasn't fair for him to be stranded on this earthly plane when he no longer belonged here. His spirit needed freedom and she intended to set him free.

"I must settle the mystery surrounding your death," she said, confirming her suspicions.

"It is my responsibility," Max insisted. "Billie is not to interfere or endanger her life."

Oran shook his head slowly. *"You haven't listened to me, Maximillian. I think perhaps you don't wish me to leave."*

Max stood, walked over to face the hearth and braced his arm on the mahogany mantel.

Billie empathized with her husband. If her mother or father had returned as a ghost she would have been selfish and wanted them to remain with her. The hurt and pain of losing a loved one was unbearable.

"I love you, Father," Max said softly.

Billie heard his pain and ached to comfort him, but she understood this was an emotional matter between father and son.

"And I you, my son, more than you will ever know." Oran paused to collect himself, choking back his tears. *"But we both knew this time would come. I must leave and Billie has done much in securing information to help me in making my final journey."*

Max turned and swallowed his pain though it shined ever so brightly and hurtful in his eyes. "I will help you."

"We both can help," Billie offered pleadingly.

Max shut his eyes a brief moment and shook his head. "Even if I order you to mind your business in this matter, you won't, will you?"

"Of course I won't and this *is* my business. After all, I am family."

"She has a point," Oran agreed.

"I'm outnumbered," Max said and threw up his hands in surrender.

"Good," Oran said and rubbed his hands together. *"Now to get down to business. I have learned that Derry Jones has been seen around St. Clair."*

"Where?" Billie asked excitedly, moving to the edge of her seat.

"You're not to go anywhere near him," Max ordered sharply. "I will see to this Jones character."

"But I thought—"

Max interrupted her. "You will pursue your investigation into this mysterious person that you insist is the mastermind behind the wreckers."

Oran reached out and patted her hand. *"He's right, Billie. You should continue to search for this person."*

Billie was about to object most vehemently when she caught the conspiratorial wink that Oran sent her. "I suppose I should. The person's identity may prove to be worthwhile."

"Precisely," Max said. "And I shall see to Derry Jones."

"Good," Oran said and stood. *"Now I shall leave you both to handle matters and bid you a good day."*

"Father," Max said anxiously.

Oran smiled sadly. *"I will return, my son, and we will talk more."*

Max nodded and watched his father disappear into a puff of smoke and fade away.

Billie walked over to her husband and reached for his hand, locking their fingers tightly together. He looked down at her and her heart swelled with sorrow for his pain.

"I thought I would never get over his death and now I must go through the pain again."

"I will be here for you," she said softly.

Max kissed her gently. "That means so very much to me."

She kissed him back, lingering on his lips until she finally whispered, "Make love to me."

Max scooped his wife up into his arms. "I don't know what I would do without you."

"You'll never get a chance to find out," she teased as he carried her out of the room and upstairs to their bedchamber where he proceeded to satisfy her request.

Billie was in the kitchen the next afternoon transferring freshly baked shortbread cookies that had just finished cooling to a serving plate when Oran materialized before her eyes on the opposite side of the table where she stood.

"Good heavens, Oran, you frightened me out of my wits," she said, her hands shaking so badly that she shook the last cookie right off the wooden spatula.

"I am so sorry, my dear, but you must come with me immediately. We have no time to waste," Oran urged.

Billie dropped the spatula and untied her apron. "Whatever is the matter?"

"Derry Jones is down in the caves with one of his cohorts."

"Max isn't here."

He rushed to the pantry and grabbed her boots, answering her on his return. *"There isn't time to wait for him."*

Billie hurried out of her slippers and into the boots. She reached for the lantern.

"You can't take that."

She shook her head. "You're right. They will see the light's approach."

He nodded and activated the lever, opening the entrance to the passageway. "You will have to trust me to lead the way."

Billie didn't hesitate, she reached for his hand. "Let's go."

Their descent to the caves below was slow and frightening, the dark dampness closed in around them, reminding Billie of demon shadows swallowing them whole.

If it wasn't for Oran's sure and steady lead she was certain she would have turned around and run away in fright, though with the thick cloak of darkness covering them she would surely have lost her way. They neared the cave where she had often visited with him and he stopped to press a finger to her lips in silent warning for her to remain quiet.

She nodded and together they edged their way closer to the voices in the near distance.

"I tell you she's going to give you trouble," the rough voice said with a hollow laugh.

Billie followed Oran as he eased them through a narrow rock entrance that brought them out to a slim space behind the crates. She barely had room to breathe, her breasts brushed the high stack of wooden crates in front of her and the back of her dress dampened quickly from the sweat of the stone wall.

She listened intently while still clinging to Oran's hand. She needed to know he was there beside her, his presence, though ghostly, gave her strength.

"She'll do as I say," Derry snapped.

"She hasn't so far," the other man argued.

Billie strained to hear a response since it wasn't forthcoming. She heard only frightened gasps.

"Le-let go," the strangled voice begged.

"She'll obey me this time, understand?" Derry said.

The man sounded as if he struggled to speak and struggled to free himself. "Ye-yes."

A thud to the ground sounded his release.

"You'll gather the others and I'll have no refusals on this wreck. They're all to participate, every last one of them or there will be hell to pay. Understand?"

The other man must have nodded because Derry continued. "I'll have the finalized date and time soon."

"What about this cave? Have you spoken with the vicar?"

Derry laughed. "That stupid fool won't give us any trouble and besides, I plan to finish him and his lovely bride off after this job."

"The information I found out in the study proved enough?"

Billie tensed, realizing the other man in front of the crates was the man who had invaded her study and privacy.

"She's all alone, not a relative to give a damn about her and the same for the vicar. The manor will sit empty long enough for us to finish the jobs planned, store the necessary booty and then we can move on."

The other man grunted as if annoyed. "If that Maximillian Radborne hadn't stirred up so much fury over the wrecks and smuggling activity we could remain."

"If you had finished him off the first time like I told you to, he wouldn't have had time to get the other lords all riled up and the magistrates involved."

The man attempted to argue. "He was a smart one, not like his father."

This time Oran stiffened and Billie squeezed his hand in reassurance.

"Yeah, you took him down fast even though he tried to protect that stupid woman," the man continued.

Billie shut her eyes. What woman would Oran protect with his life? A woman he loved? A woman that loved him? Who in the village . . .

She didn't need to hear the name that spilled from Derry's lips, she knew.

"Claudia Nickleton is far from stupid. She ran this wrecking operation with the other women for a whole year before I came along."

"Then why did she let you in on it?"

"She didn't have a choice. After I killed Oran Radborne I threatened her. She was frightened for her life as well as the lives of the other women involved."

"Why not do away with her?"

"Because she has the connections when it comes to the ships' cargos and their departure times." A throaty laugh sounded from Derry. "But when I was away I made my own connections, and after this wreck I won't need the Nickleton woman anymore. So after this wreck is when we'll rid ourselves of the old lady and the vicar and his wife."

Their voices began to fade as they walked away, discussing Claudia, Billie and Max's demise.

Billie stood frozen in disbelief. "Clau—"

"*Shhh,*" Oran cautioned with a whisper. "*Sound carries in these caves. We'll wait.*"

She nodded, her thoughts focused on all she had heard. Everything made sense now. The women were protecting themselves and Claudia. They were fearful for Claudia's life as well as their own. And Oran had given his life for Claudia because . . .

"You loved her, didn't you?" Billie whispered.

Oran spoke softly. "*Since we were young. I had wanted so very much to marry her. I pleaded with my father to secure a marriage arrangement with her family, but he refused. He explained quite calmly that she wasn't of the proper lineage to become an earl's wife.*"

Oran shook his head, his sadness almost pliable. "*I pleaded with Claudia to run away with me and marry me. She refused, insisting I had a duty to my family and she to hers. Even after my wife died she wouldn't marry me.*"

His voice quivered and Billie didn't have to see to know that tears filled his eyes.

"We remained secret lovers for all these years, Claudia not wanting to cause Maximillian any embarrassment and ruin his chance in arranging a good marriage contract.

"I hadn't known that she involved herself with wrecking. The money her family had left her fell prey to bad investments and she wouldn't dare ask me for help, though I would have gladly given it to her. By the time she did seek my assistance, she was deeply involved. Everyone assumed that it was the smugglers I did business with who killed me."

Oran shook his had slowly. *"But it wasn't. Claudia told me of a meeting with the man who had invaded her business. A business she desperately wanted to abandon. I told her I would go in her place and take care of everything. She insisted on going to the meeting with me. I argued with Derry. He threatened me. He reached for his pistol as I reached for mine and I mistakenly thought he intended to shoot me. He aimed for Claudia. I threw myself in front of her as I fired and missed him."*

"And his shot found its mark," Billie finished softly.

"With my dying breath I begged her to seek Maximillian's help, but I assumed she feared for his life, and when attempts were made on his life she probably thought them a warning to her."

Oran slowly led Billie out from behind the crates after making certain no one lingered at the mouth of the cave.

Billie sat on a crate, a chill racing through her not only from her damp dress but from Oran's story.

"Why didn't you just tell Max when you returned in spirit form?"

"I couldn't bring myself to name Claudia," he said gently, sitting on the crate beside her. *"I feared what might become of her and I feared Maximillian might turn against her once he discovered her involvement in my death."*

"He never suspected in all these years that you two were involved?"

Oran shrugged. *"He was a young man who had far more important matters on his mind than his father's personal life. He always looked toward Claudia as he would a dear aunt."*

"Do you think he'll believe me when I tell him?" she asked, doubtful her husband would open his mind to the possibility that women were involved with the wreckings.

"You may need to convince him. After he finishes chastising you for disobeying him."

Billie gave her predicament thought. "Perhaps if I convince Bessie to tell him, he'll believe her."

Oran laughed. *"No woman in the village will agree to stand in front of Maximillian and confess their involvement."*

Billie grinned. "But they would confess to the vicar."

Oran slapped his knee. *"Such sharp intelligence! You will do well with Maximillian. You will challenge and encourage him and, most of all, you will love him."*

"With all my heart and soul," she promised.

He reached for her hand and she reached for his. *"Love each other as if each day was your first and last and never, never let anyone stand in the way of that love."*

"Don't worry," Billie said with confidence. "I'm too stubborn-headed to let anyone or anything interfere in my marriage. Your son belongs to me forever and ever. We'll raise a family together, grow old together and die together. I'll have it no other way."

"Neither will my son," Oran said with a laugh. He jumped to stand and scanned the cave.

Billie stood, frightened by his unexpected actions. "Are they returning?"

"No, but your husband is and I cannot remain by your side," he said with regret. *"You must face him alone and convince him of the truth and . . . you must protect him."*

"He's big enough to protect himself," she said with a laugh.

Oran shook his head and began to fade. *"No, protect him from himself."*

"Himself?" she asked, straining to hear his parting words.

"He is the lord of the manor. He will suffer the blame on himself."

"I think not," she said, her grin wide and fully confident.

Oran faded away completely but not before he sent Billie a wink.

She was standing in the middle of the cave, smiling foolishly when her husband rounded the entrance and stormed in.

He looked all the more intimidating when he dressed as himself. He stood tall, broad-shouldered and breathtakingly handsome and dressed in shades of the softest, to the deepest gray. And his temper was . . . mercurial.

He advanced on her with such quickness that her words caught in her throat. He grabbed her and roughly tossed her over his shoulder.

"What do you think you're doing?" she demanded indignantly, pounding his back, though her flying fists did little damage to the thick muscles beneath his garments.

"I'm about to teach you obedience," he said firmly and walked out of the cave.

Chapter
Thirty

Billie found herself being dropped most ungraciously in the middle of her bed. She scurried to right herself and her disheveled clothes and blew at the wisps of hair that interrupted her vision. Not that she cared to view her husband, who steadily paced by the bottom of the bed, his expression grim and his eyes brimming with fury.

"What the bloody hell were you doing down in the caves?"

Billie was certain the room shivered along with her from the intensity of his shout. She dangled her feet over the edge of the bed, shaking the oversized boots off as she answered him. "Your father requested my assistance."

"He knows I forbade you from going down there."

"This was an emergency." Billie scooted to the middle of the bed—it was less easy for him to reach her that way— and crossed her legs, tucking her stockinged feet beneath her.

She continued. "Derry Jones—"

"He was down there?" Max interrupted with a shout.

"You must listen to me, Max," she attempted.

"No," he snapped, his pacing having picked up considerably. "You will listen to me or I will lock you in this room until you do."

"I think not," she said indignantly. "And if you would mind your tongue for a minute you might—"

He abruptly stopped pacing. "Mind my tongue?"

Poor choice of words, she thought, but having already spoken she plunged on. "Yes, mind your tongue so I may explain."

"I should mind my hand to your backside for disobedience."

Billie laughed robustly. "Max, you say the funniest things."

"You think I wouldn't?" he said, bracing his hands on the bed and glaring at her.

She got to her knees and placed her hands on her hips. "I wouldn't dare if I were you. I wouldn't take kindly to be thrashed by my husband."

"And what would you do?" He stood straight and attempted to intimidate her with his imposing size.

Billie blew wisps of hair out of her eyes, raised a tight fist and shook it menacingly at him. "I'd punch you in the nose."

Max hadn't expected a violent warning from his wife nor had he expected her disheveled appearance combined with her defiant stance to arouse him so. Her strong will charged his passion and brought a devil of a smile to his face.

"In the nose? With that puny fist?" He approached from the end of the bed, crawling deliberately slow on his hands and knees toward her until he stopped in front of her and braced himself on his haunches. "Go ahead, punch me."

His threatening invitation was whisper soft and sent a shot of desire racing through Billie. She remained defiant while her insides quivered. "Are you going to thrash me?"

He removed his jacket, tossing it off the bed. "I'm going to teach you obedience." His shirt followed his jacket.

"Does that include thrashing?"

His hands unfastened his breeches. "Oh, you will thrash, Belinda."

Her lips curved in the most sensual smile. "Promise me I'll thrash."

He shook his head and to her disappointment left the bed but only to remove his boots and breeches. Then he returned, grabbing her tight fist. "No, I insist that you thrash."

He twisted it gently behind her back and kissed her with an urgency that left her breathless and aching for more. He inched his hand beneath her damp dress, caressing her leg as he ran his hand up her thigh. He eased his fingers between her legs, gently entering her wetness and teasing her with slow, consistent strokes until she moved against his hand in a steady rhythm.

"My clothes, please," she managed to say between his hungry kisses.

He obliged her and quickly stripped her of all her garments.

She fell back on the bed and welcomed him with outstretched arms.

He dropped down over her, his knees spreading hers and it wasn't long before he was buried deep inside her and they both thrashed wildly together, exploding as one in a fiery climax.

"Promise me you will thrash me often," Billie teased, stroking his back as he lay over her, regaining his breath.

He shook his head buried in the crook of her neck and then playfully bit her shoulder before raising his head.

"Mmmm, I like when you bite," she said and moved suggestively beneath him.

"You'll be the death of me," he said with a pleased smile as he nipped at her nipples, still hard from their lovemaking.

"Don't leave me," she urged, locking her legs around his waist when he attempted to move.

He shuddered when he felt her squeeze around him and was shocked to find himself swelling again. Only in his youth had he been ready so soon afterwards. He suddenly felt young and carefree.

Billie tightened her legs around him, locking him inside her. "I won't let you go."

He laughed and flicked his tongue across her nipple. "I don't want to go." He moved inside her, slow at first and then more steady, more potent, more forceful, until Billie unlocked her legs and they both became lost in their own erotic world for the next three hours.

Billie soaked in the brass tub, filled to the brim with hot rose-scented water while Max towel-dried his freshly washed hair.

"You are a very thoughtful husband," she said with a sigh of gratitude as she sank her shoulders beneath the steaming water.

He laughed, dropped the towel to the floor along with the one around his waist and walked to the wardrobe where his clothes had been added along with Billie's. "It was only fair of me to have fresh bathwater prepared for you after having forced you to share mine and do everything but wash."

She giggled and watched with admiration as her well-muscled husband slipped into his gray silk, floor-length robe. "The last few hours have been heavenly."

Max walked over to the tub and planted a kiss on his wife's wet mouth. "More like a combination of heaven and hell."

Billie smiled her agreement and hugged herself beneath the water. She was so very happy and so very much in love.

"Now for business," he said sternly and pulled a chair up beside the tub, planting himself in the chair. "Why did my father require your assistance in the caves?"

Billie sat up and soaped the sponge that floated with her in the tub. "Derry Jones and his cohort were making plans in the cave." She paused and looked Max right in the eye. "Derry plans to do away with John and me."

Max stiffened. "When?"

"As soon as this next wreck they are planning is over."

"When is the wreck?"

"He mentioned that the time and date weren't firm as of yet."

Max scratched his chin. "What else did he say?"

Billie wasn't certain how much to tell him. She feared that if she confessed all she heard that it would send him into a fury, especially when he discovered that Derry had killed his father. She decided that she would be sparing in her information until more was uncovered about this wreck and then . . .

She splashed the water over her body to rinse the soap off. "Derry named the person in St. Clair who heads the wreckers."

Max grabbed a towel from the stack on the table and stood, holding it up for his wife as she rose out of the tub. He couldn't help but admire her body, blushed pink from the hot bathwater and, therefore, shook his head when he heard . . .

"Claudia Nickleton."

Max wrapped the towel around Billie. "What did you say?"

Billie, seeing his distraction, stepped away from him and tucked the towel securely around her before she repeated, "Claudia Nickleton."

"Preposterous!" Max said with a hearty laugh.

Billie reached for another towel to dry her freshly washed hair. "I knew you wouldn't believe me."

"That's ridiculous."

"Why? Because she's a woman?"

Max nodded and Billie continued.

"Then you'll be even more surprised to discover that many of the wreckers along the coast are women."

Max stared at her, speechless.

"Most women are far from mindless, weeping fools. We are strong and resourceful, mainly because we have no choice . . . life makes us that way."

Max gave thought to Billie being entirely on her own after her mother and uncle's deaths. She probably had friends—Billie was too gregarious not to—but she had no family, no special ties that bind. He had suffered the same when he had lost his father and he suddenly understood just how precarious life actually was.

Billie attempted further explanation. "Your father tried to help Claudia. She wished to terminate her illegal activities, but Derry threatened her."

Max shut his eyes against the obvious. "And my father lost his life in the process."

"Yes, but he doesn't regret what he did for her." Billie wanted to tell him of his father's love for the woman, but she felt that it was Oran's place to explain, not hers.

Max moved to sit on the side of the bed and held his hand out to his wife. She went to him without hesitation. He tugged the towel free and proceeded to make certain she was dry all over.

"Then all we need to do is see that Derry is captured for his crimes and Claudia freed of her involvement and protected."

Billie smiled, having had no doubt Max would protect Claudia.

Max finished drying her and tossed the towel aside.

"Matilda is going to scold you tomorrow for making such a mess," Billie teased as she watched him remove his robe and toss it to the chair.

Max looked around the room. Towels were tossed about, the tub sat full, food trays littered with remnants of their meal occupied the small table and two empty wine bottles lay next to the tub.

He laughed and reached down to toss the covers of the bed back. "I'd say Matilda is going to think we had one grand evening for ourselves."

He slipped into bed and Billie surveyed the room.

"Oh my goodness," she said after realizing the room resembled a recent lovers' tryst. "I'd better straighten—"

Billie never got to finish. Max yanked her into bed and captured her beneath him.

He teased her lips and neck with ardent kisses and Billie was soon lost to her husband's lovemaking.

Billie hurried along the shops and cottages toward the Cox Crow Inn. The message she had received just a few short hours ago requested her immediate presence at the inn. She had to wait until Max had disguised himself as the vicar and gone off to perform his duties for the day before she could leave. And, of course, Max had to reiterate his instructions from the previous night that she was to *behave*.

Since he didn't completely outline and define *behave* she felt his instructions left for a wide margin of acceptable behavior—meaning she would do as she wished.

Billie shivered as a rumble of thunder sounded in the distance. All week the villagers had been talking and whispering and worrying over the approaching storm. Consensus was that a bad one was brewing and would hit in a few days. The talk sent shivers through people and most walked around concerned and mindful.

Many feared a repeat performance of the All Hallows' Eve storm and that brought the frights to everyone, with most fearing that Lord Radborne's ghost would surely walk the village on such a ghastly night.

Billie herself felt something brewing, something being drawn to a climax and the possible outcome troubled her. She had her husband's safety to concern herself with and that of Claudia and, most of all, she had the responsibility of seeing Oran's soul brought to peace. A conclusion that would undoubtedly upset her husband and herself.

She entered the Cox Crow Inn with a flourish of a summer's wind and a blast of distant thunder. Bessie and Marlee were the only occupants in the inn and, after shoving the door closed behind her and running her fingers through her windswept hair to make it more presentable, Billie hurried over to join them at the table.

"We thought you'd never come," Bessie whispered.

"I had to wait until John left for the day," Billie explained and accepted the cup of tea Bessie poured for her.

Marlee jabbed Bessie in the arm with her elbow. "Told you that was what was keeping her. I knew my lady would come when urgently summoned."

"Of course I would," Billie insisted. "Especially when you cited that it was a matter of life or death."

"That it is," Bessie agreed with several bobs of her head.

Marlee was more direct. "Mind you now, my lady, what we're about to confide in you isn't for anyone else's ears."

"I promise," Billie said sincerely as she settled herself with her hands locked around her teacup and listened.

Marlee proceeded in her storytelling manner. "You must understand that when there's a hungry child to feed, a mother doesn't stop to worry where the coins come from. What matters is that she puts food in her children's bellies."

Billie understood perfectly, recalling the many times her mother had taken in an impoverished woman and child who needed food and shelter and help in surviving the long absence of her seafaring husband.

Marlee continued. "The women who participate—" Marlee stopped abruptly to clarify "—not Bessie or me, were ordered to participate in a wrecking that's planned soon, though the date and time aren't clear."

"When will the women be notified of specifics?" Billie asked.

"Soon, I imagine," Marlee said and looked at Bessie. Bessie nodded as if urging her to continue. Marlee did, though it appeared to pain her to do so. "This isn't easy for me to tell you."

Billie took advantage of her pause. "You mean about Claudia commanding the wreckers?"

"You know?" both women said simultaneously.

Billie nodded, offering a simple explanation while skirting the truth. "I discovered her involvement by chance."

"We're worried for her," Marlee confided and Bessie confirmed with a worried shake of her head and tear-filled eyes. "Claudia only needed to make enough coins to get by like most of the women. She organized the women to work a wrecking every now and then. And they would always make certain they never hit a ship carrying passengers. They only wrecked for the cargo. The crew was always rescued and so shocked by the fact that it was women who wrecked that they kept hushed about it, too embarrassed to say otherwise.

"When Derry Jones entered the picture, all that changed. He discovered Claudia's participation and forced a partnership to help aid in his smuggling activities. She attempted on several occasions to terminate their business dealings. Derry refused to release her."

Marlee bit her trembling lip and fought back her tears.

Billie spoke the words she was certain Marlee felt. "And Claudia became a prisoner of her own making."

Marlee nodded. "She needs help."

Billie reached out and patted her hand. "I'll make certain that Claudia gets the help she needs."

"Derry's insisting that Claudia assist him with the wreck that he's planned. He tells her that he will free her of their partnership after this one, but she doesn't believe him."

"She's wise in not believing him," Billie said, recalling Derry's intention.

"But who will help?" Bessie asked. "Begging your pardon, my lady, your husband the vicar is a wonderful man, but he doesn't possess the strength or skill to face a man like Derry Jones."

"Don't worry," Billie assured them. "I'll find someone with the courage and strength to help us."

The door opened and the summer's wind whipped another person into the inn and by Marlee and Bessie's rounded eyes, Billie knew who had entered.

"Good day, ladies," John's soft voice called out as he walked over to the table.

Billie tilted her head back and John peered down over her face. "Hello, dear wife." He pecked her on the cheek and threw his leg over the bench to sit beside her. "Sharing a spot of tea and gossip?"

"We don't gossip," Bessie said with an urgent shake of her head.

John raised his brow and his tone was that of a scolding vicar. "Is that the truth now, Bessie?"

Bessie's face rushed with color. "We're not gossiping now, it's facts we're discussing."

Marlee and Billie sent her a look that warned her to hold her racing tongue.

Bessie winced and bit her lower lip as if trying to keep herself from divulging any further information.

"And what facts might they be?" John asked, looking from Marlee to his wife, who resembled an innocent young woman garbed in silk violet casually sipping her tea. He smiled at her picture of purity when beneath, he knew, she sizzled with passion.

Marlee fumbled for an acceptable explanation when Billie spoke up. "The storm that's brewing."

"Right, the storm," Bessie agreed hastily. "It's going to be a bad one."

"A bad one," Marlee echoed. "Much like the one on the night that claimed Lord Radborne's life."

Bessie spoke in a hushed and reverent tone. "Some villagers wonder if his unsettled spirit will return with the height of the storm."

"Do you ladies believe such nonsense?" John asked with the seriousness of the vicar.

Billie joined Marlee and Bessie when they nodded their heads.

"Lord Radborne's ghost has been seen, it's a fact," Marlee said.

Bessie kept nodding her head. "That's right, he has and the whole village believes in him."

"Don't you, John?" Billie asked sweetly and hooked her arm possessively around his.

"We'll see," John said with a sparkle of devilment in his eye that only his wife recognized as controlled passion.

Billie looked at the two women and ignored her husband's hand intimately inching his way up her thigh beneath the table. "Max will visit."

Marlee and Bessie's eyes rounded all the more upon hearing their lord addressed so improperly and her husband's hand came to an abrupt halt.

"And why is that?" John asked.

Billie stared him straight in the eye. "His spirit must face the man who caused his death."

Chapter Thirty-One

"I forbid it!" Max yelled and smashed his fist down on the desk, emphasizing his command. "You almost sent those two women into apoplexy by calling me Max and insisting that my ghost would return for revenge. I'll return for revenge all right, but you won't be involved."

Billie stood her ground, her arms crossed over her chest and her toe tapping impatiently on the carpet. "Claudia will not confide in you. She will confide in me and without her valid information, you will not know when the wrecking will take place."

Max attempted to hold his temper and to do so he walked straight for the liquor cabinet and poured himself a generous glass of whiskey.

"Whatever is the problem?" Oran asked materializing through the cold hearth.

Max shook his head, taking a hefty swallow.

"My *husband*," she emphasized, "will not allow me to participate in the capture of Derry Jones."

"As well he shouldn't," Oran agreed.

"Thank you, Father," Max said in relief. "Finally someone who understands the danger in her intentions."

"Much too dangerous, Billie," Oran warned. *"This Derry character has no scruples. He kills without remorse and cares only for himself. Leave this to Max."*

Maximillian looked at his father. "Max?"

Oran shook his head. *"I am so accustomed to hearing Billie call you thus that I forget I always called you Maximillian."*

Max took another swallow before he asked the one question that had haunted his thoughts day and night. "When this is settled with Derry, you will pass on?"

Oran nodded. *"Immediately."*

A crack of thunder reverberated in the room. Billie jumped, startled by the blast, but Max and his father remained staring at one another.

"Will we have time to say good-bye?" Max asked.

Oran responded with sorrow. *"I fear not."*

"Then we must see to that now," Max said and Oran nodded.

Billie quietly slipped out of the room, slowly closing the door behind her, allowing father and son to share their last good-bye alone. She turned to hurry to the kitchen and bumped into Pembrooke.

"Max doesn't wish to be disturbed," she told him, realizing he was headed for the study.

Pembrooke winced. "His lordship may need my—"

Billie interrupted, grabbing his arm and directing him along with her toward the kitchen. "Max is presently attending to a private matter and insisted he doesn't wish to be disturbed and *I insist* his wishes be obeyed."

Matilda looked up from putting a fire beneath the kettle as Billie and Pembrooke entered the kitchen, arms locked.

She smiled at her frowning husband. "Remember what our lordship advised us."

Billie almost giggled at Matilda's reminder. After Billie had learned of his dual identity, Max had instructed the couple that the lady of the manor was a trifle different and that they should attempt to understand her unusual ways and help her to understand her duties.

Billie released Pembrooke's arm and ordered sternly, though with a smile, "I need the carriage brought around."

"My lordship has ordered that my lady is not to go anywhere without his permission," Pembrooke informed her smugly.

"When did he do that?" Billie asked.

"Upon your return from the village this afternoon."

Matilda attempted to comfort. "The storm has worsened, my lady. You wouldn't want to be out there on such a ghastly night."

Billie felt a chill run down her spine. *Tonight*, the wrecking was planned for tonight. She knew it, she could feel it.

She almost flew out of the kitchen and upstairs. She raced through her wardrobe, finding her oldest, most worn cotton dress and black high boots. She changed quickly. Grabbing her black cloak and throwing it around her, she rushed down the steps.

The front door closed behind her with a soft click, but Pembrooke saw and heard and looked with concern at the closed study door.

It took Billie longer than usual to walk to Claudia's. It was the wind that made her walk difficult. It blew at her with strength and determination, as if attempting to prevent her from reaching her destination. The heavy rain started when she was but a few feet from Claudia's front door and by the time she knocked, pellets of rain pounded the earth furiously.

The storm exploded like an unleashed temper, pounding angry rain against ground and buildings. Wind violently whipped across the land, lightning speared the night sky and thunder beat such a wild cadence that it made her cover her ears in fright.

"Good Lord, child, whatever are you doing out on such a horrid night?" Claudia said, rushing Billie into the house.

Billie threw the hood of her cloak back. "I've come to help you stop Derry."

Claudia paled and staggered back to drop down on the plain wooden bench in the foyer. "However did you find out?"

"That isn't important at the moment. What is important is that the wrecking is tonight, isn't it?"

Claudia nodded. "The ship's departure time was moved, hoping it would be out to sea before the storm hit."

Billie rushed to Claudia's side, going down on bent knees beside the older woman and grabbing her hand in support.

"I never wanted this," Claudia pleaded. "Never. I hurt the very people I loved the most and Lord, how I loved Oran. I was so wrong. So weak." She shook her head, her round eyes filled with a mixture of sadness and tears. "And tonight it ends. I have caused too much pain and sorrow for everyone. No more—it is time for me to take responsibility for my mistakes."

"What do you mean?" A shiver ran through Billie.

It was Claudia's turn to comfort. "It's time, dear, this must end."

"The ship—"

"Left port yesterday and is out to sea. There will be no wrecking."

"Derry will kill you when he discovers you betrayed him," she said, her knees going weak and her stomach tumbling.

The rapid knock on the door startled them both. Billie rushed to see who was there. The harsh wind blew in Marlee and Bessie.

Both women looked fearful. They ignored Billie, and Marlee directed her frantic news to Claudia.

"The women are hiding in their homes as you ordered and they're frightened to death."

Claudia stood, reaching for her dark green cloak on the brass hook near the door. "They'll be safe there."

"What are you doing?" Bessie asked anxiously. "You don't mean to be going out on a night like this and with that *man* waiting for you?"

"I must take care of matters once and for all," Claudia said firmly.

Marlee blocked the front door, her arms spread wide. "I won't let you go out there."

Billie spoke before anyone else could. "We need to return to the manor, Ma—" She caught her mistake and amended it to, "John will know what to do."

All three women looked at her as if she had lost her mind.

"Trust me." Billie insisted. "John will take care of everything."

Marlee partially agreed. "The manor is a safer place to be than here."

"But the storm," Bessie argued.

Billie smiled. "I know another way."

In minutes and wet, though not soaked, the three women made their way down the steps of the secret passageway in the vicarage. They followed Billie through the room where Max changed into John and John changed into Max.

The women looked about oddly and before any of them could ask, Billie said, "I'll explain later."

Billie kept the lantern high above her head, lighting the way for them to see their path clearly. She had grown accustomed to the cave's passageways, but recalled how intimidated she felt when she had first descended down into them.

"It gives you the shivers," Bessie said and felt the tingles run over her.

"A perfect place for ghosts to haunt." Marlee sounded as if she was about to recount a tale.

"We'll be hearing none of your tales, Marlee," Bessie warned her.

"I agree," Claudia chirped. "This is not a place to discuss hauntings."

"It's not a place to be talking," Billie said softly. "Sound carries and we don't want anyone to know we're down here."

"Good advice," came the sharp, male voice.

The four women froze in the narrow passageway.

"Keep walking this way, ladies," the voice ordered.

"Derry," Claudia said firmly, "I'll not have you hurt these women."

"As long as they do their job tonight no one will get hurt," he returned.

"Good Lord," Bessie whispered. "He thinks we're here to help with the wrecking."

"Come on, we don't have all night," he shouted.

Claudia stood directly behind Billie. She grabbed at her arm and whispered. "Whatever are we to do?"

"Keep Derry talking," she murmured to Claudia, "while I talk to Bessie."

Claudia called out to Derry. "There's no need to rush."

His warning response brought another retort from Claudia and they continued to exchange shouts while Billie, after handing the lantern to Claudia, made her way back to Bessie.

"I'm assuming he doesn't know how many women are here, therefore, you are going to go for help." Billie told her in a hushed voice.

"Me?" Bessie squeaked softly and in disbelief.

"Yes you," Billie confirmed. "Just a few feet ahead is a passageway that veers to the right. As soon as you come upon it, duck in there and keep walking."

"But I'll have no light to guide me," Bessie said.

"It's a curvy passageway. Use your hands to guide you and just keeping following it. You'll come to a division. Bear to the right and follow that straight until you come to a door. Take that door up the stone steps. There's a latch at the top that will open the passageway and bring you out into the manor's kitchen. Seek John's help immediately."

Bessie voiced her fears. "I don't know if I can do this."

"Nonsense, of course you can," Marlee encouraged.

"She's right," Billie agreed. "You can do this, you must. You are our only hope."

"Enough arguing, old woman, get over here," Derry shouted angrily.

Billie gave Bessie's arm a reassuring squeeze and hurried back to Claudia, taking the lantern from her.

"Let's go," Billie said and started walking.

The three women followed Derry's voice. Bessie did as Billie had directed and slowly made her way, silently praying, along the dark passageway. The women came out in the part of the cave where Oran and Billie had often met.

Derry and a short, barrel-shaped man stood with pistols pointed at them.

Derry craned his neck to look past them. "Where's the rest of the women?"

Billie spoke up. "There are no more."

Derry stared with wide, enraged eyes at Claudia. "You expect this sorry lot to help in the wrecking?"

Claudia responded with authority. "There will be no wrecking."

Derry glared at her. "I warned you not to mess with me."

"And I warned you that I no longer wanted any part of these wreckings. The ship sailed yesterday. You will not have your wrecking tonight or ever. I will no longer tolerate this arrangement. Our business association is at an end."

"How dare you disobey me!" Derry yelled, brandishing his gun with angry waves of his hand. "Did you really think I would simply let you walk away?"

"What other choice do you have?" Claudia asked bravely.

"I'll kill you."

Billie shivered at the cold, uncaring tone of his reply.

"All of us?" Marlee asked.

The two men laughed and the short one answered. "Can't have witnesses now, can we?"

"Move," Derry ordered, waving his gun for them to precede him.

Billie took Claudia and Marlee's hands and squeezed them as they proceeded to the mouth of the cave. "He'll come, don't fear."

"Shut up," Derry warned with a shout.

The rain had abated, leaving in its wake a light mist and a swirling fog. Several lanterns had been placed along the rocky shore in preparation of the wreck and the angry sea could be heard slapping the sharp outcropping of rocks not far offshore.

Billie felt the tremble of Marlee and Claudia's hands in hers. She released them and stepped forward toward Derry, hoping to buy them time. "Do you really expect to get away with this?"

"I certainly do."

"My husband will—"

Derry laughed along with the other man. "Your husband is a fool and when I finish off the three of you, I will see to his disposal as well. Then the manor will finally be empty and I will make certain that the village women help me."

"They won't help you," Marlee insisted.

Derry wore a pleased smile. "Then they'll each meet with an unfortunate accident."

"You can't," Claudia said with a gasp.

"Who will stop me? No one has been able to so far. I rid myself of Oran Radborne, the sea took care of Maximillian Radborne for me after several of my own attempts failed and she," Derry said, pointing with his gun at Billie, "and her husband will soon be dead as will you and this other woman. I may even do away with the housekeeper and that pompous pain Pembrooke. Then the manor will be completely empty and all will be mine."

"What about the ghost?" Billie asked, the damp night settling around them and reaching in through their garments to set a chill to them.

"Wh-what ghost?" the short man asked.

"There ain't no such thing as ghosts," Derry said. "She's just trying to frighten you."

"But I saw the ghost of Radborne Manor." Billie shivered, drawing her cloak more tightly around her. "Maximillian Radborne walks the manor night after night."

"You've seen him?" the man asked, his voice trembling.

Billie nodded and looked around her with anxious eyes. "He comes and goes as he pleases, appearing anywhere on Radborne property that he wishes."

The man followed her anxious look, squinting into the fog that swirled like a heavy cloak around them. "H-h-he could appear here?"

Billie fueled the man's fear. "He's materialized right in front of me. He starts out much like this fog and then, before you know it, he's taken full form and he stands large and powerful and completely invincible."

Marlee and Claudia's wide-eyed stare was fixed on Billie and their attention on her every word.

"B-but a ghost can't hurt a living creature, right?" the man asked, his limbs trembling.

"Shut up, you stupid fool," Derry yelled. "Can't you see that she's making all this up?"

Billie ignored Derry and concentrated on answering the man. "He's done terrible things to my husband."

"He has?" Marlee asked incredulously.

Billie nodded slowly. "John is afraid to occupy the master bedchamber because of Maximillian." She had all she could do to stop from laughing since she spoke the truth, though embellished it some.

"But John's a pious man," Marlee said. "The ghost shouldn't want to hurt him."

"Y-yeah," the man agreed with a nervous stutter. "The vicar is a God-fearin' man. Why would a ghost want to do him harm?"

"Maximillian does as he wishes. He is lord of this manor and he'll have no one stand in his way," Billie said and crossed herself hastily, casting a hurried glance around her.

The short man jerked his head about, searching the area himself. "I think we should get out of here."

A distant clap of thunder sounded and caused everyone to jump in alarm.

"After we get rid of them," Derry insisted and raised his pistol.

"I think we should leave now," the man said, lowering his pistol to his side and taking several steps back.

"No, we kill them first."

"What if the ghost—"

"There is no ghost," Derry said with a sharp shout. "Ghosts don't exist. Maximillian Radborne is dead and buried in the sea. His body is out there—" Derry pointed toward the sound of the crashing waves against the rocks "—in a watery grave never to return, never to walk this land again. He's dead. Dead! Dead!"

All eyes opened so wide that they looked like full moons and they stared past Derry in shocked silence.

Derry turned himself, suddenly fearful at what drew their stunned attention. He staggered back as he stared in horror at the towering black shape that walked with powerful strides out of the fog.

The figure was tall, powerfully built, garbed in black and headed right for them. The fog even rolled aside out of his path as if fearful of this mighty demon. Thunder rumbled and lightning struck as the figure fully emerged.

Marlee fainted.

The short man ran into the sea.

And Claudia screamed, "Maximillian!"

Chapter
Thirty-Two

Derry raised his pistol, Billie screamed and Claudia threw herself in front of Maximillian.

The gunshot echoed in the late night air as Claudia fell into Maximillian's arms and he held her as they slipped down to the ground together.

Billie ran, falling to her knees beside them.

"See to her," Max ordered as he caught sight of Derry scurrying off into the fog. He gently shifted Claudia to rest in Billie's arms.

Billie removed her own cloak to throw over a shivering Claudia.

"Max, be careful," she shouted into the darkness and followed it with, "I love you." She was fearful for her husband, but more fearful for the woman who lay in her arms dying.

"I never meant . . ." Claudia swallowed against the pain.

"Don't try to talk, rest. We'll get the physician." Billie spoke with tear-filled eyes, attempting desperately to hold them back.

"No, I haven't much time . . ."

A gunshot ricocheted in the distance and Billie shut her eyes and silently prayed for her husband's safety.

"Maximillian is no ghost?" Claudia asked with difficulty.

Billie briefly explained the circumstances of Max's supposed death and his pretense as the vicar.

Claudia coughed and groaned from the pain. "He always was so intelligent. You—" She paused for a much-needed breath "—perfect for him."

Billie heard the rush of footsteps in the sand behind her and prayed that . . .

"Is she all right?" Maximillian asked, anxiously dropping down beside them.

Billie silently thanked God for answering her prayers and assumed that Derry would no longer be disturbing them.

"No," Claudia answered. "I'm dying."

"Nonsense," Max argued.

Claudia reached with a cry of pain for his hand. "I must beg your forgiveness."

"There is nothing to forgive," Max said softly.

Billie cautioned Marlee to be silent with a finger to her own mouth as Marlee, having recovered from her faint, approached them slowly. She kept her distance and listened, her eyes also brimming with tears.

Claudia spoke between pauses and pain. "I never meant for Oran to die. It was my fault. I was a fool. I should have listened to him. We should have married."

Max stared at Claudia. "You loved my father?"

"Very much."

"Why didn't you marry him?"

"Because I was a fool . . ." Her breathing grew more difficult.

Max looked lovingly at Billie and then back to Claudia. "Love is the only thing that matters."

Claudia squeezed his hand tightly. "She has taught you well. Never stop loving her."

"My heart would never allow me to," Max assured her.

Claudia looked up at Billie. "If only I had possessed your courage, I wou . . ."

Her words trailed off, her eyes closed and she whispered, "Oran."

Tears ran from Billie's eyes and Marlee stood beside her, her hand braced on Billie's shoulder and her own tears falling freely.

Max continued to hold Claudia's hand after she breathed her last breath. "I never knew. It explains so much."

"Your father and Claudia loved each other since they were young. He wanted so badly for them to marry, but Claudia insisted his duty to his family came first and after your mother died she feared if she married your father it would hurt your chance of a successful marriage."

Max took Claudia's hand and crossed them over each other on her chest. He lifted her head off Billie's lap and Marlee helped her to stand. He then covered Claudia with Billie's cloak.

He slipped off his coat and threw it over his wife's shoulders, pulling her to him and resting his forehead to hers. He spoke softly. "I had once thought like Claudia of duty and family and never gave a thought to love. I realize now how much I would have missed. I love you, my lady. You are my life, my heart, my soul."

He kissed her gently.

"Good Lord," Marlee cried, startling them both.

Billie and Max turned not at all surprised to see Oran emerging from the fog. He raised his hand in a good-bye wave and they returned his farewell.

He then called softly, *"Claudia."*

All three were startled when Claudia's spirit rose from her body and walked to take his outstretched hand and together they disappeared into the fog.

Lights approached them with Bessie's voice in the lead.

Marlee looked at them both. "Take the cave to the manor. I'll relate all that happened here tonight."

"All?" Max inquired.

Marlee smiled widely. "Your father and Claudia deserve a beautiful tale told about them and I will do that tale justice."

"Thank you," he said, slipping his arm around Billie's waist to guide her toward the entrance of the cave.

Billie halted and asked another favor. "You will explain about Max not being a ghost?"

"With pleasure and delight," she assured them and waved them away.

Billie toweled herself dry, the hot bath having chased away the chills and restored her strength. She had watched her husband for the last half hour. He stood at the window, staring into the night's darkness, clad in his silk robe and freshly bathed.

She had thought he would seek her out while in the tub and had been surprised when he had not moved from his position at the window. She shared his hurt, his pain over losing his father, but she also knew that Oran would not want his son to suffer so.

Billie dropped the towel to the floor and she approached him completely naked. She startled him, slipping around in front of him and surprised him all the more when she unknotted the ties to his robe, spread it open and braced herself against him, her arms wrapping around his waist and her head resting on his chest.

"I love you," she whispered.

His arms circled her. "And I you."

She looked up at him. "I wish to name our first son Oran."

"Are you . . ."

She shook her head. "Not yet, but if we work at it I'm sure we could produce a child by spring."

He smiled. "And if it is a daughter?"

"We'll name her Claudia and immediately set to work on producing a son."

His hand drifted to her backside and he tenderly caressed her firm derriere. "And what if we again have a daughter?"

"We will just have to keep at it until we get our son, Oran."

He pulled her flat against him and she felt the strength of his desire press into her. "I would like that."

She teased his lips with hers. "The name or the attempts at producing a son?"

Max scooped her up into his arms. "Both."

They fell on the bed together and Max wasted no time in ridding himself of his robe. Their urgency to mate, to unite as one, to strengthen the bond of their love brought them together fast and furiously.

Max buried himself inside her swiftly and she cried out her need for him. Together they moved, together they cried out, together they climaxed and together they loved.

And once sated they relaxed against each other, and with sly smiles rained kisses on each other and again made love, only this time slow and teasingly. And so the night continued until, finally exhausted, Max and Billie lay wrapped in each other's arms.

A late night wind blew through the open window and the tired couple ignored the stirring until a ripple of soft laughter drifted in, followed by familiar voices.

"Good-bye, my son and daughter. Love well," Oran whispered.

"And forever," Claudia added even more softly.

Billie and Max sprang up in the bed and looked around the room.

They both smiled, hugged each other and proceeded to do exactly as Oran and Claudia suggested.

Love well and love forever.

And now for a preview of the next
Haunting Hearts romance

A Spirited Seduction

Coming in May 1997 from Jove

"We could kill him! We could poison him with something truly awful and then bury his body where no one could ever find it. Maybe behind the dovecote where all the ivy—"

"Theodore!"

Sabrina silenced her brother with a look that doused the murderous spark in his eyes. He pushed out his lower lip and she shook her head firmly. Eight-year-olds were a frightfully bloodthirsty lot.

"What have you been reading, Teddy, to put such ideas in your head?" Sabrina asked. "One simply cannot go around murdering viscounts."

"No, it's not at all the thing," Andrew put in, his youthful countenance as grave as any undertaker's.

Although only thirteen, Andrew was very mature for his age, a serious and thoughtful boy. The rapscallion Teddy, however . . .

"But Papa—"

"Papa might have been a bit daring, Teddy, but he would have most certainly drawn the line at murder. Even in a time of crisis," Sabrina asserted. "I know that you miss him—we all do—but we cannot lose our heads."

Even as she spoke, Sabrina wished she might temporarily be rid of hers. Her skull pounded with a severe case of the megrims that made it hurt even to blink.

"I can take care of this. I can. I only wish that you two had never learned of this nasty business. If it weren't for a certain someone listening at keyholes . . ." She frowned at Teddy who squirmed in his chair like a long-legged puppy.

"Now see here, Rina, you must allow me to help," Andrew insisted. "You should have told me when the banker arrived. I am the man of the family now and I will not leave you to get us out of this muddle alone."

Sabrina leaned forward and affectionately nudged Andrew's spectacles from the tip of his nose to a more secure position.

"I have had plenty of experience with muddles, Andy. Never fear. I'll keep the wolves from our door. Especially that one very odious wolf, the Viscount Colbridge."

Teddy snorted and crossed his arms across his thin chest. "Well, I say the bloke is bloody cheeky trying to steal Simmons House right out from under our noses."

"And *I* say"—Sabrina shot him an arch look—"that you ought watch your tongue, Theodore Simmons, or I'm going to triple your time at Latin exercises."

That threat served to quiet young Teddy for a few seconds, long enough for Sabrina's gaze to linger on the frayed fabric at his jacket's elbows. Not only was the coat sadly threadbare but it was also two sizes too small.

She bit at the inside of her lip. *Well, he'll simply have to make do with one of Andrew's hand-me-downs.* They would undoubtedly be too large for him, but what else could be done? With the bank threatening to call in their mortgage, she could not squander their pennies on luxuries like new clothing.

Her head pounded more fiercely and she glanced to the window where the rain pelted the glass in angry bursts. Lightning lit the sky in a flash of white, accompanied by the crackling roar of thunder. It was a dreadful night that followed a dreadful day.

Sabrina rose from the divan and felt the chill of the room sneak beneath her skirts.

"Run along to bed, boys, it's growing late. Ask Hattie if she'll tuck you in. I need to do some reading tonight."

Teddy grumbled but dutifully clambered from his chair. He cast a dubious glance at the shelves of books lining the library walls.

"How can you enjoy all that horrid reading, Sabrina? It bores me stiff, it does."

Sabrina ruffled his mop of pale yellow curls. Her youngest brother was not the scholar of the Simmons family.

"One can learn a great deal from books, Teddy. All types of things. In fact, there is virtually nothing that can't be learned by reading history or literature.

"For instance . . ."—her tone turned teasing—"these books could tell me which Shropshire native plants are most toxic to unscrupulous viscounts."

"They can?" he asked, his eyes suddenly aglow.

Sabrina bit back a smile. "You *are* a scamp. Come on now, off to bed with you."

Teddy threw his arms around her waist and gave her a brief yet sturdy hug before he bolted out the library door— no doubt intent on making one last piece of mischief before the day was done.

As his footsteps clattered down the uncarpeted hallway, Sabrina turned to Andrew. Her smile faded. "Please don't look so glum, Andy. We aren't going to lose our home, I promise you."

Andy's quiet gaze touched upon bare spots along the wall where, once, fine landscapes had hung. "We've already lost so much."

Sabrina knew he didn't refer to the paintings. They'd lost Papa this year. Mother, the year before. Times had been hard at Simmons House.

And it looked as if they were getting harder.

From what she'd learned that afternoon, Lord Colbridge had not one whit in common with his deceased relative, Lord Calhoun. "Calhoun the Old Prune," as Teddy had dubbed him, had been an irascible old fellow who'd lived a monk-like existence the seventy years he'd been neighbor to Simmons House. He'd never married, never entertained nor paid calls. He'd rarely been seen outside his home, and when he had been, he'd not once been seen to smile.

His nephew, however—if one were to believe the gossipy banker Bardwell—was London's answer to a modern-day Lothario.

At first, Sabrina had not been certain why Mr. Bardwell was sharing so much personal information with her about the stranger who wanted to purchase Simmons House. "A rake of historical proportions," the banker had called him. Interesting, yes, but so? What could it matter to her if Lord Colbridge had recently dismissed his French paramour? Why should she care if the viscount was known to be "extremely generous with his ladyloves"?

It had necessitated a broad wink of Bardwell's rheumy eye for Sabrina to finally grasp the banker's innuendo. Granted, it had taken her aback for a moment. Even two. But she was far too pragmatic to dismiss the idea out of hand. Desperate times called for desperate measures, she had said to herself. And the more Mr. Bardwell had expounded on their financial situation, the more desperate matters had begun to appear.

"Why does he want Simmons House anyway?" Andrew asked, cutting into her thoughts. "What is wrong with Lord Calhoun's home?"

"Supposedly Lord Colbridge thinks Leyton Hall too small," she answered, bending down to toss a modest scoop of coal onto the fire.

"Calhoun's place isn't exactly a Simmons House, is it?"

The pride in Andrew's voice was both understandable and a little sad. This house, their home, was all that was left of Andrew's birthright. Over the years the stables had been thinned out, the hunting lodge sold, the family jewels pawned. As the debts had continued to mount, Papa's investments had continued to go sour until eventually nothing had remained. Nothing but Simmons House.

"I really think I should speak to the viscount," Andrew insisted. "If he's any kind of gentleman, he'll hear me out."

"But he's *not* any kind of gentleman," Sabrina mumbled under her breath. "At least, not according to Mr. Bardwell."

She turned away from the fire and her heart contracted a notch to see her brother standing there with his slim shoulders squared and his fuzzy chin raised. And his spectacles once again teetering at the tip of his nose.

"Andrew, I think you're right. We should meet with the viscount and discuss our situation. However, I believe that I should be the one to speak with him."

"You, Sabrina?"

She hastened to soothe his adolescent pride. "You are very wise for your age, Andy—truly you are—but it might be better if I were to address this matter with Lord Colbridge."

Andrew thought for a minute, then gave a sober nod. "Yes, I suppose that would be the sensible way to go about it."

Dear Andy. Always so sensible. So much like herself.

"Agreed, then," she said. "Now, would you be a dear and hunt down Teddy and drag him off to bed for me? I'm sure he's driving Hattie 'round the bend."

Andrew turned as if to leave, then hesitated, his expression as easy to read as one of Teddy's old primers.

"Don't fret, Andy. I give you my solemn vow. I will do whatever necessary to make certain we don't lose Simmons House."

He gave her a weak smile, his lips a bit wobbly. "I know you will, Rina . . . And that's what worries me."

As he closed the door behind him, Sabrina wondered if it had been only overnight that her brother had gone from child to young man.

She pulled her shawl close about her, ignoring the insistent pounding in her temple. Out of habit, she walked over to the immaculately kept bookshelves and began scanning the titles, seeking counsel from her faithful mentors: Plato, David Hume and, of course, Mary Wollstonecraft.

Always, when faced with difficult questions, Sabrina had sought answers between the pages of a book. All her life, she had relied on the only people she could truly count on—history's great scholars and writers. When there had been no one else to depend on, no one else to burden with her concerns, she had always had her books.

She took a deep breath, and the smell of leather and aged paper was like a balm to her nerves. There was no other sensible alternative.

For even if she could dissuade Lord Colbridge from purchasing their home, what then? They still wouldn't have the monies to pay their mortgage and the bank's patience would not hold forever.

The words "extremely generous" echoed in her thoughts as she stared blindly at the titles before her.

What, after all, would she be losing? Her chastity was of little value without a dowry to accompany it.

On occasion, poverty might be forgiven if a young woman possessed exceptional beauty, but such was not her case. She was too thin, too tall, too ordinary.

And although she might have preferred to bestow her virtue on a man she cared for, she certainly entertained no notion of ever "falling in love."

The only risk, therefore, lay in her ability to succeed.

Slowly Sabrina ran her fingers over the contours of her face. Could she do it? Could she, with this pointed chin and these sharp cheekbones, seduce the Viscount Colbridge? Make him desire her enough to take her as his mistress?

Resolve sent her into action.

With feverish movements, she began to snatch books from the shelves. She had told Teddy only earlier this night that one could learn anything from history and literature.

Surely she could learn to become a great seductress.

Tomes piled high to her chin, Sabrina dropped onto the sofa and spilled her books beside her. She grabbed the first that lay atop the heap.

Homer's "Iliad."

Helen of Troy.

Sabrina thumbed through the pages until a passage caught her attention. She loosely translated, "Watching Helen as she climbed the stair, the old leaders said to one another: 'It is no wonder that men . . . have borne the pains of war for one like this. Unearthliness. The woman is a goddess to look upon.'"

She slammed the book shut. "A goddess, hmmph."

Helen had an obvious advantage over Sabrina. Unearthliness.

"No, I need a seductress with more commonplace appeal," she muttered as she picked up the next book.

As she stared into the dancing flames and contemplated the task she'd set for herself, doubt entered her thoughts.

"None of that," she chided herself in a stern voice. "I'm quite sure that Cleopatra didn't waste any time on self-pity when she had to save Egypt by giving herself to Julius Caesar. She did what had to be done."

Just as *she* would do what had to be done.

Nevertheless, as she returned to her reading, Sabrina was haunted by the feeling that she was not up to this assignment. Her experience with the opposite sex was confined to boys; she knew nothing of men.

Hours later, from the corner of her eye, she surveyed the pile of books still to be read.

The problem was that nowhere in literature did it explain *how* these women had seduced their men. What clothes had

Nell Gwynn worn, what fragrance had she used, to so capti-
vate Charles II? How had Cleopatra lured the world's most
powerful men into her bed?

These questions played through Sabrina's mind as she
half-drowsed, tucked into the corner of the divan.

"Lord, but I need help," she mumbled sleepily. "I need a
tutor to instruct me how to go about a proper seduction."

A draft suddenly swept through the room, colder than any
that had gone before it that night. Clinging to her soporific
state, Sabrina shivered and curled more tightly into the sofa.
In the back of her mind arose the crazy notion that she
smelled . . . frangipani.

"Coooo-ee!"

Sabrina's eyes snapped open and she found herself staring
at the ceiling.

*"Gor, what a trip that was. I'd wager me hair is mussed
somethin' awful."*

Sabrina whipped her head around in the direction of the
strange feminine voice. What she saw caused the air to
whoosh from her lungs.

It was an apparition. A hallucination. A . . .

"Ah . . . ah." Her throat had closed. Words were stuck
somewhere between her brain and her mouth. She must be
dreaming. She rubbed furiously at her eyes.

*"Oh now, don't be doin' that, luv. You'll give yourself
wrinkles, you will."*

Sabrina's fists froze in mid-air. This . . . this *delusion* was
talking to her about wrinkles?

A giggle pushed its way past her clogged throat and
emerged as a sound Sabrina would never have recognized as
coming from herself. It was a frightened sound. It was a
slightly hysterical sound.

"I've given you a start, haven't I?" The apparition
clucked its tongue like a mother hen.

"The strain has got to me," Sabrina whispered. "I had
thought I was managing, getting along well enough, but to
suffer this manner of nightmare—"

"But I'm not your nightmare, Sabrina luv—"

"You know my name?"

Sabrina fairly choked on the question. Naturally, her own delusion would know her name. That would make sense, wouldn't it? But what *had* her tortured brain been thinking to construct such a wildly improbable hallucination?

Hair bleached nearly to the color of Teddy's was curled closely to the apparition's head and topped by a bonnet that must have been some milliner's idea of a prank. It had feathers, it had ribands, it had pearls, it had lace. It had everything but a live parakeet.

The smiling face beneath the hideous headpiece could have been called pretty if not refined. A coquettishly-placed beauty mark enhanced both a cupid's bow mouth and a roundish button nose. From tiny, shell-shaped ears swung the gaudiest earbobs conceivable, fair to blinding with all their multicolored glass.

Sabrina had not known her imagination capable of such invention.

"Of course I know your name," the vision said. *"That's me job."*

Sabrina winced. Perhaps if she closed her eyes and went back to sleep, this thing would go away.

She was about to do just that when the specter's shawl slipped from one shoulder. Sabrina's eyebrows shot up.

"Immodest" was a paltry term to describe this particular decolletage. And if immodest characterized the neckline, only superfluous could describe the flesh beneath it. Good gracious, but she'd never seen the like—

Sabrina shook herself. But she wasn't *seeing* the like. She was only imagining it. She was only imagining the garish furbelows encircling the skirt of that scandalously sheer gown . . . A frisson of fear raced up Sabrina's spine.

Everything about this apparition was sheer. Why, she could see straight through her!

"Oh, dear. Oh, dear." She squeezed her eyes shut. "There must be a logical explanation for this. There must be."

"But there is."

Reluctantly, Sabrina opened her eyes to find that the delusion had come nearer. She pressed herself back against the sofa.

"You called me here," the vision said. *"Don't you remember?"*

"I . . . I called you here?"

The apparition smiled, revealing a small gap between her two front teeth and a dimple in her left cheek. *"You asked for a tutor."*

Sabrina blinked a few times in nervous succession. *A tutor?*

The specter patted daintly at the ringlets curling against her temple. *"I'm the spirit who's come to help you, luv."*

Sabrina felt suddenly light-headed. "Sp-spirit? As in ghost?"

The apparition laughed, a rich, feminine sound that jiggled her feminine attributes. *"Fancy that, I've plum forgot to introduce myself."* She held out a transparent hand. *"Nell deNuit, at your service. Or should I say . . . the ghost of Nell deNuit?"*